# THE GAMES WE PLAY

*A Novel By*

# Kathleen Haun

Cover photo by Cheryl Perry
Cover design by Brad Allen Photography & Art (allenfoto.com)

Published by Aventine Press
55 East Emerson St.
Chula Vista CA 91911
www.aventinepress.com

ISBN: 978-1-955162-35-7

# BOOKS BY KATHLEEN HAUN

My historical fiction novels cover the years 1849 to 1913. They cover early San Francisco, the towns of the California gold rush, Placerville after the rush, travel west by wagon train, and the mining towns of the Eastern Sierra and Nevada.

They were not written in chronological order. If you would like to read them in the order those years are covered, the following would be that order.

| | |
|---|---|
| *Chasing the Dream* | 1849 - 1859 |
| *Digging Deeper* | 1862 - (summer) |
| *Not Enough Forever* | 1862 – 1881 |
| Moving On | 1863 - 1872 |
| *Dear Carrie* | 1878 – 1899 |
| *No Trees For Shade* | 1880 – 1881 |
| *Declining Fortunes* | 1882 – 1886 |
| *The Games We Play* | 1888 - (June) |
| *Passing Storms* | 1900 - 1913 |

Dedicated to
those who are
dedicated to
Bridgeport

"Laws control the lesser man.
Right conduct controls the greater."

Mark Twain

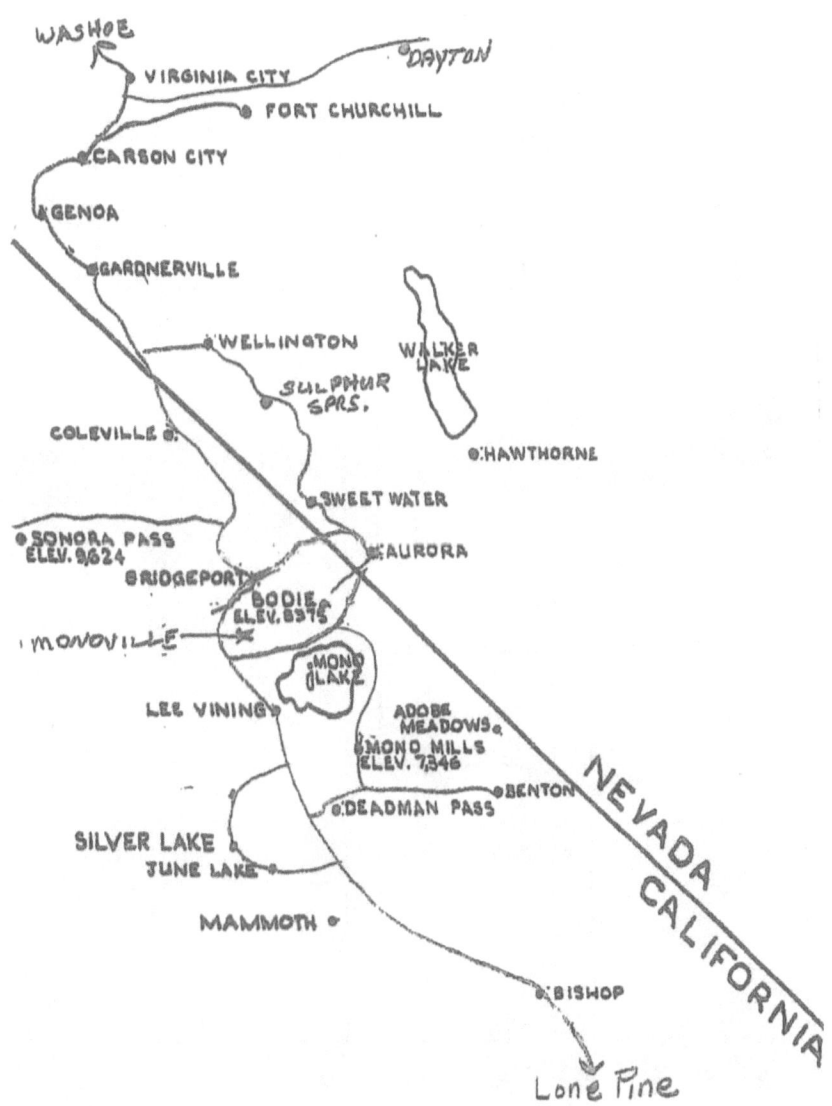

1    Leavitt House Hotel

2    Court House Corner Saloon

3    Bryant Hall

4    Turner Home

5    Allen House Hotel

6    Kirkwood Home

## Historic Bridgeport

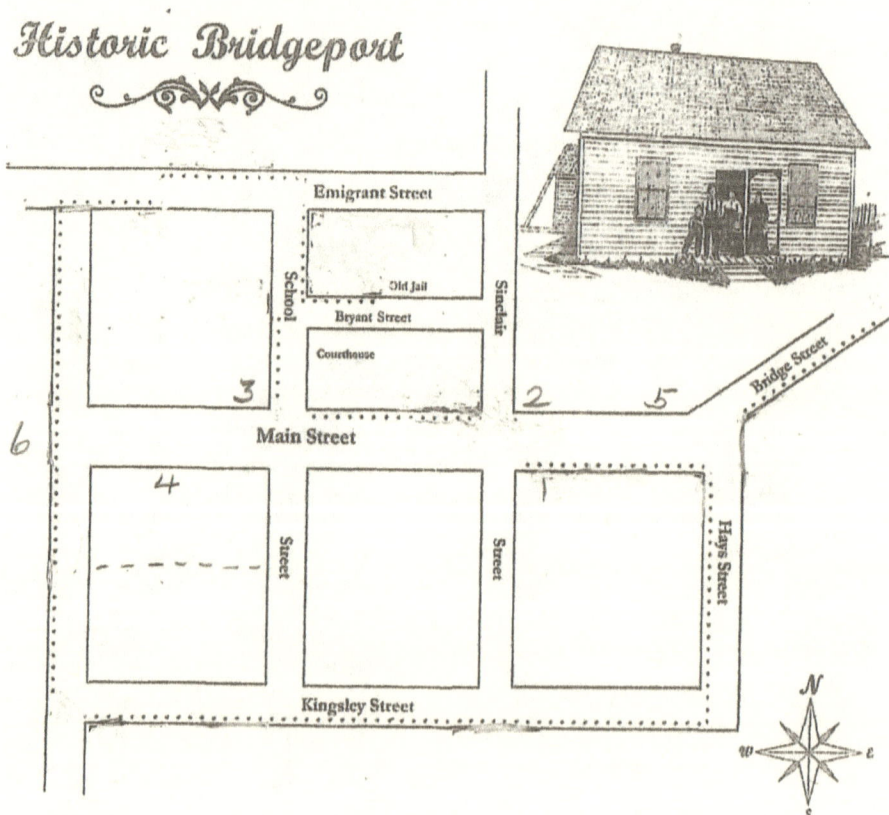

# BRIDGEPORT

The old log and stone cribbed bridge

Main Street during the 1880s, looking west. The Hays Store is on the left and the Allen House is the white building on the right next to the Bump Market and the two-story Bryant Store.

Michael Cody in the 1880s.

Hiram Leavitt in the 1860s.

A.F. Bryant about 1870.

Esther Hunewill

Sam Fales abut 1890.

Napoleon Bonaparte Hunnewell

# PREFACE

The action of this story takes place in 1888, Bridgeport, California. To clarify for the reader the values of the amounts of money discussed in the book, the equivalent value today of $1 in 1888, would be $32. Therefore, a $2 ante in a poker game would be equivalent to $64. The $20 collected from six players by the day's winner of $120 total, would be exchanged today at $3,832 in purchasing power.

The chips used in the game converted to today's value:

$1  white chip   =    $ 32
$5   red chip  =    $ 160
$10 green chip  =    $ 320

From this, one can understand why the term "penny ante" came to be used for anything unimportant, not valuable or unimpressive.

# CHAPTER I

## THE INVITATION

Spring in Virginia City, Nevada, is one of the town's most pleasant times of the year. It certainly was in 1888. Jim Murphy walked out of his favorite saloon and gambling hall, felt the softness of the cool breeze, and hoped it wouldn't become stronger. He was taking his wife, Lucy, to dinner at the International Hotel that night, and didn't want to cancel because of one of the area's infamous zephyr winds raking the town.

"Mr. Murphy, you have a letter here at Will Call." A young postal clerk, his long white apron protecting his clothes from ink and dirt, stood in the door of the post office waving at him. "It's from Bridgeport." He scratched his chin, covered in the stubble of a novice beard, and glared at Mr. Murphy's neatly trimmed mustache.

"Who on earth could that be from?" Jim mumbled. He didn't expect an answer, but he got one anyway.

"Isn't that where you were once held in jail for murder?" The clerk thought he was being clever. He often felt intimidated in the presence of this slick gambler.

Jim Murphy was a popular resident of Virginia City, and even at 54, caused women to cast friendly glances in his direction. Tall and athletic of build, his thick, dark hair was streaked with only a little gray, and his blue eyes were rimmed with dark lashes. He was an older version of his thirty-year-old son, Roger Murphy, who was also a professional gambler. A thin mustache accented his altogether handsome face, although it did tend to give him the appearance of the clichéd, back-room gambler. Roger always seemed to have an intense watchfulness in his dark blue eyes, about which the clerk's wife had commented more than once. The clerk didn't like Roger either.

Stepping into the post office, Jim Murphy glared at the postal clerk as he moved behind the counter, reaching into one of the many cubbyholes holding mail. Jim removed his new Stetson, not yet broken in, and ran his hand through his hair. He could have ignored the kid's tactless witticism, but his pride decided him otherwise. "As everyone knows, I was proved innocent of that crime several years ago."

"Oh, yes, sir."

Nevertheless, as Jim walked up the stair-stepped streets of Virginia City, the comment rankled. He was also fighting a frisson of tingling along his spine. It was not an unusual reaction whenever Bridgeport was mentioned. He gave himself a stern command to stop being a rattlebrained idiot, and passed through the gate of the white fence in front of the "B" Street house he shared with his wife.

He lowered himself onto the stone bench under the apple tree in the tiny front yard, and forced himself to relax as he looked over at his Lucy. The sleeves of her white waist were rolled up and she was wearing a long pinafore apron. Nevertheless, there were smudges of mud on her arms, as well as her forehead where she had brushed back a strand of hair.

Jim idly wondered what she would do if he picked her up and carried her into the house, stripped her down and cleaned off the mud. Instead, he once again took command of his rambling thoughts and decided to be practical, something that Lucy always professed to be important. Besides, there was this damn letter to open.

Unaware of her husband's randy thoughts, Lucy was yanking out weeds that had dared to encroach into the flower bed under the kitchen's bay window. As curious as Jim was about the letter, he took a moment to observe her. He liked that she had met her fiftieth year with grace, although that was probably because she looked and acted considerably younger. Her dark hair showed gray only along the temples, and her figure was still slender enough that she wore a corset only for dressy occasions. Her face had changed little, with skin still smooth except for little lines around her eyes. And, of course, the faint scar on her cheek, no more obvious now than a stray hair would be upon her ivory skin. Still, no one ever referred to it, not even in the family.

Walking down the street with Lucy on his arm was a matter of pride for Jim. Not because he could show off a lovely, fashionably dressed wife, but because he knew the quality of her character, as did many of those they would encounter. He also knew she was perceived by many as having too many opinions inappropriate for a woman. He considered her courageous for not hiding her intelligence. At least no one would ever assume that marriage to Lucy was boring.

Lucy walked over to her husband while removing her gardening gloves and settled herself next to him. "Who's the letter from?"

"I don't know." He looked down at the unopened envelope. "It's got a return address on it like their asking us to do now, but no name of the sender."

Lucy looked closer at the envelope. "Oh, Bridgeport." She said nothing more, but she now understood why Jim was hesitating. He had been jailed there back in 1879, an innocent man fighting lies.

Jim ripped open the envelope, and seeing who the letter was from, was both relieved and surprised. "J. B. Roberts. He has a ranch out in the Bridgeport meadows."

"Such a lovely area. But memories not so good for you, are they?"

"Well, until they arrested me, I liked the place a lot." The fact that he couldn't keep the humor from his voice, or the smirk from his lips, pleased Lucy. There had been a time when he wouldn't have been able to joke about it.

"*Falsely* arrested," she corrected him, gently nudging his shoulder with her own.

"Yes, but they didn't know that at the time. I don't hold it against anyone, though. It was a confusing time. But I didn't know J.B. back in '78, although I'd heard of him. The first time I met him was last fall in Bodie, when Roger and I were there." Jim had made many friends when he had worked in the Bridgeport sawmills back in the '70's, but also a few enemies. Those last had almost cost him his life.

"What does he say?" Lucy was finding it difficult to hide her curiosity, and was wondering if her husband was delaying just to tease her.

Jim smiled, showing that she was correct. He then held up the single piece of paper so Lucy could read what was written. The swirls of the Spencerian penmanship were moderate and neatly applied to the cream-colored stationery, which she recognized as of excellent quality, and not cheaply purchased.

*Dear Jim:*                                                  *April 16, 1888*

*I am inviting you to be part of a poker tournament at my home in Bridgeport on the weekend of June 23. Arrive on Friday, the 22nd, and leave when you want. I have also invited your son, along with Victor Turner from town, and Otto Mercer, who works at a nearby ranch. You will be made welcome and comfortable. My housekeeper, Mrs. Lewis, will make sure of that, and I have a very fine cook. And, of course, I keep a well-stocked liquor cabinet. The rules of the game will be a little unusual, and will be explained upon your arrival. Bring lots of money, and be willing to sign an IOU if necessary. If you're confident of your ability, you should have no problem with that. Respond by telegram.*

*J. B. Roberts*

*P.S. Please invite two men you know who are accomplished players. I trust your judgment.*

Lucy stood up and stretched her back. "So, I guess that means Roger has received a note like this one, too."

"I guess so." Jim looked out past the small garden. "Maybe that's why he's approaching with such purposeful strides."

Jim didn't try to hide his smile as he watched Lucy anticipate the approach of their son. But, as he so often did, he fought a wave of regret that he had not been around during his son's adolescence. The Civil War and the years that had followed it had brought about unexpected consequences for thousands of people, not least of whom was Jim and his family. But while many people had suffered permanent loss, Lucy and Roger had been without Jim for only sixteen years. Now, after seven years together again, they had settled into a comfortable life. But the memory of their time apart had only faded into the background, still casting a subtle shadow.

Roger stopped a moment to catch his breath before opening the gate, enjoying the sight of his parents together. He wondered if he would ever take such a tableau for granted, knowing what they had all gone through in order to make such a moment possible. He entered the gate, kissed his mother's cheek and plopped down on the bench next to his father.

"I see you got your letter. Is this the J.B. we met last October in Bodie?"

Lucy smiled with satisfaction as she remembered greeting Jim upon his return home from that trip. "That was the big game where you won enough for us to pay our taxes and a year ahead to the water company?"

Roger wasn't going to go unacknowledged. "I won big, too."

"Yes, dear, Amanda told me. Your wife and I enjoyed a lovely luncheon at the International Hotel."

Jim folded the letter and slid it back into the envelope. "J.B. was there delivering smoked hams to the Occidental Hotel. He has some kind of deal with them. He was one of the men we played with, and he did well for himself. Afterwards, we got to talking, and even had dinner with him."

"He had his twelve-year-old son, Alex, with him." Roger smiled at the memory. "I must say he was a very polite, well-behaved kid. He talked about their ranch like it was heaven on earth."

Jim grinned at his son. "After watching you play a few hands, the kid looked at you like you were Earp and Holliday rolled into one. No wonder you like him."

Roger grinned. "My mustache is smaller than theirs." He was often quick with a jest, but he never lost focus. "So, do we go?"

Jim turned to Lucy. "What do you think? I wish you could come along. You could be the dealer."

"That would be nice. But with my husband and my son at the table, it might not go down well with the other players."

"Probably not. But you're a professional dealer."

"Not so much anymore, dear. Just private games. Anyway, you and Roger are professional gamblers. I think Mr. Roberts is expecting it to be a masculine weekend."

Jim sighed. "I don't like leaving you here so long. The game might be over a weekend, but with travel there and back, even on horseback, we'll be gone the better part of two weeks."

Lucy laughed off his concern and rested a hand on her son's shoulder. He was such a sweet man, but she realized that even though he was thirty, he still had some of the boy in him. With the allure of such an exciting game at hand, Lucy was afraid he might not take into consideration those relying on him. "How does Amanda feel about your going?"

Roger shrugged. "Not thrilled, but she admitted it sounds like it would be a lot of fun for me."

Lucy was immensely fond of her daughter-in-law, but it was a considerable hike downhill from "B" Street to "D" Street where Amanda and Roger lived. Especially considering there was always the walk back up again. Lucy also realized that maybe she didn't always act sufficiently fawning over her toddler granddaughter.

"I'll tell you what." She walked over to the rose bush by the gate and broke off a choice bloom, handing it to Roger. "Why not ask Amanda to bring the baby and come stay here with me while you're gone? It'll be a nice break for her."

"Will Kathryn mind the extra work?" Jim asked. The Irish housekeeper, in Lucy's employ since a teenager, was now a married woman. But the loyalty of Kathryn and her husband, who owed his life to Jim, was such that she still came to the house four days a week.

Lucy reassured him. "Kathryn adores little Ellie. And we have a very capable daily girl now, so if more help is needed, she'll pitch in."

Roger held back a laugh. Before either of them had been married, he had been aware of Kathryn's crush on him, but had always pretended otherwise. Consequently, they were now good friends of long-standing. "I'm sure Kathryn won't mind," he declared. "I'm even more sure that Amanda will enjoy the change. And the extra help with Ellie."

With what he thought of as *the wife problem* settled, Roger turned to his father. The two men put their heads together while discussing their plans, and Lucy could hear the excitement in their voices. Neither one would admit it aloud, but the idea of spending so much time together, just father and son, was the greatest appeal of the invitation.

As they finished pie and coffee at the kitchen table, Lucy got up and walked to the stove. She reached for the enamel coffee pot sitting on an iron trivet atop the still warm stove. But she hesitated and turned back to the men.

"Why didn't this J.B. invite more men from Bridgeport? Why ask you to find two more players?"

Jim looked at Roger and they shrugged in unison. "Maybe he figured that being a gambler myself, I'd know men here who ..." He shrugged again. "I just don't know."

"You would think," Lucy mused, "that he'd know at least two more men he could invite."

"Well, he did invite Victor and Otto, whoever the hell they are." Jim picked up the letter and stared at it, remembering Bridgeport, once known more familiarly as Big Meadows. "It's a cattle and lumber area. Ranches, a dairy, and sawmills."

Roger, having listened to this exchange and not caring one way or another, stretched out his long legs and rested them on the empty chair across from him. Catching a stern look from his mother as she returned to the table with the coffee pot, he put them back on the floor.

Still thinking the invitation strange, Lucy nevertheless ceased to question it, not wanting to throw cold water on the men's enthusiasm. "Do you have someone in mind to ask?"

The three of them contemplated the invitation on the table before them, as though it might speak up and make a suggestion. Whether welcome or an intrusion, it demanded to be answered. Breaking the tension, Jim finally spoke. "I was thinking about Frank Eastman and Vince Perry."

Lucy frowned. "It's quite a long way for them to come from Lone Pine."

Roger, however, immediately became wedded to the idea. "The Owens River Valley isn't all that remote now. They can take the train to Benton. And then the stage up through Adobe Valley to Bodie. They can rent horses there if they want or take the stage north to Bridgeport. Or they can ride the whole way, camping out, and staying at ranches and stage stops."

Lucy looked out the window. "Frank and Emily's daughter, Whitney, is almost eight now. And Vince and Charlotte's son, Steven, is almost seven. So I doubt their wives will be coming with them. Emily and Charlotte are great friends of Amanda's, so I imagine she'll be disappointed."

"Life's full of disappointments." It was an unusually harsh statement from Jim.

Although he had mostly put behind him the difficult circumstances that had separated him from his family after the war, residual resentment still sometimes colored his perspective of events. A little perturbed at himself for what he had said, Jim stood up and walked into the parlor. He took his hat down from its peg on the wall as Roger rushed to join him.

"So, Dad, are we going to send J.B. a confirming telegram?"

"Yes. Want to stop for a beer on the way back?"

Roger laughed. "Do you want four of a kind in every hand?"

The two happy men left the house, leaving behind a wife and mother frowning as she pondered the questions forming in her mind about the unexpected invitation. That the men didn't think it strange wasn't surprising to Lucy, as they were excited about the *tournament*. Even Mr. Roberts calling it that seemed strange to Lucy.

But, always quick to give benefit of the doubt, she reasoned that maybe he was just a strange man; some old eccentric stuck out on a ranch in the middle of acres of grassy meadows, with only cattle as company. Neither Jim nor Roger had described him, so she was left to imagine based on his curt and somewhat demanding letter. But he had referred to a housekeeper and a cook, and Jim had mentioned a young son, so he wasn't a hermit. Glancing down at the envelope on the table, she noted again that the stationery was of very good quality. And her curiosity grew. Because Mr. Roberts had not mentioned a wife.

\* \* \*

Victor Turner looked at the letter once again, thinking, "Why on earth did that sonofabitch send me a formal invitation to the game? Is he trying to say he's sorry for what he did to me, or is he afraid of what I might know about him?"

Back in 1873 the owner of a large tract of land had decided not to sell to Victor after J.B. married the man's sister. Victor remained convinced that J.B. had married her just to get the land. He recalled that she had died only two years after Alex's birth in '76, and he chuckled to himself. "She probably got sick living in the barn while he built his damn house."

He clenched his jaw and only just stopped himself from grinding his teeth. Then he relaxed, remembering how sweet J.B.'s wife had always smelled, and how nice she had been to him. But, he recalled, it had gotten around that while on a trip to visit her brother, she had died. He mumbled aloud, "Boy, was I glad to hear that!" At the same time, he refused to admit why.

Victor had avoided J.B. for a long time after that, not offering condolences because he didn't want to deal with an awkward encounter. He had justified it by telling himself that J.B. had the support of friends; ones who actually liked him.

Victor hadn't always been so bitter, or at least unwise enough to let it show. Life hadn't been easy for him. He had started out in an orphanage in the East before finally being adopted at twelve. His new family had immediately started for California on a wagon train. Mom had been kind, but distant. By eavesdropping, he had learned that she had wanted to adopt a girl. But Dad had insisted on a boy so the lad could help on the trip west, and then on the farm that was planned.

They had prospered on the small farm in the San Joaquin Valley of California, selling fruits, vegetables and herbs to nearby towns. Victor had learned much about agriculture, working hard in the orchards and fields, and this had pleased his new parents. Nevertheless, Victor had soon realized that he would always be more *worker* than *son*. Besides his other duties, it had been his responsibility to care for two horses, a mule, three cows and a goat.

When he wasn't being shouted at, he was being cuffed on the ear for not moving fast enough. He ran away from the farm when he turned seventeen. But it had been the hard work that had made him physically strong, while also teaching him that you could count on animals more than people. Animals might misbehave, but at least it was in ways you could understand and forgive. Their actions didn't make you burn with resentment.

By hiring on at ranches as he had worked his way over the Sierra to the east side, he had been able to save enough money to lease a plot of land near Bridgeport and build a small cabin. Not long after, while working odd jobs, he had purchased breeding stock. Along with the wild mustangs he caught, he eventually produced a nice herd of horses. From this, he began selling to ranches as far north as Virginia City and as far south as Bishop Creek in the Owens River Valley. J.B. had been one of the local buyers. When Victor had married in '78, his life had finally become all he had ever dreamed of having.

But his wife had lost their baby, and then her life, and he had started drinking and gambling. Neither had numbed the pain of loss, and it had drained him financially by the time he pulled himself together. In order to pay his overdue bills and make repairs to his small ranch, he had sold J.B. most of his stock, with the understanding that when he could afford it, Victor would buy them back at the same price.

Victor was once again married. Two years earlier he had met a woman with two young daughters, and who was determined to have no more. He was fine with that. She kept a nice house, which she owned there in Bridgeport, and was a good cook. She had also brought to the marriage a small herd of large, sturdy horses good for pulling wagons that he was breeding and selling. She had also brought a moderate fortune that no one knew about but themselves, although he did wonder if J.B. had somehow discovered this. It might explain why he would think that Victor could afford to accept an invitation to such a player's weekend. Everyone in Bridgeport knew Victor liked to play cards, although he now had both his drinking and his gambling under control.

Victor shoved the invitation aside, then put pen to paper and wrote a quick note of acceptance. It took considerable effort, but he managed to include the words "thank you".

* * *

Otto Mercer had received a verbal invitation from J.B. when they had run into each other in town outside the Bump Market. But he wasn't surprised by it, because his friend Victor had already told him about the "tournament", as J.B. insisted on calling it. However, Otto was still uneasy with what else Victor had said during their conversation. He just wasn't comfortable about playing with so many strangers. He wasn't as good at cards as J.B., and Victor had said two of the others coming were professionals. And now, even though he had accepted the invite, he wasn't sure he was happy that he had.

Otto was a middle-aged, wiry ranch hand, almost as proud that he had remained single as he was of his generously long mustache. He was senior to J. B. Roberts by fifteen years, and he thought of himself as also senior in knowledge and skill with livestock. Even better than big-shot Roberts. He knew for sure that he was a better poker player than Victor, having won a lot of money from him recently. He looked forward to collecting on that I.O.U. soon. Maybe it would be in his favor that, unlike Victor, he wouldn't be thrown off his game by hate eating away at his gut. He didn't know what irony was, but it was underlying his laughter.

\* \* \*

Lone Pine, in the southern portion of the Owens Valley, was a ride of several days from Bridgeport, although train travel now made that somewhat faster. Frank Eastman and Vincent Perry were well aware of this, as they had first met back in 1879 when they had lived in Bodie, the County Seat of which was Bridgeport. Still having a few business interests in Bodie, once a year they made the long trip to that town.

Their wives, Emily and Charlotte, played along with the *business interest* excuse. It was true, of course, but they also knew there would be much more time spent in various gambling halls. Frank loved poker, and Vince was partial to twenty-one, often referred to as *vingt et un*. Emily Eastman and Charlotte Perry had become friends with Roger's wife Amanda not long before the Eastmans and Perrys had moved from Bodie late in 1880. Amanda had even lived in Lone Pine for a short time before Roger had married her and taken her back to Bodie.

When Amanda had given birth to Ellie in Virginia City in '86, the Eastman and Perry families had traveled north to be with her. It had been on that trip that the men had become friends with Jim, having already met Roger when he had been courting Amanda.

Bodie being not all that far southeast of Bridgeport, when Vince approached Frank with envelopes in his hand, he was thinking about the distance. And the routes they had previously traveled.

Vince was a little taller than Frank, broad-shouldered, thick through the chest but with narrow hips and long legs. And with sandy blond hair that refused to mat down even under a hat. He was cleanshaven, but only because any attempt at a mustache had produced something akin to a molting caterpillar. But it didn't matter, as he had the kind of open face that matched his friendly demeanor. Vince had a way of putting anyone immediately at their ease, and every man in town considered themselves Vincent Perry's great friend.

Frank was almost as tall, but of a slimmer build, with dark brown hair, a neat mustache, a slight dimple in his chin, and brown eyes that tended to bore into people. He was well-liked, but it was often edged with more respect than warmth. Possibly because, besides being a local rancher, he also spent considerable time in the saloons at the poker tables. He had lived in Lone Pine since the year after the big earthquake of 1872, and initially had worked for the Cerro Gordo mine owners as a mining engineer. He hadn't met Emily until 1878, when she had been a servant living in the house then owned by Mrs. Kennedy, but now belonging to him and Emily.

Frank, sitting in the wooden swing on the front porch of the two-story, yellow house facing Main Street, watched Vince approaching. Mt. Whitney, far in the background, was catching the golden glow of the early morning light on the snow still clinging from the previous winter. The tallest mountain in the U.S. stood proud just beyond the shoulder of Lone Pine Peak and the nearer brown boulders of the Alabama Hills. The contrast of these colors under a dark blue sky made Frank wish he was a painter.

That idea being laughable, Frank pulled his eyes from the far view. Instead, he focused on his friend and business partner who was approaching from the street.

"Is that the letter from the man wanting to buy our cattle?"

Vince climbed the steps to the porch, his long legs taking two at a time. He sprawled in a wicker chair facing the swing, his back to the street. "No. It's a letter addressed to the two of us. I thought I'd let you open it."

Puzzled, Frank opened the envelope. "It's from Jim Murphy." He read it aloud, after which the two men looked at each other with mixed feelings. "So," Frank concluded, "it's actually J. B. Roberts who's having this poker tournament in June."

"Yes, but he asked Jim to invite two friends, and I guess that's us." Vince laced his fingers over his chest and grinned. "Could be fun."

"We only met Jim that once when we brought the wives to be with Amanda at the birth of her baby."

"Yeah, that was an odd trip." Vince cast his mind back. "I remembered Roger and Amanda from when they got married out front of your house under the sycamore trees before they returned to live in Bodie. But we didn't know anything about Roger's family at that time. I only knew Roger as a square gambler in Bodie, mostly dealing Faro. I hoped like hell that Amanda knew what she was doing."

Frank grinned. "Evidently, she did."

"Yeah. She's a nice, decent gal. I'll never understand how she got involved with that bad apple, DeRoche, who got himself hanged."

"I enjoyed that visit in Virginia City. Jim and Lucy Murphy were great hosts, and I could see why our wives are so fond of Amanda."

"I don't think Amanda liked that Jim and Roger took us into town so often." Vince smiled at the memory.

"Oh, I don't know." Frank chuckled. "It gave the wives time to help with the new baby. And talk about us."

Vince ignored the probable truth of that last part. "So, are we going to accept this invitation?"

"What do you think we should do?"

Vince shook his head. "I asked you first."

After a moment's hesitation, Frank answered. "Honestly? I want to go. It sounds interesting."

"If not somewhat strange."

"Yeah, that too."

Vince let out a sigh of obvious relief. "Okay, then." He stood up and stretched, an old injury left over from his Bodie days making his leg sometimes stiffen, and causing a slight limp much of the time. "Now all we have to do is tell the wives."

That turned out not to be as difficult as the men had anticipated, as both Emily and Charlotte wanted to get started making jam and canning vegetables. And without having to spend hours each day cooking for hungry, sometimes demanding husbands. They each had a daily girl who took care of the cleaning chores, but they had only themselves to do the cooking.

Learning of the men's plan, Emily and Charlotte decided that Charlotte would move in with Emily while the men were gone, as Emily's kitchen was the largest. Charlotte would bring her seven-year-old son Steven, who would be thrilled because it would allow him to spend time with Emily's daughter, Whitney. Less than a year separating them, the children had been best friends their whole lives, the townspeople considering them brother and sister. What the two friends wouldn't realize until they were young adults, was that what can bond people together can also break them apart.

With all the invitations accepted, the invitees began making their plans for the tournament weekend. The events that would follow were now lined up and in place, and like a deadly boulder rolling downhill, they would follow their inevitable course.

* * *

Jim and Roger Murphy left Virginia City, Nevada, on the early morning train out to Carson City, then switched to the stage heading to Genoa. The small agricultural town at the foot of the Sierra was one of their favorite places, and they spent the night there. After a good breakfast and a visit with the friend from whom they borrowed two well-conditioned horses, they only covered the first eight miles of their seventy-mile journey.

They stopped in Gardnerville for the night. The town was barely ten years old, but because it was on the route to the Esmeralda Mining District and Bodie, it had become a popular stop for the huge freight teams carrying supplies and mining equipment. Some tandem-hitched wagons had carried a load so heavy that it took two dozen horses to pull. Now, in 1888, with the dwindling number of mining areas, the town was developing into a farming community. Consequently, the two men had no problem finding a hotel for the night. That it was next door to a saloon with room enough for two tables, one of which had a poker game open, made it all the better. Roger played while Jim sipped a beer at the bar, and the next morning they had enough money to cover the hotel and livery stable bills.

After a long day of riding, they spent their next night at Holbrook Station at the turning to Wellington, Nevada. Considering how stiff he was upon rising the next morning, Jim wondered how he would feel after another day in the saddle. Roger maintained his father's dignity by pretending he didn't notice his awkwardness in mounting his horse. He also used it as cover for his own strained effort to mount. These men were gamblers, not cowboys, and right then they were only too aware of the fact.

Jim and Roger spent their third night in Coleville, California. Although they had broken their journey into fairly moderate distances, Jim still dismounted hard onto the ground, wishing they were in their usual evening haunt and their favorite saloon.

They were made welcome in the Barnett Hotel, a large white house surrounded by orchards, and joined by a number of freight teams there for the night. Roger was happy, as the freighters were eager for a game of chance. Jim was eager only for bed. Roger won several hands, enjoyed the beer and the company, then artfully lost back some of the money to the freighters. Consequently, everyone retired for the night in a companionable mood.

In the morning, they enjoyed peaches and plums, along with lots of fresh honey on their pancakes. They were invited to see the apiary, but they declined, not anxious to get all that close to beehives.

Late in the afternoon, they approached Fales Hot Springs, a popular toll station on the main route north and south. Having that day spent their longest time on the trail, they were grateful that they were now only 15 miles from Bridgeport.

Jim had once met Sam Fales and his lovely wife Diana, considerably younger than Sam, when they had all lived in Bodie. Having heard about the station and the delightful hot springs, and feeling the aches and pains of the long ride, Jim announced to Roger that they were stopping there for the night. Roger would have been happier completing the last fifteen miles to Bridgeport and spending the night in a nice hotel. However, he realized that might be pushing it for his father.

From the road above, they looked down at the layout of the hot springs resort nestled in a shallow hollow. They admired the two large, two-story buildings, with the hot tub shacks beyond, the well-maintained out buildings, and the several large corrals full of horses and mules. Since a number of buggies were parked in front, as well as two freight wagons off to the side, it was obvious that this was a popular place. The smell of minerals rose in the air, carried by the steam from the hot springs bubbling up in a large pool. It was all very inviting to anyone as sore as were Jim and Roger.

Even more welcoming was Sam Fales and two other men coming out to greet them as they rode down the road onto the property. Sam was easily recognized by his bald head covered by an old hat, and his long gray beard feathering out in the breeze. The hired hands with him took up the men's cloth valises and heavy saddlebags, and headed to the long white building to the right of the plain, two-story house.

It was then that Jim and Roger noticed that Sam had been followed by a large, vocal turkey introduced as Brigham. He was displaying the breadth of his wing span as he strutted along, leading a dozen chickens mostly interested in scratching up the earth. After the handshaking, reassurances that the horses would be cared for properly, and a short discussion of how lovely was the area, the three men made their way inside.

After being shown to a room with several bunks, Jim and Roger placed their jackets on the beds where their things had been deposited. Taking up the large towels also on the beds, they made their way to the baths housed in sheds. Each shed looked to be decades old, although this was simply because the boards used in their construction were spaced to allow for the entering of the steam from below.

Jim turned to his son with a facetious grin. "Are you going to have a mud bath?"

Roger scoffed at that most decidedly. "I just want to soak in hot water. The water in the pitchers in our rooms along the way have been tepid at best."

"True. But the pool might be nice."

The pool, however, was currently populated to capacity. Men were splashing each other, trading jokes and jibes, and all the while tossing a bar of lye soap back and forth. Father and son found a couple of the square wooden tubs free in a shack, and settled in for a soak. The water piped straight from the hot springs was 180 degrees, but it was tempered by that from a cold spring nearby. All in all, the whole arrangement was very well designed and maintained, and was the reason for the station's popularity.

They dressed quickly in the cooling evening air, muscles no longer screaming at them, and headed back to their room. They passed two women with towels over their shoulders approaching a nearby shed, each dragging a wriggling young boy by the hand.

"Harry, if you don't mind your manners, this bar of soap is going to end up in your mouth! It won't kill you to be clean for a change."

"You like the hot tubs, Hershel," exclaimed the other woman. "Get along now! And be careful how you step on the floor boards."

"Awwww ..." This was the only response both mothers received in return. But one of them was smart enough to remind the boys that there would be cake afterwards, and cooperation was suddenly afforded as they entered one of the steamy shacks.

The dining room was a delight. The lovely Diana Fales had just finished placing platters and bowls of food on a long table, and her daughter was playing the piano with a skill that was surprising. Sam had married the widow when she had been supporting herself and Minnie by managing lodging houses, first in Aurora until it's decline, and then in Bodie as it prospered. It was there in Bodie that they had met and married, he enchanted by her beauty and self-sufficiency, and she recognizing a kind and gentle man with ambition that matched her own.

Roger marveled at the number of different fruits in bowls at each end of the long table. The freighters passing through from Sonora were always most generous with what they shared from their hauls. Lucy Murphy's yard had apple trees, but citrus was a rare delight in arid Virginia City. The long freighting distances to get it there meant it was expensive and rarely without blemish. An orange and a pile of berries quickly sat on Roger's plate, along with fried chicken and mashed potatoes covered in gravy. He happily paid the fifty-cent charge for himself, as well as Jim. Children were twenty-five cents, and that included their bath.

As darkness descended and everyone finished eating, a neighbor arrived with his fiddle and the furniture was cleared away for dancing. Because there were more men present than women, the dances would be mostly schottisches and square dancing. Much laughter accompanied the choosing of the men to wear a bandanna around their upper arm to designate them as a stand-in female. Roger and Jim politely declined to participate, lured away to their beds by their fatigue. They were sound asleep by the time the others sharing the room came to their bunks.

Leaving early the next morning, the Murphy men arrived in Bridgeport early afternoon. They had taken their time, as they were enjoying their travel through lush green meadows cut by rivulets of melted snow, and accented by low, rocky hills. It was an exceedingly pleasant route that boosted their spirits, and encouraged the return of their eagerness for the weekend's gambling. As they approached Bridgeport, they were met by a soft breeze that brought to them the welcoming fragrance of damp earth and wild flowers, spiced by the familiar scent of cattle herds.

They were on a wide trail between pastures teeming with cattle, oxen used at the sawmills, and a number of large mules used for hauling heavy wagons. Far in the distance to their right was the Sawtooth Range with lingering snow along its crest, not unexpected since the town they were nearing was almost 6,500 feet in elevation. In the distance east of the town they could see the Bodie Hills, while to their left they could see ranches spread out in the lowlands north of town, the Walker River cutting through them with the Sweetwater Mountains as the backdrop.

"No wonder," Roger commented, "that the land here is so fertile. The town sure doesn't lack for water and feed."

Every animal they saw had its face buried in sweet, green grass or one of the many streams running through the fenced meadows. Entering the town proper, not far to their right were a cluster of barns and corrals past a large house. In fact, behind many of the houses they were passing were barns of various sizes. Buggies or wagons, along with feed and firewood could be stored there, and in the larger ones even animals. The elements in the Big Meadows area, as it was still sometimes called, could be brutal. Summers were pleasantly warm, but never severe. The winters, however, saw feet of deep snow and temperatures well below zero.

As the men passed down Emigrant Street, the main road entering the town from the north, they passed on their left a number of clapboard-sided, whitewashed homes. That several of them were trimmed in blue was a reminder of the first settlers' New England roots, and an architectural style common throughout the town. Also common was the presence of hop vines growing up the side of a house, or along a surrounding slab rail fence.

Jim and Roger turned right onto School Street, passing the newspaper offices on their left just behind the large, white courthouse that faced Main Street. In order to merge into the traffic on the wide main road through town, they had to wait for an opening among passing freight teams, farm wagons, big-wheeled black buggies, and riders on horses. A lumber wagon had just passed, heading east. The wagon was nothing more than flat boards on wheels, now loaded with ten trees skinned of all branches, and so heavy that it took ten large horses to pull it.

While father and son waited, they took the opportunity to admire the courthouse on their left and Bryant's Hall on their right. Both buildings were on land donated to the town by Amasa Bryant, whose ranch spread out to the north toward the flow of the river that crossed the land of seven ranches.

When a break in the traffic allowed them to move forward, they settled their horses at the stables to the west of the Leavitt House hotel. Hesitating on the small, raised porch and looking out at the town, both men nodded with approval at the neatness of the painted buildings and carefully maintained wooden walkways. What surprised them most was the number of large trees between the buildings, with more on the streets running behind Main Street.

Ladies dressed in summer calico, a light shawl over their shoulders for modesty, were out doing their shopping, hemp bags or baskets over their arms. Several small groups of them were gathered on the wooden sidewalks, enjoying short conversations. Men were doing the same, most dressed in denim and high-necked, cotton shirts under leather or cloth vests, but several were sporting business suits.

Dust from the road filled the air, but was being wetted down by a horse-drawn wagon passing slowly along the road edge so as not to block the passage of the wagon traffic. It consisted of a large barrel on its side, held up by two large wagon wheels on a frame, with the driver seated on a small buckboard seat toward the front. The wooden, horizontal barrel was filled through a hole in the top, and with the removal of boards beneath, small holes were revealed that allowed just enough water to sprinkle out to wet the road.

Having seen a similar wagon in Virginia City, Jim and Roger watched this one for only a moment before turning around to enter the hotel. They were faced by the *Gentlemen's Entrance* to the left and the *Ladies Entrance* to the right of that, each entrance so noted by the words painted in small white letters above the doors.

Choosing the appropriate entrance, they entered directly into the lobby. To their immediate right was a doorway that opened onto the area at the foot of the stairs to the second floor. Women entering through their entrance would find themselves at the foot of the stairs and could go immediately to their room without having to mingle with men in the lobby. Evidently, when built in 1877, this was something which the builders had assumed would be of importance to women. Whether or not it had been important then, in 1888 few women paid attention to the distinction.

Of course, this may have been helped by the fact that the dining room, accessed through a door at the foot of the stairs, served both men and women; even those women who were unescorted by a man. Society's rules in the late 1800's might have been somewhat ambiguous, but people seemingly had no problem sorting them out to suit their needs.

Jim and Roger crossed to an unattended counter between a small alcove to the left and a door to a back room to the right. After tapping a brass bell on the counter, they turned to a group of local women gathered in the far corner of the lobby. Sitting on the two velvet sofas, the women had a large quilt spread between them on a frame and each was busily applying a needle to the area in front of them. The men tipped their hats to the ladies before turning back to the counter to greet a young man in black pants, a white shirt buttoned to the neck, and a black vest.

"How might I help you?"

"I telegrammed ahead," Jim told the young man. "Jim Murphy. Two rooms."

Looking down at a large ledger, the man's smile disappeared. "Oh, I'm so sorry, Mr. Murphy. I have it down as one room with two beds. And we're full up."

Roger stepped forward before his father could speak up, knowing how short his temper could be when he was tired. "That's okay. My father and I can share a room." Roger signed the register while the clerk called over a well-muscled youth. He threw a saddlebag over each shoulder and picked up their valises before effortlessly walking up the steep stairs. Carrying only their room key, the exhausted gamblers followed more slowly.

It was the afternoon of Thursday, June 21, and they weren't due at J.B.'s ranch until the next day. This gave them time to recover their energy with a hearty meal in the hotel's dining room before heading out into the town. Although it had several shops and five saloons, and even a newspaper office, along with all the other basics of any settled town, it didn't take them long to see it all.

They chose to spend an hour at Joe Spark's Tonsorial Parlor, better known locally as *the barber shop*. It was in a small brown building on Main Street with a bath house out back, and the Murphy men arrived just as the two barbers were finishing with two men in nice suits. Roger figured they were locals, since they didn't pay before leaving, and Mr. Sparks was making notations in a ledger.

As Roger settled into one of the vacant chairs, he admired the row of fancy, personally labeled shaving mugs lined up on the counter. Above was a large mirror in a carved, wooden frame.

Mr. Sparks was a middle-aged man with a thin but ready smile and a luxurious mustache. His hair was slicked back with a gel he made himself, and which he sold for two bits a jar. While nimbly holding a comb in one hand a scissors in the other, he clipped at Jim's hair as he talked. Roger, preferring his hair on the long side, had settled for a shave from the other barber introduced as Leroy. He wielded the single-edged straight-razor with a dexterity and gentleness that impressed Roger, but he nevertheless focused on remaining still. And was glad that Leroy wasn't a talker.

"You fellas visiting or passing through?" Mr. Sparks asked.

Jim grinned at him. "How do know we don't live here?"

Mr. Sparks took that as a great joke, and barked out a good laugh. "Ah, my friend, I know every face in town. Man or woman. Yep, I trim a lady's hair from time to time."

"We're visiting," Jim told him. "Out at the Double R."

There was a longer pause than expected while the barber glanced over at Leroy. "Oh, yeah?" It was as much a statement as a question, and had just a little underlying wariness in it. It made Jim and Roger wonder at the kind of guests usually associated with J. B. Roberts.

"So," Roger began, hoping for more insight into their host, "you know him?"

"Everyone knows J.B.," Leroy said. "Not well, mind you. But he's been good to the town. We're planning on putting in a ditch across Main for the snow melt to drain out to the low lands north. He's contributed to that."

Jim felt the need to reassure the barbers about the casualness of their acquaintance. "We only met him once last year when we were all in Bodie. He's invited us and some others for the weekend to play poker. Just a friendly game."

Both barbers seemed to relax. "Oh, well," Leroy said, "he's known for liking his gambling. Goes to Bodie and Virginia City every once in awhile for that, they say."

Now that he could fit these strangers into his knowledge of Bridgeport society, Mr. Sparks asked, "Anyone from town invited?"

"Two. Victor Turner and Otto Mercer. You know them?"

"Oh, yes. Vic lives here in town and Otto works out at the Valley View ranch south of town." Simple words, but he was frowning, which was explained by his next statement. "Not men I'd expect J.B. to socialize with."

Not knowing how to respond to that, Jim said nothing in reply. Roger simply wondered what they had gotten themselves into. It seemed, however, that Mr. Sparks had expended all his comments on that subject.

"Did you read about the big statue they've put up on an island in New York Harbor?" Mr. Sparks asked. He liked to show how well informed he was. "It's supposed to be the goddess of liberty. Several stories tall, it is. Made of copper plates, and shines like gold in the sun."

"Copper, you say?" Roger was fascinated. "It'll be interesting to see how the salt air affects that."

"Oh, say, I hadn't thought of that." Mr. Sparks brushed loose hairs off Jim's neck and tightened the drape over him. "What'll happen to the statue, do you think?"

Jim looked at his well-educated son with a raised brow. Roger explained, feeling a little like a trained dog given the command to perform. "It'll turn green, I suppose. Copper does that as it ages."

This was a new fact for Mr. Sparks and Leroy, and they were both thrilled to have something new to tell their customers. Leroy summed up his feelings. "Well, I'll be!"

Roger paid their bill, and, as was the commonly accepted custom, Mr. Sparks assured them that the good weather would surely hold. Whether it would or not wasn't the point. It was the duty of a loyal local to have faith that it would.

They shook hands, thanked the barbers for doing such a grand job, and walked out into the sunshine. As they turned to their left toward the river, and past several nicely painted buildings, they looked back. Mr. Sparks was locking his front door while Leroy hung an out-to-lunch sign on it. The barbers then quickly walked in the other direction to the nearby Kirkwood Saloon.

Jim kept his voice down. "I wonder if his first report will be about us and J.B.'s poker game, or the Statue of Liberty?"

Their attention was diverted when they saw Joe Brown's store. On the wall outside the store, an advertising poster declared that Mr. Brown sold "Yankee Notions, gun stuff (powder caps, shot and cartridges), groceries, and stationery". In smaller print it was noted that "shirt fronts and ladies cuffs and neckware" were also within. They found a couple of shirts they liked, and also purchased two pairs of socks and several handkerchiefs.

They passed by "Hays & Bros., General Merchandise, selling groceries, hardware, liquor, clothing, boots and shoes, and agricultural implements". At Bryant's Store they purchased a bottle of red wine as a gift for J.B., and had it packed in a hemp bag with lots of straw. There were a number of fancy boxes of locally crafted chocolates stacked neatly on a table, but they managed to resist them.

Outside on the wooden sidewalk, they hesitated. They considered following a short stretch of stone sidewalk to the big Allen House Hotel, not far from the bridge that spanned the East Walker River and gave the town its name. But they decided to walk back into the heart of town.

Spotting Mrs. McKinnon's Millinery Shop nearby, Roger thought back to his mother's first job when he and Lucy had arrived in Virginia City.

"Did mother tell you about working in a millinery shop when we first got to Virginia City back in '75?"

"Yes, but she didn't go into any detail."

"She probably doesn't want to think about it. Her fingers were always raw at the tips from sewing feathers onto hats. She was told that she wouldn't be allowed to do anything else for some time. I was sure glad when she was able to give that up."

Jim still found such reminiscences uncomfortable. Lucy and Roger had been lost to him during that time, and it wasn't until 1881 that he had reunited with his beloved wife. And then, only because he had stumbled into Bodie and found Roger over a year earlier. His son had hidden him from those searching for him, and had nursed him through a long illness that neither of them had been sure Jim would survive. They had kept Lucy in the dark, letting her think Jim still dead until they were sure he would fully recover. That was not a time in either man's life they liked to remember.

# CHAPTER 2

## SETTING UP THE GAMES

The next morning after one of the Leavitt House's hearty breakfasts, Jim and Roger took their time riding down the road out of town. Living in the land of sagebrush, they were overjoyed to find themselves surrounded by lush green meadows filled with cattle and oxen. The morning air was mild and the breeze gentle, carrying to them the chortle of black birds sitting on the wire fences. It all felt like a friendly welcome. Not far past the second bend in the road they could see the ranch in the distance off to their left.

Jim was impressed. "My God, it's huge!"

Stacked stone supported the house, the rest made of locally harvested timber, and with an imposing stone fireplace at the near end. Behind the house were two large barns and several other good-size buildings, a large and a small corral, and a round pen for close work with horses. Beyond all that was a pond with a windmill on its edge. On the east end of the house, near a small grove of willows, they could just make out a hog pen, chicken coop, and a turkey run. Next to a narrow creek behind those was a laundry house with clothes lines along both sides. A black smoke stack poked through its roof, no doubt from the stove within where water was heated. A cold house straddled the creek, where milk, cheese, crocks of butter, and other perishables were kept in quantity. It was next to a shed they assumed was the ice house.

Reaching the turn-off to the house, the Murphy men looked up at a large iron medallion at the top of an entrance arch made from tall, skinned trees. The ranch's brand, the *Double R*, was formed by a circle of iron around two joined letters R. The men assumed correctly that it was for J.

B. Roberts and his son Alex. The townspeople joked that it meant no one else need apply, especially women looking for a wealthy husband.

As they started down the long road to the house, they admired the long-leaf pines fronted by lilac bushes along its length. They were past their spring bloom, but their green leaves were shining in the sun, someone having cut off the spent blooms so they couldn't form ugly brown seed pods. Once closer to the house, they noted black smoke stacks extending through the roof in several places. Counting them, they speculated that other than the kitchen stove, there were probably three rooms upstairs that had warming stoves in them.

Observing the property, a combination of grandeur and utilitarian practicality, Jim's first thought was that Lucy would find it pretentious and possibly a little too masculine, but nice for a visit. It was much different from their simple Victorian house in Virginia City. Roger's first assessment of the house was much the same, but that Amanda would happily move in to stay. Their house was very small, and although she hadn't said anything, Roger knew his wife wanted to find something larger for their little family.

The men tied their horses to the railing provided near the split-log steps while looking up to the porch. A woman stood there looking down at them, her hands clasped at her waste. She was tall and thin, her imperious attitude displayed on a face off-set by a sharp nose and gray eyes like those of an angry eagle. Her black dress was cinched wasp-like at her waste, and its white collar off-set black hair pulled back into a tight knot. The white cuffs gripped her wrists so tightly that it was a wonder the buttons didn't pop off.

She made a minimum effort to smile, and although she may have meant it to be welcoming, it came across as disdain. It was her usual pose when greeting guests, as she thought it gave others the most befitting impression of status. J.B. may have built the house, but she was determined that everyone understand that the one in charge of it was Mrs. Lewis. No one on the ranch or in town knew her first name, and wouldn't have dared use it if they had.

Slipping around from behind her, a small but distinguished looking Chinese gentleman, somewhere in the vicinity of thirty, skipped down the steps to greet them. Dressed in black pants, a white shirt and a white coat similar to what a chef might wear, he nevertheless had a traditional, Chinese braid of hair. After a quick glance up at the woman, he murmured to the men, "That Mrs. Lewis, housekeeper. I am Sing, cook and houseman." His genial smile showed brilliantly white teeth as he made a slight bow to them. At the same time, a ranch hand appeared and led their horses away.

They would find that the furthest building from the house was the large horse barn, conveniently located next to the tack room and feed barn, as well as a tool shed. Nearest the main house was the bunk house, behind which was a bath house and several storage sheds. All were painted a serviceable dark red. Hitching posts and water troughs were strategically placed among it all, with the privies hidden behind the buildings.

In the small corral not far from the bunk house, and within view of the house, were currently five yearling horses, all bays with various markings. With them was an older, light gray mare that the younger horses treated as though she was their mother.

Sing led the men into a large, open room much too large to be called a parlor, over which loomed a huge stone fireplace on the far wall to their right. Embedded into the wall on the far side of it was a long and deep, stone-lined niche in which logs were tightly packed, awaiting their turn in the maw of the fireplace. The rest of the firewood was housed out back in a shed that held a dozen cords.

The fireplace was fronted by two long sofas that faced each other over a dark wood coffee table, leather easy chairs at both ends. On the same wall as the fireplace, and near the large front windows, was an upright piano. Jim, who played well, looked forward to feeling the ivory keys beneath his fingers. Then he noticed the game table centered under the windows, a chair on either side facing a chess board ready to be played. It was a reminder of the reason they were there.

Roger noted the same items, but also that brass and glass kerosene lamps of various designs were everywhere. A great reader, he was thankful for that, as he figured there would be plenty of time when they weren't playing poker. Beneath it all was a scattering of colorful rugs, and equally colorful blankets over the backs of the sofas. The room could have looked almost chaotic, but instead somehow managed to be inviting.

To their left was a large dining area with a long, rectangular table surrounded by an odd assortment of wooden chairs. But it was the curio cabinets against the wall at either end of the dining room that caused most people consternation. There were three on the outside wall and two on the wall at the other end of the room. At first glance, they noted a set of gleaming white fine china, silver serving bowls and platters, crystal stemware, and highly decorated porcelain vases and biscuit jars. The silver frames without photos gave Roger the creeps.

The door to the kitchen was open at the back of the dining area and revealed a large kitchen with a deep sink under a window looking out over a small garden, an iron pump handle on the right side of the sink. A center work island, and a huge stove dripping with chrome against the outside wall to the left gave evidence that in this room no expense had been spared. Further proof of this was hidden from their view to the right of the door; two large ice boxes and a walk-in pantry. Just visible to the left was the edge of a small round table of highly polished pine. This might have been a kitchen, but it was also Sing's domain, where no expense had been spared.

Not far in front of those entering through the front door, and backing to the kitchen, was a small fireplace with a raised hearth, faced by a small sofa. Beyond that cozy arrangement was a flight of stairs that led to the upstairs rooms, each one facing a railed, open hallway that looked down over the great room below. At the back of the great room, on the wall below the railing, was a large cabinet with doors tightly closed.

The walls of the hallway above and the great room below were hung with tapestries, oil paintings, a few photographs, and kerosene-filled wall sconces. These last were lit by Sing at dusk each evening, and turned down after everyone retired for the night.

But among all they surveyed, the most impressive embellishment was a duplicate of the iron medallion first seen at the ranch's entrance. It loomed over the room from the top half of the stone fireplace. No one was allowed to forget they were now at the Double R Ranch.

A comely young woman in her late teens or early twenties entered the room from the kitchen. Her blonde hair was pulled back from her face and the ringlets held in place by a black ribbon, a few dangling curls at the temples accenting an attractive face the very image of youthful vitality. Roger smiled as he noticed that her black dress rustled under the sway of hips that as yet had not learned how to remain rigid. Even the white pinafore apron over the dress could not successfully conceal the movement.

This young vision of loveliness, as a local had dubbed her, was carrying a tray with a coffee pot and several mugs, which she carefully set on the table between the sofas. When she stood up, she offered a demure courtesy while still managing a bold sweep of her eyes over the new arrivals. She rustled invitingly as she walked past them, her eyes primly cast down while leaving behind the light scent of lilac.

Roger glanced at Mrs. Lewis standing by the door to the kitchen, watching the girl with a critical eye as she approached to stand next to the housekeeper. But there was a slight softness in the housekeeper's expression, and Roger realized that this dour woman actually liked the girl. He wasn't sure what to do with this knowledge, but it made him feel a little less intimidated by the housekeeper.

In a throaty voice with a slight rasp to it, Mrs. Lewis announced, "This is Sara. If you need anything at any time, you may inform her or Sing." In other words, Sing and Sara were trained not to bother her unless absolutely necessary, and no mere visitor should even think about it.

Mrs. Lewis walked toward the sofas and held out an arm as an invitation for Jim and Roger to sit where they could enjoy the coffee. When Sara noticed Sing picking up the Murphy's saddlebags by the front door, after placing the packaged bottle of wine on the dining table, she cast a quick glance at Mrs. Lewis. Receiving a nod, Sara hurried to get the men's two valises.

Roger watched her as she followed the houseman up the stairs, the hem of her skirt just short enough to allow her to ascend without the necessity of lifting it. This meant showing the tops of her high-button shoes and therefore the turn of trim ankles, but Roger assumed that Mrs. Lewis allowed it for the sake of safety and efficiency. And Sara was, after all, young and just a servant. Roger blushed when he caught his father watching him. Jim merely smiled and poured coffee into their cups.

A stamping of feet could be heard on the rug just inside the back door, which was at the end of a corridor off the great room between the small fireplace and the foot of the stairs. The hall continued to the back door, past the kitchen on the left and two small bedrooms on the right for Sing and Sara, and one large room for Mrs. Lewis. In fact, Sara's tiny room had at one time been a walk-in closet used for storage.

At the sound of the stamping feet, Mrs. Lewis had suddenly come to life. Her color deepened, her eyes took on an eager shine, and she hurried into the kitchen. She immerged with a large mug in hand and set it on a small table next to the leather chair nearest the fireplace. Anyone sitting there would have within their view the entrance into the house, the great room, the dining room, and the upstairs corridor. Roger thought of it as a throne awaiting the king.

And indeed, after Mrs. Lewis hurried into the corridor, they heard her say, "Your coffee is next to your chair."

A pleasant masculine voice answered with a breezy, "Thank you, my dear."

Into the room walked a tall man of average build but broad through the shoulders, with thick brown hair, smokey gray eyes, a strong jaw, and what is often called a *winning smile*. His denim pants, sky blue shirt and brown leather vest might have been simple and even dusty, but nothing could mask their obvious quality and perfect fit. This was especially true of the man's snake-skin boots.

He hesitated a moment before moving toward his guests, holding out a hand as Jim and Roger stood. "My first gamblers! It's so nice to see you both again. Welcome to the Double R."

"Hello, J.B.," Jim answered. "Thank you for inviting us."

"Thank you for accepting." His smile was warm and friendly, but it didn't quite reach to his eyes. Which, Roger noted, had darted around the entirety of the room in that split second before he fully entered.

After J.B. walked to his chair and picked up his coffee cup, he held it up as in salute, a picture of pleasant anticipation. "I think this is going to be a memorable weekend for all of us." Little did he know how prophetic those words would be.

It wasn't long before the others began to arrive. Three days before, Frank Eastman and Vince Perry had taken the train to Benton Station north of Bishop Creek, spending the night at the California Hotel. The next day they took the stage west to Mono Mills. Although the *Bodie & Benton Railroad* from there to Bodie was not supposed to take passengers, its reason for existing being the transport of wood, if you knew the right people, it was occasionally allowed. And both Frank and Vince knew those people.

After spending the night in one of the employee boarding houses, they got on the first train leaving in the morning. There wasn't much to see, what with the huge expanse of Mono Lake to their left and desert scrub to their right, but they still enjoyed the trip. After all, the journey on a train, even one not meant to accommodate passengers, was better than enduring a longer ride on a horse or the jostling of a stage. The only part they didn't care for was the crossing of the 250 foot-long trestle, 50 feet over a deep gorge.

When they got to Bodie, because the train station was at the far eastern edge of the town near the mines on the hill. A freighter saw them get off the train and asked if they needed a ride into town. They gratefully accepted, tipping the man two bits. It would buy him a drink at any of the saloons.

They wasted no time meeting up with a man who owed them money, which they used at the Kingsley Stables to rent horses for the ride to Bridgeport. From what people in Lone Pine had told them about the Double R, it was further out in the meadows than could be reached by a quick walk from town. But beyond that, they were a little uneasy about the strangeness of the invitation, and thought it best to have the ability to leave whenever they felt like it.

This feeling was enhanced by a conversation had with the hostler at the stable in Bodie, a man they had known since '81 when they had both lived there. After a brief conversation about the changes in Bodie since they were last there, they mentioned where they were headed. They immediately sensed a reserve in their old friend. When Vince gently prodded, the man simply shrugged, looked around to be sure no one else was within range of their conversation, and took a step closer.

"It's just that…" The man checked again to be sure no one else was nearby. "Well, J. B. Robert's background is kinda murky. Men say it's real hard getting friendly with him. No one seems to know anything about him before he came to the meadows in '73 and settled on the land. He had a hand with him, Hank, who still works for him. They built the bunk house first, where they lived while building the big barn and the corrals. At the same time, J.B. had a good-sized crew building the house."

Frank broke in. "I thought he was married when he came to the Big Meadows area."

"Oh, he was. She showed up from wherever she'd been just before the house was finished. Fine lookin' woman!" He sighed and shook his head, but didn't explain its meaning. "He added the porch across the back of the house just recently." He took another step closer and lowered his voice. "Now, all that takes a lot of money. Of course, people say he's a right good gambler. But you've got to wonder where he got the money to build all that, what with him being so young. He's only thirty-six now, and all that building was fifteen years ago."

"How does he make his money other than gambling?" Frank was always interested in that subject.

The hostler looked down at the ground and rubbed his chin. "He has a big spread. Lots of cattle. Breeds horses and hogs, too. *Investments* is what some say. Others say his late wife brought a good amount to the marriage." Again, that big sigh. "Beyond all that, I don't know."

Vince thought to himself that most of what the man claimed to know was really just rumor and surmising. It made him wonder how many unfounded stories about himself and Frank circulated around Lone Pine unbeknownst to them. He and Frank agreed that their weekend in Bridgeport was going to be at the least a diverting adventure, and possibly an interesting tale to tell when they got back home.

After an uneventful ride down the toll road, broken at Murphey's Station and a short stop at Dogtown, they moved on. They broke free of the high rock walls forming the winding pass known as Bridgeport Canyon, the southern entrance into the meadows. It was the first time in ten years that they had been there, and that had been in late fall when the pastures were brown and the cattle sold or moved elsewhere in preparation of the harsh winter to follow. On this day, their first view of the vast area once called Big Meadows was far different. Acre upon acre of lush, green grass spread before them, filled with cattle, oxen, mules, and horses.

A flock of sheep were bunched together in a long, narrow pasture to their right. It was backed by low, rocky outcroppings, but barbed wire fencing ran along the base of them, as well as along the road. Branches and scrap wood acted as posts, but it had proven quite serviceable over the years. Two large, shaggy dogs nipped at the heels of the sheep whenever they got too close to the road edge, commanded by a Basque sheepherder by a series of whistles.

Half an hour later they were crossing over the pounded earth and stone bridge spanning the East Walker River that served as the portal to the town. There were, however, still a few of the original town buildings to their right just before crossing. They were weather-worn from twenty-five years of severe winters, and some walls were missing boards, but that didn't mean the buildings weren't being utilized. Most were used for storage, but a few were being used by a small contingent of Chinese who traded with the nearby Piute tribes.

One was a small store run by a Chinese man named Ah Quong Tia, who was tolerated by the Indians even though he sometimes cheated them when gambling with them. He also sold them whisky and opium. It was a situation fraught with potential disaster, and three years later it would erupt into Bridgeport's most violent episode.

Once onto Bridge Street, Frank and Vince encountered on their left the Wedertz Store. It was backed by a small lumber mill and was next to the new two-story, Victorian house of the Towle family. To their right was a small marsh that raucous black birds were finding a source of food and shelter. It was to this area where the runoff of melting snow was channeled in the spring, using ditches that were cut across the road and bridged by boards.

Merging onto Main Street, they found most of the buildings, barns and houses built of whitewashed wood and only a couple of brick. The busy Hughes Blacksmith Shop was the exception, being an old, weatherworn barn with double doors opening right onto the street. Vince's unease about their trip was only partially laid to rest by the town's tidy attractiveness. But the friendly, welcoming smiles from those they passed did the trick and he felt himself relax.

Nevertheless, he told Frank, "We've been in some strange situations before, but this feels a little like walking blindfolded through a boggy marsh. Like the one we just passed."

"You feel it, too?" Frank was relieved to know he wasn't alone in his uncertainty. "I've been looking forward to being here. It's a beautiful area." He looked over at a house, neat and well-maintained with hop vines along the slab fence in front of it. But it was also very small. "I'm just concerned about so many of us being crammed together in someone's home. It doesn't really appeal."

"Yeah, but it'd be downright rude of us to insist on staying in town."

"Not to mention expensive." This fact settled the question for Frank.

At the far end of Main, they faced the Kirkwood home and were forced to make a decision. Turning right would take them onto the short length of Sinnamon Lane. If they had wanted to connect with the road leading out of town to the north, they would have had to turn at the courthouse to access Emigrant Street. But they were headed out into the meadows, so they turned to their left, passed the Kirkwood barns and corrals, and continued out into an immense expanse of green grass dotted with the black and brown of cattle, and the beige of oxen.

The meadows spread all the way to the Sierra foothills known as the Sawtooth Range. It created a wall that curved around the southern half of the valley, and which supported the forests that had inspired the first settlers to establish sawmills. Shingle and planing mills had followed. These mills had produced the lumber for the expansion of the town, as well as the buildings of early Monoville, Aurora, and especially Bodie during its boom in the late 1870's.

After the road jogged a couple of times, they stopped their horses on the road and looked up at the large medallion mimicking the ranch's brand. The circle of iron encasing two letters R absorbed the sun's rays and bounced it back at them. Neither man believed in portents and mystical signs, but in that moment they both had a sense that more lay in store for them than just a typical weekend of gambling and drinking. Their eyes followed the road leading from the entrance to the big, two-story house of log and stone, with the barns, out buildings, corrals, and pond in the distance.

Vince grinned at Frank. "I don't think we have to worry about being crammed in anywhere."

"No, sir!" Frank was not only relieved, but fascinated as well. Here was a grand residence like no other he had ever seen outside a drawing in a magazine. Considering the current growling in his stomach, he was hoping the kitchen was just as grand.

Vince almost laughed aloud when he saw the carefully choreographed greeting awaiting them as Mrs. Lewis came out to stand on the high porch, introducing herself and welcoming them to the Double R. Although Sing stood by her side, one could tell by his frown that she must have done something to irritate him that morning. As soon as she stopped speaking, he announced, "Mrs. Lewis is Double R housekeeper. I am Sing, cook and houseman." He thus managed to make it clear that she was not *the lady of the house*, but just a servant as was he.

Looking happy once again, Sing joyfully took their things from them while saying, "Anything you need, you ask."

Vince noticed Frank sporting his signature smirk that was somewhere between laughter and tactful reticence. But he knew Frank well, and looked forward to later sharing opinions about their first impressions.

Not long after, they found themselves sitting across from Jim and Roger. They had greeted one another with enthusiasm and whispered inquiries about where J.B. might be. Jim and Roger could only answer with shrugs, as their host had suddenly gone to his study upstairs a short time before.

With their cups of coffee in front of them, Sara arrived, batting her lashes reminiscent of a stage star. She asked if the men would prefer something *different* than coffee, with a subtle implication that she might be that something, although everyone knew she really meant liquor. The offer was politely declined. She gave a small curtsey, accompanied by a wink that left the men a little non-plussed, and hurried back to the kitchen. Nevertheless, all four men watched with interest the swing of her hips, and didn't bother to hide their appreciation.

J.B. came down the stairs to make the acquaintance of the new arrivals, a bright smile on his face. Only Vince had perceived that he had been watching his guests' interactions from the upstairs hallway for the last several minutes. He wondered how well the acoustics of the room might be, allowing J.B. to hear what was being said.

As their host passed into the room, Mrs. Lewis emerged from the kitchen and handed him his large coffee mug. On his way to his chair by the fireplace, he stopped to shake hands with Frank and Vince. It allowed Roger to smell the strength of the brandy in J.B.'s mug. By the raised brow on Frank, it was obvious to Roger that he wasn't the only one to have noticed.

After taking a large swallow of his generously laced coffee, J.B. turned to Frank and Vince. "Jim tells me you both like a challenging game of poker."

While Frank merely smiled, Vince said, "Yes, we do. But Frank here is much more of a gambler than I am. I used to own a large merchandise warehouse in Bodie until half of it fell on me, and Frank was a mining engineer there. This was back during the boom. We honed our skills at the tables there." Vince seemed to hesitate as though waiting for a response. When it came, it was not what he expected.

"Well, let's face it," J.B. grinned, "anyone who's ever lived in Bodie has to be somewhat of a gambler." He turned to Jim and Roger. "We met last year when you were there, but did you once live there, too?"

Roger nodded. "Yes. I met my wife there in '80. I'd been working at Wagner's Saloon since late in '78."

"And in '79, I spent a year there," Jim added, glancing sideways at his son. "But it was under his care while I took my time recovering from a pernicious form of pneumonia." He didn't say more than that, wondering if J.B. knew about his stint in the Bridgeport jail just before that, and the circumstances under which he had left it.

As though in answer, J.B. looked at Jim more intently, his eyes suddenly alight with interest. "Oh, right. The death at the sawmill." Then he brightened. "Well, as they say, 'everyone has a past'." But more than the words, it was the crooked half-smile that accompanied them that caused his guests to keep quiet. For Frank and Vince, it brought to mind their conversation with the man at the Bodie livery stable.

A small commotion coming from the front porch switched their attention to the thin, clean-shaven man entering the house, somewhere in his late forties or early fifties. So thin was he that there was a gauntness to his cheeks, making his eyes seem even larger than they were. Looking around, the man removed his hat to reveal a bald head, as well as an aquiline nose and full lips. From his denim pants and jacket, to his general appearance, the first impression he generated was one that attracted interest. Men thought he might be good company while leaning on a bar sharing stories. Women wished they could feed him.

J.B. stepped forward, introducing the new guest as Victor Turner, the man tossing his hat and jacket onto the back of the sofa in front of the small fireplace. Mrs. Lewis moved swiftly from the dining room, giving Victor a scathing scowl. Her lips pursed, she took up his things and hung them on the coat rack by the door. She then retreated into the kitchen, leaving the door slightly ajar.

None of this made an impact on Victor, who didn't bother to acknowledge the other men. Instead, he told J.B., "Thanks for inviting me." When he spoke, his voice had a strained quality to it that made Roger wish he would clear his throat. The other oddity noticed by Roger was that Victor at first glance seemed completely bald. But when he turned his head, one could see thin, fuzzy patches at the crown. No explanation for this came to mind, so Roger tried to ignore it.

"This should be a great weekend, J.B.," Victor said, a little louder than was required. "One of your better ideas."

J.B. seemed somewhat rattled, and Roger wondered whether it was Victor's jovial attitude or his words that had startled their host. He turned to look at his father and noticed a frown between his eyes as he reached for his coffee mug. But Jim didn't drink from the cup. He simply held it and looked up at the medallion on the fireplace with an intensity that puzzled Roger.

Sara approached with a fresh pot of coffee to be switched out with the one on the tray, as well as adding a bowl of brown sugar while giving Victor a sly smile. As she turned to leave, she made sure to bat her lashes in what had become her signature style, and once again wiggled her way back to the kitchen.

Victor was obviously impressed. "I guess I still have it." But when he laughed, there was a bitterness underlying. "On the other hand, according to my wife, I never had it."

The men chuckled, as a good male audience should, but there was no mirth in any of it. Frank poured out and handed Victor a mug of coffee, after which he dumped in two heaping spoons of the brown sugar, of which he was obviously very fond. Roger looked at the other men and realized they were all a little uncomfortable, without understanding why. Wondering if he was missing something, he made a greater effort to pay attention.

Victor, sitting at the far end of the conversation area from J.B., focused on his host. "I dropped off my things out in the bunk house. Otto Mercer told me he too was invited, and had been assigned to stay out there. But I told him he could have the guest room here instead of me. It'll be a treat for him to stay in a big house like this. Besides, after the wife and girls and their yammering, I'd enjoy some quiet time. I know you're only using town laborers right now, so the bunk house has plenty of available beds. I hope you don't mind."

"No, not at all." And indeed, he seemed only slightly thrown by the news. "I'll go tell Mrs. Lewis."

Of course, no one commented as J.B. left the room. But Roger wondered if the others thought, as he did, that Victor's changing the arrangements had been exceedingly presumptuous. Especially considering that they were under the impression that J.B. and Victor were only casual friends.

Victor took a big swallow of his sweetened coffee and sat back with a sigh of obvious contentment. It was followed by a spasm of pain that seemed to surprise him. Placing a hand on his stomach, he sat up straighter and smiled at the other men. "Too many beans with dinner last night, I guess."

Everyone quickly introduced themselves to Victor, mentioning the town where they lived and their enthusiasm for the tournament. Victor laughed at the use of J.B.'s term for the weekend, but he made no comment about it. Instead, he showed interest in the route each had traveled to Bridgeport, which took up several pleasant minutes.

Roger was curious about the man. "Do you live in Bridgeport, Mr. Turner?"

"Oh, please, first names, okay? I have a house on Main across from Bryant's Hall. It was my wife's before we married. She'd been a widow for some time. I also have a small spread north of town, where I pasture horses that I sell. But it's only got a small cabin, although it's next to a creek."

"Your wife doesn't mind you spending your weekend gambling?" Vince asked.

Victor looked at him, his light tone suddenly dropping away. "Probably not. But she's gone to Sacramento for a few weeks with the girls to be with her sister. She doesn't even know I'm here."

It seemed no one knew how to respond to that, so there followed a communal sipping of coffee. Victor walked over to his jacket and reached into a side pocket, pulling out a dark brown pipe and a small leather bag of shredded tobacco. He returned to his chair and proceeded to fill his pipe, tamping it with his finger. He took a match from the small glass jar next to the ashtray near him, and lit the pipe while sucking air through the stem with hungry enthusiasm. He looked up at the other men, who had been watching him with the intensity they might have given a stage play.

"Any of you smoke a pipe?" he asked. "No? I find it one of life's greatest pleasures, especially coupled with a small glass of whiskey." He grinned and sat back, looking over at the large iron brand high on the stone fireplace. "It must have taken some effort to get that up there. But then, J.B. doesn't shirk at any effort to get what he wants."

When their host returned, he explained where everyone would be sleeping. The arrangement of the rooms upstairs along the hallway, from left to right, was first Otto in a small guest room at the head of the stairs with its door facing down the hall. Vince and Frank came next in the corner guest room that was small, but had big windows on two walls. Jim and Roger were next in a larger guest room that connected through a dressing area to the room of J.B.'s son, Alex. The two last doors were to J.B.'s study, which he often referred to as his office, and his bedroom at the end, its door facing the length of the hallway. And, of course, there was Victor out in the bunk house in what usually housed six men in the bunks lined up along the wall, each with an armoire against the wall opposite.

However, the cattle had been brought into the pastures from their warmer winter quarters, the branding of the calves had been completed, and the haying season wasn't yet upon them. This meant that the ranch was being run with ranch foreman Hank, and several men who came in from town each day.

No one knew Hank's last name, or anything about him before he came to the Double R, even though many got the impression he and J.B. went back a long way together. Tall and thin, Hank was probably in his late thirties, with skin darkened by most of those years outside in the sun. His black hair was perpetually held in place by an old brown Stetson that he kept remarkably clean. He had been one of the first at the Dave Hays Store to purchase a pair of the new 501 denim jeans with the rivets on the pocket corners, and these too were always clean. The most surprising thing to many people was that on the rare occasions when he put more than two sentences together, it became clear that Hank was highly educated. Other than the additional fact that he could handle any horse he straddled, no matter its nasty temperament, that was about it.

That Friday night all of J.B.'s guests sat around the large dining table with an array of enticing food before them. J.B. sat at the far end, his back to the outside wall. His son, Alex, sat at the other end with the kitchen door to his right, through which wafted enticing aromas. Between the host and his son, facing the great room was Frank, Jim and Victor. Facing the kitchen was Vince, Roger, and an empty chair to Alex's left because Otto had not yet shown up. No one knew whether he was arriving later that night, or early the next morning. But, as Victor noted, at least no word had arrived that he was not joining them.

The pork roast was succulent, and the bowls of roasted potatoes, coleslaw, and pickled beets were plentifully full. Hot rolls sat next to a crock of fresh butter, with two kinds of jam from which to choose. The generous plenty of the meal did not detract from their enjoyment of the berry cobbler served for dessert, accompanied by a generously used pitcher of heavy cream. Sing received abundant praise, which he acknowledged with a modest bow before scurrying back into the kitchen.

There was little conversation during the meal, but over the coffee that followed there was discussion of the fine hunting and fishing available in the area. However, it soon became obvious to them all, that now that their stomachs were full, they were ready to retire for the night. It was on everyone's mind that over the next two days they would be very much in one another's company; and that they would possibly be tense much of that time, depending on the shuffle of the cards. No one was willing to admit that traveling to the ranch had been arduous and fatiguing.

Dawn did not arrive quietly that Saturday morning. Bedroom doors flew open and heads looked out into the hall when Hank was heard pounding on J.B.'s bedroom door. When it was opened, they all heard the same news. "Someone stole the new horses last night." Hank turned to the guests now standing in the hall, shirts or pants hastily pulled on, but no one wearing both. "Not the horses in the barn where yours are," Hank assured them. "It was those in the small corral next to the bunk house."

"Did you hear anything during the night?" J.B., his pants hastily pulled on, had finally struggled into his shirt, catching every other button in his rush to get outside.

"No, not a thing. I woke up Vic. He was snoring like a hog on clean straw, just like he had all night. He hadn't heard anything either."

J.B. seemed surprised, asking, "Are you sure?"

Hank didn't bother to answer, racing down the stairs and out the back door.

Finally dressed, J.B. rushed down the hall, calling out, "Sorry fellas. You might as well go back to sleep. There's nothing you can do."

Roger noticed young Alex in the doorway of his room, his arms folded across his chest and his eyes large in fear. Approaching the boy, he said, "You're not about to go back to sleep, are you?"

Alex shook his head. "Why would someone steal our horses?"

Roger put a hand on his shoulder. "I imagine that's what your father is wondering right now, too. But he's right. We can't do anything more than he's doing, so how about we get dressed and go down to the kitchen."

"I don't know if Sing's up yet. Can you make coffee?"

"Do you drink coffee?"

"With enough cream and sugar, I do."

"Yeah, I like that, too. And I can probably manage to make it."

Alex darted back into his room and Roger returned to his next door. Jim was already dressed and pulling on his boots. "I heard what you told the boy, but I'll bet you anything Sing is already in the kitchen. Why don't you look after the boy and make sure breakfast is in the works? I want to go see what happened."

What Jim found was a confab of J.B., Hank, Victor and two hands just arrived from town. They were standing next to a small corral that was conspicuously empty, except for horse droppings giving evidence of its recent occupation.

J.B. turned to Jim as he approached. "We had six new horses in here. They were damn expensive. Good stock from a breeder in the Owens River Valley. They got all this way without injury, just to be stolen." He took off his hat and slapped it against his thigh, putting it back on with a muttered oath.

Jim leaned on the wooden enclosure, folding his arms along the top rail. "How long have you had them, J.B.?"

"Only four days. They were barely broke to ride, but were easy to handle. They'd been halter broke almost from birth. How in hell did the thieves know they were even here?"

Jim looked at J.B. and nodded. "That's the real question, isn't it?"

J.B. turned to look at the two hands, one Piute and the other Mexican. When asked, both vehemently denied having mentioned the horses to anyone, not even their families. Manuel stepped forward. "You've been very good to us, Mr. Roberts. We wouldn't betray your trust, or lie to you now if we'd told anyone."

The man called Indian Joe stepped to his side. "And if we had, we'd tell you, so you could ask them if they told anyone. We want those horses back!"

J.B. put out his hand and shook both of theirs. "I know. You're two of the best workers I've ever had, and I've seen how gently you've worked with these horses."

Hank looked down at the ground in front of the corral's gate. "You can see where they were herded out and down the back road to the main road."

Jim looked where Hank was pointing. "So you have a road out of here other than the one coming up to the front of the house? That must be why the horses didn't get close to where we were all sleeping."

"That's right." J.B. looked at Hank. "And they did it so quietly that you didn't hear them. That's something."

Hank looked over at Victor. "Well, truth be told, it would have been difficult to hear anything over his snoring. I was in my room in the front corner and I still had a pillow over my head in order to get to sleep."

Victor turned a darker color. "Yeah, that's one of the reasons I thought it best to stay out in the bunk house. My wife and I can't even share a bedroom because of it."

Each man smiled, all of them having had the same experience at some time in their lives, whether in a bunk house, a trail camp, or a thin-walled hotel. But Hank was wasting no time talking, going into the barn and saddling his horse.

Leading it out, he announced, "I'm going to follow the tracks as far as I can."

J.B. asked Manuel, "Do you mind going into town and telling Sheriff Cody what's happened? If you have to fill out a report, your handwriting is good. And you can describe each of the horses."

"Yes, sir. I'll do it right now."

"Had they been branded yet?" Jim asked.

"Yes."

"They had?" Startled, Victor looked over at the empty corral. "I saw them yesterday when I arrived and I don't remember seeing a brand."

"We did a small neck brand under the mane."

Victor started to say something, but they were all distracted by a rider approaching. "Hi, everyone." The man dismounted, tied his horse to a rail of the corral, and walked up to the group. "Sorry I couldn't get here until this morning. The boss wouldn't let me go yesterday."

J.B. mumbled, "Jim, this is Otto Mercer." He was shorter than any of the other men, with a large handlebar mustache that didn't detract from brown eyes so dark they were more like little chunks of coal. He wore an old straw hat that flattened short black hair salted with gray, and he approached with a slight swagger. Jim wondered if it was injury or attitude.

Otto accepted Jim's outstretched hand and shook it with a crushing grip that belied his small stature. "Nice to meet you, Jim." Otto grinned. "You're the gambler from Virginia City I've heard about? Looking forward to playing with you. Did your son come, too?"

"Yes. He's inside making sure breakfast is getting started for us."

Otto suddenly tuned into the tension around him. "Is something wrong?"

J.B. nodded. "Six of my horses were stolen during the night."

"Oh!" Otto looked at his friend Victor, who nodded. "Are you all getting together as a posse to go after them?"

"No." J.B. ran the back of his hand over his forehead, feeling sweat beginning to form. "The sheriff is being notified. And Hank is out tracking."

"Ah!" Otto nodded with approval. "He's a great tracker."

Accepting that there was nothing more to be done in the yard right then, J.B. turned to Otto. "Come inside and put your things in your room. We'll be having breakfast, and then getting started with the game at ten o'clock."

J.B. didn't look nearly as enthusiastic about his tournament as he had the day before, but he was determined not to let the theft of his horses put a damper on everyone's fun. After all, most of them had traveled a long way, and he doubted that Otto's employer at the ranch where he worked had given him the weekend off with pay. In fact, he was surprised Otto had been given the weekend off at all.

Sing made sure everyone was fed a good breakfast of thick gravy filled with big chunks of sausage over the biggest, fluffiest biscuits any of them had ever seen. To balance the richness of the meal, there were spiced apple slices on the side. As he served, Sing kept up a jovial chatter, somehow getting the men to swap stories of their most memorable times around a felt-covered table.

First to speak up was Roger, with a humorous tale about his biggest loss due to the fact that instead of focusing on the game, he was thinking about a pretty girl he'd just met. She turned out to be Amanda, his future wife. Thus inspired, the others chimed in with stories of their biggest losses. This resulted in joking and laughter, along with a degree of unity that hadn't been present before. Only Otto told a story of a big win.

After breakfast, the men returned briefly to their room or visited the privy. On his way back into the house, Roger noted that Victor and Otto were the only ones to grab a quick smoke. They were on the covered porch that extended along the back of the house, a place Roger thought might be an inviting place for a quick nap later.

Entering the kitchen, Roger greeted Sing, who was busy washing dishes at the sink. He then joined Jim and Frank for a last cup of coffee at the small table in the corner of the kitchen. Their conversation wasn't about cards, but rather wondering how Sing gave the coffee a unique underlying flavor. As they left, Sing reached over and gently pushed close the drawer where he kept his expensive oriental spices.

When they all gathered back in the dining room just before ten, the breakfast things had been cleared way, and a table leaf had been removed. It was now a little smaller and covered in a cut-to-fit, green felt cover. At J.B.'s place was a stack of fresh cards still in their sealed boxes next to a round, walnut chip holder. But its columns were empty, the chips having been evenly distributed around the table. The white, red, and green ivory chips seemed to beg those present to fondle them.

Being the first to arrive at the table, Roger looked from the chips to young Alex, standing beside him. "That's a fancy set of chips from that caddy."

"He won it in a game." It was a proud declaration by a proud son. "From the guy whose house they were playing in. The guy was out of money, and it was too bad because he thought he had a pretty good hand. Dad said he'd take the chips and caddy for any size bet the man said."

No one needed to say who had won that hand. With a dawning realization, Roger looked around the dining room at the hutches filled with their odd assortment of items. Seeing this, Alex grinned up at him. "Yeah, a lot of it was won the same way. Especially the silver stuff." He glanced into the great room and back. "Even some of the stuff in there he got that same way." Pointing to a set of white dishes in the hutch behind J.B.'s chair, he said, "Those were my mother's. Dad says she brought them to the marriage, and was always proud of them." He spoke with a nonchalance that showed he had said it many times before. "She died shortly after I was born in '76."

"I'm sorry to hear that, son."

"Oh, it's okay. My dad and I are the Double R." His tone seemed to warn that no one should dare to think otherwise. "And, of course, we have Mrs. Lewis to take care of us." His sudden frown was one of puzzlement. "And now Sara."

"Don't you like her?"

"She's okay, I guess. But Mrs. Lewis always seems to be worried about her, and Mrs. Lewis isn't a worrier." Alex looked up at Roger. "I'm off to the Hunewill ranch for the rest of the weekend. They're having a passel of guests staying with them. That means lots of games and fun things to do."

"You like it there?"

"Oh, sure. Mrs. Hunewill is the best!"

Before Roger had time to wonder about the kindness of mother substitutes, the others began arriving. Alex headed into the kitchen, where he grabbed a large cookie off a serving plate and headed to the back door. Sing pretended not to notice, something Roger was beginning to realize the houseman was very practiced at doing.

It was a lovely, sunny day with a cool breeze coming off the mountains where canyons still harbored the previous winter's snow. Roger smiled, thinking that no boy would be content to stay indoors on such a day, especially when he thought a bunch of "old men playing cards" was the main entertainment.

In fact, J.B. had earlier offered his son the suggestion that he could spend the day in his room reading a book or working on schoolwork. Alex hadn't wasted any words, the roll of his eyes and a disbelieving laugh his only reply.

It had been the response J.B. had expected, and wanted. He especially didn't want Alex's presence during this particular weekend.

# CHAPTER 3

## THE GAMES BEGIN

It was ten minutes before their start time of 10 o'clock, but J.B. had not yet joined them. While waiting, the other players stood around the kitchen table. Undeterred by their earlier breakfast, they drank coffee and ate plump, fried donuts rolled in sugar. Sing continuously thrust a bowl of apple slices and juicy plums at them, but it was ignored. The tall, ceramic coffee pot on the table, however, had been refilled three times and the cream jug twice.

"Hey!" Roger startled everyone. "I read in the paper that this is a leap year."

Frank grinned as he responded. "Why do you care? You're already married."

Victor cut in. "Maybe that's why he brought it up. He'd like to leap... off a cliff. Marriage will do that to a man."

No one laughed or commented, but Victor didn't seem to mind. He was too busy chuckling at his own witticism.

They heard the front door open and close, and everyone hurried into the dining room, eager to begin the game. But J.B. was not alone. Sheriff Michael J. Cody was with him. He had only recently been elected to the office, having moved from Bodie where he had been the Land Office Receiver. Roger's first reaction was much the same as most people meeting the sheriff for the first time; respect and admiration, followed by just a little trepidation.

In his mid-thirties, the sheriff was an inch over six feet, which put him an inch over any of the men before him. He cut an imposing figure, with his broad shoulders and long legs, barbered short hair, and a well-trimmed but full mustache that curled up a little on the ends. He wore a dark suit rather than the more casual clothing of someone who worked on the land, although his hat was decidedly western. He kept his badge on his vest, so his coat's lapel covered it most of the time, but allowed for a quick reveal of it when necessary.

What lent him an assumption of authority, even without the badge, was the way his blue eyes locked on people with whom he spoke, especially when they were being interrogated. Having been a miner in Bodie as well as its Land Receiver, he had demonstrated not only his physical strength and courage, but also his intellect and integrity. Being newly elected, he was hoping to prove this in Bridgeport before anything happened that might put it in doubt.

Mrs. Lewis walked into the room from the back hallway and stopped at the foot of the stairs, her gray eyes alight against the black of her hair. Her hands clasped at her waist and her back ramrod straight, she appeared to be braced for whatever was to come. Nevertheless, when Sheriff Cody turned to her, she focused on him and remained silent. Roger thought her prepared-for-battle posture odd, since the sheriff's demeanor was calm and pleasant. But more than one miscreant had realized too late that they had underestimated Michael Cody.

"Good morning, Mrs. Lewis." He removed his hat, exposing thick brown hair, and held it loosely in his hands.

"Good morning, Michael. How are Catherine and the children?"

"Catie's fine. So are the kids." His face had immediately softened at the mention of five year old Ella, four year old Mary Louise, and Edmund only 18 months. Little did he know that there would be three more children in the next decade.

The sheriff's eyes swept the room. "Where's Alex?"

Mrs. Lewis answered quickly. "He's staying the weekend at the Hunewill place. We thought this weekend might be a little too adult for him. In fact, I was just leaving to join him there."

"I won't detain you further, then."

"Thank you." She left somewhat hesitantly, not wanting to miss what was to follow, but realizing that she had been tactfully dismissed. She might not have thought of herself as a mere servant, but she was aware that most others did. She considered this assumption an offense that lacked recognition of her superior status, and it was a perpetual annoyance that she had not yet managed to change.

As soon as she had left the room, Sheriff Cody turned to look at Jim, who was hanging out on the far side of the dining room. The sheriff didn't waste words or bother to preface his comment. "I wasn't Sheriff back in '79, but we did meet once."

Jim stepped around the table and looked the law man in the eyes. "Yes, it was before the arrest."

"I know you were innocent." Noting that the sheriff's smile was friendly, Jim fought to breathe more calmly and ease the tightness in his chest as Cody continued. "I thought so at the time, but it wasn't any of my business. But the fact that you escaped, rather than let the court decide, was a problem."

"If you were here, you know the atmosphere. I never would have had an impartial jury. The scaffold from the recent hanging hadn't been taken down for a reason. And later, the judge in Virginia City eliminated the charge over my method of leaving, calling it self-preservation."

Expecting an argument and ready to defend himself further, Jim couldn't help but wonder why, if Cody had been in Bodie in '80, he hadn't also recognized Roger. Maybe he hadn't spent his spare time in gambling halls. Jim was brought back to the moment when the Sheriff grinned. "I spent some time in Virginia City back in the early '80's. The judge was a good man. I believe your wife knew him very well indeed."

Before Jim could decide whether or not to offer an objection to what he perceived as an improper suggestion, the sheriff turned to J.B. "Other than these men, the only people on the property when the horses were stolen were of your household?"

"That's right."

"Don't you have a new gal?" Nothing like town gossip to keep people informed of a basic fact. However, the sheriff knew that raised brows and pursed lips accompanying the telling of "facts" were always open to interpretation.

"Yes, Sara Dulong." J.B. fought to keep himself from smiling. "She's a maid that works under Mrs. Lewis." Everyone glanced at Victor, and Roger was surprised to see him blush, although he remained silent. "Nice girl, just barely out of her teens and still learning how to do a proper job of serving and such like. One of my hands took her into town early this morning on errands for Sing and Mrs. Lewis."

After J.B. explained where everyone had been sleeping the night before, Sheriff Cody turned to Victor. "Do you consider yourself observant?"

Victor was quick to respond. "Maybe, but not when I'm sleeping sound like I do when I'm really tired. Hank had to practically slap me awake."

J.B. laughed. "Hank said he heard Vic snoring all through the night."

The sheriff locked eyes on J.B. as he asked, "What about Hank himself?"

J.B.'s pleasantness disappeared, replaced by a thunderous glare. The sheriff held up a hand. "Okay, okay. I know Hank, too. No way he'd do anything to hurt you."

J.B. forced himself to control his knee-jerk reaction to defend Hank, and made himself show only a passionless calm. As cover for his ire, he said, "I keep trying to think of anyone I know who'd do this to me."

"Why would it have to be someone you know?"

"Well, the horses hadn't been here all that long. And I think we all got the impression that there had to have been some planning behind the theft. I mean, one of the keys to keeping them together was that there was a bell mare with them."

The sheriff's eyes scanned the others. "What about the rest of you? Any idea who could have done it?"

Victor shrugged while Jim, Roger, Frank and Vince all shook their heads. Otto was the only one to speak up. "I wasn't here until yesterday morning. The day before, Thursday, I was at the ranch, still working until about ten o'clock that night, when I went to my bunk. And I had chores to do early yesterday morning before I could head out. When I got here, I was greeted with the news. I was pretty tired out, and glad we weren't starting until today."

J.B. put a hand on Otto's shoulder. "Yeah, you looked it. But I'm glad you made it. You're a good player." He turned to the sheriff. "Mike, can we get started with our game? I thought all of this would have been done and over yesterday."

"Sorry I couldn't get out to you before now. Something came up in town."

"Of course," J.B. grinned, "if you want to sit in, the ante is $2."

The sheriff quickly declined and returned to his horse tied up out front. As he rode away, his thought was on the ante. "I could buy Ella a new doll with just one ante." With that judgmental thought, he hurried home to Catherine and the children. He would have been pleased to know that little Ella's future as a teacher would bring her back to Bodie where she had been born, and where in 1904 she would become Mrs. David Cain.

As they listened to the rapidly retreating hoofbeats of the sheriff's fleeing horse, Victor quipped, "Now I know how to get rid of a lawman."

The others laughed, but any inclination to levity was cut off when J.B. began directing them to what he had decided should be their placement at the table. J.B. sat in his usual place at the far end where he could see the kitchen door to his left and the great room to his right. And no one could pass behind his chair. To his left he had placed Roger and Victor, with Jim and Otto across the table facing him. Vince and Frank were to J.B.'s right, the only ones without their backs to a wall. Being a professional gambler himself, Roger wondered if this meant that J.B. considered Vince and Frank the most trusting of those present. At the same time, Roger acknowledged to himself that he was not in that trusting category.

Eager to hear the rules of play, everyone turned to J.B. with a tense expectancy. "First off, I haven't played with these rules before. They may be somewhat strange, but I think it'll make for a friendly and interesting game. It's after ten o'clock now. We'll start tomorrow at exactly ten o'clock. I'm assuming no one here minds missing church for a change." He ignored the various chuckles and smirks as he continued. "We'll be ending at four in the afternoon. There'll be a short break around the beginning of each hour if anyone requests it. We're none of us in our twenties anymore."

Jim, Victor and Otto, all over forty, didn't bother to comment, thinking J.B. was being tactful on their behalf. Truth be told, Roger was glad to hear they could take a break. He was still sore and a little stiff from the unaccustomed long ride to Bridgeport. And although J.B. was only in his mid-thirties, he obviously had a lot on his mind other than poker. He had really liked those six horses, and had paid good money for them.

J.B. continued. "At Noon, we'll break for an hour to eat dinner, and so I can go out to check on things with Hank. An alarm clock will be wound up at the beginning of the breaks, so everyone will know when to be back at the table." He suddenly grinned. "I've been told it's annoyingly loud. If you're more than a minute late, you're out of the play until the next break. I'll start the deal, and it'll pass to my left with each hand.

"Each day, we all start out with the same chip pile." He went on to explain how he had calculated that, and everyone held back their questions. "All antes are $2. The white chips are $1, the red ones are $5, and the green are $10. If you want a black chip at some point, you'll have to exchange it for five of your green chips. The last hand is the one that's in play when the clock hits four o'clock. The winner at that point is the one with the most money in chips over the original pot, and that day's game is over. But instead of the value of the chips, the winner gets $20 in real money from each of the other players. Then tomorrow, all players go back to having the same basic chip pile as you're starting with today. That means it's possible, at the end of the weekend, for two of us to be a big winner."

Vince spoke up. "It also means one of us could be a really big winner if they win both days."

J.B. smiled. "That's right. But it means, too, that you could lose all the chips in front of you and still actually only lose $20 to the day's winner. I wanted this to be a friendly weekend."

Frank cleared his throat. "Maybe, but a $20 payout from six players is a lot of money to win."

"Yes, and as host, I'll only take ten per cent from the winner." He looked around at everyone's degree of surprise, calculating their personality from their reaction. This was information he figured he could use if any of them tried to bluff at some point.

It was Jim who quickly spoke up when he saw Victor and Otto frowning. "That's only fair, considering all the food and booze you're supplying for us."

"Thank you, Jim." J.B. wondered if Jim's generous reaction might mean that he had a conscience that would affect the way he bluffed. But he only said, "To show I want to be fair, if I'm the winner of either day, the winner of the other day doesn't have to pay out to me."

Victor was the only one who didn't nod in agreement, but J.B. didn't seem surprised by that. At the same time, Otto looked like he was trying to figure out a particularly complicated math problem, which in one sense he was. However, when he looked over at Victor and saw that he was unperturbed and relaxed, he too relaxed.

Roger was puzzled by the way J.B. had smirked at Victor while conveying that he could afford to be generous. It seemed to imply that he was pleased that Victor was a little out of sorts at the idea. It was obvious to Roger that there was some kind of history between these two men. Had J.B. been suggesting that he was so well off that he could show such largesse, but that Victor could not? Was J.B. suggesting an uncomfortable comparison in that regard? Roger didn't think he'd want Victor as an enemy, but maybe J.B. didn't feel that way. All in all, Roger thought those men invited to this game were an odd collection of personalities.

While J.B. had been explaining the rules, Roger had been considering these men through the eyes of a professional gambler. Neither Victor nor Otto looked like what one would picture as a gambler, but Roger knew from experience that some of the best he'd played with had looked like they lived under a rock. The one thing the two men shared was a lizard-like concentration so intense they seldom blinked. When they did, it was usually to glance at each other before quickly looking away. But then, they were longtime friends, and Roger admitted that he had to resist glancing at his father as often as he wished.

It was obvious to Roger that Frank and Vince, although focused on what was being said, were there to have an enjoyable new experience. They were probably already looking forward to sharing descriptions of everything with their wives, as was he. Amanda was a pretty good poker play herself, and his mother was a professional dealer, so he and his father would have a good audience upon their return.

Roger had played backgammon, chess and checkers with his father many times. But they had avoided gambling with one another at the same table. There hadn't been anything said about such an avoidance, but both had thought it best, mainly because money would be involved. And now, here they were. Roger had no illusions about his father's competitive nature, or his own for that matter, so he knew that neither of them would hold back. The only relationship that mattered that weekend was that between a player and his cards.

Still, Roger wondered, "Is it an advantage or a disadvantage to know well at least one other person at the table?" Because that applied to everyone present. Of course, it wasn't unusual for personalities, habits, and reactions common in everyday life, to change dramatically with the rise and fall of the chip pile. Roger decided to keep his main focus on J.B., sensing that it was from him that most of the table's tension was emanating. At first, he had assumed J.B. was feeling unease about the stolen horses, but now he was thinking something more than that was on their host's mind.

Frank looked around the table as everyone was dealt their first five cards, and wondered why he was feeling an uncharacteristic uneasiness. It wasn't about the game. He would of course like to win, and be able to present to Emily a bundle of money, but they weren't in a bad financial condition. And the way the rules were set up, no one man would come away a very big loser. He therefore decided to just enjoy the game, the ranch, the incredible food, and the interesting company. But he still wondered why he was so uneasy.

Vince, as he often did, felt a little left out of things. He gambled far less than his friend, and had not developed an immediate friendship with Jim Murphy, as had Frank when they had all first met in Virginia City two years earlier. And although he and Frank were the same age as J.B., their host seemed older, having a maturity that Vince surmised had been developed by more than just years lived as a rancher. It occurred to him that although they had been told much about J.B. from the time that he had acquired the ranch land, nothing had ever been mentioned about him before that. And with all his hail-fellow-well-met charm, Vince sensed a ruthlessness in J.B. that was at the core of who he was.

Jim's thoughts were not focused on those around the table, but rather his eagerness for the play to get underway. No, he realized, that wasn't quite true. He was impatient for the weekend to be over. He was missing Lucy, and was trying valiantly to deny the fact that he would rather be at home with her. It was probably just the lingering effects of having been separated from her for so many years following the war. Whenever he thought he'd left behind those traumatic years, a memory would pop into his mind unbidden at the oddest times. It was like a spellbinding flash of light in his head, but he felt it as a punch to the chest, sometimes even taking away his breath. But what he felt now was different, and he was forced to admit that he simply didn't like the atmosphere here at the Double R.

It was a beautiful spread, a luxurious house, and the food was terrific, but for Jim, it all lacked substance. It was as though J.B. was trying to convince the world of his worth; not only his financial wealth, but also the esteem of respectability and belonging. Giving himself a mental shake, Jim picked up the cards dealt him, trying hard not to smile as he looked at them. It felt good to be holding cards again. The cards had a nice slick feel, the edges clean with no shaving, and he was ready to see where Fate would take him.

Otto found it hard to concentrate on his cards, not because he didn't like them, but because he kept looking over at his friend Victor. He wasn't sure what he was expecting to see. Maybe it was some kind of reassurance. He chuckled to himself. Maybe it was just because he was uncomfortable without his old slouch hat on his head, and wondered if it would be in bad taste to request that he be able to wear it indoors.

Otto puzzled Roger. He was short and stocky, with a large nose that somewhat took away from the length of the thick mustache hanging like a horseshoe down his face. His arms were well muscled and his hands showed ware that gloves had not protected. He also had the leather-like skin of someone who had spent most of his forty-plus years outdoors. Roger found Otto's appearance unexceptional, so he decided that what bothered him about Otto was how much he fidgeted and seemed unable to relax.

Victor had no problem concentrating on his cards. He asked for only one to replace his first discard, and sat back to await everyone else's play. He felt a remarkable sense of calm, unusual for him when playing cards. But then, he really didn't care if he won or lost. He was there to eat Sing's food, drink J.B.'s liquor, and enjoy the scenery, not least of which was the young maid. Mainly, he just wanted distractions so he didn't have to think about his marriage and other pressing problems in his life. He wondered when the saucy wench Sara might return. Saucy wench? Where on earth had he heard or read that? He chuckled to himself. Then he looked over at Otto who had seen him smiling. Victor frowned at the alarm he saw on his friend's face. "What the hell does he assume I'm thinking about? I need to have a word with him as soon as possible."

A break at the eleven o'clock hour was suggested by Roger, but welcomed by everyone. The privies were utilized, the coffee pot drained, and the last of the morning's donuts gulped down. Still, none of the players had a problem being in their seats when the alarm clock went off. J.B., however, made it into his chair while it was still ringing, causing everyone to rib him about his strict rules. The lighthearted banter helped ease any tension felt earlier.

There was little talk during the game's action, although while the cards were being shuffled and dealt, some few words were exchanged. After Otto lost a third hand, Victor said, "You're not playing up to your usual standard today."

"I guess not." Otto looked at his friend and grinned. "Too bad we're not playing backgammon. I might be able to win some of what you owe me."

J.B. looked at Otto and smiled. "Our Victor isn't very good at the game?"

"Nah. He's got a terrible imagination."

After that, the brief comments ranged through the nice weather holding on, the rowdiness of a few teenagers in town, the growing number of sheep in the valley, and wondering about what delectable treat Sing might be preparing for their dinner at noon.

When it was Frank's turn to shuffle and deal the cards, Victor stared at him. "I bet the ladies go wild over that dimple in your chin."

"Yep." Frank's refusal to be baited irritated Victor, but there wasn't anything he could say that wouldn't make him look ridiculous, so he kept silent.

J.B. had glanced at Victor several times with a slight frown. "I like your cleaned-up look, Vic. And you've lost a lot of weight."

Victor grunted an acknowledgement and gathered his cards together, fanning them out in his hands. "Well, with the heat of summer approaching..."

He left the sentence dangling, and those new to the town assumed that Victor's lack of facial hair must be something new. But J.B. didn't focus on that. "You trimmed up your brows. Your wife has been a good influence."

"Yeah," he grunted, "an influence."

Whereas most of the men merely smiled and focused on their cards, the conversation immediately forgotten, Otto seemed flustered. His glances at Victor were cast more often, and he seemed to be uncomfortable in his seat.

J.B. finally took notice. "Otto, are you okay? You're sweating a lot."

"Ah, just a bit of headache. Do you mind if I get a glass of water? I'm feeling a little queasy."

"No, go ahead."

And indeed, the man who regularly turned to something stronger than water, practically drained the pitcher sitting on the sideboard next to the kitchen door. As he returned to his seat, he rubbed at his chest and took a deep breath.

Victor looked at his friend. "Geez, Otto, you don't look so good. Why don't you go lay down for the next couple of hands?"

"Oh, you'd like that!"

Taken aback by his sharp tone, J.B. stepped in. "It's up to you, of course, but if you decide you want to do that, feel free. We'll wake you for lunch."

"Thanks." He took a deep, somewhat labored breath. "I'll stick it out."

In an effort to give Otto's embarrassment some cover, Vince spoke up. "I must say, J.B., I really like your location. We're not used to so much green around our ranches."

"Yes, I was very fortunate to have found it."

Victor let loose with, "Yeah, right!" J.B. glared at him with visible irritation. Victor stared back, undaunted by an intimidation that everyone knew J.B. wanted Victor to feel. "You must admit, J.B., you were fortunate to have married well."

"Yes." J.B.'s jaw tightened. Startling Jim, he turned to him to explain. "The property originally belonged to my wife's brother before I bought it from him." Victor's smile as he heard this was hard to read. It disappeared when J.B. boldly added, "Vic here was also interested in purchasing the land."

Victor shrugged as though it had been a small matter, but Roger suspected that he was disappointed that J.B. had removed the sting from his caustic insinuations. However, the need for concentration being so great, everyone immediately turned their thoughts to their cards.

When that hand had been dealt with, Roger commented, "My wife would be happy to know there's a millinery shop here. She loves hats."

J.B. responded while looking at his hand. "Mrs. McKinney is looking to sell. I think Mrs. Crowell, who lives next door to the shop, is thinking of buying it." He grinned as he discarded one card and picked up his new one. "The ladies are abuzz over the prospect. You'd think it was a major happening."

He laid down his hand. The diamond flush was met with groans from the others. It was clear that his smile had not been about the sale of a shop, but rather about the status of his hand.

Roger asked, "Do you ever wonder what ole Mr. Bolton is doing now?"

"You're referring to the man known as Black Bart?" When Roger nodded, Frank continued. "Yeah, after he was released from prison this New Year's day I heard he was greeted at the prison gates by a bunch of reporters. He said outright that he wasn't going to return to a life of crime."

"They said he'd learned how to work in a pharmacy while in prison."

"Yeah, the San Quintin warden during his time was very much a proponent of rehabilitation. Evidently it worked with him, because nothing has been heard about Black Bart since he got out."

"And," Otto said, "what has been said turned out to be baseless rumors."

"I think I'm okay with that." When everyone looked at Vince, he shrugged. "I mean, he was such a legend back in the day. Who wants to think of him as ending his days doing something mundane like sweeping floors in a saloon?"

Roger nodded. "I understand what you mean. Did you ever see a photo of the guy? He looks like a banker or a minister, or someone's grandpa."

The only other comment was from J.B. not long before they broke for lunch. "I was sorry to hear that Doc Holliday died last November."

"Yeah." Roger shook his head. "I would have loved to sit at a table like this with him."

Victor turned to him. "You think you could have out drawn him?"

Roger smiled. "Only at cards."

While the others laughed, Jim looked at his son and cocked a brow. He had seen Roger in quick-draw competitions, several of which he had won. Professional gamblers all carried a gun, even if not conspicuously, and it was best to know how to use it.

In a tone of extreme casualness, Victor looked at Jim. "Speaking of guns, didn't you or Roger here kill Terry Miller in Virginia City a few years ago?"

The name mentioned brought to mind for both Roger and Jim a very bad memory. Roger's throat was suddenly too dry to talk, but Jim managed to say, "No, we didn't. He was about to kill us when some unknown person behind him shot him in the neck."

"Yeah, that's what the newspapers said." Victor gritted his teeth. "It also said no one tried to find his killer."

"That wasn't our decision." Jim looked square at Victor. "And, after all, he was the one who murdered Jimmy Mack, who I was accused of killing." Knowing he probably shouldn't say it, he nevertheless snapped out, "Neither one of them was a loss to society!"

Victor's eyes narrowed. "They had no family, but I was friends with both men."

Roger found his voice. "If they'd cared anything about anyone but themselves, they would've lived a different kind of life!"

"Okay, fellas, let's get back to the game." More than his words, it was J.B.'s tone that made it clear he wasn't going to allow the conversation to accelerate.

Only later that night, as Vince and Frank would lie in their beds, would they share speculation about the underlying meanings being batted back and forth between J.B. and Victor. They would also discuss the deaths of Jimmy and Terry, Jim's false arrest, and his escape from jail. Frank's main question would be whether or not Victor was friend or foe to J.B., and if the latter, why had J.B. invited him to be in this tournament?

But for now, the late morning play proceeded. Roger won a hand with a full house, and everyone congratulated him amid the bemoaning of their bad luck. It stopped when Otto stood up, swaying a bit before heading to the stairs.

"I need to lay down." The look of pain on his pale face, now mottled with red, gave evidence of the need for that.

Once his door closed, with everyone's alarm visible, Victor assured the others. "He's had turns before. His digestion is kinda dicey and he gets headaches. One doc told him he had an ulcer. Another said something about his liver."

Frank pointed out the obvious. "But he still drinks whiskey. That can't be good for either."

"Sing!" J.B. hollered. When the Chinese cook hurried in, he was asked if he had noticed anything odd about Otto that morning.

"No. He okay at breakfast. Ate donuts, drank much coffee. Same at break. Went out back for short walk after."

"Did you see where he went?"

"Headed to back porch." Sing turned to Victor. "You come in back door with him end of break from game."

Everyone transferred their eyes to their fellow player. He nodded as he said, "I was coming up from out back where I was having a quick smoke, and joined him for a few minutes." He looked down at his stack of chips, then back up again with a frown. "He was eating something. I think a donut."

"Yeah," Roger said, "I saw him chewing something, but it wasn't a donut. He had berry jam on his mouth."

"I not see him take anything before he leave kitchen." Sing shrugged. "But could have."

J.B. thanked Sing, which he took as dismissal and retreated to the comfort of his kitchen. Concern, along with unvoiced confusion and curiosity, had invaded their good time, and the men were wondering how to rescue it.

"Maybe he was having a chew of tobacco?" Roger posed.

Victor nodded, but not with conviction. "He does do that, but not often."

J.B., whose turn it was to deal the cards, focused on what was important to them. "Let's get on with the game. We'll check on him when we break for lunch."

This exchange having taken only a couple of minutes, no one felt it had overly disrupted the flow of the game, and they eagerly continued. There was little talk between hands, and the one that concluded at noon left Frank the only one smiling as he looked at his chip pile.

Victor stood up. "I'll go check on Otto."

He came back almost immediately. "He's in a lot of pain and he's sweating like a sponge. I think someone should go for Doc Sinclair."

Within minutes, Sing was mounted on his pony and bouncing his way into town. Dr. Clark Sinclair's arrival half an hour later had an immediately calming influence on everyone. His round face, receding hairline of short hair, his neat mustache, and especially his kind eyes, were perfect for a doctor.

Having lived in Big Meadows since the 1860's, he was a beloved citizen. He had set their bones, sutured their cuts, and had delivered their babies. He had also saved all but one citizen during the Scarlet Fever outbreak that had affected forty townspeople. The flock of sheep that Frank and Vince had passed as they entered the valley had been his, purchased the year before as a new venture. The doctor had arrived at the Double R on horseback in order to speed his arrival, leaving his wife and occasional nurse at home with their children, William and Flora.

Doc spent a good fifteen minutes with Otto while Victor hovered at the foot of the stairs. When he came out and joined them, he didn't look relieved. "I think all the excitement, rich food, and too much booze has upset him. But I don't know why he's having so much difficulty breathing, and his blood pressure is way up there. His heart doesn't sound good either. If you can hitch up a wagon and make up a bed in back of it, I'd like to take him to my surgery."

Victor asked, "What's wrong with his heart?"

"It's beating very erratically."

"Why?"

Doc looked at Victor, not hiding his impatience. "I don't know yet. That's why I want to monitor his condition."

With Sing gone off to tell Hank about the need for the wagon, Sara was summoned from upstairs where she was cleaning the guests' rooms. And, of course, from where she was listening to the conversations taking place in the room below.

J.B. looked her over. "You know how to ride, don't you?" She nodded enthusiastically, eager to please. "Have a horse saddled and go get Mrs. Lewis from the Hunewill ranch. There's a lady's side saddle you can use."

"I can ride without a saddle if I'm allowed to ride astride."

J.B. ignored the valiantly fought smiles of his guests. "I think not. Hank will saddle your horse for you. Now, get going, please." They watched her hurry down the hall to the back door, where she hung her apron on the coat rack before rushing out. There was nothing flirty about her now.

"The wagon should be ready in a few minutes," J.B. told the doctor. "Should I get some of the hired men to come help bring Otto down?"

"Don't bother." Frank glanced at the other men as he spoke. "We can do it." Roger, Vince and Jim all nodded.

The doctor looked relieved. "I've given him a small shot of morphine to help with the pain, so it should make it easy to carry him down." With that, the doctor went up the stairs and opened wide the door to make room for the men filing up the stairs behind him. However, they were met by his upraised hand commanding them to stop. As they waited, he retreated into the room for a moment before coming back out. "I'm sorry. He's dead."

The stunned silence that followed, and the statue-like stillness of the men, each on a different stair tread, greeted Mrs. Lewis as she came in the back door. She had been on her way back from the Hunewill ranch after learning upon her arrival that everyone had left for a picnic in the hills. Sara hovered behind, peeking over her shoulder. Their entrance broke the men's shock, and everyone turned around and descended into the great room.

"What's happened?" Mrs. Lewis didn't sound overly concerned, what with her eyes on J.B. and knowing Alex's whereabouts. No one else in her universe mattered to her.

Sara, meanwhile, sensing that trouble was brewing, retreated into the kitchen to question Sing. She knew he would have been listening to the proceedings while keeping out of the way.

"It's Otto," J.B. told Mrs. Lewis. "He just died."

He moved to her side, not sure how she might react, her being a woman and all. She looked up at him and heaved a sigh. "Stroke or heart attack?"

Although surprised at the question, the doctor moved forward, ever the professional. "What makes you ask that?"

Her snort of disdain was not muffled. "He drank like an old sot, he gulped his food, and I saw him huffing snuff up his nose not long after he arrived."

It wasn't often that people saw J.B. thrown off balance, but right then he was. Always in control, always the leader of every group, he was now dealing with sudden death in the heart of his empire. And a woman responding in a way he didn't think a woman should.

Jim moved to his side and put a comforting hand on his shoulder as Mrs. Lewis retired to her room with a dismissive gesture. J.B. turned to the doctor in confusion. "Clark? What happens now?"

"Can you send someone into town to fetch the undertaker? He'll have to close his furniture store, but I need him to bring his wagon and take charge of the body. He needs to see it in place, so he can agree with me as to the cause of death. I don't think there'll be an inquest, but you never know."

J.B. hollered for Sara. "Go tell Hank that we won't need our wagon. Also tell him to go into town to fetch the undertaker and his wagon."

"Yes, sir." She curtsied and ran out of the house.

J.B. turned back to the doctor. "Do you know what he died of, then?"

"I think he'd over-stressed his heart for some time, probably for a long time. And all the hurry to get here and the excitement that followed, along with too much food and drink, was just too much for him." What he didn't say was that some of what he had seen didn't quite conform to that. He planned to do an autopsy, but they didn't need to know that.

With the body upstairs awaiting the coroner, no one felt like staying in the house. Except Mrs. Lewis, that is. She told the men to go into town, and that Sing would feed the doctor while they waited. "Besides," she explained, "it's a woman's job to sit with the dead."

The men didn't argue, going as a group to the barn for their horses. The ride into town through the wildflower strewn meadows dotted with grazing cattle was pleasant, and helped blur the unexpected event that had disrupted their game. A hearty meal at the Allen House Hotel, a drink at the Stanton Saloon nearby, and conversation about totally unrelated events, gave them a grateful and satisfying respite.

By the time they returned to the Double R, the body had been removed and the room scrubbed by Sara under the strict direction of Mrs. Lewis. Sara had then transferred her things from her present tiny closet of a room into the freshly cleaned guest room still smelling of lye soap. She was so happy to be further away from Mrs. Lewis, that she didn't particularly care that someone had died in the bed only hours before. Sachets of lavender, made during the previous year's harvest, were stuck around the room and soon overcame the smell of the soap. After changing the water in a vase of purple flowers on the table by the open window, Sara was the happiest she had been since being hired.

Dinner was eaten in the kitchen so the table with their cards and chips would be in place whenever they could return to playing. J.B. was eager to do just that. "Having lost out on this afternoon's play doesn't mean we can't play for a few hours tonight instead." He looked around the table where they were gathered in such tight quarters that shoulders touched. "Unless anyone has an objection to that."

Frank asked for one clarification. "And the winner at the end of the night will be the winner for the day?"

"Yes, and collect his twenty dollars from the others."

When they all eagerly agreed to the proposal, J.B. couldn't help show his relief, being once again the host in charge. The men spent the next two hours playing. Although Frank had come out ahead that morning, the day's winner turned out to be Vince. Only a little less surprised than everyone else, he gratefully accepted their money in a combination of paper and coin.

Frank was the least surprised of them all. Vince wasn't flashy, outspoken, or bold. But Frank had many times seen his friend carefully weigh different choices, sometimes while having to ignore Frank's impatience. But he always produced positive results for their partnership. And now Frank knew that Vince's approach to business also influenced the way he played cards.

J.B. spent the rest of the evening in his study, while Jim settled himself in the great room with a book found on one of the shelves lining the walls of the back hallway. Vince sat on the front porch, enjoying the cool night air. Frank relaxed at the kitchen table with the latest edition of the *Bridgeport Chronicle Union* spread out before him. Victor took an older edition with him back to the bunk house. Roger retreated to a chair on the back porch, and with light shining down from J.B.'s study window above, wrote a few lines in a small notebook. Mrs. Lewis was in her room teaching Sara the fine art of mending socks. But by midnight, they were all tucked up in their beds.

Early Sunday morning, with dawn just starting to cast shadows, and while Sing was still gathering eggs, Roger stood looking out the window over the kitchen sink. He had spent a restless night, and was drinking his second cup of coffee while admiring the kitchen garden and beyond to the sheds, pens and coops. It was an admirable assemblage of self-sufficiency, and almost made him wish they had as much in Virginia City. Chuckling, he reminded himself that it was a safe bet that he wasn't cut out to care for and slaughter animals.

Roger was brought up short when he heard Mrs. Lewis and Sara in the hall. Rather than make his presence known, however, he froze in place. As ridiculous as he felt, he decided that if they discovered his presence, he'd pretend that he hadn't heard them.

"I'm not flirting with him!" Sara sounded petulant, and Roger could picture her with hands on hips.

"Sara, I've seen how you smile and bat your lashes at Victor."

"I'm just being friendly. He may give me looks like he's interested, but lots of men do that and it seldom means anything. Some men just like to flirt."

"How on earth would you know that?" Mrs. Lewis was obviously scandalized.

"I have friends! They tell me things. Things a girl should know."

"No good girl responds to such a thing from a man. You need to let him know you're a decent girl who won't stand for any nonsense. Especially from a married man."

"Okay. But how does a girl let a man know she's interested?"

Mrs. Lewis hesitated, followed by a short laugh from Sara. "You don't know, do you? You've never had a man."

"That's been my choice! Just because an opportunity arises, doesn't mean a woman must accept."

At this point, Roger was expecting some chastising words from Mrs. Lewis about Sara not knowing her place. Instead, it was Sara who spoke up.

"One of my friends told me that Vic's wife has left him. That she's not just away visiting."

"How would your friend know that?"

"Otto told her husband, and the husband of course told my friend, and she told me. That's the way gossip works, you know."

"Oh, I know only too well!" Mrs. Lewis's voice was sharp. "And it means it's probably not true."

"I think it is. Have you noticed how Otto is always watching Victor? I think Otto is worried that Vic knows he's the one who spread it around about his wife."

"Well, yes, I did notice." Mrs. Lewis sighed loudly and with conviction. "We need to get on. Sing is coming up from the hen house and in an hour the guests will be gathered for breakfast. I've been invited to join Alex at the Hunewill ranch for my breakfast. It'll give me a chance to check on him."

"Oh, heavens, he's fine." Sara's voice reeked with impatience. "You're worse than a mother hen when it comes to that boy."

"That boy, as you call him, is the future of this ranch. He needs to grow up knowing that."

"Oh, he does!"

And with that, their conversation ended, Sara going out the back door as Sing came in, and Mrs. Lewis following Sara. However, once outside, Mrs. Lewis headed straight to the barn where the wagons were kept so Hank could hitch up a horse to the small black rig she always preferred. She claimed it was beneath her dignity to ride a horse.

The maid at the Hunewill ranch had suggested to Mrs. Hunewill that such an invitation would give "poor Mrs. Lewis" a break away from all the men gathered for the poker tournament. Mrs. Hunewill, however, thought it was so the maid could get the latest gossip regarding all that was happening at the Double R. Esther Hunewill was known to be a very smart woman.

# CHAPTER 4

## A NEW DECK UNWRAPPED

Sing greeted the men Sunday morning with platters of corn and bacon fritters accompanied by a pitcher of warm maple syrup and a crock of blackberry jam. The syrup had been purchased from a freighter passing through town from San Francisco, the major source of goods shipped in by rail from the East, and Sing only brought it out on Sundays.

The enjoyment of their breakfast was interrupted in a most unexpected manner, consisting of loud whistling, the thunder of horse's hooves, the hollering of men, and pounding on the back door. Closely following J.B. as he strode to the back door were Jim, Roger, Frank, and Vince. Victor finished his last bite of fritter before joining the others. The door opened to Hank, just outside the back door, dancing around like he had ants in his pants. "They're back! They're back!"

J.B. stared at his foreman. "What?"

"The stolen horses are back!"

Reaching the corral that had been the site of the horses' kidnapping, they all stopped to gawk. Looking none the worse for their experience, the horses clustered together at the fence and looked at the men with mild curiosity. The men looked back in shocked awe. Indian Joe and Manuel began pouring buckets of water into the trough in the middle of the corral, and the horses quickly gathered around, eager for a drink.

J.B. turned to Hank. "How?"

Hank looked back to the big barn and waved his hand to someone to come join them. A tall, muscular man with a bulge of tobacco in his cheek approached, spitting on the ground as he slowly approached. Everything about him was casual, from the way he walked to the way he wore his soft gray hat slouched forward to shade his weather-worn face and long, drooping mustache. He walked up to J.B. with his hand extended and introduced himself by his first name, which was the only one he ever used. "Morning. I'm Mort."

J.B. shook his hand for longer than he usually did anyone. "Do I have you to thank for this?"

"Yeah, well, me and the boys." He turned to two men sitting on the fence of the larger corral next to the horse barn. Both African-American, both young and handsome, when they saw everyone looking in their direction, they grinned and held up a hand in acknowledgement. Victor walked over to them and shook their hands, engaging them in conversation unheard by the others.

"I think we've hired those two during branding. Brothers Jeb and Rudy, right?" J.B. turned to Hank and when he nodded, turned back to the man before him. "So, Mort, where'd you find the horses?"

Mort looked toward Victor. "In his pasture."

Not having heard this statement, Victor approached with a slow shuffle. "Hey, Mort, how you doin'? Haven't seen you in town for a while."

"Been working north."

"Did you find the horses?"

"Um, yeah."

"Wonderful! Where?"

Frank burst out with, "In your pasture!"

Victor's brows raised in surprise. "Huh? Which one?"

"How many do you have?" Vince asked.

"Well, a small one north of town on the big curve, and a bigger one out back of town on the toll road. I lease both of 'em."

Mort turned to J.B. and said, "It was the one north."

J.B. removed his hat, ran a hand through his dark hair, and replaced his hat with a sigh. "I know that one. It'd be easy to cut the wire so close to the road and herd the horses in."

Jim walked over to a curious horse at the fence and ran a hand down the long white blaze on its face, stopping at its soft muzzle. He glanced at Hank. "Could one man do that, or would he have to have help?"

"These are well-broken horses that were never any trouble." Hank shook his head. "They're used to being herded together, especially if that gray mare over in the corner is in the lead."

Roger joined his father at the corral, next to Hank. "Wouldn't someone have to know that? I mean, being familiar enough with the horses to know there was such a mare with them?"

Jim, rubbing the horse's ears, responded to Roger loud enough that everyone heard him. "Or be told by someone who knows."

Every man there familiar with the ranch had to fight the urge to look at those around him. To break the tension, J.B. turned to Hank. "Why don't you go into town and tell the sheriff that they're back. And maybe you should hire those two on the fence to stand guard for a few nights. Where are they working now?"

"They're not."

"Good. Oh, and Hank..." He stopped to fish some coins from his pocket, handing them to his foreman. "Have a good breakfast at the Allen House after you report to the sheriff."

"Thanks."

"And you might find out if Mort wants a job here."

"He used to be a blacksmith in Bodie."

"Even better. We know for sure he's got a good way with horses."

"Will do." Hank put the coins in his pocket as he walked to the barn to saddle his favorite horse.

"Okay, gentlemen, let's get back to the house and our game. We also have a funeral to arrange this afternoon after the undertaker gets home from church. We'll set the funeral for tomorrow." He looked at Jim, Vince and Frank. "You may want to send a telegram to your wives that your return isn't going to start tomorrow. I'm sure the sheriff will want us all available for a while longer. Vic, you have anything in town you have to take care of?"

"No. Not a thing."

"Okay, then, let's get back to our game." J.B. didn't wait for anyone's opinion, just setting off for the house at a brisk walk. They played, but it was without enthusiasm, each man finding it difficult to concentrate.

Trying to get a little normalcy back, Jim commented, "I noticed a lot of fresh produce in your markets."

"Yes. We get the berries and honey from the farms north in Antelope Valley. We supply lumber and shingles when they're building, and they give us produce."

"Give?" Frank scoffed.

There was general laugher as J.B. clarified. "No, we both pay, but at fair negotiated prices."

With the general atmosphere lightened, J.B. found his rhythm before the others, and was ahead when they broke at noon. J.B. left for Bridgeport with Frank and Jim, with plans to eat in town before meeting with the undertaker and the minister of the local church. The others stayed at the ranch to try and find something to occupy their time after consuming sandwiches set out by Sing. Vince and Roger decided on a game of chess, while Victor took a newspaper with him out to the bunk house.

After one game, Vince laughed at Roger's drooping eye lids. However, both of them admitted that a nap sounded good, knowing the return of the others from town would wake them. Vince sprawled out on one of the sofas in the great room, not bothering to remove his boots since Mrs. Lewis wasn't around. It floated through his mind to wonder where Sara might be, but since he didn't really care, he drifted off.

She was, in fact, busy weeding the kitchen garden with Sing. Roger thought of keeping them company, but was afraid he'd be expected to help. Digging around in the dirt was not his preferred activity. Instead, he went around to the back porch facing the barns and corrals. Deeply cushioned wicker chairs were lined up along the wall and Roger took up residence in the one with an ottoman.

Shortly afterwards, Sara passed him heading for the tack room. Having several times seen flirtatious by-play between Sara and Victor, Roger wondered if she had mistaken the tack room for the bunk house. But once inside, she didn't immediately come out. As Roger began to nod off, he pictured all that she would be seeing: harnesses, bridles, halters, collars, horse blankets, ropes, saddles and pieces of saddles, and tools she probably couldn't identify. Like counting sheep to settle into sleep, this did the trick and he dozed peacefully.

When Roger awoke, it was over an hour later. There was no activity around the barn and corrals, and feeling refreshed yet bored, he went into the kitchen for a drink from the pitcher next to the stoneware water filter. He glanced into the other room and saw that Vince was still sacked out on the sofa. But the men had returned from town, their hats on the rack by the door, and their horses tied up out front. Roger figured Jim and Frank had gone to their respective rooms, as had J.B., maybe they too eager for a nap.

He sat at the kitchen table, playing solitaire while watching Sing clean what he had harvested from the garden. Roger was always most comfortable with a deck of cards in his hands, and it actually helped him focus on any conversation.

Roger discovered that Sing had immigrated from China when a child, with parents who had come to the United States during the California gold rush. They had learned very little English, and never spoke it at home, but he had made a determined effort to learn all he could about American customs and cooking. Nevertheless, he had never had the courage to cut off the entirety of his braid, or queue. He kept it short, and the front portion of his head wasn't shaved as was traditional. Instead, his long hair was simply slicked back into the braid.

"I am American," he stated to Roger. "I am not loyal to any dynasty in China. But I respect ancestors and what they were forced to do."

The main thing that Roger learned was that Sing loved his work at the Double R. He respected J.B., loved the child Alex, tolerated Mrs. Lewis, and was intimidated by Hank. Most recently, he was puzzled by Sara. But it was the Double R itself that he dearly loved. He thought of it like a large, demanding child that often challenged the patience of everyone, but was loved nonetheless. To him, working at such a highly regarded spread was proof that he was a person of consequence, and it gave him prestige among his Asian friends in Bridgeport, as well as in Carson City. His self-esteem was also sustained by J.B.'s obvious respect of him. Roger chuckled to himself. "I'd treat well anyone who could cook like Sing, too."

Roger settled back into what was now his favorite chair on the back porch, anticipating that evening's supper. It was the warmest part of the day, and other than a large horse fly that buzzed past, there was little activity.

Seeing Mort in the doorway of the blacksmith shop stretching and yawning, Roger realized he must have just awakened from a nap. He had a small room in the front corner of the barn, as did Hank at the front of the bunk house. Roger wondered if the hostler knew the men were back. Should he tell him so the horses tied up out front weren't too long without water? Was Mrs. Lewis still at the Hunewill ranch, where they had agreed to extend Alex's visit? What had he learned from the poker game they'd played, besides the fact that Victor never tried to bluff? Such were the lazy thoughts anyone might entertain while enjoying shade and a cool breeze on a warm afternoon.

Roger could see Hank at the small pond beyond the arrangement of out buildings and corrals, and the two newly hired night guards with him. They were pulling vegetation from around the edges of the pond fed by a spring, making sure it remained open and the water available. Roger was surprised by a slight sense of guilt as he pictured his life spent mostly indoors. This was followed by a surge of gratitude. Ranch life might seem an energizing and appealing life, but he now realized that it was a daily grind of hard work. No matter the weather, or how one might feel, people and animals had to be fed and cared for. "Of course," he mumbled, "if one has a lot of money like J.B., you can hire others to do all that." That brought to him a keen realization. "This place must take one hell of a lot of money to keep going!"

After completing a mental inventory of the ranch's occupants, Roger realized that he couldn't account for Sara or Victor. However, just then the girl came hurrying past him, heading toward the barn area. He smiled when he realized that she was not wearing her apron, and had pinned on a white lace collar. When she reached the bunk house, she glanced around, taking note of where everyone was before walking boldly inside. Roger grinned. "I wonder if ole Vic is expecting the girl with the sexy wiggle."

Almost immediately, however, Sara came back out, leaned against the door jamb, and screamed. When she found her voice, the only words that came out were, "Help! Help!"

Roger bounded off the porch and arrived at the bunk house with Mort, who had emerged from the blacksmith shed with a heavy glove still on one hand. The other men were not far behind.

The picture before them was one of horrific consequence. Victor hung from a cross beam of the ceiling, a rope around his neck, and a wooden chair not far away.

Hank told Jeb, "Go up to the house and get J.B." Hank then turned to brother Rudy. "Ride into town. We need the sheriff and Doc Sinclair right away." Looking up at Victor's body swaying in the breeze from the open door, he added, "And if you see the undertaker, you might tell him to bring his wagon."

Roger told Rudy, "My dad's horse is still out front. The dark bay with the star on his forehead. You can take that one."

"Thanks." The young men sprinted away to fulfill their orders. Jeb disappeared into the house through the back door, not bothering to knock. He was followed back out almost immediately by Jim, Frank and Vince. Sing stood on the back porch, caught between food that was cooking and his curiosity. But remembering his place, he returned to the kitchen. After all, curiosity could wait, but the chickens in the oven needed basting. And the boss needed wakening.

"Where's J.B?" Roger asked Jeb.

"Sing couldn't raise him. He could hear him snoring in his room through the door, though."

Hank took charge, telling the others to stay where they were just inside the door. He walked slowly to the body and after taking hold of Victor's hand, turned back to the others. "He's not cold. He must have done this a short time ago."

Frank's voice rang out in the quiet room. "How?"

"What do you mean?" Hank stared at Frank in disbelief. "Isn't it obvious?"

Maybe it was because they were standing further away and had a wider view of the room, but Vince had picked up on the same thing that had Frank. "The chair he would have been standing on is several feet away."

Hank turned and looked at the chair. "That's probably where it landed when he kicked it away."

"No." Frank shook his head. "If it had been kicked away, it would be on its side, not upright. The floor boards are too uneven for it to slide that far away and remain upright."

Disobeying Hank's order, Roger wandered over to the small table next to the bed Victor had been using. "Look here. His pipe is freshly packed, but not smoked. And he'd poured himself a whiskey. Remember, he told us it went well with a pipe. The newspaper I saw him take from the house is open on the bed." He looked at Hank with a frown. "Is all this the picture of someone about to give themselves a hemp neck massage?"

No one knew what to say to that, ignoring the popular, flippant slang term for hanging. But at least Roger had startled them into looking differently at what was before them.

When Sheriff Cody arrived an hour later, he stood in the doorway and took in the scene. Hank briefly explained where they had all been when they heard the screaming. The sheriff walked close to the body and looked up at it while slowly nodding his head. But he didn't say what he found so agreeable about it. The sheriff, Mort, and Hank managed to cut down Victor's body and get it into the back of the ranch's buckboard. After Rudy left for town with the wagon, the sheriff went back inside, scanning the room. The others stood as sentinels by the door, watching every move he made.

"Did anyone handle or move anything in here?"

Roger spoke up immediately. "No. I was the first one to reach the door and the screaming Sara. Mort was the next to arrive, since he was in the blacksmith shed nearby. Then Hank, along with Rudy and Jeb, came up. Hank told us to stay by the door and we did."

Hank spoke up. "Then I told Jeb to go up to the house for the others, and told Rudy to go get you."

"Right." He scanned the area again, focusing on the old wooden chair off to the left side of where the body would have been hanging. "Could Sara have moved the chair?" When no one said anything, the sheriff asked, "Where is she now?"

Roger glanced over his shoulder toward the house. "She ran back up to the house as soon as we arrived."

"Understandable." Sheriff Cody looked around once more before turning to Hank. "Does this door lock?"

"Yes, sir."

"Then give me the keys. And everyone, please go back to the house. I'll join you in a moment. But first, can anyone tell me why J.B. isn't here?"

The answer to that became evident as they turned around. J.B. was walking off the back porch and approaching them, none too steady on his feet. At the same time, Mrs. Lewis arrived home, bringing the black rig to a stop nearby. Mort, walking back after having retrieved the two remaining horses from the front of the house, took them to the barn. But he immediately returned for the rig, which he also brought over to the barn. The sheriff, knowing Mort would be busy for some time caring for the horses and cleaning the buggy, decided to question him later.

Meanwhile, J.B. had stopped before the assembled men. "What's up? Sing told me something was happening out here." He turned to the sheriff.

"Good morning, Mike. I came home from town and took a longer nap than I'd planned. You come to tell us who stole the horses?"

"Didn't you hear the screaming, or the wagon going to town? It would have passed right by your bedroom window."

Startled by the question, J.B. looked over at Hank, who shook his head and turned away. J.B. answered the question with a tight jaw. "No! What the hell's been going on? The horses get stolen and I don't hear that, and now something else happens while I'm sleeping, and that doesn't wake me either?"

"Huh!" Everyone turned toward Jim, who put up his hands as though to ward off a blow. "Sorry. It's just that I had a strange idea."

"What?" Roger knew the wisdom of listening to his father's hunches.

Jim turned to J.B. with a frown. "Do you by any chance have a bottle of whiskey in your room?"

"So what?" J.B. was immediately on the defensive. "There's one in all the guest rooms, too."

"Yes," Jim smiled. "And thank you for that. But do you take a drink to help you sleep? Even this afternoon before your nap?"

"Again, so what?" J.B., feeling that for some reason he was being criticized, no longer looked like a friendly host.

"Just that I wouldn't drink any more from that bottle until it can be checked for an added sleeping powder."

Everyone looked at the sheriff, as though he might have the answer. The best he could give them was a shrug. "It does sound reasonable. I'll take the bottle with me when I leave."

J.B.'s color was deepening by the minute as his irritation increased. "Will someone tell me what's been happening out here?" He looked around at the group. "Where's Vic?"

The sheriff rested his eyes on J.B. "Victor's dead."

Considering the rapidity with which J.B.'s face fell into slack-jawed surprise, Roger half expected him to faint. "What? How?"

"He hanged himself."

"No! He'd never!"

The sheriff nodded. "That's pretty much what I'm thinking. Come look at the room."

After looking up at the rope over the beam with its cut end dangling down, along with the chair off to the side, J.B. backed out of the room.

Leaning against the outside wall of the bunk house, he took a deep breath and turned to Vince. "Who found him?"

Sheriff Cody stepped outside and placed a hand on J.B.'s shoulder, answering before Vince could speak. "It was Sara. I haven't been able to talk to her yet."

Roger told them, "I saw her go inside the bunk house. She popped back out almost immediately."

J.B. shook his head. "What a terrible thing for a young girl to see!"

Roger felt like a cad, but he still asked, "Why did she go into the bunk house in the first place?" The only response was a lot of frowns aimed at him.

"What I'd like now," Sheriff Cody told them, "is for everyone to go back to the house and gather in the great room. And make sure Sara is with you."

He turned to Mrs. Lewis standing at the edge of the group. By the startled faces of the men, the sheriff could tell they had forgotten her presence. But he hadn't. Within the group around him were several men whom he had known, and liked, for some time. Nevertheless, he knew people often had hidden secrets they'd go to dire lengths to hide. It meant that he needed to stay alert, since he realized these men were going to bunch up like sheep in a thunderstorm. He was determined to be the dog that sorted them out.

He turned back to Mrs. Lewis. Her hands were clutched at her waste and her back was stiffly erect. At first glance she appeared a marvel of self-control, but the paleness of her face told a different story. Using the soft voice he reserved for elderly women and nervous animals, the sheriff told her, "Maybe you'd better go check on Sara."

Mrs. Lewis said nothing, the only sound the crisp fabric of her black dress swishing around her legs as she walked rapidly toward the house.

After everyone left the area, Hank with them, the sheriff took a moment to take a mental photograph of the bunk house. After a walk through, he stood looking down at the table next to the bed, and then at the bed itself. It didn't appear to him as though someone had been lying on top of it napping or reading. It was too mussed up, with the open newspaper half on and half off the bed, like there had been a struggle. It might account for the red patch of skin he had seen on the side of Victor's head when they were moving his body. If he had lived longer, it might have turned into quite a bruise.

When recently reading Mark Twain's novel *The Tragedy of Pudd'nhead Wilson*, the sheriff had been fascinated by the courtroom scenes involving friction ridge skin imprints. The sheriff picked up the whiskey glass and carried it to the window at the far end of the long room, careful to hold it by the edge of its base. He held it up to the low light offered by the late afternoon sun, not sure how he would be able to match any handprint to Victor, or anyone else. Still, he thought he might be able to tell something by the size of the hand or fingers. The only problem was that there was not one print of any kind on the glass.

Frowning, Sheriff Cody put the glass back on the table where it had been resting. "So, Victor either wore gloves when he poured the drink, or someone else poured it and wiped off the glass. Not too many people would know to do that." Remembering that there had been no gloves on the body, he looked around and found no gloves anywhere.

More and more convinced that this had not been a case of suicide, the sheriff joined the others in the house. They didn't look pleased with being made to wait, especially J.B., who Cody realized was suddenly finding it awkward to present himself as the master in charge. J.B. had met that challenge by ordering Sing to bring in coffee, which he accomplished with Sara's help. J.B. then told the girl, obviously still shaken, to sit.

Sheriff Michael Cody stood with his back to the sofa facing the small fireplace, Sara curled up in the large chair to his right, and Mrs. Lewis perched on the arm of it. "Sorry to keep you waiting." Attempting to look more relaxed than he felt, he half sat on the back of the sofa, keeping one foot on the floor. He had only been sheriff for a matter of days, and he was very much aware that those in town considered every day a test of his ability.

Ignoring the knot in his stomach, the sheriff's eyes swept the room. J.B. was not only a friend, but also a major land owner in the valley. And, therefore, a man of consequence. But in the towns where they lived, this was also true of J.B.'s guests.

The sheriff scanned the faces before him. Frank Eastman and Vince Perry were simply looking curious, and just a little bit eager, probably wondering what they'd gotten into by coming to the ranch. Besides curious, Jim and Roger Murphy also looked a little tense and watchful. No one more than Jim knew how quickly a situation like this could turn into a calamity for an innocent person if not handled just right.

Mrs. Lewis and Sara kept exchanging what they thought were surreptitious glances, but which everyone saw while pretending they had not. Both women sat stiffly with folded hands tightly clasped in their laps. J.B. drummed his fingers on the arm of his chair, barely holding back his impatience.

The sheriff turned to Sara. "I'm sure that you're still in shock over what you saw. And I won't keep you long. But when you went in, did you touch anything?"

Sara looked up at him, her eyes large and a slight quiver in her chin. "It was awful! I never imagined something like that! I got out of there as fast as I could."

"Yes, yes. I'm sure you did." His voice was as gentle as he knew how to make it as he asked, "Now, my dear, just why did you go to the bunk house?"

Sara sat at attention, ringing her hands and trying hard not to whimper. She stared straight ahead, sounding like a school child reciting in front of a classroom. "I went to tell him that the men were back from town, and that dinner was going to be a little later than usual."

The sheriff didn't miss the startled look that Mrs. Lewis rained down on Sara before quickly looking away. "Who," he asked, "told you to go tell him that?"

"Well, um, no one." There was more twisting of fingers as she forced herself not to look away from the sheriff. "I just thought it would be a polite thing to do."

"Sing didn't tell you dinner was going to be late?"

"No. I...I just thought it would be."

Roger spoke up, addressing the flustered girl. "You'd been out to the tack room earlier."

"Yes." She pursed her lips, telling the sheriff, "I was looking for an awl so I could enlarge a hole in a belt. I couldn't find one, so I hurried back to the house." She turned to Roger, snapping out, "I suppose you saw that, too!"

"Actually, I had fallen asleep."

"Thank you, my dear." The sheriff was adept at moderating his tone depending on the person before him. He was courteous to women, kindly to youngsters, and forthright with men. Somehow, he managed all of this without being condescending or threatening. Besides his reputation for integrity, his charm was part of the reason he had just been elected to his current position. "If you'd like to go to your room and lie down, Sara, it's perfectly alright."

"Do I have to leave?" Sara had an oddly stubborn set to her jaw.

"Uh, no." Sheriff Cody glanced at Mrs. Lewis, only to find her staring at the girl with an expression he couldn't interpret. She was obviously surprised that Sara wanted to stay, as was everyone, but it was more than that. The sheriff didn't press the point, realizing that even if she went to her room, she could easily crack the door and hear what was said.

"Mr. Eastman and Mr. Perry? I'm not sure how you fit into this group. How do you know J.B.?"

Frank spoke up when Vince turned to him with brows raised. "We didn't know him until we got here. We were invited by Jim and Roger. We met them a couple of years ago through our wives, who are good friends with Roger's wife."

"And Mr. Murphy knew you liked to gamble?"

"That's right."

After a moment's thought, the sheriff asked Jim, "Mr. Murphy, did you or your son know Victor or Otto before this weekend?"

"No." Jim ran a hand over his face before looking across the coffee table to Roger. "But I had the strangest feeling that I'd met Victor before."

Roger shook his head. "Not me."

"I think it might have something to do with when we were in Bodie last year." Jim turned to the others. "We played with a lot of men. Several times when Victor spoke these last few days, that game would flash into my mind."

J.B. leaned forward, as he did when he was eager to make a point. "Vic was in Bodie several times last year. But he would have looked very different then. He had an eyebrow that was practically a single, and a thick beard often with shreds of tobacco in it."

Roger stood up like he'd been bitten on the butt. "That was him? Dad, remember? That was the guy who lost a pile to you that night."

"And to you, too, if I remember right. He played at your table before mine." Jim looked at J.B., still trying to accept what he had just been told. "So that was Victor. I never knew the guy's name. But, boy, was he angry when he stomped out of the gambling hall!"

Roger sat back down. "I'll say he was. He accused you of cheating, of having unmarried parents, and being a cur dog. All in terms I'd never repeat in front of a lady. Oh, and he said you were someone who should die a bad death."

"Really?" Jim didn't look overly disturbed. "I didn't hear everything he was shouting."

"Yeah, well, I followed him out. You didn't see me do that. You'd gone out back to the privy. But I wanted to see where he went. I waited a few minutes and then followed him. His pockets weren't weighed down with a gun, but I wanted to be sure he didn't have one in his saddlebag. He was already on his horse, riding down Main toward the Bodie Toll Road."

"And that was the last you two ever saw of him, until you got here?" The sheriff kept his voice even, no hint of suspicion showing.

Jim cleared his throat. "But there's something else. It came up while we were playing Saturday morning. He was a friend of Jimmy Mack and Terry Miller. He blamed me for both their deaths, when in fact I didn't kill either one."

"So, he resented you for that, whether justified or not. And also, maybe because of the game in Bodie. Interesting." He turned to J.B. "Did you know about any of this when you invited Victor to be in a game with these two?"

J.B. looked back at him with confusion clear on his face. "No!" After a moment's hesitation he added, "And to be really accurate, it was Vic's idea to invite Jim and Roger. He said he'd heard about them when he'd been in Virginia City recently." J.B. stopped talking, but everyone could tell there was something more he wanted to say by the way he cocked his head to the side. "I'd heard he'd been there. But when I asked him why, he very pointedly changed the subject. I didn't press him."

Roger shook his head. "I can't believe I didn't recognize him. I'm usually good at remembering faces." Roger turned to J.B. "During our first game you said something about him being cleaned up. Was that about his facial fur?"

J.B. nodded. "When I saw him in town last month, he still had his brow, although his beard was gone. In fact, his hair had thinned out, too. We had a beer, and got to talking. I hadn't seen him for months. We talked about games we'd played lately, and where, and that's when I told him about a big game I was hoping to host someday. He thought it was a good idea." J.B. looked out the front windows and frowned. "Come to think of it, it was Vic that said we should do it this summer. 'No time like the present', he said."

"How did you react to that?"

"I agreed, obviously. But I told him beyond the two of us, I didn't know who else we could ask. He suggested Otto. I knew him from some time ago. I have to admit, I was a little surprised Victor would suggest him. He knew that at one time we weren't on the best of terms."

"Why not?"

"Oh, it was a long time ago. Maybe two years. Otto had worked for me for a short time. But I didn't like the way he worked with the green-broke horses. He had no patience. After he left here, he asked me for a reference so he could get a job at the Circle H, the Hunewill place. I declined, and instead he got a job at another ranch south of town. Only thing is, they paid less."

"So, he resented you?"

"I don't know about that." J.B. thought for a moment. "I never heard that he was unhappy. I know the foreman there, and he's never said anything against Otto."

The sheriff turned to Jim. "But you knew J.B.?"

"Yes. We'd met J.B. in Bodie just before last winter set in. I played at a small table of men with him. We got to talking afterwards, and after Roger's table folded, we shared supper with him. I gave him my address in Virginia City and told him to stop by if he was ever in town."

"Did he?"

"No. His invitation to this weekend was the first I'd heard from him." He turned to J.B. and smiled. "We were happy to accept. It promised to be an eventful weekend." The minute he said it, he was sorry he had. Thankfully, no one pointed out the irony, still too shocked by the morning's discovery.

Sheriff Cody finally asked the question everyone had upper most in mind. "Does anyone know why Victor would want to take his life?"

That got an immediate shake of the head from everyone present. And for the first time since gathering together in the great room, they became aware of Hank's presence. "I saw him several times swallow some tablets."

"What were they for?" The eagerness in the sheriff's voice was obvious.

"Hell, I don't know," Hank declared. "It wasn't any of my business."

Hank's reticence was understandable. Sheriff Cody thought of his wife and her friends, and in that moment wished that one of them had seen Victor take the pills. Women wouldn't have hesitated to ask him about them. This would have been helpful, as there had been no pills in the bunk house or on the body.

J.B. ran his fingers through his hair, something Roger noted he did often when he was perturbed. "It just isn't what I'd expect from Vic. He's had a rough life, but he's always moved forward."

"What kind of a rough life?" The sheriff wasn't sure it mattered, but while people were in a talking mood, he was going to grasp at any straw he could.

"Well, he lost his first wife and child. He turned to the bottle and it took him a long time to get his life back on track. I loaned him some money to help him out once when his ranch was in financial trouble. Then he met and married his current wife. She has two girls, and he was fond of them. His life was finally going well."

"Not really," Mrs. Lewis volunteered. "It's gotten around that his wife has moved out with the girls."

"Not just for a visit?" J.B. asked.

"No. A neighbor of theirs told the maid at the Circle H that the decision to leave was sudden, since nothing was said about it the day before. Evidently, Mrs. Turner was wiping tears from her eyes as the stage left town, while the youngest girl was openly weeping."

J.B. frowned. "I'm sorry to hear that." He then looked around the room. "But is a break in his marriage enough for him to take his life?"

That's exactly what they were all thinking. Although a few were also thinking that there was the possibility that Victor had not taken his life. And once again there was a determined effort not to cast suspicious looks at one another.

It occurred to Roger, alarmed at the thought, that when they next had to go into town, people there wouldn't be so circumspect. Gossiping and speculating was a major sport in all towns, but especially in one so small. And especially in a town already a little uncomfortable with J. B. Roberts.

Ever practical, Frank asked, "Does anyone know how to get ahold of his wife?"

"Oh, God, that's right." J.B. turned to Hank and then the sheriff. "Did either of you find a note? Doesn't someone taking their life, who has a family, leave a note?"

Both men shook their heads, the sheriff saying, "I'll ask around in town about the wife. And I'll check their house, too."

"It'll take some time for that to be done," Frank said, "and to get her back here."

Mrs. Lewis pointed out the obvious. "If she even wants to come back."

Frank looked at her and nodded. Accepting the reality of the messy situation in which they found themselves, he said, "I guess that means we have another funeral to plan."

J.B. once again ran his fingers through his hair. "Yeah, I'll pay for it. We'll be in town in the morning for Otto's funeral, so afterwards we'll make the arrangement for a Wednesday funeral for Vic."

"Where's the cemetery?" Vince hadn't remembered seeing it on the way into town.

The sheriff answered. "Just off Main back of Bryant's Hall at School and Emigrant. But there's a new one east of town and he'll be buried there."

Jim spoke up, determination underlying his words. "I think we should all pitch in a few bucks for the burial. It's only fitting." He got no argument from anyone, and J.B. was too surprised and grateful to know what to say.

Sara sat forward, her voice hesitant and low when she spoke. "Otto's funeral is tomorrow, and Vic's on Wednesday?" She looked up at Mrs. Lewis. "Should I wear my black work dress with maybe crocheted collar and cuffs?"

Roger, thinking back to the conversation between the two women that he'd overheard, thought to himself, "So that's what Mrs. Lewis looks like when scandalized." He almost chuckled, but caught himself in time.

"Sara, dear," Mrs. Lewis told her, "we should talk about that later at a more appropriate time."

Sara sat back and refolded her hands on her lap. By her pout, it was obvious that she was feeling the chastisement as unfair. Whatever she had felt about Victor, she wasn't as bothered by his death as the men expected her to be, and they were not comfortable acknowledging this.

The sheriff, realizing that he had gotten from everyone what was possible right then, expressed his gratitude for their cooperation. He had Sing retrieve the whiskey bottle from J.B.'s room, and immediately left without further conversation.

He was, however, thinking that he would soon be back. There had been a number of things said that he wanted more time to consider before approaching certain individuals. With only his horse to hear him as he rode away from the Double R in the day's lengthening shadows, he murmured, "This investigation is far from over."

# CHAPTER 5

## DISCARDS

Otto's funeral was appropriately solemn, held in the newly established cemetery on a hill east of town off the Aurora Road. The old and very small cemetery in town being full, there were now over a dozen burials that had taken place in the new one, as it also served Coleville, Dog Town, the Sweetwater Valley, and Bodie.

Some few graves had a fancy, upright stone headstone, but most were marked by carved, wooden headboards. The "unknown" deceased, moved from the town cemetery, were noted by small white crosses. Two had iron railings around the grave, both for decorative purposes and to discourage disturbance of the graves. The blacksmith charged a good price for those. The entry arch between a row of young trees was still unpainted raw wood, but rows had been set aside for future burials using wooden stakes to denote burial plots. An area at the north end had been designated for the tribal members who had accepted the Christian faith.

Roger wondered how Otto would have felt about his parting being attended by only half a dozen townspeople. Mrs. Lewis had kept Sara at home with her, much to the girl's displeasure. But it had been brought home to Sara that her first responsibility was her job, not gossiping among her friends in town.

It certainly didn't go without notice by everyone from the Double R, that those half-dozen townspeople made a decided effort to keep themselves at a distance from J.B. and his guests. The minister read two passages from the Bible, followed by a short prayer. When the public was invited to speak, no one stepped forward. Normally, such a brief service would have encouraged people to stand around and visit afterwards. But on this day, everyone immediately walked away to their wagons or horses while trying to look as though they had urgent business elsewhere.

The minister shook hands with J.B., who after all had paid him for the service, but he spared only a quick nod in the direction of J.B.'s guests. He then pulled out his watch chain and checked the time on a cheap, metal timepiece given him by a grateful congregation. After uttering a somber reference to time flying, he didn't wait for a response before long strides brought him to the entrance where he climbed into the back seat of a black buggy. He was barely inside before he said something to the man in the front seat, whereupon he was whisked off down the hill.

Frank moved to stand next to J.B., close enough that their arms almost touched. Vince did the same on J.B.'s other side. Seeing this, Roger motioned to his father and they moved to join the trio. It may have been meant as a supportive gesture, but those townspeople looking back saw it as a closing of ranks. It only increased their suspicion that something untoward was going on out at "that strange man's ranch".

Adding to their speculation was seeing Sheriff Cody standing in the shadow of a tree by the entrance arch, having kept himself apart from the service and those attending. After the last of the townspeople had departed, the sheriff mounted his horse and rode away without speaking to anyone. This last was ignored, however, when it was reported in town that the sheriff had avoided J.B. and his guests. It was enough to kindle a flare-up of gossip that swept through the town like unchecked wildfire.

It was a small community, allowing word to spread quickly about the deaths at the Double R. Some people thought it strange that Otto and Victor, known as long-time friends, had died at the same location only a day apart. Of course, people weren't saying one of the gambling party had done anything lethal, but most agreed that it was an odd coincidence. And until it was all fully explained, most people thought it best to stay away from J.B. and his guests. Because even if J.B. might possibly be in the clear, and one never knew about him, what about those he had invited?

J.B. was unaware that his past interactions with many of the citizens had set him up for this mistrust. Some of them had always been a little uneasy about J. B. Roberts, mainly because they simply knew so little about him. Some men had found to their detriment that he was a skilled, somewhat cut-throat gambler, unlike themselves who played for amusement. A number of ranchers had vied for horses or cattle at stock auctions, and had been unable to top his bids. Shopkeepers and feed suppliers knew him to be a shrewd bargainer and trader, resulting in at least a small cut into their profits.

And, in general, J.B. wasn't one to stay long in a saloon to visit and gossip. And when he did, men would later realize that he had done more listening than talking. On the other hand, people had to admit that J.B. always stood a round of drinks, so he did have at least one redeeming quality.

As for women, a few of the older ones had hoped he would cast his favor upon their daughters. He had not. Several younger women had unsuccessfully tried to attract his attention before settling for their current husbands. These were the women who were harboring resentments that made them all the more eager to hear talk against him. And they didn't hesitate to pass it on.

It didn't help that men who were popular like N. B. Hunewill, Amasa Bryant and "By" Day were known to have spent considerable time with J.B., and yet declared not to know much about him. Nor would they say anything against him. These, and some of the other older men, didn't hesitate to say that J.B. was a gracious host with a fine property, a wonderful cook, and an odd but efficient housekeeper. They were also quick to point out that J.B. had readily joined in when ranch hands had been scarce during the haying season, or when town projects needed just a little more funding. Although this was readily acknowledged, it didn't change the fact that many people would have been happier to have been told something villainous.

J.B., Frank and Jim, having ridden their horses to the funeral, rode to the undertaker's office to arrange for Victor's funeral on Wednesday. They followed this task with a quick drink at The Brick, a saloon owned by Jack Severe, one of the early pioneers of the town. The men patiently listened while Jack talked of his desire to sell out to Pike Richardson. It may not have been of particular interest to them, but they were happy to be treated like a friend and paying customer instead of a plague carrier.

While J.B., Frank and Jim had headed to the saloon, Vince and Roger had gone to the dining room of the Leavitt House for pie and coffee before returning to the ranch. They settled themselves in front of the great room windows, hoping to block out the morning's unpleasantness with a game of chess. They both knew they would soon be leaving, while their host could not. It felt as though they would be deserting a friend in his time of need, but they also didn't want to over-stay their welcome.

Supper Monday night was a somber occasion, with little conversation. No one shared a story, no one cracked a joke, and only after Roger complimented Sing on the meal did anyone else think to thank him. However, they did discuss whether or not they could have another game Wednesday afternoon following Victor's funeral. They all agreed that would be pleasant, but also that they should wait and see. What they were waiting for, and what they thought they might see, was not defined.

Roger was curious about Otto. Spearing another roasted potato and placing it on his plate, he asked, "Did he have any family here?"

J.B. could only shake his head. "I don't think he had family. At least, I never heard him refer to any."

In a low voice, Jim shared what the others were thinking. "It was very generous of you to take care of his burial expenses."

"Someone had to do it." J.B. looked down at the coffee cup in front of him as Sing cleared away the plates. "I didn't want him buried in a potter's grave. The people at the ranch where he worked are going to arrange for a headstone."

It wasn't until they were in their room getting ready for bed that Jim shared his thoughts with Roger. "We never did decide if we're going to have a game after Victor's funeral."

"But we did decide to have a group dinner at the Leavitt House after the funeral."

"Yeah."

Roger looked up from polishing his boots, setting them aside. As he crawled into his bed, he asked, "Dad, what's bothering you?"

"There's something about Otto's death that feels wrong, and I can't put my finger on what it is."

"Something someone said, maybe Otto himself?"

"No. I don't think so." Jim walked to the open window and looked out into the darkness, feeling a kinship with what could only be defined as inky shadows. "I just don't know."

"Well, let's get some sleep. It'll come to you if it's meant to."

"God, you sound like your mother!" Jim lowered the wick on the oil lamp, effectively turning out the light.

Roger only smiled. He couldn't think of anyone whom he'd rather sound like. Glad that they were in the dark, he asked, "Dad?"

"Hmmm?"

"What you said about going out to the privy when we were in Bodie? Right after the game where Victor lost to you? Is that true?"

"Why wouldn't it be true?"

Thinking that was an odd way to word a reply, Roger called up his courage. "I went back to the privy myself, and I should have passed you leaving it to go back inside the hall. And I didn't."

"Maybe you were watching Vic riding away longer than you thought." Leaving no time for further questions, Jim announced, "Good night, son."

Roger tried hard to accept that explanation, but he was not very successful. His father was holding something back, and although he knew it was probably innocuous, it bothered him that his father wasn't being totally forthcoming with him. But within two minutes both men were sound asleep, which was a good thing, considering the day that was to follow.

The household was just waking up on Tuesday morning when knocking on the front door brought Sing out from the kitchen. He was greeted at the door by Sheriff Cody and Doc Sinclair.

"Good morning, Sing. Can you go tell all those in the house that I want to talk to them?"

"Now?" That his boss and his friends should be disturbed this early in the morning was an affront to his sense of order and hospitality.

"Yes." The sheriff's voice brooked no argument. "If you don't mind?"

"Oh, yes. Oh, yes. I go now." However, before charging up the stairs, he stopped to knock on the door of Mrs. Lewis. A quick, whispered exchange between them resulted in the hard closure of her door. Sing then ran up the stairs and knocked on J.B.'s door. Another hurried exchange resulted in his door also closing hard. Sing made his way to the door of Jim and Roger, then Frank and Vince. All the men ducked back inside their rooms to dress. When Sing got to Sara's door, however, there was no answer. Sing flapped his arms, shook his head over the laziness of the young, and scurried down the stairs and into the kitchen.

As J.B. entered the great room, followed by the others, they could hear him mumbling under his breath, "Just once I'd like to start the day with the rooster's crow instead of someone pounding on doors." When they were altogether, he confronted Sheriff Cody. "Morning, Mike. Why are you here so damn early?"

"I know it's going to be a busy day for everyone, but I wanted you to have the latest information before it gets around."

"Okay, but let's get our coffee first."

They all moved to the dining room table, where Sing served them with cups of coffee from a big enamel pot sitting on an iron trivet in the middle of the table. He made sure everyone's cup was filled, after which several men generously doctored their cups from the bowl of sugar and a large pitcher of fresh cream. Roger vaguely noted that there was no brown sugar, but then realized that Victor had been the only one to ever use it.

Meanwhile, Sing brought in platters of hard cooked eggs that were halved and sprinkled with herbs, a bowl of spiced peaches canned the year before, and another of applesauce made the day before. The platter of large biscuits drew instant attention. Everyone pulled out a chair and filled their plates. When J.B. invited the sheriff and the doctor to join in, they accepted gratefully.

Several minutes were spent enjoying their food before the sheriff turned to the physician. "Why don't you take over from here, Doc?"

Doc nodded and swallowed a mouthful of egg. "As far as we can tell, Otto died because his heart stopped. And it stopped because of a lack of oxygen, or what we call asphyxia. How that occurred, I can't tell, but the eyes showed it." He held up his hands as Roger and Frank started to speak. "Before you go jumping to conclusions, he wasn't suffocated by anything over his face. And there was no bruising on his neck. All I can say, at least until I can confer with more experienced colleagues, is that for some reason there was inadequate oxygen to the cells of his body, including his heart. The death certificate will say he died of asphyxia brought on by an unknown cause."

Sheriff Cody reached for another biscuit. "That's all we can do unless something more definitive comes to light. It's my job to sign the certificate, and investigate the death if suspicious, but I can only do that if there's evidence of foul play."

"Geez!" Vince looked around the table. "Poor guy!"

The doctor was quick to reassure everyone. "I don't think Otto suffered. He probably just passed out."

At that moment Mrs. Lewis joined them, standing against the wall by the kitchen door. She asked no questions, everyone assuming she had been listening from the kitchen. It was their opinion that she was usually listening the other side of most doors.

Vince was not appeased by the doctor's reassurances, but he decided to move on. "What about Victor?"

"Ah. That's different." Doc poured himself more coffee before answering. "He definitely died from hanging. There was a clear ligature furrow on his neck from the rope, and the signature inverted 'V' configuration, with the apex at the point of suspension."

"So what you're saying is that he wasn't killed some other way and then put up there?"

"Well..."

J.B. leaned forward. "Spit it out, Doc!"

"There was some slight redness that was probably on its way to becoming bruising. It was on one side of his head above the temple. But even if he was hit, it wasn't hard enough to kill him."

Frank leaned back in his chair to better see everyone seated around the table before asking, "Would it have been enough to stun him for a few minutes?"

"Possibly. I can't say for sure." Doc had seen his share of bruising from fights, falls from a height, being thrown by a horse, and simple clumsy tripping. But he was puzzled by the damaged skin he had seen on Victor's head.

Everyone reacted to the doctor's vague response in their own way. Frank and Vince looked at one another and sat back with arms folded cross their chests as they looked toward J.B. sitting silent at the head of the table. Jim and Roger boldly looked around at everyone else, hesitating at Mrs. Lewis who was still standing by the kitchen door.

Jim asked her, "Why isn't Sara here with us?"

She looked back at them with pursed lips, but managed to explain. "She broke out in itchy red spots on her arms and neck yesterday. She'd been out in the garden weeding. I put some calamine lotion on them last night. She's probably too embarrassed to come down. I'll go check."

J.B. and Sing, if you had asked them, would have said that Mrs. Lewis was incapable of typical female reactions, but she proved them wrong. From Sara's room came a muffled scream. The sheriff and the doctor reached Sara's bedroom at the same time, pushing through the door. Sara lay across the bed, a short-sleeved nightdress bunched around her legs. One arm, outstretched and wrapped around a chamber pot, was splotched with a pink lotion. The other arm, also dotted with pink lotion, was pressed against her chest. Next to her on the bed was a large box of chocolates with only a few remaining.

The sheriff led Mrs. Lewis to the landing outside the door before closing it in her face and returning to stand beside Dr. Sinclair next to the bed. J.B. hurried upstairs to his housekeeper, leading her down into the great room. Placing her on the sofa in front of the small fireplace, he wrapped her shoulders with the small blanket kept over the back of it. When Sing brought her something in a cup, J.B. raced up the stairs. He opened the bedroom door and stepped inside, braced for what he would see.

The doctor and the sheriff were looking at the scene before them, and ignored J.B.'s presence. Sheriff Cody, his face showing deep emotion, clenched his jaw. "What the hell is going on around here? How did she die?"

Doc Sinclair shook his head. "I don't know. But I want to take that box of chocolates with me. She was obviously sick before she died. And her face is slightly swollen. Looks like poisoning to me."

The sheriff looked closer at the outstretched arm. "I wonder what she was handling to get a spotty, red rash like that."

"Could be any number of things." The doctor spoke from years of vast experience, but it didn't help him with a quick answer now.

The sheriff looked at the chamber pot on the bed and quickly looked away. "We'd better lock the door of the room and send someone into town for the undertaker. Again."

The doctor was deep in thought. "I can see her death being somewhat similar to Otto's, although he wasn't sick. But how can either of their deaths have anything to do with Victor hanging himself?"

"If he did."

"Well, yes, I've thought the same thing." Doc stroked his small mustache. "That mark on the side of his head. But how possible is it that someone could lift a stunned man up onto a chair and get his head into a noose? He'd have to be incredibly strong, wouldn't he?"

The sheriff stared at his friend. "Is that the way you see it happening?"

"How else?"

J.B. started to say something, but held himself in check. After a moment, the sheriff answered. "Put the rope around the neck of someone unconscious in the chair, and pull down on the rope's slack already over the beam. And then just hoist. They'd only have to be strong enough for that. Then tie off the rope, and cut off the excess length so it would look like it did when we found him."

"Good lord!" He looked at his friend, respecting his imagination. "But, Mike, the body had the signs of a typical drop hanging."

"Would the same signs show if he was hoisted up like I described?"

The doc thought a minute. "I don't know. I guess it could look the same. I've just never seen such a thing to compare it to."

J.B. spoke up. "Wouldn't the beam show the rub of the rope being pulled over the wood?"

Mike turned to him. "I thought of that, but he was strung up from one of several places where something heavy had been hanging at one time."

J.B. pressed the point. "So the wood was too messed up to tell?"

The sheriff nodded and glanced over at the bed. "About Sara. I wonder if she saw or heard something she wasn't supposed to."

"Maybe." Doc's knowledge of people caused him to speak his mind. "If so, did she try to profit from that knowledge in some way?"

"I hate to say this about someone I saw only a few times around town, but I think she was the type." The sheriff frowned and looked out the window, past the dainty arrangement of purple flowers on the little table. They had been there when they'd found Otto, too, and it saddened him to think that the young girl had thought them so pretty that she had left them for herself to enjoy.

The meadows looked especially green because of clouds passing over the area, with just a hint of sunshine bouncing off the wet grass. The sheriff thought again of the young girl, lying dead only a few feet away, who might have enjoyed being out on such a day. Or even seeing it through her window like he was doing. In fact, his daughter Ella was probably doing just that while writing a thank you note for a party recently attended.

Before he could fall further into sentimental reflection, he remembered that he was the sheriff now, and had an important job to do.

"This can't be a coincidence," he said aloud. "Three people dead, I mean." He turned to the doctor, who was watching him closely. "If I find that someone caused their deaths, I'll happily see them behind bars."

"But Otto did have health issues," the doctor reminded him. "And everyone who might have killed him seems to have been together at the time he died."

J.B. cleared his throat. "Well, that's not exactly true. Vic and Otto met up on the back porch for a few minutes during our eleven o'clock break from the game."

Sheriff Cody took a moment to consider that. "But were you all together around the time Victor died?"

J.B. shook his head. "I don't remember."

Doc tried to inject reason into the conversation. "Vic may have been more despondent than anyone knew about. My wife told me that his wife and the girls have left him. And aren't coming back."

"I'll need to find Vic's wife somehow." Sheriff Cody sighed, not looking forward to dealing with an hysterical widow.

"Oh, my wife knows the address. You can send a telegram."

"Thank you!" Grateful for one thing that could be crossed off his list, the sheriff was still focused on the recent deaths. "The others might have died by disease or suicide, but you can't say Sara died either of those ways. And I have to face the fact that there were five men in the house who weren't always within sight of each other."

The doctor looked uneasy. "Mike, J.B.'s your friend."

Michael Cody, a look of doom on his face, dragged his eyes from the dead girl on the bed and back to the doctor before looking at J.B. "Not that I think you'd be capable of murder, but on the other hand no one who could do this is my friend."

J.B. looked back without flinching. "I completely understand, Mike. I feel the same way." He turned to the doctor. "But how did she die?"

"Well, I'm not sure how she died, but it sure as hell wasn't natural causes."

After the doctor got a jar and a bag from Sing, he took a sample from the chamber pot and closed the lid on the candy. Putting both items into the bag, he joined the sheriff on the landing and locked the door of the room. When they descended the stairs, they found everyone seated in the great room silently waiting. He handed the room key to Sing, who put it in his pocket while avoiding Mrs. Lewis's outrage.

Since the doctor had his own horse, he declared that he was going back into town and would notify the undertaker. "He'll have to close his store again, and he'll grumble." Before stepping through the front door, Doc turned back to J.B. "I hope you realize that with these three deaths, there's going to be a lot of flapping jaws in town."

"Oh, yes." J.B. ran a hand over his face. "We've experienced that already. Otto's funeral was tense. I expect no better at Vic's funeral tomorrow. Especially if word has gotten around about Sara."

The doctor got the message. "I won't say anything. But once the undertaker has the body, all bets are off."

As soon as the door shut behind the doctor, Sheriff Cody sank heavily into the chair that had once been occupied by Sara. He looked at the coffee table between the sofas, now cluttered with cups and pots of coffee. He was surprised that Sing would allow such a mess, but noises from the kitchen told him that the houseman was dealing with his shock in his own way.

Waiting for the sheriff to speak, everyone's eyes were riveted on him. Turning toward Mrs. Lewis, who had moved to sit next to J.B., the sheriff told her. "I'm sorry. I think she was poisoned. Doc thinks so too, but he won't say for sure yet. Something in the chocolates, possibly. Do you know where she got them?"

Mrs. Lewis pulled a handkerchief from her skirt pocket and pressed it against her mouth. J.B. surprised everyone by putting a consoling hand on her arm. Pulling herself together with an effort, she announced, "I bought them in town on Friday. Vic had seen them in the store, and when I told him that Sara's birthday was on Monday, he gave me the money to buy them for her."

"When did you give them to her?"

"Sunday night. We both ate one. It was a box of different kinds. Nothing happened to either of us, so they couldn't have been poisoned."

"What did she do with the box after that?"

"I told her she should wait to eat them when it was actually her birthday, and she agreed. I retied the ribbon that had been around the box, and then put it on the table by the window. It was a fancy blue ribbon. She said it matched the flowers." She once again pressed the hanky to her mouth before taking a deep breath.

"So, the box was out in the open, in her room, all day yesterday?"

"Yes. I saw it still there in the morning, with the bow I'd tied untouched. I remember thinking that she hadn't opened it yet, and I was surprised. She didn't usually have that much restraint."

Frank leaned forward, his voice angry and his face red as he confronted the sheriff. "You're insinuating that someone here snuck into her room and poisoned the candy. We were all gone part of the day at Otto's funeral. Vince and I are new to this area, and didn't know her. Same for Jim and Roger. And J.B. had no reason to want a kid like her dead." He turned to his host. "Did you even know her?"

"Not before she came to work here."

Vince spoke up. "Victor might have known her. He didn't specifically say. But by the way he flirted with her, it was obvious he was trying to make time with the girl. Probably why he bought her the candy."

The sheriff looked around the room. "No one has wondered how she might have been poisoned if it wasn't the chocolates."

Roger frowned at him. "That doesn't mean we're not thinking it. We're still trying to accept that she's dead, much less murdered. Or how."

Roger and the sheriff locked eyes, and it was then that Sheriff Cody realized that this young man was deeply shaken by the girl's death. Roger certainly hadn't been so moved by the death of the two men. Then again, this was the sudden death of a young, vibrant and pretty girl, and they were all obviously shaken.

J.B. sat back in his chair and rubbed his eyes, as though trying to remove the picture of what he had seen upstairs. "Can Doc figure out what poison could have killed her?"

"I don't know. He took the candy with him, and we'll see if he can find out."

Mrs. Lewis made a sound of disgusted impatience deep in her throat. "But I ate one of them on Sunday! So did Sara. And we both chose at random. I can picture them in the box, and none of them looked tampered with in the slightest."

The sheriff looked around the room at every person there. "I can't explain it. But I sure would like to know what the hell is going on here. You guys gather for a weekend of poker, and people start dropping dead."

J.B. couldn't hide his irritation. "Yes, but only the girl seems to have been murdered. Otto had some kind of heart or liver condition, and Victor decided to kill himself. Although, God knows what triggered him to do it here and when he did."

"Not wanting to be too blunt about it," Jim said, "but might Victor have somehow poisoned the candy after it was given to the girl, and then regretted it? Along with whatever other sins he might have committed?"

Pointing out the obvious, the sheriff said, "That's possible only if he knew the girl before this weekend and something had happened between them."

Mrs. Lewis raised her voice, her anguish naked and raw. "Sara! Her name is Sara! Not 'the girl'. Sara!"

Everyone mumbled their apologies. They were unable to explain that sometimes in horrendous circumstances, it was easier to disassociate from the humanity of the victim in order to focus on the search for answers.

Roger got them back on track by asking, "How old was Sara?"

Mrs. Lewis took a deep breath. "This was her eighteenth birthday."

J.B. turned to her, his face a display of incredulity. "I thought she was twenty-one. That's what you both said."

"I know." She looked down at her lap where she was twisting the hanky into a knot. "We lied so she could get the job here. I wanted her to be with me."

J.B. tried hard not to sound accusatory. "Why?"

Instead of looking at J.B., she addressed herself to the sheriff. "Because she was my sister."

Roger barely kept himself from interjecting, "Ah, ha!" He was thinking of the conversation he had overheard between the two women, finally understanding why Mrs. Lewis had tolerated impudent behavior on Sara's part.

Sing came in from the kitchen, breaking the spell of surprise and J.B.'s awkward search for an appropriate response. "Dinner served in one hour. Mr. Cody, will you be joining us?"

Ignoring that Sing referred to him as *Mr.* instead of *Sheriff*, he stood up. "No. I think right now I'm like the grim reaper casting a shadow."

"Oh, Mike, that's just bull!" J.B. came forward to stand next to his friend. "You're just doing your job. We know that. You're welcome to stay."

"Well, thank you, J.B. But I need to get back into town. Catie will be expecting me, and I want to check with Doc on some things. I also have to write up a report."

Soon after the sheriff had left, the undertaker arrived with his assistant. While Mrs. Lewis went to her room and everyone else found an excuse to be in the kitchen, Sing unlocked the room for them. He then joined the others in the kitchen while Sara's body was wrapped in a canvas shroud before being carried out to a spring wagon.

While the men picked at the sandwiches set before them on the kitchen table, Mrs. Lewis and Sing cleaned the bedroom. They stripped the bed, bundled the sheets into a ball, and mopped the floor. While Sing removed the chamber pot to the privy out back, Mrs. Lewis opened wide the bedroom window so the room could air out. After picking up the sheets in order to carry them out to the wash house, she closed the door with a finality that was heard all the way downstairs.

The quality of the food, and Sing's cheerful chatter, allowed the meal to end more pleasantly than it had begun. They also agreed that the diversion of a few hours with the cards would be welcome, but with penny ante stakes. That way, the game would be without the pressure of their high-stakes play. Their conversation, although intermittent, covered a number of somewhat banal but absorbing topics.

Roger asked J.B, "How cold does it get here in winter?"

"Damn cold. The clerk at the courthouse has to put his bottle of ink in the safe at night or it freezes by the next morning."

"How long has Cody been sheriff?" Jim asked.

"Just elected. Mike came here from Bodie."

Jim and Roger exchanged glances, as they often did when Bodie was mentioned. J.B. saw it this time. "You two lived there at the same time, didn't you?"

Jim answered quickly, before his son could give out more details than he wanted him to do. "Yeah, back in '79."

Frank, sensing Jim's unease with that topic, quickly redirected the conversation. "How long have you had a telegram office here?"

"Since '81. We can thank Amasa Bryant for that. Just one more of his generous contributions to the town."

"The courthouse land was his, too, wasn't it?"

"Yeah. And he brought the building used for Bryant Hall here from Bodie and fixed it up. We hold everything from meetings to dances there."

Jim skipped to another topic. "I heard about the big fire up canyon in Lundy last August. How has the town rebounded?"

"It hasn't much." J.B. didn't look happy about that. "Most of the buildings were lost and few have been rebuilt. A lot of people have left for other towns."

Vince threw his hand in and sat back. "One thing that has prospered is Tom Rickey's setup."

J.B. grunted. "Yeah, Rickey. The *Cattle King of the West* some people call him. He's been buying up all the land he can get, over 47,000 acres they say."

"I hear he's calling it The Rickey Land and Cattle Company," Roger said, "with the headquarters in Topaz. We passed by there on our way here. Lots of buildings."

J.B. nodded. "Got a post office, stores, a hotel, a few homes for his workers, and of course, lots of barns and sheds. Yeah, quite a spread. Lots of men working for him."

After the game, in which everyone won at least one hand, showing how evenly matched they were, they went in different directions. There wasn't much to do until supper that evening, the aroma of it cooking causing a great deal of eager anticipation, even while still full from their mid-day meal.

Frank and Vince went for a walk out to the corrals, Roger found a book he liked on a hall shelf and spread out on a sofa, and Jim decided to relax in a rocking chair on the front porch. Mrs. Lewis kept to her room after meeting with Sing about the supper menu. And J.B. declared he had paperwork to do in his office.

Jim was just about to doze off when he was awakened by the crunch of wheels on the long drive up to the house. He walked to the edge of the porch to see who it might be, everyone connected to the day's activities being accounted for in his mind. For a moment, he thought that he might possibly still be asleep, and having a most peculiar dream.

There was a single woman inside the black buggy, her gloved hands keeping a tight grip on the long ribbons of rein as she pulled up at the foot of the steps. Deep in the shadow of the buggy's canopy, Jim could just make out a small bonnet adorning upswept curls, and a short cape covering the shoulders of a dark blue dress. Then she leaned forward and her hair caught the sparkle of the late afternoon sun. And Jim caught his breath. It was his Lucy.

# CHAPTER 6

## QUEEN HIGH STRAIGHT

Jim barely managed to tie the buggy's horse to the rail before helping his wife down and sweeping her into his arms. It took a great degree of will-power for him to wait that long. He then pressed his lips to hers with a passion that made the usually stone-faced Mort smile as he arrived to see if he was needed. But then, Mort liked Jim, who came often to the barn to check on his and Roger's horses, bringing with him apple or carrot pieces.

"Would you like me to stable the horse, sir?"

Jim turned to Lucy. "How long are you staying?"

"I'll be returning to town before dark."

Mort nodded. "I'll have your rig back to you in time for that. I just want to give the horse a rubdown and some water." He didn't wait for approval before climbing up onto the seat and bringing the buggie around to the barn.

Unsure if the man could hear her or not, Lucy called after him, "Thank you!" She then turned to her husband. "Who was that?"

"That, my dear, was Mort. No man loves horses as much as he does."

"No wonder the man at the stable looked pleased when I told him where I was going."

"Come sit on the porch with me. You can meet everyone later." Once seated together in the wicker loveseat just big enough for two people, he put his arm around her shoulders and pulled her close. "Not to sound unwelcoming, but why are you here?"

"When we received your telegram Sunday, I knew immediately that it would be more than a couple of days before you'd be able to leave here. We threw some things together and caught the last train out to Carson City.

Yesterday, we took a stage to Wellington, arriving just at dark. Because the moon was bright, we went on to Sweetwater Station, where we spent the night. Then early this morning we came directly here down the East Walker River & Munckton Toll Road. I guess the stage was unusually direct, because our only other passengers were two men in suits wanting to reach the courthouse as soon as possible."

Jim put a hand on her arm to stop her flow of words. The trip for her may have been an adventure, but his curiosity was in another direction. "You keep saying *we*. Who's with you? And where are your things?"

"My things are at the Leavitt House in a very nice little room upstairs. And in another room is Emily Eastman. She and Charlotte Perry left Lone Pine right after Frank and Vince, but they took the train from Keeler to Mound House, Nevada, then on to Virginia City by stage. It was a surprise for Amanda. We were having a wonderful time together until we received your telegram. Emily, like me, had the impression that strange things were happening here."

"You're right about that!"

"Charlotte is staying at our house with Amanda and our granddaughter." Lucy held back a laugh. "Not that Charlotte didn't want to come, but Amanda talked her into staying."

"Good thing our house isn't a boarding house anymore." Jim then remembered comments by Frank and Vince. "Emily and Charlotte both have young children, right?"

"Yes, but a good friend, Mrs. Carrington, is staying with them at Emily's house in Lone Pine. Having heard that lady's story, I'm sure she'll have no problem coping. And a friend of Lucy's is helping, too. Dolly Robbins, I think her name is."

With his thoughts focused elsewhere, he didn't inquire further. "Is your bed at the Leavitt House big enough for two?"

"Yes, dear. You don't think I wouldn't have thought of that, do you?" And together they laughed, not unlike two teenagers anticipating a few stolen moments in a hayloft.

"The Allen House would have been cheaper," Jim told her.

"Have you won any money this weekend?"

"Well, yes."

"I figured as much. So don't complain."

Grinning at her confidence, he stood up. "I think we should go in so you can meet everyone and get caught up on what's been happening."

"Do you know the cause of death?"

"Whose death?"

She stopped before he could open the door, staring at him in surprise. "There's been more than one death?"

He held up three fingers, enjoying her look of startled surprise. It wasn't often that he got one up on his wife.

"What in the world is going on here?"

"That, my love, is a question that's been uttered several times over the last few days." He held the door open for her. "Come in and meet the current cast of characters. And I do mean characters."

Roger's jaw literally dropped when he saw his mother standing just inside the front door. But his astonishment didn't stop him from rushing to wrap his arms around her. After kissing her on the cheek, he led her by the hand to the chair at the near end of the sofa arrangement before seating himself on the end of the sofa next to her.

"Have you come to rescue us? Or to tell the sheriff he's blind and the doctor a fool?"

"Oh, Roger!" She laughed at her son, happy to see he was his usual teasing self. Still, Jim thought Roger was probably not far off the mark.

"Where's Vince?" Lucy looked around the big room with curiosity, but also a growing admiration of the house in which she sat. It passed through her mind to wonder why she had not thought of it as a *home*, but she quickly forced herself to focus. But then her eyes came to rest on the fireplace and the large Double R brand. Her only reaction was a slight smirk and a murmured, "Oh, I see."

Roger chuckled, knowing his mother's acute ability to quickly size up people and situations. But he said nothing. He wanted her to meet J.B. without any prejudicial input.

Lucy turned back to her son. "I have a note for Vince from Charlotte."

"I think he's out back with Frank."

At that moment, however, the back door opened and the two men walked into the room. Frank greeted Lucy with a big smile. "I thought the woman being described by Mort might be you." He glanced around the room, trying to look only mildly interested, but doing a bad job of it. "Emily not with you?"

"No. But she's here in town. Just resting in the room she's taken at the Leavitt House for the two of you." Turning to Vince, she told him, "I'm sorry to say that Charlotte stayed in Virginia City with Amanda."

"Oh, that's okay." His hat in his hands, he twirled it in a show of nonchalance as he walked to the rack by the front door. It may have released a little dust, but it didn't release him of his disappointment, even while trying to put a good face on it. "They're great friends and it's a chance for Charlotte to do a lot of shopping."

These were men who were not ashamed to admit that they were happily married. No one ever heard them make "wife jokes" or disparaging remarks about marriage. More than one man they knew had wondered if these wives were exceptional women; or if just possibly they had not been appreciating the good woman to whom they were married.

Charlotte's kind and gentle nature had garnered for her many friends over the years, and she was admired by everyone who knew her. Possibly because she was willing to keep her opinions to herself. Emily was closer to Lucy in temperament, both of them a little more outspoken than most women of their generation. Still, both Emily and Lucy were usually tolerated when speaking up. They were, after all, credited with having caring and generous natures, especially as they so often contributed freely to community projects.

Sing hurried out of the kitchen and Roger rose to introduce his mother. She beamed upon Sing her most gracious smile. "So, you're the wonderful cook about whom my husband raved in his telegram to me. All he said was 'great food', but that was enough."

The houseman gave her a little bow. "Happy to please. May I get you refreshment? Supper in two hours."

"I would enjoy a glass of cold water."

He gave her a conspiratorial wink. "And maybe a pot of tea?"

"Oh, Sing, you are indeed a wonderful man." And together they laughed, the other men clearly not understanding. But Sing had over time served many a woman of Lucy's generation, and he knew how fond they were of tea.

That wonderful man, as Lucy often referred to him in the future, simply hurried from the room. And Roger once again wondered at how easily his mother ingratiated herself with people, no matter how dissimilar they might be. It was a talent many people recognized as also present in Roger, but because he always compared himself to Lucy, he failed to see it in himself.

Lucy turned to her son. "Where's Mr. Roberts? I'm eager to meet him."

"I'm not sure, but he'll show up in his own good time."

She leaned back in her chair. "Okay, now tell me what's been happening. Start with what's known about Otto's death."

Even with all four men pitching in, it still took half an hour to give her not only the pertinent facts about all three deaths, but also their individual observations. And, of course, their opinions, although those were still pretty vague. The tea pot was refilled twice, a coffee pot added to the tray, and a plate of cookies emptied. And the men were all wondering when J.B. would appear.

Finally, as they concluded their discussion, J.B. entered the room from upstairs. Roger immediately surmised that no one needed to tell him about the conversation just ended.

"Well, and who do we have here?" Jim and Lucy stood up and faced him, Jim feeling a tingle of challenge and wondering at it. Lucy, however, cast her most charming smile upon her host.

Before Jim could speak, J.B. stepped closer to Lucy and smiled. "Let me guess. You're the incomparable Lucy Murphy. Every time Jim speaks of you, his eyes light up. Now I know why."

"I am indeed Lucy Murphy." Lucy generously offered her hand to him, as it was not considered polite for a man to offer his hand to a lady first. For Lucy to do so, it was a sign of acceptance, if not trust. For a younger woman, it might also have suggested attraction.

J.B. smiled as he took her offered hand, turned it backside up, and for a moment considered kissing it. But the narrowing of Jim's eyes, and the slight widening of Lucy's, kept him from it. However, he did hold it slightly longer than was socially acceptable, looking into her eyes as he did so. If the term *cougar* had been coined at that time, it would have defined the atmosphere.

"Welcome to the Double R, Mrs. Murphy."

Lucy was quick to respond. "Aren't you a kind young man!" Her mention of his youth along with her light laughter, prompted everyone else to smile. She took out any sting remaining by adding, "And, please, call me Lucy." It didn't need to be said that she would call him J.B., since everyone did.

Sing entered with a fresh pot of tea and more cookies, placing them on the tray between the facing sofas. He turned to his employer. "Whiskey?"

"I'll get it." J.B. walked to the liquor cabinet against the wall under the upstairs corridor, and opened its doors to reveal a well-stocked interior. He poured himself half a glass of his favorite brand, closed the doors to the cabinet, and moved to his chair by the fireplace.

Sitting on the sofa across from his wife, Jim announced loudly to no one in particular, "Frank and I are returning to town with Lucy in her rig. We'll take her and Emily to supper tonight."

Frank leaned forward. "When are we leaving?"

Understanding Frank's eagerness to be reunited with his wife, Jim told him, "As soon as Lucy has refreshed herself and Mort has brought the rig around to the front." Sing took that as a hint, and immediately left for the barn.

That night at supper, with two of their number having left, J.B., Vince and Roger decided to eat at the kitchen table in a more informal style. Fewer steps filling Sing's busy day was certainly welcomed by him.

At the end of their meal, Alex bounded noisily through the back door, slinging his jacket in the general direction of the coat rack. Sing went out to hang it up as Roger stood up, welcoming the cherished progeny with enthusiasm. Alex grinned at Roger, but it was on his father that his eyes came to rest. J.B. said nothing, but he looked happier and more relaxed than he had all day. Alex pulled out a chair, and even though he had eaten before leaving the Hunewill home, he smiled up at Sing as a piece of apple pie was placed before him.

Swallowing a mouthful, he said, "I heard about Victor and Sara." At the sudden stillness of the men, Alex told them, "Everyone in town is talking about it. Probably at the sawmills and most of the ranches, too. Everyone I run into asks me about *all the deaths at the Double R*." That he piped the last words in a high voice indicated that most of the questions were from women. "I just say I don't know because I wasn't here. It's also gotten around that you paid for Otto's funeral. Most people seem to think that was decent of you."

Roger thought there was more Alex wanted to say. "And what do the rest think?"

Alex shifted his weight uncomfortably, wiping his mouth with his napkin and asking for a glass of water. "Some think it was prompted by guilt." He reached for a walnut from the wooden bowl always on the table and cracked it open with the metal nut cracker. He looked down at the pieces in his hand before looking up at his father. "When you all go into town, be prepared for funny looks and whispers."

Since they already had experienced that, no one was unduly disturbed. J.B. did, however, have a question for his son. "How did they find out that I paid for the funeral?"

Alex slewed his eyes to the hallway door and lowered his voice. "Mrs. Lewis told the Hunewill maid. She was just trying to show how kind a man you are."

J.B. said nothing. He didn't have to, as his deep sigh eloquently expressed his exasperation. He would, of course, say nothing to Mrs. Lewis, giving her benefit of the doubt that she had been trying to be helpful.

Roger looked carefully at the boy, realizing that in some ways he was close to becoming a man. He might have been almost thirteen, but he had the manner of someone older. Just like his father. No one thought of J.B. as only in his mid-thirties, although it was the average age for those who had demonstrated solid success. But with J.B., there was always the sense that you were not quite his equal. Although equal in what way, people found it difficult to pin down. Roger thought that Alex was going to be much the same as an adult; kind and generous, but always just a little aloof, and therefore considered by those in town as "not quite one of us".

When the Eastmans and Murphys entered the Leavitt House dining room that night, it was to discover Sheriff Cody and his wife Catherine just finishing their meal. After introductions had been made to Lucy and Emily, the sheriff turned to Frank and Jim. "I'm coming out to the ranch in the morning around nine o'clock. Will you be there?"

Frank answered for them both. "Certainly, if that's what you want."

"I think you'll find it interesting. I have a report to make to you all." With that, he tipped his hat and ushered his wife Catherine, known as Catie, out into the still evening.

As soon as they were all seated, Emily picked up her water glass and took a sip. She carefully placed it back on the table and looked at the others. "I hope he realizes that Lucy and I will be there, too!"

The two men looked at each other, each fighting a smile. Lucy looked at Emily and nodded her agreement. It had been a long time since Lucy had felt so completely at ease with another woman. Although twenty years older than Emily, Lucy recognized in her new friend the same eagerness for adventure and the same tendency toward unconventional ideas. Emily did not sit passively on the sideline of any issue, and more often than not expressed her opinion freely. Lucy could relate to that. She also knew very well people's reaction to such behavior, which was divided between admiration and harsh judgement, if not outright condemnation.

Society was most comfortable with the image of women as the saint-like keeper of the home, and men its brave protector and provider. It was an unrealistic, almost mythical ideal, and especially ignored the reality of rural life. Women plowed fields, churned butter, and cooked all the meals. At the same time, they tried to keep the house clean as well as the clothes on their family. In their spare time, they carded and spun wool into yarn, milked the cow and the goat, and slaughtered a chicken for supper. Occasionally, they fit in the bearing of a child, or nursing the family through an illness. But no matter what she did, or how capably she did it, it would not earn her the right to have a say in the running of her town, or God-forbid, her country. Jim and Frank knew all this because they had heard all this from their wives on more than one occasion.

Frank looked at Emily with open pride, and catching him out, she felt a surge of gratitude for the fact of him in her life. She knew how lovely he thought her, although she herself was only too aware of her flaws. She had once described herself in a letter to her dear friend, Carrie, as having '*a pleasant balance of my father's proud chin and my mother's slanting green eyes, but my dark brown hair is all my own.*' She had added, '*As your cousin once pointed out, my high cheekbones, fair complexion and regular brow line may be nice, but the whole is more ordinary than I might hope.*'

Emily was not quite as tall as Lucy, and her hair had as yet no gray in it, but she was old enough to have transitioned from *pretty girl* into *handsome woman*. Neither of them had need of a corset for more than the smoothing of their dresses, and on the rare occasion when they dared to wear make-up, it was subtly applied. The two women had discovered that when together they often attracted admiring looks cast in their direction. It was a pleasant realization, what with Emily just entering her middle years and Lucy being well into them.

With their dessert consumed, Emily glanced at Lucy, trying to find a tactful way to suggest they all retire to their rooms. Jim saved her the trouble.

"Well, we're done here," he declared. "I say we call it a night. I have the feeling we're going to want to be rested when we hear whatever news Cody has for us."

With that, they climbed the steep stairs from the small vestibule up to the second floor, one behind the other with Lucy in the lead. Frank clutched the brass key in his hand and fought to control his eagerness to be alone with Emily. Jim didn't bother to hide his eagerness. In fact, he had to resist the urge to give his wife a friendly *goose* as she carefully ascended in front of him. But she was holding up her skirts with her right hand, her other on the railing for balance, and he didn't want to startle her. Or shock Emily, although he had a hunch she would have laughed.

The two couples arrived at the ranch at seven-thirty on Wednesday morning, to be greeted by a dining table set to accommodate comfortably all the people expected, along with Mrs. Lewis and the sheriff. Upon inquiry, Roger was told that Alex had already eaten and was helping out at the barn. The table was laid out with coffee and tea pots, a basket of biscuits next to a crock of butter and another of blackberry jam, a platter of corn and ham fritters, and a big bowl of spiced apple slices.

While waiting for Sheriff Cody to arrive, Mrs. Lewis remained out back in the kitchen garden. Roger and Vince finished a game of chess in the great room, and Jim went upstairs to pack those things he hadn't taken the night before. Frank took Emily, an enthusiastic horsewoman, out to the corrals to see the horses that had been stolen and returned. That left J.B. and Lucy, who made themselves comfortable on the front porch wicker rocking chairs.

Lucy noticed that J.B. looked as though he had not slept well the night before. "This must be a stressful time for you. I know it would be for me if three people had died in my house. Not to mention your normal routine disrupted by our extended stay."

"I'm actually enjoying having you all in my home. I very much like your husband and son. Frank and Vince are men I admire, and they have a way of never seeming to be in the way." A gust of wind blew a lock of his dark hair down over his forehead and he reached up to push it aside. He wished he had his hat, as it not only kept his hair in place but also gave him a sense of security by casting a shadow over his face. "But I can't figure out these deaths. It's not like they all died the same way." He barked out a bitter laugh. "Those in town will probably start saying the ranch is cursed."

"I wish I could argue against that, but I can't. I'm too familiar with people's readiness to think badly about others."

"The thing is," he continued, "Otto was obviously ill. Vic took his own life, which is odd given the type of person he was. But maybe I'm just not aware of all he was dealing with. Hopefully, his wife will give us some idea when she gets here from Sacramento." J.B. shook his head and looked out at his cattle in the meadow. As Lucy watched him, it was as though he derived comfort from seeing the bovines there as part of his domain. But if such reflection had worked in the past, it didn't seem to last long this time. "Then there's Sara." He looked closely at Lucy. "Mrs. Lewis keeps saying she must have choked on a candy, but I wonder. I know Mrs. Lewis is a stoic woman who rarely shows her true feelings, but this has really thrown her. I can tell, because she's appearing even more impassive than usual."

"How long has she been with you?"

"Since Alex was a baby. My wife wasn't a well woman after his birth. With her gone, Mrs. Lewis filled the void in the household. She was nursemaid to Alex, and housekeeper for our home." He looked at Lucy and boldly winked. "I think people wonder if there's something between the two of us, but that's never entered the picture. As she would say, she knows her place."

But the way he said it so casually, Lucy wasn't sure if that was a quote from Mrs. Lewis, or his own attitude. She couldn't deny that J.B. was a handsome man. Along with a good deal of money, he also had status in society. It was easy for Lucy to imagine that many a woman had cast him in the role of potential husband, even those a few years older such as Mrs. Lewis. She was, after all, not unattractive.

Lucy glanced toward the front door. "I'd offer to help in some way, but with the incomparable Sing and the highly efficient Mrs. Lewis, I can't imagine there's anything I could do."

J.B. smiled and rested his hand on the arm of her chair near her wrist. But as familiar a gesture as it might have been, Lucy didn't feel as though he was taking liberties. He rocked slightly in his chair as he said, "You're right, of course. Sing and Mrs. Lewis always have things well in hand. But the offer is kind, and I thank you for it."

Lucy rose up. "I see the sheriff coming down the road." And together they went inside to alert the others.

Sheriff Cody didn't hesitate to walk into the house after a quick knock. Possibly it was because it was beginning to feel to him more like a hotel than a home, but more likely it was due to the fact that he was a good friend. He and Catherine had spent several pleasant evenings at the Double R being fed and entertained. He only hoped that the conclusion of this investigation didn't change that.

Frank and Emily had seen the sheriff riding down the long entrance road and had returned to the house just in time to seat themselves at the table as he entered. Sing was just leaving the dining room after bringing in a pitcher of filtered water.

"Ah, Mike, welcome." J.B. walked toward his friend as Cody hung his coat on the rack by the door. After shaking hands, J.B. motioned toward the table. "We're all ready to sit down together, enjoy some breakfast, and hear what you have to say. I understand you met Lucy and Emily last night."

The sheriff nodded to the women and murmured, "Ladies, good morning."

Everyone gathered around the table, J.B. placing Lucy to his right, but allowing everyone else to choose their own place. Mrs. Lewis, who took the place to J.B.'s left, shoved Roger aside to do so. She glared across at Lucy with what could only be interpreted as sulky resentment. Seeing this, Roger held back a smile, thinking that after all, the mistress of the house should be seated on the master's right. Then Jim pulled out the chair next to his wife with a determination that did make Roger smile.

As the hungry gathering helped themselves to the breakfast items, Sheriff Cody observed them, thinking, "They sure don't look like people with a guilty conscience." What he said aloud was, "I won't keep you guessing. First, about Sara. She wasn't poisoned. There was nothing wrong with the candy. It was a typical arrangement of filled chocolates with nuts and such, and many just the chocolate common to them all that was infused with strong peppermint." He turned to Lucy and Emily. "The local candy maker is known for her mint." He smiled, as did J.B. and Mrs. Lewis, the candymaker's inclination toward peppermint being a bit of a local joke.

Emily asked, "How can you be sure grains of something hadn't been added?"

"We checked each piece carefully and couldn't see any signs of tampering." He chuckled in such a way that it alarmed them all. "Also, one of my deputies arrived for work and saw the box on my desk where Doc had returned it. He helped himself to the three chocolates left in the box while I was out of the room. I thought he'd been informed about them, but he'd been off duty the last few days."

There were a couple of gasps, but everyone was alert to what the sheriff had to say next. "Nothing happened to him."

J.B. stared at his friend. "Then how the hell did Sara die?" He was so upset that he didn't bother to excuse his language.

"Doc figures it could have been just an unfortunate accident. The way her face was somewhat swollen, he figures she might have choked on one of the candies, although there wasn't one in her throat. Or maybe she had some kind of bad reaction to one of the ingredients. It does sometimes happen. Especially berries and nuts."

Everyone looked at Mrs. Lewis, who was staring at the sheriff as though he had said something offensive. "That's ridiculous! She was a healthy girl, raised on a farm in Oregon. We ate just about everything that could be grown."

Frank spoke up. "And as far as nuts go, I saw her crack and eat some from the bowl on the kitchen table."

J.B. was showing signs of impatience. "So what? Who the hell can't eat nuts?"

Sheriff Cody spoke up. "The Doc says he's known of a case where peanuts made someone's face swell after eating them. But they didn't die."

"What exactly was in the rest of the candy?" J.B. demanded.

"Just the normal candy fillings. Jam made from last year's raspberries, blue berries, and black berries, with mint in the chocolate. I checked with the woman who made them."

Mrs. Lewis stood up, clutching the napkin from her lap. "So, in other words, nothing she ate could have killed her. She's eaten berries her whole life. And we had lots of spearmint and peppermint plants on the farm. Sara and I harvested and sold mint to neighbors for extra money. There's even some in the kitchen garden here." She threw her napkin onto her plate and turned to the sheriff. "So, no one knows how she died. Not you or the doctor. But she *is* dead! Incompetent fools!" She turned and left the room, the slamming of her bedroom door heard clearly.

J.B. started to get up, but Lucy put a hand on his arm. "She'll be okay. Her anger is just her way of coping with her grief. It's emotional survival."

J.B. sat back in his chair, his eyes wandering past Lucy as he muttered, "Yeah, survival."

It wasn't the great room or the corridor upstairs that held his gaze as he spoke. It was the large Double R iron medallion affixed to the rock fireplace. Lucy surmised that he was thinking about Alex. The boy was his much-loved child, but also the beneficiary and future caretaker of all J.B. had thus far been able to attain.

Frank, following through with the point Mrs. Lewis had made, took that moment to summarize the situation. "So, two natural deaths, Otto and Sara, even though we're not sure how they died. And one man who took his own life, although we don't know why he would do that."

"That about covers it." To say that Sheriff Cody didn't look happy would have been an understatement. "Although I do have some doubts about Victor's death."

Lucy focused on the sheriff. Not only was he taller than any of the other men present, but he was also very attractive. His blue eyes were deep set, his mouth below a trim mustache was full, and his chin strong. But it was the intelligence in his eyes as he studied them, individually and as a group, that held her attention. "Did you deduce something from the body?"

"No. It was more from what was around him."

The men having seen the bunk house, and having had some questions themselves, were interested to hear what the sheriff thought. However, Roger noticed that J.B. was the exception to that. He was looking down at his plate, his fork poking at a partially eaten fritter. Whatever he was thinking, the little frown between his eyes showed that the topic worried him.

"Here's what I found odd." The sheriff glanced around the table. The women stopped eating to give him their full attention, while the men continued, even helping themselves to more fritters. "First of all, the chair was too far from where the body had been hanging if he had stood on it and then kicked it away so he could drop. Not only that, but it would most likely have been on its side."

"That's what I thought!" Roger and Frank had both spoken at the same time.

The sheriff merely smiled at them before continuing. "If he'd been hoisted up, one would think the beam would show the rub of the rope. But unfortunately, it was pretty worn from other items having in the past hung there. Observing the table next to his bed, it looked like he'd been preparing to enjoy a glass of whiskey and a smoke of his pipe, then changed his mind. Or was interrupted by someone."

"But," Jim interjected, "it was also something he might have done as a last act before taking his life."

"Yeah," Roger chimed in, "but he hadn't lit the pipe."

The sheriff nodded in agreement. "That's right. Why fill it if you're not going to immediately smoke it? Also, his bed looked like there had been a struggle on it, like someone trying to subdue him. About his drink, he hadn't taken a sip of it. But there's something about the glass you don't know. No one had touched it."

"What?" That was a collective question from several of them.

"That's right. I held it up to the light and there were no traces of anyone having held or even touched it."

Roger was trying to picture the scene. "Could it have been a clean glass on the table that he poured straight into?"

"He would have had to handle the glass to put it on the table."

"Oh, right."

Emily found herself enjoying this conversation, delighted at being included in a reasoned discussion among men. Too often she was shunted aside when men gathered, as were most women. But she felt these men would not do that, so she was emboldened to comment. "So that means Victor had handled it, but someone wiped off the glass for some reason. They must not have noticed the freshly packed pipe."

"That's right," Lucy chimed in. "Otherwise, why would they leave anything that would cause doubt that Victor committed suicide?"

"They could have taken the pipe away," Roger suggested.

"No," Frank countered, "because we all knew he had a pipe. It would have looked suspicious if it was missing."

Emily nodded. "And there wouldn't have been time to light it. So, the killer would have had to just leave it where it was. Again, if he even noticed it, or thought it significant."

Lucy added what she felt the others must be thinking. "Of course, that's working with the idea that he was murdered by someone who wanted it to look like suicide."

Sheriff Cody looked at the two women, reminded of his very capable wife, and thought, "Men who consider women inferior are either ignorant or single." Aloud, he asked, "But why bother to wipe the glass clean? The whole idea of impressions on glass left by hands that can be traced to an individual is a very new idea. Not many people even know about it." He was met by several blank stares to confirm that. "I read an article about it in a magazine, or I wouldn't know either. And Mark Twain made it part of a court trial in his book *The Tragedy of Pudd'n Head Wilson*. That got me interested in the idea." He had everyone's attention, so he expanded on the concept. "A man called Sir Francis Galton, a British scientist and a cousin of Charles Darwin, has made a study of fingerprints and has even made up a way to use them as a means of identification."

Hoping they wouldn't ask for more details, which he didn't have, he quickly added, "All that might be helpful someday, but for us now, all I know is that it's very suspicious to have a glass of freshly poured whiskey that doesn't show being handled."

Lucy shrugged. "Maybe the killer read that book, too. Just because he's depraved doesn't mean he's illiterate." Lucy sat back in her chair. "Have you been able to contact his wife?"

"Yes. She should be here late today." He took out a small timepiece from the watch pocket of his vest and glanced at it before putting it back. "In fact, I should be getting on."

"Wait a minute," J.B. stopped him. "What about Otto's death?"

"Nothing more to report. He was ill and he died. And you buried him." The sheriff stood up, thanked J.B. for the nice breakfast, and left. No ceremony about it, and no promises of more to come on the various deaths.

Everyone scattered in different directions, finding something to fill their time until they would be leaving for Victor's funeral in the afternoon. Frank and Emily decided to ride horses out along the road through the meadows and up toward the twin lakes, the mountains around them still showing snow in the canyons. Roger and Vince returned to the chess board, but then decided to play cribbage instead. Jim was too restless for games, so he went out to the barn to visit with Hank. Alex had left for town with a school friend.

Before approaching the barn where he saw Hank at the door, Jim stopped by the privy out back of it. By the time he got to the barn, he could hear voices inside. Realizing J.B. was with Hank, he hung back. He didn't do it with eavesdropping in mind, but that's how it turned out. There was a long pause in the voices and Jim was about to step forward when Hank spoke.

"Um, J.B., I was wondering about something."

"About what?"

"Do you think that Vic knew about our pasts?"

A short pause and then J.B. spoke, so low that Jim had to strain to hear. "I don't think so. Why?"

"Well... Oh, nothing."

"Hank, I didn't kill Victor." It was said with such nonchalance that Jim actually believed him.

"Oh, no, I didn't think..."

"You might well have wondered, considering what he did. And I did think about it. But I would have shot him, or cut his throat."

"Yeah. That's what I figured."

"Hank, are you the same now as you were seventeen years ago?"

"No. Not even close."

"Neither am I. It was realizing that fact that stopped me from seeking revenge." Jim heard a soft chuckle. "At least lethal revenge."

Thinking their conversation might be close to ending, Jim ducked back around the corner of the barn. He was just in time, as J.B. came out and headed for the house. Waiting for him to be well out of sight, Jim took a minute to do some basic math. Seventeen years prior would have been 1871, a year that evidently had great significance for both J.B. and Hank. Maybe he would visit the newspaper office in town when he had the chance.

Jim strolled into the barn, but seeing Hank leaving through the small back door, walked directly to the stalls where his borrowed horses were being kept. They certainly didn't need grooming, so he gave them the carrot pieces in his pocket before also going out the back door. A good, long walk was what he wanted right then.

Lucy was also walking, but it was through the kitchen garden while admiring Sing's crops of cabbage, squash, melon, and herbs. She was so deep in thought that when J.B. approached, she jumped.

By way of greeting, she told him, "I wish I could have a small vegetable garden like this."

He stopped beside her, smiling. "Yes, it is nice, isn't it? I never cease being grateful for Sing. You have no idea how often others try to lure him away to work for them. But he just laughs them off."

"You must pay him well."

It had been a casual comment, but J.B. reacted to it as though it had been an implied criticism. "He also understands loyalty to those who are loyal to his needs."

Surprised at the defensiveness in his tone, Lucy was quick to respond. "Of course. It's obvious how much he respects and admires you."

He looked at the ground as he kicked at one of the stones edging the path. "I'm sorry I snapped at you. It's been a trying week, and I haven't been sleeping well. I could use some coffee. How about you?"

"That sounds lovely."

Stopping in the kitchen, they filled large mugs from the pot on the stove, after which J.B. led them to the front porch. He settled back in one of the wicker rocking chairs and took a big swallow from his mug. Lucy sat in the other rocker and sipped her coffee. Several minutes were spent just enjoying the cool breeze and their view of the green meadows around the Double R. A covey of quail ran through the yard in front of them, the youngest just past the gray puff-ball stage and struggling to keep up with the adults.

Sharing a moment of laughter worked to lighten the mood between them, but their laughter ceased when they heard the sound of a shot gun in the distance. "Don't be alarmed," he reassured her. "It's probably just someone shooting a coyote."

"Why?"

"Other than the fact that they're not wanted near calves, the County pays a few dollars a head, literally. After tallying the kill to an account, they pile the heads in the dirt lot near the courthouse and burn them. That way, they don't attract wildlife into town."

Aware that sometimes her sensitive nature and love of animals clashed with her knowledge of country ways, she changed the subject rather than comment. "Tell me about Victor."

He looked down at his cup, set it on the table between them, and began twisting a gold, snakehead ring on his left pinky finger. "There's not much to tell."

"Yes, there is." She smiled at him, a reminder that she was a friend that could be trusted. "Often when his name comes up, you look down. When a boy, Roger did that whenever he was feeling guilty about something."

J.B. laughed and shook his head. "I'll have to keep in mind just how perceptive you are." He took a deep breath and while looking across the green landscape before him, also looked back into the distance of time. "Oh, Lucy, I've done some things in my life that I'm not proud of. I'm not the same person I was in my youth, thank God. Some of what I did was bad enough to haunt my dreams, and some just regrettable. My relationship with Victor is one of those."

Not sure which "those" he was referencing, she resisted the urge to ask for clarification. Instead, her compassion took the lead. "You earlier reacted to my mention of survival. We've all done what we had to in order to survive. Some of us look back and wonder how we could have made the choices we did."

"Surely, not you?"

She looked at him and boldly stated, "My mother was buried outside the cemetery in San Francisco during the rush."

"She was a soiled dove?"

"It's how she kept us fed and housed. Until she died when I was twelve."

J.B. shook his head. "She must have loved you a lot. My father loved me, too. But I was a wild kid and I left home when I was only sixteen. After I got in trouble a few years later, he got me out of jail, but I refused to go back home with him. I never saw him again. I deeply regret that."

"Now that you're a father with a son?"

"Yeah."

It was Lucy's turn to look into the distance, as though seeing an old memory. Realizing this, he told her, "I guess I never think of regrets being true of women."

"Well, those of us who lived during the gold rush had quite a time of it. I could have turned in a man wanted for stage robbery. But I didn't, because he had been kind to me." Her hand went to the slight scar on her cheek. "He had once been a doctor, and I saw goodness in him. Besides, I figured he'd be caught sooner or later. One could debate whether or not my decision was the right one. I only know it was right for me at the time."

"Was he captured?"

"Yes." She closed her eyes for a moment, took a deep breath as she opened them and looked directly at J.B. "And he was hanged."

J.B. rested his head on the back of the rocker and looked up at the blue sky dotted with the white of clouds. "I sort of cheated Victor out of this land. We both wanted it, and he'd put in a fair bid. We both had. But I knew the owner's sister, and I asked her to marry me." He looked over at Lucy. "Oh, don't get me wrong. I was very fond of her. It was a sincere proposal that she accepted." He looked away from Lucy and out *to* the abundance of cattle scattered across the meadows. His voice softened. "She knew she wasn't the love of my life, but to make me happy, she talked her brother into selling me this land. Because she knew I did love that."

"And how did Victor take it?"

"Not well. But time went on, and he married a nice woman who bore him a child. They had a little spread down the toll road, along the East Walker River. Nice little place, and he was breeding horses and selling them. Then his wife and daughter both died, and I think he thought life had turned against him. He drank heavily and gambled himself deep into debt. To help him out, I bought almost all of his horses. It gave him the money to pay off his debts and get himself sorted out, which he did. I admired him for that."

"There's a 'but' coming, isn't there?"

"Yeah." As he hesitated, Lucy noticed again his nervous habit of twisting the ring. "For some reason, he thought he could buy back the horses he'd sold me for just what I'd paid him for them. But I asked him for the current value of them after I'd broken and trained them. He couldn't come up with that much money."

"Did he start drinking again?"

"No. He went out and caught some mustangs and broke them. And he started building his ranch again from those. But to get back at me, he made a play for my wife. She was horrified at his boldness. She didn't tell me all the details of what he did, but I suspect she had to fight him off."

"Did you press her about it?"

"I might have, but I lost her not long after. She was always on the fragile side."

Lucy had the feeling there was more that could be said about the actions of both men back then. But it was clear that J.B. had given all the details he wanted to give. "Why did you invite him to this weekend then? Did you think the past between you was well and truly buried?"

A frown formed between his eyes. "I didn't actually invite him. Not initially. We got to talking after running into one another in town, and I said someday I'd like to have a small poker tournament out at my place. The next thing I knew, I was having one. And inviting Jim and Roger." It wasn't until later that Lucy realized he hadn't answered her second question.

"So, this weekend was actually Victor's idea."

"Well, no, I..."

Lucy's laughter cut him off. "You men! You have to claim all ideas as your own. But think about it. It was actually Victor who said you should do it?"

"Well, he did say, 'No time like the present'."

"Were you thinking of doing it this soon?"

He rubbed his jaw for a long minute. "No. I was just idly talking."

"There you are. Now the question changes. Why did Victor want to do it, and as soon as possible?" An idea struck her that had been niggling away at the back of her mind for some time. "And why invite Jim and Roger? He'd only met them once, back when he lost to them in a Bodie poker game."

J.B.'s frown deepened. "I didn't know about that at the time."

"Let's put that aside for now." She didn't want to give away an idea that she was forming about Victor. "What was your relationship with Otto?"

"I didn't have one. He worked for me once for a couple of weeks. I didn't like the rough way he treated the horses, so I let him go. He was a bronc buster and I don't do it that old way. When he asked me for a recommendation so he could apply for a job at the Hunewill place, I refused."

"He resented that?"

"Oh, yeah. He made that clear to anyone in town who'd listen to him. But then he got a good job at the old Valley View Ranch south of town."

"You had to know he might still be resentful. Why did you ask him to be here for the game?"

"Um, I didn't." He forced himself to look at Lucy, feeling the warmth of embarrassment spreading over his face. "Vic said he thought Otto would enjoy such a weekend. They were pretty good friends. In fact, I was going to put Otto out in the bunk house, but Vic switched with him. He said Otto would get a kick out of staying in the main house."

"It sounds like Victor was maneuvering things to suit himself." That thought having occurred to J.B. as he was talking, he simply shrugged, wanting to avoid thinking about where that realization might lead. Therefore, he flinched when Lucy asked, "But why would Victor go to all that trouble?"

J.B. shook his head, finding it difficult to admit that he had been so artfully manipulated. He looked at Lucy, who was looking at the meadows, and made up his mind not to waste time feeling foolish. "After all," he thought, "this weekend has had its good points."

# CHAPTER 7

## OTHER GAMES TO PLAY

Victor's funeral on Wednesday was much different from Otto's, although both graves were close together. There were, unlike at Otto's funeral, a large number of people in attendance, including Alex and Robert Folger from the *Bridgeport Chronicle Union* newspaper. Evidently, Victor was news, but Otto was not.

Amasa Bryant, owner of Bryant Hall, as well as several other businesses, was also there. He was easily recognized even from a distance by his thick mutton-chop side whiskers, but also because he was hardly ever seen alone. A popular early pioneer, this afternoon he was standing with Byron "By" Day, another early pioneer. Sheriff Cody and Doc Sinclair were also in attendance, surrounded by Doc's friends of long standing. None of these people, although they nodded in J.B.'s direction, came over to shake his hand or speak to him. Although the addition of a woman in their midst did spark curiosity.

Lucy kept her mounting exasperation under control and said nothing during the burial service. At the end, however, when everyone who hadn't immediately departed was still standing around, she sauntered up to Mr. Day.

"Hello, Mr. Day. You don't know me, but good friends of mine made your acquaintance back in the fall of '62 when they were traveling through. Robert and Dolly Robbins. They had a covered wagon, and another lady with them, who Dolly said didn't spend as much time around the campfire listening to your stories as they did."

"Oh, my goodness, yes." His smile expressed his delight in the memory. "I do remember them. And you are?"

"I'm Mrs. James Murphy, but please call me Lucy."

"Well, Lucy, I remember how interested they were in the whole area. Where did they go after leaving here?"

"They traveled through Dogtown to Monoville, and then on to Aurora."

"Ah, but they wouldn't have stayed there too long, I'd imagine."

"After a year or so they did move to Carson City."

"Yes, I'd think that would fit the ladies better. Especially at that time."

He was referring to the lawlessness and violence that had been prevalent in Aurora. Before he could focus on that, Lucy continued. "I just wanted to say hello to you. They were impressed with your kindness to them at a difficult time in their lives, and I know they'd want me to pass on their gratitude."

"Oh, well." He removed his hat and turned it in his hands. "That's very kind of you, I'm sure. Are you living here now?"

"No. I'm here with my husband. We're guests of Mr. Roberts at the Double R."

There was just a momentary flicker of surprise, ineptly hidden, before he smiled. "Oh, that's nice. Your husband is one of the gamblers invited to J.B.'s tournament?" The emphasis on the last word was not missed by Lucy.

Laughing lightly, she nodded. "It's so unfortunate that Otto's ill health overtook him just then." Glancing over at Victor's gravesite where two cemetery workers were shoveling dirt into the grave, she added, "And that Victor should succumb to his despair when he had friends around him who would have been willing to help him."

"Yes," Mr. Day nodded. "Looking forward to a bad end can't be easy, though."

Lucy looked at him, trying not to appear overly interested. "Bad end?"

"Some diseases take one quickly, but his wouldn't have done that. Not from what his wife told mine."

Trying to sound knowledgeable, but actually speaking from assumption, Lucy nodded sagely. "So true. And, of course, that's why he sent his wife and the girls away. They took it hard, even seen weeping as the stage pulled out of town."

"Yes." Mr. Day slowly shook his head, a puzzled frown between his eyes. "But Sara Dulong dying! That's something altogether different, right?"

"Yes." Lucy tried not to show her disappointment in losing the thread of Victor's illness. But hoping there was something she could learn about Sara, she focused on that. "Doc seems to put it down to having choked on a chocolate."

"By" Day showed his surprise. "Oh, really? I heard she had a bad reaction to something in the candy."

"I suppose that's possible. But all the ingredients were fruits or nuts she had eaten in the past."

"I was told they came from the candymaker here in town. She's known for using way too much mint in her candy, but other than that, they're very popular." He gave a slight smile before adding, "Especially among the courting couples."

Lucy laughed, forcing herself not to ask what he might mean by that.

"Oh, well." Mr. Day put his hat back on and gave Lucy a big smile. "It was nice talking to you." He then did the most audacious thing. He took a step closer and said, "I'll be sure to pass it around that the occurrences at the Double R have nothing to do with J.B. or any of his guests."

Lucy gave him her most winning smile. "You're very kind."

With that, Lucy turned to find that J.B. and the others were conversing with a man who she later learned to be Mr. Hunewill. This was "N.B.", Napolean Bonapart Hunewill, one of the first arrivals in the area. His sawmill had made the growth of the town possible. When more settlers had come to Big Meadows, it had been his wisdom and kindness that had contributed to keeping peace with the local tribes.

Lucy had seldom seen a man so distinguished, even reminding her of drawings of European kings. Possibly it was his long nose and high forehead, but mostly it was the way he carried himself with a bearing that was of natural authority. Then she heard his deep laugh, and realized he must be a very jolly monarch. Which explained why Alex so loved spending time at his Circle H ranch.

J.B. looked to be enjoying himself, so Lucy chose to move away, looking at nearby headstones as were Frank, Jim and Roger. Looking up a moment later, she noticed what she considered an odd couple standing near the entrance.

The man was large, muscled and had a square jaw like a stud horse. His thick brows formed the arch of a scowl over dark eyes that were scouring the cemetery, as though daring anyone to approach. The woman next to him, who Lucy presumed was his wife, was small and delicate, with eyes that were scrupulously cast down, as were the corners of her mouth. Although the air was not chilly, she huddled beneath an almost thread-bare shawl. But it couldn't hide the plain, obviously homemade dress she wore. The words *brute* and *drudge* came easily to mind, and Lucy felt an urge to somehow rescue what she perceived as an unfortunate woman.

Lucy watched the man and woman walk to a nearby spring wagon, the back filled with bags, barrels and farm equipment, the evidence of recent errands in town. The woman turned to her husband with eyes that rose to meet his, whereupon he lifted her up and placed her gently on the seat as though she were a child's doll. He received from her a smile that lit up her face, displaying bare, naked adoration. As soon as he was seated beside her, he reached over and helped her adjust the shawl over her shoulders while whispering something in her ear that caused her to laugh. As their wagon rolled away, she with her eyes cast down and he with his scowl in place, people glanced in their direction and quickly turned away. And Lucy paused to think about how little we know about people because we're so quick to judge by appearances.

J. B. shook Mr. Hunewill's hand before his fellow rancher walked away, then came over to Lucy. He looked down at the headstone nearest them, one of four with the same last name, that of Stewart. "John Stewart was one of the very first of the settlers here. A grand old man. He died in '83." J.B. looked saddened by whatever memories he was entertaining, and fell silent.

Lucy looked around them and shook her head. "So many of those here are young children. Some just babies."

"I know. Life so often greets children with promises unfulfilled." He pointed to one such child, reciting a few details about the parents that showed he liked them. He then turned his back on the small collection of graves and looked far into the distance toward the Sierra. "During funeral services, have you noticed how people often talk about what a sterling life the deceased lived?"

"Oh, yes. I guess the best we can ask is that people will acknowledge our life as honorably lived."

THE GAMES WE PLAY

J.B. looked at her, startled by her words. "Do you think most people are honorable? Or is it just something said about them because they're dead? If we're honest, don't you think we can seldom claim any such thing about most of those we know?"

"I don't know." By the look of disappointment on his face, she could tell he had hoped for something more profound from her, so she tried again. "Whether we've led an honorable life or not, it's too late for us to change that once we're dead. We have to accomplish that while we're alive. And it's never too late to start."

J.B. said nothing, simply offering her his arm for support over the uneven ground on the way back to Jim's side. He also said nothing before walking away toward the horses tied along a rail near the entrance.

Jim helped Lucy into J.B.'s black rig where Emily was waiting, the top folded back so the occupants could be seen. Noting that Emily had a firm grasp of the reins, Jim was glad she was so adept at driving a team. He knew Lucy to be much better on a horse than behind one.

A second such rig had already left with Mrs. Lewis sitting rigidly straight, and Sing at the reins looking neither to the left nor right as they passed through the town to Kirkwood Street. There were people on the corner as they turned left toward the meadows, but no one waved when Sing looked in their direction.

Mrs. Lewis didn't mind, but she knew Sing would be upset by such cool treatment. "Don't mind them, Sing. In a few months everything will be back to normal, and they'll claim they just didn't see us. And we'll pretend we didn't notice their rudeness." Sing smiled at her, moved by her effort to be kind.

But her tone was bitter rather than encouraging as she murmured, "And life will then go on as usual."

J.B. and his gamblers, as some of the townspeople had begun calling them, were mounting their horses as Sheriff Cody approached them. Each one of them tensed. But the sheriff simply shook J.B.'s hand and nodded to the others. "I'm sorry people are being so stand-offish. It won't last. But you know how people are."

Frank didn't mince words. "Yes, we know how *people* are. But J.B. has a right to expect better from his *friends*."

When J.B. said nothing, the sheriff looked down at the ground and nodded. "You're right, of course." He then looked up, taking them all in. "But you have to admit that three deaths in as many days is a lot for people to accept without question."

"And," J.B. said, "we're wealthy ranchers and gamblers."

Frank interpreted this accurately. "Easy to ignore until something out of the ordinary happens. Then, the sanctimonious hypocrites are quick to pass judgment."

"And old resentments rise to the surface," Jim added. "Like wolves picking up the scent of wounded prey."

"Oh, come on, fellas." The sheriff looked around uneasily. "It isn't quite as dramatic as all that."

J.B. mounted his horse and looked down at his friend. "Maybe, Mike. But right now it sure as hell feels like it to us." As he started to turn his horse, he looked back and asked, "Want to join us for a drink at the Court House, Mike?"

Knowing J.B. meant the Court House Corner Saloon, he shook his head. "I wish I could, but I have to get back to the office."

J.B. took it as a mere excuse. "I understand, *Sheriff*."

What Mike Cody might have felt was lost to the men, who were focused on keeping up with J.B. as his horse loped down the road toward town. They didn't slow down until they approached the narrow river and crossed over on the bridge, passing the Wedertz store and the new Towle home, and merging into Main Street traffic.

They skirted around a freight wagon and tied their horses at the rail out front of the saloon while glancing to their left at the gleaming white courthouse. There was talk going around town of plans to fence off the wide dirt area in front along Main and School Streets. This would keep wagons from cutting across from one street to the other, sometimes coming so close to the building's corner that a post had been set in the ground there to protect it.

With J.B. in the lead, the men stepped over the saloon's raised door sill onto the wide planks of the wooden floor. J.B. headed directly to the long, dark wooden bar to their right. The others followed, each resting a foot on the brass rail running along the bottom of it. A long mirror faced them, reflecting the stacks of glasses and bottles sitting on the low backbar.

Dark wood wainscoting ran around the walls, the wallpaper above showing a repeating pattern of widely spaced fleur de' les. A few advertising posters decorated the walls, but there was nothing fancy or overblown about the large room. No velvet or lace was to be seen, and of course, no women either.

There were two spaces off the back of the room, one to the left covered by a curtain and used for storage, and the other nearer the bar with an arched doorway. Roger was pleased to note that the floor was well swept and the bar wiped clean, with a small and highly polished balance scale sitting at the far end. Although men now usually had coins with which they paid for their drinks, it was there to weigh gold dust if that was offered in payment. With the low tin ceiling and a pot-bellied stove at the front end of the bar, Roger found it a welcoming place.

Roger left off his observation of the room to watch those at the billiard table in the middle of the floor, one of the men having just sent a ball into a crocheted corner pocket. The ball hung there like a large bird egg safely at rest in its nest. A man behind Roger entered, carrying a chair from the line of them on the front porch, and settled himself in a far corner to watch the game. One of the players fetched the spectator a beer, which when brought to him was gratefully accepted by a nod and a smile. That no money exchanged hands intrigued Roger, but he said nothing.

They received friendly greetings, not only from the bartender, but also from the three other men at the bar. No reference was made to the deaths at the Double R, all comments being general. This was a place of refuge not only from the world outside, but for some, from lives filled with difficult challenges. And definitely from feminine influences. Here, men could relax and even let down their hair; where debate might take place, but differences would not turn to exclusion.

A surprisingly thin man in overalls, leaning on the bar next to J.B., asked, "How's Alex doin' in school? My boy's doin' better now that his ma's makin' him read more."

"Alex is doing fine." The pride in J.B.'s voice couldn't be missed. "Looking forward to going away to Berkeley High School in the bay area."

"A lot of the boys from here go there." He nodded his head and then changed the subject. "Did you hear that there's steam comin' out of one of them islands out in Mono Lake? That's one strange place!"

"Sure is!" As the man turned to a new arrival on his other side, J.B. looked out the front window at a busy Main Street, feeling his spirits lift. He didn't care that the conversations were about commonplace issues, that the man next to him smelled of horse and hay, that the spittoons could use a good cleaning, or that a man in the back room had a laugh that could be heard all the way up front. He only cared that it was cool inside and no one was talking about death.

J.B. ordered himself a second drink, Jim refusing the offer. He was content with his beer, visiting with Frank and Roger, and watching the billiard game. The man next to J.B. started complaining about his wife, but stopped talking when J.B. offered him a free whiskey. J.B. watched with interest as the man slowly sipped the amber liquid, giving its quality consideration as it slid down his throat. He seemed to approve, since he took another sip. But this time he followed it with a contented sigh, indicating definite approval. J.B. looked down at his own drink, wishing something so simple could bring such contentment to himself.

The man had several times coughed into a none too clean handkerchief, after which he would take a moment to breathe deeply. After he left, Jim expressed concern and the bartender explained. "That was Almond Huntoon. Nice fella. Owns Huntoon Station north of here. He's married to her who was Elizabeth Anne Butler, once married to ole Kernahan of Bodie. She and Almond had a boarding house in Bodie, but what with the mines failing, they moved away. His brother, Lansing, has a saloon here. In fact, his brother Sydney owned hundreds of acres northeast of here. He sold 800 to James Sinnamon, before selling his whole ranch to John Murphey in '64. Went off to Canada. Colorful family, all seven brothers."

In September of 1890, Almond, tired of his ill health, would commit suicide; and Elizabeth would marry businessman Jesse McGath. The house he built on Green Street in Bodie would still be there through the next century, and even into the one after that.

While the men from the Double R were enjoying what to them was a respite amid normal people talking about normal things, Lucy and Emily had returned to the ranch. There, they stood in the middle of the guest room that had housed both Otto and Sara. The bed was stripped down, the rug on the floor rolled up, and the curtains drawn, giving the room a feeling of abandonment not soon to be changed. Contributing to the sense of despondent gloom that hung over the room was the water in the crystal flower vase that had turned a slimy yellow. The last of the blue petals had fallen onto the table around the vase.

As Emily pulled back the curtains, flooding the room with light, she looked down at the table. "I always think it's sad to see what was once a sweet arrangement begin to fall apart. This must have been put here by someone who thought it special."

"What are those flowers," Lucy asked. "I haven't seen them in Virginia City."

"They're delphiniums." Emily touched a stem and the last of the petals on it fell. "I saw their tall, blue spikes growing in some of the town gardens."

"I wonder if I can get some seeds off this and get them going in my garden."

"You might. But I'd be careful if I were you. They're somewhat poisonous, at least the young parts are. A friend lost a dog that way."

"Maybe I won't take them, then."

Both women looked around a last time, wondering why they had bothered to enter the room, so deplete of personality or presence was it. Almost at the door, however, they stopped and looked at each other with eyes wide.

Emily was the first to speak. "When those flowers were first here, there would have been a lot of young leaves and new flowers."

"That would have been when Otto was using the room."

Emily nodded. "We need to ask the local doctor if he knows anything about the symptoms of someone ingesting the toxic parts of such a plant."

"Where did you learn about it?"

Emily thought a moment. "I think it was from Mrs. Kennedy, the woman I lived with when I first came to Lone Pine in '78. She had an extensive garden, and I used to help her in it."

"If we're correct in what we're thinking, then Otto didn't die a natural death at all. He was poisoned. Does that mean that Sara was also poisoned?"

"The sheriff said the candy was okay."

"But she had blotches on her arms and neck. And she'd been sick." Lucy scanned the room and shrugged. "She certainly reacted to something."

"Yes. Frank says Mrs. Lewis doctored the welts before Sara went to bed with a book and the box of chocolates. What do you suppose she'd handled that caused that?"

"The doctor said there wasn't anything in her stomach except the candy and some tea. Which he said was not poisoned."

At that moment, Sing came into the room. "Ladies need something?"

Lucy turned to him. "Maybe just the answer to a couple of questions?"

Sing clasped a hand to his head. "Oh, so many questions lately. But you ask."

"Was there a cup of something in her room when she was found?"

He nodded. "Yes. I cleared out room, and cup here."

"Could you tell what had been in it?"

"Yes. Tea."

Lucy asked, "How did these flowers get into the room?"

"I put there."

Emily was puzzled. "I didn't notice any delphiniums growing on the ranch when Frank and I were walking around outside."

"Oh, no. Mr. Otto bring with him. He tell me to put in room. To cheer it up, he say."

"Do you know where he got them?"

Sing shook his head. "Don't know. Many ladies in town grow pretty flowers."

After he left, Emily and Lucy followed, closing the door to the room almost reverently. However, they had with them the vase of dead flowers, now mostly stems. Upon reaching the back porch where they were blocked from the breeze, they laid out each individual stem and looked at them carefully. It was evident that toward the bottom of several of them, leaves had been stripped off.

Emily pointed out the obvious. "It doesn't mean that they were used to poison anyone. Just that they were removed."

"I know. Sometimes I do that just so more water will saturate the stems of an arrangement."

"But at least it opens the door to a new theory. We need to tell the sheriff." Emily carefully wrapped the bouquet in butcher paper given them by Sing. At Lucy's suggestion, they hid the bundle in Roger's room before coming down the stairs just in time to join the men, who had returned in time for supper. Lucy and Emily sat at the far end of the table from the men, out of the way of their current discussion about cattle prices.

The stew's gravy was thick, and the vegetables still a little toothsome, just the way J.B. liked it. The corn bread was better than either woman had ever made, and after a low conversation between them that greatly amused the men, they were eager to quiz Sing. All in all, the atmosphere was the lightest it had been for days.

As everyone sat around the dining room table enjoying the bounty of Sing's food, Emily managed to slip in that the flowers in Otto's room had been of a toxic nature. She held back the conclusion she and Lucy were forming in order that she might observe the reactions of the men.

J.B. found what they said particularly interesting. "I saw Otto ride up when he arrived." He looked around the table and frowned. "Some of you were there, too. It was Saturday morning just after we had discovered that the horses had been taken. I don't remember seeing him with any flowers."

The men shook their heads in concert, obviously puzzled. Roger ventured an idea. "I guess he could have had them wrapped up in the valise he had tied to the back of his saddle."

J.B. nodded. "It just seems an odd thing for him to bring with him."

Lucy looked at him, and thinking of their earlier conversation, raised an eyebrow. "Maybe someone suggested it to him?"

After a moment of blankness, J.B. realized what she was indicating. "You mean Vic suggested it?"

"That's right."

"But... but... You're suggesting that Vic poisoned Otto with the flowers? And planned that before the weekend even began? And that's why he suggested that Otto stay in the house?"

"Yes."

Roger perked up suddenly. "Wait! Remember, I mentioned that when I came in for the start of the game after the break that I passed Otto and Victor on the back porch? I told you Otto was chewing on something."

Jim frowned. "Vic too said he'd seen Otto chewing on something."

"If he'd given Otto that something," Vince reasoned, "if he knew that Roger had seen Otto eating something, he would have had to say that he had, too."

J.B. felt like he should play Devil's advocate. "But Otto was okay when we started to play again."

"Yes," Frank shrugged, "but maybe there was some kind of a delayed effect. It was about an hour after we started that Otto began feeling bad. And it was a while later that we found him dead."

"Okay," J.B. argued, "but why on earth would Vic want to kill Otto? They were friends."

In her most gentle voice, Emily said, "Otto probably thought so, too."

Frank completed his wife's thought, although not so gently. "And maybe for some time, even before our weekend, that's what Vic wanted everyone to think. That way no one would suspect him if he killed Otto."

"For some reason unknown to us," Vince added.

Following that train of thinking, Jim asked, "J.B., can you think of anything that might have transpired between them to cause hard feelings?"

J.B. just shook his head, the idea not only new to him, but abhorrent as well. "I thought I knew both of them pretty well. But I guess I didn't."

Lucy had to force herself not to roll her eyes. "You know your experience with each of them, but did you ever try to get to know them beyond that? Did you ask them about their lives?"

J.B. looked at Lucy, then down at his plate. "You're right. I kept our relationships as surface as possible."

"Oh, hell." Vince felt someone should come to J.B.'s defense. "Most men do that. Unless we decide there's a good reason to put forth effort. Like family or close friends. Maybe business."

Lucy thought that J.B. might go further in keeping everyone at bay. An male acquaintance wouldn't ask him questions about his past, but a friend or a woman might. She wondered if that would require him to lie, knowing as he did that lies often find their way to the light. Safer to just keep relationships shallow.

Roger asked, "During our first game, didn't Otto refer to money Victor owed him?"

"Oh, yeah," Vince said. "Money Vic lost to him when they played backgammon."

J.B. sat back, eager to change the subject. "Okay. You're going on the assumption that Vic planned ahead to poison Otto while here. So he asked Otto to cut a bouquet of flowers to put in his room, just so he could use them later."

"Yes," Emily agreed, "but not just any flowers. He probably specified which ones."

"Men like Victor and Otto don't care about pretty flowers." Lucy thought a moment and added, "Victor must have told Otto that he wanted them brought so he could give them to a woman."

She turned to Emily, who exclaimed, "Sara!"

Roger liked the idea. "And Otto would have had to be the one to bring them so they would be in his room. All ole Vic would have had to do is slip into Otto's room and snip off the parts he wanted, grab something out of the kitchen and feed it to Otto during the break."

"Or," Vince put in, "keep something off his own plate at breakfast that morning."

J.B. was still finding it hard to believe that Victor would have done such a thing to Otto. "But when could Vic have gotten to the flowers so he could take off the leaves? He wasn't the cleverest man around!"

The men looked at one another, each one weighing the repercussions of speaking up. But it was Frank who pointed out the obvious. "We were all going in different directions that morning. Not only could he have done it, but any one of us could have, too."

Lucy turned to him. "I wonder if the sheriff realizes that. If he does, he's considering everyone who was here that morning as a suspect."

J.B. frowned at her. "But Mike hasn't suggested anything like that. Or acted like he thinks it. He was fine at the funeral."

Emily again felt it necessary to gently correct his thinking. "Well, he would be, wouldn't he? I mean, it's obvious he's an intelligent man. He wouldn't want to alert a suspect to his way of thinking."

The men stared at her as though she had told them she thought a woman would someday serve on the Supreme Court; a shocking thought even more profound than a woman serving on a local jury, as the suffragists demanded. Emily simply looked back at them and bit her tongue.

"But why suspect us?" Roger asked, surprising Lucy, who wondered why Roger found the thought so disturbing. "We weren't on the back porch with Otto just before the game started. Victor was."

Lucy told her son, "There's only your word for that, which puts you there, too."

"Mom!"

"Well, dear, it's best we look at this from every angle. Sheriff Cody certainly will."

Emily was following her own line of thought. "If what we're posing is true, and Victor had some kind of plan worked out, is there more to it that we haven't yet realized?"

Roger sat forward. "I keep wondering why Victor wanted it to play out here."

"Maybe," Lucy surmised, "Victor's suicide was the rest of the plan. Although, if he wanted to take his own life, why not do it in his house in town?"

Roger reached for another piece of cornbread. "Someone might not have found the body right away. Not with his wife gone. Here, they certainly would." Everyone turned to him after he had spoken, realizing that there was a lot that could be said about bodies not found right away. But realizing it was an indelicate subject for the dinner table, no one did.

J.B. looked around at his guests, twisting his pinky ring like it was on fire. "Okay, let's say that's all true. If Vic wanted to kill Otto, why make it look like a death from illness?"

Roger poured honey onto his cornbread. "Yeah. Wouldn't Vic be taking a risk to expect that everyone would believe it was a natural death?"

Jim thought he had the answer. "Why not? He'd already primed our reaction by telling us that Otto had health problems. And that's been repeated several times by others as an accepted fact. But was it really true?"

Lucy nodded. "Probably planted in the minds of so many people recently by Victor that after awhile, no one can recall how they know."

"Boy," Roger declared, "Vic was some kind of master at manipulating people!"

Vince looked around the table. "Doc Sinclair is a trusted medic here in town. So, if he says Otto died because he had some kind of underlying illness, then no one is going to argue with him. And they haven't."

"But," Emily said, "how did Doc know about Otto's health problems?"

J.B. shrugged. "I assume he was Otto's doctor."

Emily didn't want to make an issue of this, but she made a mental note to ask Doc about Otto's health later.

Roger looked suddenly enlightened. "If Otto had died in some way obvious of murder, it would have triggered an investigation. And that might have gotten in the way of what else Vic wanted to do."

"You mean, kill Sara?" Lucy asked.

Lucy's bold question brought J.B.'s focus to her. "You don't hesitate to face brutal facts, do you?"

"They can't be solved if they're not faced." Lucy looked carefully at J.B., trying to form her next words as tactfully as possible. "You told me about Otto working for you. Other than the way he handled the unbroken horses, how was he with them?"

"Pretty good, I guess."

"Good enough that he might have stolen them Friday night? Could that have been why he was late getting here on Saturday morning?"

The men stared at Lucy with a type of awe. Then Jim grinned. "She's good at word puzzles, too."

It was an opportunity to release their tension, and they all laughed while Lucy colored in response. "I think it's just that I wasn't here like you men were, and I don't have a past relationship with Otto and Victor to get in the way." She looked directly at J.B. "You were dealing with the stolen horses, people coming and going, and a game that was supposed to start soon. You were probably trying to be a good host at the same time as dealing with the horse theft. It must have been a chaotic time."

"Yeah, it was."

But, thought Lucy, you're not about to admit just how much that's true. Instead of commenting on that, however, she asked about the tea in Sara's room.

Sing joined them when J.B. rang a crystal bell next to his plate. He was asked about the tea given Sara. "I make earlier for Victor day he get here, to settle his stomach. He say mint tea very good for that."

"But you also gave some to Sara?" Lucy asked.

"Yes. Mrs. Lewis come in Monday night and tell me Sara not well. I tell her what Victor tell me. We make tea and she pour into big mug. She say it might help Sara relax and sleep."

J.B. couldn't contain himself any longer. He stood up and began to pace around the great room. "Okay. We know how several things got into Sara's room. So what? Even if Otto was killed by the flower parts, Sara wasn't. And the chocolates and the tea sure as hell couldn't kill her, so what does all that matter?"

He turned back to the table, looking first at Emily and Lucy, who had been demonstrating how clever they were. But they only looked back at him, no answer on offer. Any pride the women had been feeling about their deductive ability evaporated, to be replaced with the same befuddlement felt by everyone else. Sing, sensing the sudden tension in the room, scuttled back into the kitchen.

In town on Thursday morning, Sheriff Cody was sitting in the small parlor of a house facing north on Main just west of School Street. He was nibbling a cookie from a bakery bag he had brought as a gift, and drinking tea poured into his cup by Mrs. Turner, Victor's wife. He wanted as casual an atmosphere as possible when questioning the recent widow. While getting their refreshments organized, she apologized for not making it back in time for Victor's funeral. Sheriff Cody quickly brushed it aside as nothing for which she need apologize.

He had met Laura Turner when he had campaigned for his current job, as he had canvassed door-to-door for support. She was a woman somewhere in her fifties, and looked ten years older, the evidence of a hard life clinging to her like dust. She pushed at the gray hair hanging loose from her bun. "I should have put a ribbon in my hair, but I've been so busy." The sheriff thought a comb would have been better put to use.

He smiled and held up a hand. "I'm sorry to interrupt you, but I need to talk to you."

"Oh, yes, I suppose so." When she turned her eyes full on him, he saw that her face was tracked over with both laughter and worry lines. But it was her green eyes that immediately drew his attention, as they were set amidst thick, dark lashes under perfectly arched brows. The sheriff remembered her as having a quick smile, and much appreciated for her community involvement.

Laura was also known to be quick to repeat the latest gossip. This would have been par for the course among many of the town women, except that it was often discovered that what Laura Turner repeated was not always perfectly accurate. It had never been settled among her friends whether this was because she didn't listen carefully, or because her kind acts were a front for gathering bits of gossip.

"This is nice tea," the sheriff commented. "I don't think I've ever had any like it before."

"It's mint tea. I grow mint alongside the house where it's mostly shady." She looked at the man she knew best as Michael Cody, and set her cup in its saucer before placing it on the table in front of her. "Mike, I just can't believe he's gone. Not this way."

Rather than commiserate and end up having to deal with a woman in tears, he cut right to the point. "I understand that the two of you had separated?"

"Yes, but that wasn't because we were unhappy." She looked out the front window and then back at her visitor. "Well, at least not mostly because of that. He'd been given a bad diagnosis from a doctor in Virginia City."

"Oh?"

"The doctor said he had a tumor in his bowels. But the doctor also said he was sure they could do surgery to cut it out. On the other hand, they wouldn't know if it was cancerous and had spread until they did that."

"So that was the pain he felt sometimes?"

"Yes."

"When was he going to have that surgery?"

"Oh, he declared he wouldn't undergo surgery. He was convinced he was nearing the end. He said that if the good Lord wanted him to go, he wouldn't fight it. I never knew him to be a religious man, but that's what he said. He just took laudanum when the pain got too bad."

She had hesitated, as though she wanted to say more, but was unsure if she should. The sheriff put his cup on the table and gave her his full attention, his steady gaze giving her no relief. "Was there something else he said?"

"Oh, well, he said that before he died there was some unfinished business he had with some people."

"People? Not just a person?"

"That's what he said. But he was always saying stupid things like that. It didn't mean anything."

"So why did you leave?"

"He told me to go." She pulled a hanky from beneath the cuff of her dress and dabbed her eyes. The sheriff thought they seemed pretty dry to him. "He said he couldn't handle watching me watch him, and that it would be too terrible for the girls." Her lips pinched and for a moment she looked outright angry. "It was the first time he'd ever shown such consideration for any of us."

"Oh?"

"Yes." She smoothed her skirts and took a deep breath. "He wasn't a very pleasant man to live with. Being nice like that made me think he had something up his sleeve other than an ace."

Ignoring Mrs. Turner's attempt at humor, he asked, "Like what?"

"Frankly, I thought he might accidently take too much laudanum when the pain got severe." She looked stricken at having said that, putting a hand to her mouth. Still, she couldn't help but add, "I thought he might mix it with whiskey, which makes it more potent, and that'd be the end." She clenched her jaw. "God knows, he drank like a fish! I certainly didn't think he'd hang himself!"

"I'm not sure he did."

"What?" Her surprise was genuine, but there was also a glimmer of salacious excitement that shocked the sheriff. "You saw him after he was found, didn't you?"

"Yes. But there were things that made me wonder if he might not have been stunned and then hanged while semi-conscious."

"You mean *murder*?" There was that glimmer again. "Who would do such a thing?"

He decided to change the subject instead of trying to answer her question, realizing suddenly that whatever he said might be repeated, and probably not accurately. "Did you know Otto Mercer or Sara Dulong when you lived here?"

"I know Otto fairly well. Victor used to drink with him sometimes, and they'd play checkers for pennies once in a while. He'd never hurt Victor. What does he say?"

"Nothing. He died a day or so before Victor."

"I...I hadn't heard."

Her stunned reaction gave the sheriff the opportunity to continue, making sure to keep his next question in present tense. "Do you by any chance know Sara Dulong?"

"Of course, I do."

"What do you mean by *of course*?"

"Well, we had her to dinner often. Before she went out to the Double R, she worked for the milliner where I get my bonnets repaired. My daughters took to her. Sara would come stay with them whenever Vic and I wanted to go out for an evening. Why do you ask about her?"

"I'm sorry to have to tell you that she's passed away."

"No!" He watched the color drain from her face, then return with a flush. "How?"

"We're not sure. She may have choked on a piece of candy."

"Well, I'll be jiggered!"

Her surprise may have been profound, but that of the sheriff wasn't far behind. He was trying to absorb the fact that Victor had known Sara before seeing her at the Double R. Why had Vic denied it? Did Mrs. Lewis know that Sara had cared for Victor's step-daughters? Why had Sara been so flirtatious with Victor? Was there more to their relationship than Mrs. Turner knew? So many questions filled his mind that he decided to change the subject.

"Are you going to stay here in town or go back to Sacramento?"

"As soon as I can sell the house, I'll go back. The girls like it there and my sister will let us stay with her until we can buy our own place. This house is mine outright, you know. I'd already put it up for sale before I left, and I have two people wanting to buy it. I'll complete the sale and then leave."

On his way out, Sheriff Cody passed the pretty blue flowers growing along the front of the house. Mrs. Turner, watching him leave, stepped forward. "I see you're admiring my delphiniums."

"Yes. I've seen ones just like them recently."

"I look forward to them each year. They self-seed, as they call it."

"Well, they're quite nice."

"Thank you. I think some of the neighbors cut some while I was gone, but that's okay. They should be enjoyed."

"Would you mind if I cut a few to take to my wife?"

"Help yourself." Then she hesitated. "But you have young children, don't you? Then I wouldn't if I were you. If they put things in their mouth like most little kids, it could make them very sick. Maybe even kill them."

The sheriff stared at her. "Really?"

"Oh, yes. I don't know if it's happened here, but it has in Sacramento. My sister is the one who told me about it."

As the sheriff walked down the street, he added another question to his growing list of them. Only this one was for Doc Sinclair.

# CHAPTER 8

## BENEFITS OF A POKER FACE

Lucy's comment that what was true of Victor and his movements was equally true of the others staying at the ranch, continued to haunt Frank and Vince. They discussed it in the privacy of what was now just Vince's room.

"You do realize," Vince said, "that we're the only ones here who have absolutely no motive to kill any of those who've died?"

"Yes." Frank thought a moment. "But Jim and Roger didn't lose when playing in the big game with Vic in Bodie. They won."

"Unless," Vince posed, "there was more to that incident than we've been told."

"But Victor lost," Frank insisted. "So there might have been a motive of revenge, but only on Victor's part, not theirs."

"True. But they did know Victor, so it lets them in for some of the speculation that's going on. Maybe not with those in town, but surely with the sheriff."

Vince couldn't have been more correct. Sheriff Cody sat in the office portion of his house next to the new stone jail, but he wasn't idle. He was working with a stack of papers, each one headed by the name of a man who had been present at the Double R that fateful weekend. And Jim and Roger definitely were in the stack. Once he had a piece of paper headed by a name, he filled in below what he knew about their connection to Otto, Victor and Sara, if any.

When that was complete, he was still left with crucial questions. Why did those who had died, need to die? If, that is, their deaths were not exactly what they looked like. And, although he had no proof, he was thinking more and more that they were not. If Otto and Victor had been the only two to die, one by illness and the other by suicide, such a coincidence might be possible to believe. But, with Sara's death added in, the sheriff found all the deaths suspect. Of course, he told himself, her death could be the most natural one of the three."

Hearing the door open, his ruminations were cut short. Although surprised, he was delighted to see Lucy Murphy and Emily Eastman walking into his office. After a fulsome greeting, he hurried to pull up two chairs to the front of his desk. Lucy looked askance at the old, straight-backed chairs with their sagging cane seats, but she gently lowered herself onto one of them. Emily followed her lead. Their eagerness to talk was so evident that Sheriff Cody merely waited for them to begin.

They described their time in Sara's room as succinctly as they could, excluding anything they figured might not be pertinent to the subject at hand. They knew how irritating it was to men when women veered off topic. So they succinctly explained their knowledge of the flowers in the vase, and how pieces of them might have been the source of Otto's symptoms. They did, however, make the mistake of wondering if the doctor had known of such a possibility.

Mike didn't tell the ladies that this had already occurred to him, or that he had brought up the idea to Doc Sinclair. Or that the doctor hadn't been willing to seriously consider the possibility. Because he was irritated with Doc and wasn't willing to admit to that, he became a little defensive on Doc's behalf. He therefore told the ladies about the autopsy in more detail than was necessary, hoping it might cause them some dismay, if not squeamish repugnance. But he might have been describing the weather for all the reaction it got him. If he had known their history, he would have expected nothing else.

Brushing aside the sheriff's defensiveness, Lucy offered simple logic. "If Doc hasn't had to study about toxic plants for any reason, he certainly can't be expected to look at some purple flowers and think 'that's it'."

The sheriff relaxed and decided he would be better off not jumping to conclusions so easily, wondering if he did this in all areas of his life. But he quickly refocused on the matter at hand. He also decided to tell these *unusually intelligent women*, as he would later describe them to his amused wife, about an interview he had tackled earlier.

"You've no doubt met Hank and Mort." The women nodded, but said nothing, unwilling to share their opinions. "I never met two men who were so opposed to forming words. 'Yep' and 'Nope' seemed to be their whole vocabulary." The sheriff was still perturbed, as he considered the men's reticence at answering his questions a show of disrespect for the badge, if not himself.

Emily had no patience with such self-indulgence. "Yes, but did they have anything interesting to contribute?"

"Not much. But Hank did say that he'd seen Victor swallowing pills from some druggist's envelope on several occasions. Mort said he got the impression that Victor had moments of extreme pain, and turned to whiskey more often than people probably knew. They'd both seen him double over suddenly. But there were no pills anywhere in the bunk house or on the body. Well, there were some Tutt's Pills in the cabinet. Hank said they'd been there for some time. For stomach upset after a night of drinking."

"If he was killed," Lucy mused, "why would the killer remove pills if they were for pain?"

Emily frowned. "That's right. If the killer wanted it to look like a suicide, he'd want it to look like there was a reason for Victor to take his life. And pills imply ill health."

"Which," Lucy finished the thought, "might be considered a very good reason for ending one's life. If that life was deemed too difficult to continue."

Emily asked the obvious question of the sheriff. "So why were the pills not there?"

Sheriff Cody looked at the two women and wished fervently that women law officers were possible. Then, laughing to himself, he thought, "That'll be the day!" He shrugged and told them, "Maybe it's as simple as his having taken them all. Or the fact that Victor did, in fact, take his own life."

Lucy wasn't ready to accept that. "Did you at least find the paper envelope the pills would have been in, given him by the druggist?"

"No. Not in the room or on him."

Emily changed the subject. "I was told that Mort discovered the stolen horses and brought them back to the Double R."

"That's right. He saw them in the pasture where the thief put them. It was one of Victor's leased pastures. They were probably put there because it was right on the road. A couple snips of wire and the thief had access. He was probably going to retrieve them the next night, but Mort found them before he could."

"How did Mort know they belonged to J.B.?"

The sheriff smiled slowly. "Yeah, I wondered about that, too. Turns out he was stroking the neck of the friendly mare when it came up to the fence. He saw the fresh brand under her mane and recognized it. He'd heard in town about the theft, so he found where the thief had cut the wire, with only a hasty mend. He then simply herded the horses back to the Double R. An apple he had in his saddlebag he gave to the mare, so she followed him willingly. And, of course, the other five followed her."

Lucy decided to tackle another subject. "Could Doc tell what caused the mark on the side of Victor's head?"

"No. Just that it wasn't made by a sharp instrument. Not even the butt of a gun. More like something flat."

"Like the back of a shovel?"

"You have a good imagination, Mrs. Murphy. But I guess it could have been that."

Lucy and Emily exchanged a look that the sheriff couldn't interpret, but he didn't want them holding anything back they might have discovered. Deciding to take a firm stand with them, he opened his mouth to speak. But before he could question them, they rose up, thanked him for his time, and moved to the door.

Calling out, he stopped them. "One thing. Be careful, ladies. Someone has killed, and very cleverly. Be sure you don't get in their way. Anything you know that you think might be pertinent, even slightly, you need to tell me."

"Of course." That they had said it in unison didn't go very far to reassure him. He stood at the front window and watched them walk to their rig, climb in and head toward town. He was somewhat surprised to realize how much he appreciated their coming to him with their questions. Their deductions certainly gave him something to think about. Maybe he would keep them at least somewhat informed of his progress as the investigation progressed. It might be unorthodox, but at this point, he really didn't care. These deaths weren't the only town issues demanding his attention.

Emily and Lucy stopped at Bryant's Post Office Store, where the candy eaten by Sara had been purchased. Along with boxes of chocolates, they found gauze bags of clear rock candy piled in a basket. Emily couldn't resist one of those, although she said it was for Frank. Lucy wasn't fooled, and as she put one in her basket, she freely admitted to being partial to it, even while saying, "Of course, I'll share with Jim."

The clerk looked up at the sound of their laughter. "Can I be of service to you ladies?"

"We're finding your store delightful."

"Thank you. Are you looking for anything in particular?"

Lucy stepped forward. "Maybe your stationery."

The man walked to a shelf on the far wall, taking down three boxes. "This is all I have. The plain cream, the pale blue, and the bright white. The cream is the best quality, but the blue is very popular."

Remembering the paper upon which J.B. had written the invitation, Lucy looked at the price marked on the box. She had been correct about its expense.

Emily approached the man. "I notice your boxes of chocolates. Are they fresh, or have they been there for a while?"

"I don't let them sit longer than a week before I give them to one of the ranchers for his hogs. Those boxes are fresh out this morning. But they're always the same."

"Oh?"

"Yes, ma'am. Filled with jam from whatever fruit is available, either grown around here or brought in with freighters. Sometimes nuts, but not too often."

"That's all?"

"Well, I have to admit the chocolate is usually flavored with mint." He was quick to add, "But it's very refreshing."

"Thank you, but I think I'll stick to the hard candy today." She turned to a nearby table where handkerchiefs with embroidered edges were displayed. "Oh, and I'll take two of these."

"Certainly, madam." He took her purchases to the counter, followed by Lucy with her candy and box of blue stationery. While waiting for their purchases to be wrapped, Emily noticed three women huddled together in a far corner. Startled, she realized they had been watching with interest while she and Lucy had shopped.

After Emily stood aside at the door for Lucy to pass through before her, she turned back to the women, raising her voice. "Good day, ladies."

The women quickly looked away, pretending to be inspecting a bolt of cloth. Lucy told Emily, "Yes, I saw them. I just chose to ignore them as they were ignoring us."

Emily put their purchases on the back seat of the buggy, helped Lucy to climb in and went around to get in. "I guess the men aren't the only ones under suspicion now."

"Oh, I just think it's because we're married to the ones who are. They probably just don't know what to say, the situation being too awkward for them."

"Hmmm. You're more generously inclined than I am." She gathered the reins and they headed back to the ranch before the rising breeze turned into wind.

After thinking further about the delphiniums, Sheriff Cody went back to Dr. Sinclair, aware that he had completed Otto's autopsy. Otto, having no relations to question such a procedure, Doc had not hesitated to do it. When the sheriff arrived, Doc was just finishing with a patient who left with a bandage on the back of his hand. Cody took a seat next to the desk in the front parlor, waiting for the doctor to finish writing on the front of a paper folder

Cody once again raised the subject of toxic flowers as a means of death. This time, Doc grudgingly admitted it was possible that death could have occurred by the ingestion of poisonous plant substances. He had found in the stomach partially digested blackberry jam, along with what he assumed was biscuit and coffee.

"The jam and coffee together," the doctor explained, "would hide any bitterness from the plant material, especially if there was a lot of it."

"For instance, if the plant pieces had been mixed into blackberry jam and used as the filling in a biscuit sandwich?"

"Something like that. And washed down with black coffee, especially if it had lots of sugar in it. But I couldn't tell if there was something toxic in any of it. Any plant parts must have been mashed up fine so no actual pieces of plant were present. If there was any at all. Without actual pieces of plant, I just don't have the expertise of a big city laboratory. If it was arsenic we suspected, I could do a Marsh test."

It would be years into the future before toxicology would become a well-developed forensic science in the United States. In the 1840's in France, it had begun to be introduced in court cases, but only when arsenic was suspected as "the husband killer". However, once women were allowed to sue for divorce, that became much rarer.

Sheriff Cody prepared to leave. "Anything else, Doc?"

"Yes. If someone dies from the introduction of a slow-acting poison, I do know that it would affect their heart, especially for anyone with any degree of existing heart problems. But the dead body would only show what looks like asphyxia." Doc sat back and ran his hands over his face. "In other words, I could tell there was a lack of oxygen to the heart, and even other cells in the body, but not why that occurred. Frankly, I have even more questions about Sara. Like why she had a rash on her chest and arms."

Remembering a question Emily had asked him, Cody turned to the doctor. "Were you Otto's doctor?"

"No. I don't know who was. Maybe someone at the County hospital in Bodie." Doc moved to the wash basin and began scrubbing his hands. Over his shoulder, he told the sheriff, "His heart and liver looked okay to me. But that doesn't mean he wasn't having problems with them."

As the sheriff returned to his office, he was deep in thought. He passed two people he knew without even looking in their direction, which when they repeated the incident, began a whole new onset of gossip.

The sheriff had been thinking about the death of Sara. Of all three deaths, that one puzzled him the most. Otto could have been poisoned by the plants, and Victor could have been stunned and then hanged. But there was nothing to even suggest that Sara had died by another's hand. And yet he felt in his bones that she had.

Since the men at the Double R had been told not to leave town until given permission, Jim and Roger decided to give their horses some exercise. The horses had been well fed and comfortably housed since their arrival, and were not too happy about being disturbed. Nevertheless, once out onto the road heading up toward the tree line and the twin lakes, they

settled down.  Roger chose to think they were enjoying the ride as much
as he was.

Both men had spent most of their lives on the western side of the Sierra
among green forests, cascading waterfalls, and meandering rivers.  They
had even lived for a time near rolling foothills covered in golden grasses
beneath acres of gnarled oak trees.  Those environments had been a world
away from their life among the dry scrub on the eastern side of the Sierra.

But they had grown to appreciate and even admire the drier climate
of brush appropriately named brittlebush, rabbitbrush, and creosote bush.
Nevertheless, they had to admit that they were enjoying the luxury of green
meadows through which trickled rivulets of snow melt.  The presence of
cattle in the midst of it didn't take away from its beauty, but rather enhanced
it.  Whether the cattle were lying down in the tall grass with only the tops
of their heads showing, standing knee deep in a stream while drinking,
or lounging by the fence with their big, brown eyes watching them pass,
father and son enjoyed their presence.

Jim turned to his son.  "Have you talked to Alex recently?"

"We went for a long walk yesterday evening.  He's feeling a little left
out of all that's going on, what with him being sent to spend so much time
with friends when not in school.  But I convinced him that J.B. is just
looking out for him."

"He sure idolizes his father."

"Don't worry, he'll get over it."

Jim was a little startled.  "Oh, yeah?"

"Yeah."  Roger turned to his father with a big grin.  "We all do."

Jim chuckled, familiar as he was with his son's sense of humor.  Jim's
memories of his father were vague and blurred through a lifetime of only
early memories to recall.  But he had not forgotten the strict discipline that
had often been physically painful, and dealt out only because his father had
been easily irritated.  Consequently, he had early on made up his mind to
raise his son with what he called a *constructively lenient* hand.

Lucy had suggested that all Jim really needed to do was listen to his
young son when he was trying to explain his actions.  In this way, almost
from infancy Roger learned that there was a difference between *making
excuses* and *offering reasons,* with each treated differently by his parents.
His punishment for the former was usually confinement to the house for

a week without cards or friends. This had been torture, but it had forced him to entertain himself by reading books and helping in the kitchen, which in the long run turned out not to be such a bad thing. If, however, the reasons he gave for his actions were logical, it simply brought on what he thought of as a boring lecture from his mother on proper behavior in a cooperative society. Or his father's equally boring diatribe about what a real man did or did not do. As an adult, Roger had several times benefited from recalling the points of those lectures. But he wasn't about to tell his parents that.

Sitting on the covered back porch, Emily and Lucy watched Jim and Roger riding away from the ranch. Emily sighed as she turned to Lucy. "I wish we'd had another child. Maybe a boy." Then she laughed. "But Whitney is quite the tough little girl. She and her best friend, Steven, play marbles in the dirt and race their horses through the hills. She refuses to ride side saddle, although I don't judge her for that, even if some people do."

Lucy leaned toward her new friend. "I never use a side saddle on the occasions when I ride."

Waiting for a reaction, she was surprised that the one she received from Emily was laughter. "Oh, me too! I have a very nice riding habit with a split skirt."

"That's what I wore when riding alone from Placerville to Genoa back in '75. I even brought it with me on this trip. It's also nice for hiking in the hills."

"I'll have to remember that." She gave Lucy a look of mock surprise. "And to ask you later about that long ride."

Lucy laughed. It had been quite an adventure, she had to admit, but at the time she hadn't felt it to be overly dangerous. Other people, however, always seemed to react with horror at the thought of a woman alone traveling the Placerville Road over the Sierra. And on horseback, at that. Maybe, she thought, it had been the underlying urgency of her journey that had blocked out any other consideration. It was Roger she could blame — or thank -- for that.

Emily sighed. "The best I can do with Whitney is to get her to wear a shortened skirt over boy's pants."

"Amelia Bloomer would be pleased," Lucy commented. Both women laughed at that, knowing how controversial the bloomer garment had been back in the 1850's. "I once saw a woman wearing her bloomer dress on a wagon train I was on. It was very practical. A full, below-the-knee skirt over wide-legged pants tied at the ankles certainly made it easier getting in and out of a wagon. And her limbs were as covered as if she'd been wearing a dress."

"Yes, but it wasn't." Emily considered for a moment. "Unfortunately, Mrs. Bloomer abandoned her effort to change women's mode of dress in order to make inroads with the suffrage movement."

"A wise choice, I think. After all," Lucy reasoned, "our fashions change all the time without causing much comment in society. Paris and New York designers declare hoops, crinolines, or bustles, and we fall in line."

"Not so much in the West, you have to admit."

"True." Lucy smiled a little sheepishly. "I only wear light petticoats, and often not even a corset. The same as most women I know."

Emily nodded. "Oh, yes. I have enough laundry to do. Servants in Lone Pine are rare, except those women who go from house to house washing clothes or cleaning kitchens."

Lucy avoided looking at Emily, as she was wondering why her friend didn't mention that those women were most often local Piutes. It was the same in Virginia City, although there, much of the daily help were Irish girls and women. Did Emily take for granted Lucy's knowledge, or did she think Lucy would disapprove? Either way, for a change, Lucy decided to keep silent and let the moment pass.

Emily looked at Lucy with a raised brow, her thinking still mired in the topic of fashion. "But women wearing pants like men? That certainly is a bit too far, even for the most liberal of suffragists. In most counties, it's even illegal."

"Oh, I know." Lucy decided not to tell her friend about the numerous times she had worn men's clothing as a disguise that saved her life. But she had been young then, and had been actively chasing her dreams on the other side of the Sierra.

Emily looked at Lucy, realizing her thoughts were far away. Drawing her back to the present, Emily said, "I was never brave enough to break out too far from expectations. I mean, I've never traveled by wagon train or dared to wear anything controversial. I came west on the train in '78, and as a young woman traveling alone, I dressed very conservatively." She smiled, unable to resist adding, "And I kept my opinions to myself." She gave Lucy a wink. "That last was the hardest part."

Lucy asked, somewhat tentatively, "At eight years old, Whitney has a horse?"

"Actually, it's closer to a pony in size, but she has a fit if someone calls it that."

Lucy changed the subject rather abruptly. "I have friends living in Lone Pine. Dolly and Robert Robbins."

"Oh, I know her. Such a nice lady. She's helping Mrs. Carrington tend to my daughter and Charlotte's son while we're gone."

"I get letters from her detailing her life in Lone Pine. She seems to like it there."

"It's a nice town. We're certainly happy there."

Emily didn't seem of a mind to add more, so Lucy again changed the subject. Unusual for Lucy, she felt comfortable enough with Emily to express something she had never told anyone before. "I would have liked to have had a second child, too. Especially a daughter. But these things happen for a reason. My behavior in both Placerville and Virginia City was handled well by a boy, but it would have been more difficult for a girl."

"Your behavior?"

"To support us after Jim left during the war, I dealt cards in the back room of a saloon. Consequently, when Roger and I ended up in Virginia City in '76, I did the same thing. Oh, I tried more acceptable work, but I couldn't make nearly as much money. And female dealers there weren't all that unusual. I was circumspect, and only a few of my female friends even knew that I did it."

"How exciting!"

"It sounds more so than it was." Lucy looked over at the men busy at the barn. "But I did meet a lot of interesting people."

"I'm surprised you didn't meet J.B. at some point. Sing told Frank that he goes to Virginia City quite often."

"Really?" Lucy thought a moment before shaking her head. "If he was ever at my table, I don't remember it."

Emily lowered her voice and looked around to be sure they couldn't be overheard. "I'm sure you would have remembered. He has the most glorious eyes, and his hair curls over his ears like he hates barbers."

Lucy remembered how J.B. had greeted her upon her arrival. "Or like a woman just ran her fingers through it. He's quite handsome."

"Good heavens, yes!"

Then, their eyes meeting, the two women broke into exuberant, conspiratorial laughter. This was followed by several minutes spent simply watching the activity around the barns and corrals. There seemed to be considerable movement among Hank, Mort and three hired men from town, especially near the blacksmith's shed. Horses were being led to the shed, as well as away from it, some to the big corral and others into the barn.

Lucy was curious. "What do you suppose they're doing?"

"They're checking all the horse's hooves to see if any need trimming. When they look in their mouths, they're checking their teeth. Some horses may need their teeth filed down so they can eat more comfortably. The men are just making sure they're all in good physical condition."

"I often see a horse playing with the bit in its mouth. Why do they do that?"

Emily shrugged. "Could be the horse has teeth problems, or its easily bored, or it might just be a nervous habit."

"You know quite a lot about horses, don't you?"

Emily smiled at the acknowledgement. "I learned it all after arriving in the west. My teen years were spent as a city dweller in Chicago. My parents died in the great fire of '71. After that, I lived with an uncle. But when he was traveling, which was most of the time, I stayed with a friend's family." She sighed deeply. "Ah, dear, dear Carrie." She turned to Lucy. "How about you?"

"I spent my early teen years working through California gold rush towns as an indentured servant. In my late teens, for a little while I was a cook in a parlor house."

That got a startled reaction from Emily that made Lucy laugh. Emily was quick to explain herself. "Don't take my surprise as judgement. I just didn't expect that from you."

"Oh, I know how it sounds. It's a long story, but as I said, I was chasing my dreams. Growing up so poor, my dream was of having a big life. But I eventually realized that I only wanted a good life. Jim gave me that." She looked pointedly at Emily as she said, "And I only cooked." Not wanting to go into more detail about that time in her life, Lucy brought up their visit with the sheriff. "You realize the meaning of what we're putting together, don't you?"

"Oh, yes." Emily had been trying to find a tactful way to bring up the topic, although she now realized that with Lucy, one didn't have to beat around the bush. "We were supposed to think that Otto and Sara died naturally. Now we're thinking otherwise. But not for sure, because we don't know why anyone would want them dead."

"I do think we, and maybe the sheriff, are convinced Otto was poisoned by ingesting the flowers in his room."

"Yes," Emily agreed, "and Victor is the most likely one to have done that. He had the opportunity when alone with Otto on the back porch during the break from the game."

"But," Lucy reminded her, "Sara wasn't poisoned by those flowers, or by anything toxic. And the doctor said there were no marks of violence on her, although her face was a little swollen."

"You mean like if she had been strangled?"

"Yes, but J.B. saw her body and he said there were no marks on her neck."

Emily asked, "What do you suppose caused the blotches on her skin that Mrs. Lewis treated?"

Lucy stood up and walked to the edge of the porch, looking out over the ranch. "I've heard of people with reactions to substances that looked just like that. I had a friend who started using a new laundry soap, and ended up with red blotches all over her body. Since the same thing showed up on the daughter, it wasn't difficult to figure out the cause."

"Oh, you can't trust half the things you buy." It was an oft heard complaint by women. "There's especially no telling what's in things like cosmetics and tonics."

"Some people say products sold to the public should be regulated. Or at least that the public should have to be told what's in them. They only do that with imported goods."

Emily stood up and stretched. "If it means more expense in manufacturing, such an idea will be fought hard. Only if Congress makes it a law will anything change."

In fact, it wouldn't be until 1906 that President Theodore Roosevelt would sign into law the Pure Food and Drug Act. In 1888, it was still a *buyer beware* society when it came to the wild promises accompanying the many tonics, pills, and lotions on the shelves of every general store and drugstore. The fact that many contained high concentrations of opium, and even mercury, was not unknown. But the consequences of ingesting or applying to the skin such substances over a long period of time, was yet to be realized. It may be one of the reasons that the average life expectancy in 1888 was only 55.

"Oh!"

Hearing Emily's exclamation of surprise, Lucy turned to her. "What?"

Emily was looking toward the far corner of the house. "I haven't noticed those outside stairs before."

"Neither have I. They're painted the same dark brown as the back of the house. And quite narrow and steep, too. The door at the top would be about where Alex's room is located."

"Do you think they're there as an emergency exit?"

"I would think so."

Emily noted, "We have a two-story house and we have a rope ladder in our bedroom in case of a fire downstairs."

"Yes, so do we. Only, we keep it in a chest at the far end of the upstairs hallway. Years ago, I ran our home as a boarding house, so everyone needed to know where the ladder was."

It was noon, and a brass bell outside the bunk house was being rung by Hank. The ranch hands took their mid-day meal, cooked on the stove in the far corner of the bunk house. Being summer, they did so with the back door open, and thus the aroma of searing meat reached the women. They left the back porch and went inside to see what delights Sing had made for their mid-day meal. The discovery of the stairs and the likelihood of a fire was immediately forgotten as they approached the house and the aroma of baked beans.

They were pleased to find that there was a large platter of sandwiches on the dining room table, along with a bowl of spicy beans, a bowl of sliced peaches drizzled with honey, and fried green tomatoes. There were also stacks of plates next to cutlery wrapped in napkins, the cloth of which had been boiled bright white. Glasses sat next to cold pitchers of lemonade and water. Lucy's main focus, however, was on the chocolate cake on a crystal cake stand.

Interpreting this layout as a buffet, Lucy and Emily helped themselves, settling side by side on the sofa that faced the front windows. Placing their food and drinks on the low table in front of them, neither wasted time *tucking into their grub*, a phrase Lucy remembered from her youth that always made her smile.

Shortly after, Jim and Roger came in from outside, the lingering scent of horse with them. They too filled their plates, positioning themselves on the sofa facing the women. Frank and Vince came down the stairs, spotted the food, and joined the others with their own full plates. For several minutes, no one spoke, simply enjoying their food.

Finally, J.B. came down from his office, which Roger was beginning to think of as J.B.'s secret hide-away. Although he had seen into every other room in the house, no one had even caught a glimpse of that one.

Having heard his boss descend the stairs, Sing met him at the bottom of it with a glass of whiskey-doctored lemonade. Stretching out his long legs as he relaxed in his chair, J.B. took a swallow of his drink before turning to Lucy. "How did you ladies spend your morning?"

"We did a little shopping in town and then enjoyed the view from your lovely back porch. It was a good opportunity to get to know one another better."

"It's a fairly new extension of the house," J.B. told them, his pride on full display. "One of my better ideas." He was glad Hank wasn't present to correct the accuracy of that statement, although he probably would have done no such thing. Hank was happy to let *the boss* take credit for whatever he wanted, just glad that he had a home at the ranch.

While winking at Emily, J.B. addressed Lucy in his most winning tone. "And did you learn anything fascinating about your charming new friend here?"

Ignoring his hint of condescension, Lucy told him, "I did, actually." He looked a little disappointed that she hadn't responded to his baiting with a smart remark, as he had purposely tried to rile her. It could have made for a spirited exchange. But Lucy had been a dealer in Virginia City for years, and he had no idea all that she had put up with from men playing at her table in the Crystal Saloon. She made her point to him by saying, "I discovered that Emily's family didn't fare well back in the fall of '71."

Roger wondered if anyone else noticed how suddenly J.B. went white in the face. In fact, everyone did take note of it, even if too polite to comment. For Lucy, however, it was confirmation of something she had earlier surmised about J. B. Roberts.

J.B. quickly turned to Emily. "What did she discover?"

Emily simply said, "That my parents died in the great Chicago fire that took out much of Chicago."

Each person present wondered if it was their imagination, or had J.B. been holding his breath, and now released it with a rush? He took another big swallow of his strong drink before leaning back in his chair, struggling to adopt an air of relaxed detachment. He tried to affix a smile on his face, but the result was less than successful. He ended up looking as though he'd just run a marathon foot race; breathing hard and very much relieved that it was over.

# CHAPTER 9

## CHIPS FALL WHERE THEY MAY

One of the things the sheriff had shared with Emily and Lucy just before they had left his office was what he had learned during his conversation with the widow Turner. The main thing being that Victor had known Sara. Therefore, at breakfast in the Leavitt House dining room on Friday morning, Lucy and Emily PASSED THIS ON TO their husbands. They also told them that they wanted to visit Mrs. Turner before the woman left town for good. Frank and Jim agreed it would be a good idea. So it was that rather than going immediately out to the Double R, the ladies walked west the two blocks to Mrs. Turner's house.

Frank and Jim caught a lift with a ranch hand going to work at the Hunewill spread so their wives would have use of the rig. After being dropped off under the big Double R medallion at the ranch's entrance, the men walked down the long drive to the house. Frank turned to Jim with a sly smirk. "I wonder if anyone has died while we were gone."

Jim looked at Frank and started to laugh, then caught himself, sharply clearing his throat instead. "That shouldn't be so damn funny, but it unfortunately is. More like irony, really, but the whole situation seems fantastical."

"Great word!" Frank grinned, rolling the word around in his mouth like a piece of candy tasted for the first time.

"Yeah." Jim chuckled. "I read it in a magazine. I've been wondering when I could use it in a conversation."

Frank sighed as he looked ahead at the house. "Do you think that maybe we're supposed to think it's all a fantasy? Something we can see, but should know better than to believe?"

"What do you mean?"

"Well, it feels like we've been pawns in some bizarre game that began before we even got here. The invitation to you was certainly unexpected, right? And pretty much everything that's happened since we got here has been strange."

"Yeah." After a moment of reflection, Jim said, "Like we only need to be a little more imaginative and we'll see a whole, bigger picture."

"I bet our wives have that kind of imagination."

Jim's only response was to grunt in agreement, as they had reached the steps up to the house. When they entered, they found Vince and Roger at the chess board at the game table, both deep in thought. Sounds of Sing in the kitchen came to them as reassurance of tasty treats for their later enjoyment. Not seeing J.B., they assumed he was in his study upstairs. Wondering about the whereabouts of Mrs. Lewis didn't occur to either of them.

With nothing else to occupy their time, Frank and Jim took a book from the shelves in the hallway and stretched out on one of the sofas where light from the big front windows could fall on the pages. They were grateful for everyone's occupation, as it meant no one asking them to explain the whereabouts of Lucy and Emily. Explaining their wives' behavior had always been a big part of their lives. However, interest in reading quickly palled, so the two men decided on a game of cribbage at the kitchen table.

Mrs. Turner responded to the knock on the door with an eager smile that immediately fell. Emily realized she must be expecting someone else and apologized for their arriving unannounced, explaining that they were the wives of friends of Victor.

"Oh, how nice! Come in!"

The woman was genuinely pleased to see them, and stood aside for them to enter. They introduced themselves to the plump, rosy-cheeked woman standing before them, her hair once again straying from the small bun at the nape of her neck. As she led them into an almost empty parlor, she removed her dark blue apron and tossed it over a wooden chair piled high with folded newspapers. Two half-filled hemp bags and a small wooden crate sat nearby, evidence of a move in process.

"Oh, my dears, please take a seat. I'm adrift right now, waiting for the man to come with the paperwork on the house so I can leave town. I've just been wiping out the pie safe to keep busy, so I welcome the company. And the coffee's still hot."

As happened so often with both Lucy and Emily, they were immediately considered *friend* rather than *new acquaintance*, and were invited to use first names.

While Laura Turner was in the kitchen, they looked around them. The walls of the room were bare, with the only furniture remaining being a small seating area of sofa, coffee table, and two wooden chairs. Taking the chairs, Lucy and Emily accepted a mug of coffee poured from a porcelain pot with a chipped spout that matched well the chipped mugs, all of which Mrs. Tucker carried in on a tray with no cloth. They were glad they could drink coffee black, because nothing more was offered with it.

They chatted about the warming weather, the charm of the house, and the new shipment of fabric at the Hayes Store. Ready-made clothing for men was commonly available, but women still had to make most of their own outer clothing unless they could afford a dressmaker. Most girls learned to hold a needle soon after being introduced to a fork and spoon. If they were poor or single later in life, sewing could well be a means of *acceptable* support.

"I heard that the Wedertz Store down by the bridge is getting in some white waists." Laura Turner rolled her eyes as she added, "And now I'm leaving. Oh, well. In Sacramento, they have quite a number of ready-made skirts and waists for women."

"Is that where you'll be living?" Lucy asked.

"Yes. With my sister. I have two daughters and they love it there."

"They weren't Victor's children, were they?"

"No. My first husband died just after my ten-year-old was born. The other is twelve, almost thirteen."

Emily shook her head and added a sympathetic "Tsk". But eager to get out to the Double R, she wasted no more time and deftly turned the conversation to the real reason for the visit. "And then, so soon after Victor's death, you were confronted with the death of your friend Sara."

"Yes. Such a tragedy. But, you know, it's very strange that they don't know what killed her." Laura Turner lowered her voice to a conspiratorial level. "She was really more of Victor's friend than mine."

Lucy carefully placed her mug on the tray, composing her words carefully. "She was quite young, wasn't she?"

Laura chuckled. "Oh, my dear, I love how tactful you're trying to be. I was a few years older than Victor, and he was a good twenty years older than Sara. I wouldn't say they had a father and daughter relationship, but close to it."

Lucy was quick to respond. "Oh, I didn't mean to imply there was anything unseemly in their relationship."

"The sheriff was surprised that Vic even knew her at all, so I suppose everyone out at the Double R is, too." Mrs. Turner looked out the window that allowed a view of the front walkway and Main Street beyond. But she didn't seem eager to end the visit. "Of course, there may have been more to their friendship than I was willing to admit." She looked at the women and decided to be frank. "I don't mind leaving. People think I didn't know right from the beginning that he was marrying me for my money and property. Of course, he did. And I married him because I had two girls to raise and didn't want to be alone. There was no great love between us. I did think that maybe such would grow eventually, but it never did."

"You're certainly not the first woman to marry for practical reasons," Lucy acknowledged. "Especially when there are children to consider."

"Well, I paid for it." It was stated with a nonchalance that startled Emily. Lucy, however, was not so easily shocked by such a revelation. "Victor was a somewhat erratic man. One day kind, the next day volatile. I must admit that I feel, not exactly relieved, but, well ..." She drew herself up and left that sentence incomplete. "You see, Victor and Sara had quite a lot in common. I was raised in a big city, but Victor had spent much of his life on a farm. His adopted father sold produce of all kinds and Victor helped him. And Sara had spent her whole life on a small farm up north before coming here to Bridgeport."

Emily spoke up. "So, shared experiences."

"I suppose so." She didn't look like she cared. Her thought had obviously moved on to something else. "The first time Victor had me make her his favorite tea she was thrilled. Mint grows out back like a weed. Sara said her mother used to give her mint tea to settle her stomach when she ate too many sweets, which she dearly loved. Victor bought them for her quite frequently." Mrs. Turner frowned. "But the last time she was with us, just before I left for my sister's, she said the tea made her feel funny. Kind of tingly she said, and her mouth sore."

"Oh, really?" Emily almost bit her tongue, not wanting to appear overly interested.

"I told her it was probably the chocolate candy made by that woman in town Victor thought so wonderful. God knows, he always had boxes of it around for Sara. She loved chocolate!"

Mrs. Turner picked up the coffee pot from the tray and poured into her mug. Consequently, she missed the look of startled awareness on the faces of her guests.

Emily spoke somewhat hesitantly. "Laura, would it be possible for us to cut some of the mint you grow so we can take it to Sara's sister, Mrs. Lewis?"

"Oh, my goodness, yes. Pull up a whole bunch, roots and all, if you want. It goes dormant in the winter, but it always comes back."

Lucy veered off to another topic. "Did Sara talk much about Mrs. Lewis?"

Mrs. Turner twisted her lips into a grimace. "Well, not a lot, I must say. I don't think there was much loving feeling between them, but I do think Mrs. Lewis was trying to be some influence over Sara. I know she didn't like Sara living in town by herself in a rented room."

Lucy remembered something she wanted to ask about. "I was wondering where Sara had been living before going out to the Double R."

"She had a small room in a house over on Kingsley, the one with the big red barn facing north. She said the woman was nice enough, but very much under the thumb of a nasty husband. They have a young daughter, Irene, that he bullies and berates more like a servant than a daughter. Even though she felt sorry for the girl, Sara spent as little time there as she could. She even spent some nights on our sofa when it got too bad over there."

"How generous of you," Emily enthused. "It's not always easy having another woman in the house."

"Well," Laura shrugged, "she didn't get under foot. It was usually on my night out at the quilting circle, and she was always up and out early the next morning."

Lucy didn't know what kind of a response to make to keep her talking, so she just said, "Your girls must have enjoyed that."

"Oh, they were usually with me. I think it's so important to get girls practicing their sewing as young as possible. They like making some of their own clothes, and quilting is good practice for learning various stitches."

Leaving further speculation until alone with Lucy, Emily asked, "Did you know that Mrs. Lewis and Sara both lied about Sara's age and relationship to Mrs. Lewis in order for Sara to work at the Double R?"

"Oh, yes." It must have been a fond memory for Mrs. Turner, because she suddenly softened. "It was great fun for all of us, keeping such a secret to help poor Sara."

Feeling that they had stayed long enough, Emily rose up and Lucy did the same. "Do you have some newspaper that we can wrap around the mint plant?"

"There's a stack on the chair by the door. Help yourself." She held out a hand to both women in turn. "And thank you so much for coming by. It was so kind of you, and made my waiting so much easier."

A noise on the front porch alerted them to the fact that Laura's wait was at an end. Emily and Lucy were shown the back way out, which was next to the line of mint plants mounded up against the house in the shade. It was a drab yard with one small tree badly in need of water. Flower beds along the edges were full of weeds and dead bushes, showing a lack of care of long standing. The property backed up to an empty lot on Kingsley Street, with a slab fence running horizontally between the two and stopping just short of a shed to allow a narrow pass-through. Looking over the fence, one could see across the empty lot directly behind, and across Kingsley Street. There, behind a small, dilapidated house was the big red barn mentioned by Mrs. Turner.

Lucy pulled up a clump of mint that looked to be the core of a spreading mound, dropping it onto the newspaper Emily had spread on the ground. She inhaled the strong scent of the torn stems as she slowly stood up, hesitating a moment before asking Emily, "Would you mind bending down to wrap it up? My joints are a bit stiff today."

Emily quickly scooped up the newspaper bundle, having had it brought home to her that no matter how youthful Lucy might appear, she was after all twenty years older. Climbing into the light rig, Emily gathered up the reins and headed out across the meadow to the ranch.

Emily couldn't hold back any longer. "So Sara and Victor were sometimes alone in the house."

Lucy recalled the few quilting parties she had attended in both Placerville and Virginia City. "The quilting circle probably meets at least once a week. It would give Sara and Victor plenty of time to talk privately."

Emily couldn't hold back a chuckle. "Yeah, *talk*."

"Well, yes," Lucy smiled. "But whatever else they did, it was the perfect opportunity to plot and plan."

"Especially if Victor needed Sara's help in some way."

As they traversed the narrow road through the meadows, Lucy asked, "Why did you want some of the mint from the Turner house?"

Emily surprised her. "I'm not really sure, except that it must have been from those plants that Victor always made his tea."

"Surely not the tea made on Monday that was given Sara by Mrs. Lewis."

"No. That must have been from the plants in Sing's kitchen garden."

"I wonder how strong it was," Lucy mused. "That could make a difference if you were trying to get a lot of mint into someone who had developed a reaction to it."

"Helped by the mint in the candy," Emily added.

After a moment, Lucy asked, "Would Sara have had to handle much of the mint plants in Sing's kitchen garden in order to have blotches on her arms and chest?"

"I would think so. Someone said she'd been working out there pulling weeds. Maybe she cut back some mint that was spreading too much."

"Hmmm, yes. And handling the cut stems would be more irritating to the skin than just pulling up a whole plant like we did at Mrs. Turner's."

The women hurried from the barn while Mort was still unhitching the horse, eager to tell the others what they had discovered. Emily deposited the newspaper bundle under the bed in Sing's room, then stopped by the kitchen to tell him.

"Sing, had Sara been working in your garden Sunday or Monday?"

"Yes. Both days." He sighed and shook his head. "Always weeds."

"Did she handle the mint, too?"

"Oh, yes. Peppermint spread too much if not cut back. Nice smell."

Entering from the kitchen, Emily joined Lucy in the dining room where the men were engrossed in a game of poker. Being wives of men who made at least part of their living from gambling, they knew better than to interrupt with any issue not life or death in importance. No one was speaking, the only sound the clink of ivory chips tossed onto the pile in the middle of the table. For some reason, the sound made Emily recall the first time she had seen Frank back in '78. He had been sitting at a poker table then too, and also in a private house.

The women settled onto a sofa just as Jim declared, "Three of a kind, fellas!" Various comments followed, unheard by Lucy and Emily. They had put their heads together and were talking in low voices.

But while Jim's back was to the great room, Roger was facing them. He would never let on to his parents, but having spent his formative youth and his early adult years with just Lucy, he was often more in tune to her than was his father. And right then he could tell that his mother had something on her mind that she was eager to share.

As soon as the next hand had been won by Frank, teased by Vince, and mourned by the others, Roger proposed that they take a break. Jim started to object, but then realized there was something suggestive in his son's tone as he glanced toward the women. Since everyone was amenable to a break, they followed Roger into the great room.

J.B. smiled down on Lucy and Emily, wearing his *benevolent host* face. "And how are you ladies this bright morning? We missed you at breakfast. Were you out spending your husbands' money in the shops?"

Lucy started to say something sharp in response to such a patronizing assumption, but Roger cut her off. "I think they did a little sleuthing, didn't you?"

Lucy curbed her ire, easier to do now than when she was younger. Years of practice had allowed for the development of restraint. "Yes, we did. We paid a visit to Victor's wife, Laura Turner. It was informative."

"Let me guess," J.B. told them. "Vic knew Sara before last weekend. Mike told us. He stopped by on his way out to Buckeye Canyon." When the women reacted with surprise, he grinned. "Unexpected news, right? Or hadn't you figured that out?" He stretched out in his chair and laced his fingers over his stomach. "Is there something else?"

"The sheriff did a fine job in his interview with Mrs. Turner," Lucy acknowledged. She stopped talking as Sing entered with a tray holding cups and saucers, and a tall porcelain pot painted with yellow roses. He placed it on the low table in front of Lucy, and with a slight smile, quickly retreated.

Lucy was well aware, as was everyone else, that J.B. was in a less than hospitable mood. Lucy figured it was the result of the morning's game.

However, she didn't go out of her way to improve his attitude. Instead, she took more time pouring out the coffee than was necessary.

In an age when women were discouraged from speaking their minds, or demonstrating their intelligence, they learned that small actions could act as compensation. When Roger saw his mother add a dollop of cream to her coffee and slowly stir it in, he knew what she was doing. Lucy finally looked up at J.B., ignoring his frown. "No woman will ever be willing to open up to a man in the same way she will to another woman."

"But you were complete strangers to her." J.B. wasn't going to relinquish the point easily, barely able to suppress his quarrelsome tone.

Lucy decided not to bait him further. "Yes, but Emily and I seem to have the ability to quickly establish a rapport with people. Especially those who are feeling the need for someone trustworthy in which to confide."

J.B. leaned forward to reach for the coffee pot, and Jim heard him mumble, "Yeah, I've noticed."

Emily, having had enough of this by-play, brought the discussion around to what was important. In fact, she startled everyone by boldly announcing, "We think we know how Sara died." Greatly satisfied with everyone's attention now focused on what was important, she continued. "Mrs. Turner let it be known that Victor's favorite beverage was mint tea. And he shared it often with others."

"Oh, that." J.B. sat back and smirked. "We already knew that, also from the sheriff. So what?"

Emily looked directly at J.B., not caring about his sour mood or the reason for it. "Do you also know that the last time Sara drank it at the Turner house, that she had a 'tingly' reaction to it? And a sore mouth? And did you know that she had also been handling mint on Sunday afternoon, as well as on Monday not long before she broke out in blotches?"

She allowed her audience a moment to process what all that might mean. Frank smiled at his wife. "No, dear, we didn't know that. What do you think it means?" He wasn't going to allow anyone to step on her moment.

Emily smoothed her hands over her maroon, cotton skirt in a gesture of self-satisfaction. "We think it means that she had developed a bad reaction to mint, and that Victor knew it."

Vince was the first to put into words what they were all thinking. "Are you saying that Vic got her to ingest mint candy and mint tea, hoping that it would put her out of action? Maybe even kill her?"

Emily nodded. "Sara had told Victor and his wife that as a child her mother had given her mint tea to settle her stomach. So, it was logical that Mrs. Lewis would give it to her after dosing her itchy blotches with calamine lotion on Monday night. Especially since Victor had made some of it on Sunday before he died. He told Sing it was good for anyone feeling ill."

"Which," Lucy added, "if Victor expected Sara to be ill, would be good for Sing to remember."

"But," Vince put in, "if Vic planned for mint to do damage to her, he was taking quite a chance that it would. He couldn't know if Sing would give her mint tea at some point. Not for sure."

Roger chimed in. "If Vic hadn't died, he would have been around to be sure she ingested a lot of it. Which is another reason to believe that he was killed instead of committing suicide."

"As it was," Vince pointed out, "it didn't matter that he wasn't around."

J.B. asked the obvious question. "What could Sara have done to Victor to prompt him to do such a Machiavellian thing as all that?"

All eyes turned on J.B., some questioning and others puzzled. He was immediately on the defensive. "What? I read!"

Vince simplified the point. "Why would he want her out of the way?"

No one had an answer. The silence that followed, however, was abruptly broken. "What the hell are you all saying?"

Mrs. Lewis, forgotten by everyone, had emerged from her room. Lucy and Emily were immediately contrite for having ignored her, but she had never presented herself as someone in need of comfort from other women. She walked up to the gathering and glared around at everyone present, her face red with rage.

Lucy went to her and placed a hand on her arm. "I'm so sorry, Mrs. Lewis. Please join us, won't you?"

Emily fussed over the tray. "Let me get you a cup of coffee."

Mrs. Lewis looked at Lucy, tall enough to be eye to eye with her, and slowly relaxed her jaw. Realizing that Lucy was trying to be kind, she allowed herself to be helped to the big chair at the near end of the conversation group. In accord with society's cure-all tradition, Emily added considerable sugar to the coffee before bringing the sweet liquid to Mrs. Lewis.

Upon returning to her place next to Emily, Lucy waited for J.B. to say something. When he didn't, she told Mrs. Lewis, "We know that all of this coming on top of your grief for your sister must be hard to hear. But we're just trying to get to the bottom of what's been happening here this week." Lucy looked around at the others and added, "Before one of us is falsely accused of anything." She refused to add that with three people dead, there could possibly be more to follow.

Mrs. Lewis drained her cup, her face returning to its normal paleness. "It was bad enough when I thought she had just choked on a candy. But to think that Vic might have arranged for her to die, well, it's very hard to think about." She faced them with a determined glare. "I swear I didn't know she had developed some kind of bad reaction to peppermint. Like I said before, she's been around it her whole life! As children, we used to harvest and sell it."

"She didn't say anything to you about feeling odd after having a cup of mint tea with Victor and his wife?"

"No. Before I put the calamine lotion on her, I did notice that she was a little unsteady on her feet. But I thought that was because she was complaining of a headache. That's when I went to the kitchen. I was going to get her water, but Sing told me that Victor had reminded him that strong mint tea was a general cure-all, and that Sara really liked it. So, I made a pot and brought her a big mug of it. When I got back to the kitchen, Sing and I both had a cup."

Roger stopped himself just in time from commenting on the fact that the mint tea might have been the thing that had sealed Sara's fate. Instead, he asked, "How was she when you returned to her with the tea?"

"About the same, I guess. She'd been eating chocolates all the time I was gone, and was reaching for another. She was very drowsy, and I remember thinking she should put the candy aside and get some sleep. But I didn't want to be a nag." She looked down at her lap, pulling a hanky from the pocket of her dress. "I should have stayed with her."

"You can't blame yourself," J.B. told her. "It wouldn't have occurred to anyone that she was having a reaction to something she had eaten."

Roger asked, "Was it peppermint that you grew on your farm?"

"Yes, it was. And also some other flavors of mint, like chocolate and spearmint."

"The doctor would know better," Roger mused, "but might her early exposure to it be the key here?  Can someone, instead of building up a resistance to something, go the other way?  I mean, can a person become overly sensitive to something because they've had too much exposure to it?  Maybe starting in their youth?"

It was a thought new to them all, and no one knew how to answer him.  Truth be told, if Doc Sinclair had been present, he might not have known the answer either.  Reactions to various foods had been known for centuries, but the study of just how it worked in the human body had only recently begun.  The list of common foods known to cause negative reactions was very short in 1888.  And mint was not on that list.  In fact, it would be decades before it would be, and even then, considered a very rare reaction.

Mrs. Lewis was thinking through all that she had heard.  "Are you saying that Victor had worked out that Sara could die from eating and drinking a lot of mint?"

"Maybe." Roger, having talked to Sing earlier, told them, "Especially if she had also been handling it.  Sing told me that he'd heard Victor point out to Sara that the garden needed weeding.  Of course, Sing agreed because it always needs that, and it was an opportunity for someone to do a job he'd been putting off."

Mrs. Lewis shook her head in confusion, trying to reason out an explanation.  "If she was a danger to him, and he had a way of eliminating her without putting suspicion on himself, why would he commit suicide?  If she was dead, she couldn't be a threat to him about something he didn't want to face."

"The sheriff thinks he might not have committed suicide," Roger told her.  "That he was killed, and it was made to look like suicide.  Whoever killed him wouldn't have known what he had done to set up Sara's possible death."

Mrs. Lewis looked down at her empty cup.  "Maybe he didn't want her to die, but just be warned off about revealing something she knew that could be harmful to him."

"I guess that's a possibility," Roger said, although he thought it an undeserved, charitable assumption about Victor.

"So," Mrs. Lewis addressed them, "if he hadn't been killed, and everyone had assumed the deaths of Otto and Sara were natural, what had he planned to do next? Leave the area?"

"Who knows?" Jim answered her. "The question remains as to why he needed to kill either one of them."

Lucy decided it was time to introduce a supposition she and Emily had discussed. "What if Victor had gotten Otto to steal the horses? Victor wouldn't have known they would be traced back to the Double R, at least not so soon."

"That's right!" J.B. stood up and began pacing along the front windows. "He didn't know about the brand under the manes of those horses. He was startled when he found out."

Roger said, "Maybe that gave him a reason to kill Otto, to shut him up. Although why Vic would want to steal your horses is a mystery to me. And even if it had been discovered that Vic had gotten Otto to do that, so what? J.B., you wouldn't have pressed charges against Victor."

J.B. looked at him in surprise. "Of course, I would have! It's horse stealing, for God's sake! Even if he'd put Otto up to doing it. I'd have pressed charges against them both."

Roger was taken aback not only by J.B.'s fierce words, but also by the look of abject hate on his face. Still, Roger spoke his mind. "But no one was hurt or stranded, and the horses weren't in danger of harm."

"It doesn't matter!" J.B.'s red face was twisted beyond anger into rage. "It was at least grand theft, considering the value of the horses. He deserved to be punished!"

"Well, yes." Roger quickly backed off. "That's true, legally speaking."

No one dared remind J.B. about the remark he had made earlier in the week; that the horses had not been hidden and were sure to have been discovered sooner rather than later. Still, according to the law, not to mention tradition in the West, horse theft was an exceedingly serious offence. Many a horse thief had realized that too late when a noose had been slipped over their head.

As Roger sat back, deciding he had mouthed off enough for a while, Vince asked, "But what about Sara? Did she do something for him that was illegal? Did she know he'd set up Otto to steal the horses?"

Mrs. Lewis's voice was low and hard as she spoke up. "And in all that he did, was there help from one of you? Certainly not J.B., but the rest of you could easily have had contact with him before last weekend."

"Not Vince and me." Frank was frowning at her. "We just met him."

"But he could have met you before." She looked at Frank with a steady glare that made his skin grow cold. "He sold horses in the Owens River Valley where you live. We get a lot of produce from there, along with turkeys, honey, feed and flour. Mr. Flenniken at Bishop Creek sends us eggs. And Victor did some teaming from there. And, like him, you're a gambler. I don't suppose you spend all your time only in Lone Pine." She looked around at all the men who had been on the ranch the day Victor died. "So, one of you, or two together, could have killed Victor."

It was a statement, not a question, and each of them looked at her as though she was a bug that needed squashing. Not because what she had said didn't make sense or couldn't be true, but because they had all thought it at one time or another. Hearing it put into words just made it impossible for them to continue ignoring the idea.

But Jim wasn't one to avoid unpleasantness; not after all the difficulties he had experienced in his life. "Yes, Mrs. Lewis. We could have, but we didn't. And you're wrong about one thing. J.B. should not be left out when the subject of an alibi comes up."

"What?" No one could have expressed more indignant outrage in a single word than she had.

J.B. cut in. "I was here in my office. I came downstairs once to get a drink. Sing saw me."

But her disbelief and J.B.'s denial didn't keep Jim from continuing. "Each of us has to admit that around the time Victor would have been hanged, we don't have a solid alibi. It's just that none of us had a good motive to kill Victor."

"That we know about," Mrs. Lewis insisted. Before anyone could object, she asked, "What about Mort? He's new here. What do we know about him?"

J.B. shook his head. "Mike said he's pretty sure Mort is in the clear. I'll take his word that he thoroughly checked him out."

"And," Roger pointed out, "like the rest of us, he has no motive." Seeing Mrs. Lewis start to speak, he quickly added, "Or at least any obvious motive."

More speculations and accusations were curbed that Friday afternoon when Sing announced that dinner was ready. This was not a group that ever turned down a free meal, especially ones as excellent as those prepared by Sing. Even more important, J.B. wasn't the only one eager to escape the current topic of motives and whereabouts at the time of Victor's death.

# CHAPTER 10

## SHUFFLE AND DEAL

It was the middle of the slightly overcast Friday afternoon, and Sheriff Cody had arrived at the Double R. He was delighted to discover that the men were all out of the house, as he really wanted to talk with Lucy and Emily alone. However, he hadn't known how to arrange that. Unknown to the sheriff, after J.B. had uttered a colorful oath upon seeing the sheriff approaching, a rapid exodus of men had taken place.

With Sing out back tending to the garden, and cups of coffee on the kitchen table in front of them, the sheriff felt free to speak his mind to Lucy and Emily.

"Chronology! That's what's been bothering me!" Lucy and Emily were paying rapt attention to what he was saying. "Has it occurred to you that the order of the deaths isn't really what it looks like?"

Lucy answered for them both. "We did wonder something about that. But what exactly do you mean by it?"

"Everyone keeps saying 'the deaths of Otto, Vic and Sara'. But the planning of Sara's death actually came before Vic's death. The candy was chosen before the weekend began, before anyone had died. And Vic was making suggestions about the mint tea on Sunday before he was hanged."

Emily sipped her coffee, deep in thought. "If Sara had eaten the candy Saturday or Sunday, she might have died before Vic. Some people might then have thought his hanging looked like his reaction to her death. As though there was something more than friendship between them and he decided not to continue without her. Although I don't think he was the type for that."

"Right!" His eagerness to share his ideas was still high, but he realized he might be expressing himself too forcefully. Catie had once explained to him that, combined with his height and robust physique, when he raised his voice, he sometimes came across as a little 'too much'. Reminding himself that he wasn't talking to town toughs, he took a swallow of coffee and lowered his voice. "The candy was a present for her birthday, which was on Monday. Vic told Mrs. Lewis that she shouldn't give the candy to Sara until then. Although she did give it to her earlier, Sara didn't over-indulge in it until Monday night."

Lucy shook her head in wonder as she once again thought of Victor and all she had heard about him. "It certainly seems like Victor was arranging things to suit some plan of his own."

The sheriff pictured the bunk house as he had seen it immediately after Victor's body had been removed. "If Victor arranged the death of Otto with the flowers, and the death of Sara with the mint in the candy and tea, who arranged the death of Victor? And why?"

"Let's take the death of Otto." Emily removed a piece of paper from her pocket, upon which she had made several notes.

Before she could continue, however, the sheriff said, "Yeah, about him. The foreman at the ranch where he worked said Otto asked for time off starting Friday afternoon. And it was granted him. Otto told those here that he couldn't get away until Saturday morning."

Both women smiled, and Emily told him, "That ties in with what we've been thinking."

When Lucy also pulled some notes from a side pocket of her dress, the sheriff thought, "I bet Catie would like these women."

Lucy told him, "It's Friday night that's important, I think, since the horses being stolen pretty much started all that went wrong during the poker weekend."

Sheriff Cody stood up and began to pace. "I see where you're going with this. Otto must have stolen the horses and put them in Vic's pasture." He stopped pacing and returned to his seat. "But he wouldn't have done that without Vic knowing. Mort seeing the horses there and knowing who they belonged to couldn't have been foreseen by anyone. It only happened because Mort stopped to look over the friendly mare at the fence and saw the brand."

Lucy said, "Jim told me that Victor had been unaware of how J.B. had branded his new horses."

"That's right. But if we're thinking that Victor asked Otto to steal the horses for him, why would he do that?" If he was expecting an immediate answer from one of the women, he didn't get it. He therefore continued his logical flow of thought. "The horses certainly weren't hidden. Eventually someone, maybe even Hank or J.B. himself, would have seen them in that pasture. So, what did it accomplish?"

"It upset J.B.," Lucy responded. "More than he let on."

Emily frowned. "Enough that it might throw off his concentration during the game?"

Sheriff Cody shook his head. "I'd think J.B. too experienced a player for that."

"So," Lucy mused, "maybe it was just a prank to divert everyone's attention enough for him to do the rest of his plan. Whatever that was."

Emily spoke up somewhat hesitantly. "Could the plan have been to kill Sara? Was she the real danger to him?"

"Or," the sheriff mused, "maybe something more was supposed to happen later with the horses. Maybe he was going to sell them to someone, and because they were found so quickly, that couldn't take place."

Emily told the sheriff, "You wouldn't know, but Frank said that during the first game, there were several odd exchanges between J.B. and Victor."

"Yes." Lucy tried to recall the details of what Jim had told her about the cross-talk during the game's play. "Jim said something about it being as though Victor and J.B. were talking in code, each knowing what the other meant. But, of course, no one else would."

The sheriff ran a finger over his mustache. "That's interesting. The two men did have a history, and I don't think the animosity between them had improved much."

Lucy recalled J.B. alluding to Victor accosting his wife, but said nothing. It didn't seem pertinent, and it had been told her in what she considered a private, almost confessional, conversation. Loyalty was very important to Lucy, and was probably why so many of her friends entrusted her with their secrets both mundane and tragic. They knew they wouldn't hear them repeated at the next gathering of women, at least not via Lucy.

After a moment's reflection, the sheriff returned to one of his initial questions. "We might well ask, 'What did killing Otto accomplish?' Well, Vic didn't have to worry about him getting drunk and bragging about Vic putting him up to steal the horses. Or spill to someone whatever else he might know about Victor. Something he was very likely to do, knowing Otto."

"We might ask the same question about Sara," Lucy said. "What did her death accomplish?" When no one else offered a response, Lucy gave her opinion. "It kept her from ever telling anyone about their having what was possibly an intimate relationship. More likely, it was to keep her from telling anyone what she did that he put her up to."

"Yes," Emily agreed, "but what was that?"

"Um." The sheriff fought to find a tactful way to ask a delicate question. "Do you really think there was more than friendship between the two of them, and she was threatening to tell his wife?"

Both women shook their heads, but it was Emily who answered him. "I don't think so. Oh, not that it couldn't be true. But I just don't think he'd care all that much about such a thing becoming known. His marriage was mostly one of convenience, and he had already sent Laura away."

Returning to an earlier point, Lucy asked, "What could Sara have done for him? If it was just about this weekend, as it was with Otto and the horses, the most important thing she did was to find him in the bunk house."

"And what do we know about that?" The sheriff summarized by describing his walk through the bunk house once he had been left alone there right after Victor's body had been removed.

Both women listened carefully, trying to picture the room in their minds as he talked. When he finished, Emily said, "I want to see it."

Lucy's smile made it clear she agreed. The sheriff's immediate response was surprise at such a request from what he considered refined ladies. He then scoffed at himself. These were not what he thought of as typical females. What, he wondered, were their stories? Relegating that to some other time, he stood up and said, "Okay. Let's go out there now."

Upon reaching the bunk house, the sheriff opened the door for the ladies to precede him. But he almost bumped into them when they stopped short just inside the door. It flashed through his mind that they might be overcome by being in a room where someone had been hanged. Then, recalling who they were, it leaped into his mind that they just might want a broad view of the room. He was wrong on both counts.

The table usually in front of the stove in the far corner was now in the middle of the room. On it was scattered cards, poker chips, and smoldering cigars in ash trays next to bottles of beer. And sitting around the table were the missing men. While Roger laughed outright at the looks on the faces of the unexpected arrivals, Jim, Vince and Frank presented chagrinned smirks. Hank looked downright guilty as he stood up and faced the women and the sheriff. Only J.B. looked perturbed at the interruption, grumbling, "Hi, Mike." He looked up at his foreman. "Oh, sit down, Hank. It's your turn to deal."

The women stepped aside so the sheriff could enter further into the room, figuring that he might have something to say. The men thought this as well, uncertain whether or not they were in for a tongue lashing. But when the men saw Mike Cody trying valiantly to suppress a smile, they relaxed.

Jim asked him, "Want to join us?"

"No, thanks. I came out here with Lucy and Emily to show them the bunk house. I thought it was still as I'd left it."

J.B. and Vince looked at the women and back to the sheriff. Their surprise was obvious, and Hank was outright scandalized at the thought that Cody would do any such thing with the women. Frank and Jim, knowing well their wives, didn't even look up from their cards.

The sheriff was quick to defend himself. "It was their idea."

Lucy moved over to the group and walked around the table, looking down at their hands with the best non-committal poker face any of them had ever seen. She was, after all, a long-time Virginia City professional dealer, and an occasional player. Her only comment as she turned to face the rest of the room was a noncommittal, "Hmmm!"

Emily said, "Sheriff, maybe you could describe again the placement of the bed, table, and the body as you saw it."

Instead of immediately returning to their game, the men variously relit their cigars, got another bottle of beer from the kitchen, blew their nose, and stretched their backs. Even after they went back to playing, they listened to what was being said. A couple of them also kept a cautious eye on the sheriff.

Cody walked through the room, painting a clear picture of the way it had been when Victor had been found.

When he finished, Lucy asked, "And the whiskey in the glass was tested, right?"

"As much as Doc could. It was also fed to a rat and a rabbit. They were fine. Only odd thing was that the glass had been wiped free of hand prints."

Emily walked to the back where she could look out the window. "And other than the rumpling of the bed clothes, you didn't see any sign of a struggle?"

"Just that strange mark on the side of his head. There was no particular shape to it, just general redness that Doc said probably would have turned into quite a bruise if he'd lived longer."

The sheriff was surprised when Lucy showed more interest in his comment than he thought it warranted. She walked around the perimeter of the room, looking closely at everything within sight, even looking inside the armoires.

After a few minutes of this, the sheriff couldn't keep his curiosity in check. "Are you looking for something in particular?"

"Yes." But she didn't explain, and the sheriff chose not to question her further. Not only because he didn't want to admit he didn't see her point, but also because he didn't want any of the men to hear what she might say.

After the women had spent all of fifteen minutes in the room while taking in even the smallest detail, the sheriff led them toward the door. He stopped briefly by the table that had been used by Victor, but spent only a moment there before approaching the gamblers. No one looked up, and he proceeded to the front door.

As he prepared to follow the women out, J.B. called to him. "You know where we are if you need us."

Cody didn't answer back, unsure if J.B. was baiting him or mocking him. Once back in the house, the sheriff excused himself, announced that he had business in town, and left as suddenly as he had arrived. He was well down the road before he remembered that he hadn't asked Lucy to explain what she had been looking for in the bunk house. Oh, well, he'd do it the next time he saw her.

Emily stood at the front window, watching the sheriff ride away. "Well, that was interesting. Do you think anything new occurred to him?"

"If it was about the mark on Victor's head, I don't think so."

As Emily walked toward the kitchen, she told Lucy, "Well, if it hasn't occurred to him yet, he'll probably get there eventually without our help. The man's not lacking brains."

"True." Sniffing the air, Lucy smiled. "What do you suppose Sing is making for supper?"

As for the game in the bunk house, it felt to Roger as though it was winding down. He could sense a change in everyone's initial enthusiasm and asked, "Is Alex staying at the Hunewill ranch?"

J.B. shook his head. "No, he's in town. He's got several school friends whose parents invited him to stay over the weekend."

Roger nodded his approval. "That's nice of them. They probably realized that what was happening here might be too, um, intense for a child."

J.B. frowned, and it wasn't because of the cards in his hands. "He's not a child! He's a young man now."

Jim felt the need to come to Roger's defense, which made Roger smile. "Of course, he is. But you gave your permission, so you must feel he's better off away from here."

J.B. said nothing, Hank giving his opinion instead. "They probably want to pump him for information about what's going on."

No one was particularly perturbed at the thought. They all knew that Alex had not been around much over the last week. He therefore couldn't tell any nosey questioner anything worthy of spicy gossip.

While Frank was shuffling the cards, Hank sat back and looked around the table at his fellow players. "There's something about what happened that I haven't told anyone."

Everyone froze and stared at the foreman. J.B. focused on him with an intensity akin to a warning. It hit Roger hard that J.B. had something to hide. At the same time, the realization felt more like a validation. Almost from their first meeting, Roger had sensed something a little unscrupulous about their host, and it had been hovering at the back of his mind ever since. He wondered if its genesis lay far in the past.

Hank realized that he had created a sensation, so he continued quickly, talking directly to J.B. "Right after the horses were stolen, I mentioned to Vic that you were really upset. He smiled. As though he was happy that you were upset. But more than that, it was as though he knew something I didn't and he treasured the knowledge."

"Really?" J.B. gathered the cards just dealt him and held them in his hands. Seeing his hands trembling, he put them face down and crossed his arms across his chest as he looked at Hank.

"Yeah. It reminded me of a Christmas morning when I was a kid. I'd opened one of my two presents the day before, and then rewrapped it. It gave me a sense of power when everyone else was trying to guess what was in their packages. I liked that."

J.B. shrugged. "Vic was always a strange guy."

Hank merely nodded as he picked up his cards and looked at them. No one else said a word, eager to move on from what they felt had been a conversation that should have remained between J.B. and Hank. And wondering why it hadn't been. After a few minutes, the intensity of the game took hold and everyone's focus remained on the cards.

Their supper that night was chicken pot pie with a flaky crust and lots of vegetables, and served with wilted cabbage quarters in a vinegar dressing. The meal was followed by diced fresh fruit drizzled with honey. Sing figured it was the only way he was going to get them to eat fruit. Not because he thought it particularly healthy, but so it wouldn't go to waste.

After such a filling meal, no one felt much like conversation, and the men had actually had their fill of cards for the time being. Jim, Frank, Vince, Roger and Emily decided to play a board game they found among the books on the hall shelves. It had become popular before the Civil War and was called *The Mansion of Happiness*. It utilized a board in two pieces that was shoved together to look like one, and was decorated with a colorful spiral track. It led to the middle where the player would find *eternal happiness*. By using a spinner to determine the player's advancement over titled squares, it avoided the use of dice. The creators had thought dice a tool of gamblers and the devil. Simply put, the players moved forward when landing on a *virtuous* square, and backward when landing on a *vice*. There was a lot of laughter and teasing as the game progressed, since they all found the rules exceedingly funny.

"WHOEVER possesses PIETY, HONESTY, TEMPERANCE, GRATITUDE, PRUDENCE, TRUTH, CHASTITY,

SINCERITY...is entitled to Advance six numbers toward the Mansion of Happiness. WHOEVER gets into a PASSION must be taken to the water and have a ducking to cool him... WHOEVER possesses AUDACITY, CRUELTY, IMMODESTY, or INGRATITUDE, must return to his former situation till his turn comes to spin again, and not even think of HAPPINESS, much less partake of it."

To avoid the raucous hilarity emanating from the kitchen, J.B. and Lucy retired to the back porch. They put their feet up on foot stools and watched the sun sink in the west, casting the porch with gentle crepuscular light that was not unlike the softness of candlelight. Neither Lucy nor J.B. spoke for some time, each lost in their own thoughts. When J.B. finally spoke, it was almost jarring. But then Lucy heard in his voice a suppression of strong emotion.

"Lucy, do you think God makes us pay for our sins by casting us into a place of torture called Hell?"

She kept her voice low, not far above a whisper. "I don't think people have to wait until they die. I think life does that to us, one way or another, whether we're tortured by guilt, or the self-justified fouling of our lives. Someone once classified our life experiences as 'like produces like'."

"Do you think it's proportional?"

She was startled by how worried he seemed by the idea. "You mean punishments that are an eye for an eye?"

"Sort of." He was barely talking loud enough for her to hear him. It would have helped if he had not kept his face turned away from her.

She refused to give him the hollow comfort of some platitude. "I've seen a lot of situations in my life that sure seemed like equal justice."

"Oh, hell!"

The irony of his oath struck Lucy as funny, but she realized it had come from a place of pain and she didn't laugh. She looked over at him, and in the dim light saw that he was looking past the barns to his property as it stretched beyond the buildings and corrals. She wondered what had occurred to put him in such a pensive mood. She remembered once hearing a man tell the bartender in the saloon where she worked that the *black dog* was biting at his soul. Was the concept of divine punishment something J.B. often contemplated?

Marshalling her courage, Lucy asked, "I noticed the other day that you had a very strong reaction to the mention of 1871. Was I correct?"

J.B. hesitated, looked at her, then quickly away. He twisted the snake-head ring on his little finger. "You're right. That was a very difficult time in my life. It was just before I turned twenty and I met Alex's mother."

"And then bought this land," she completed the idea.

"That's right."

"You were pretty young to have had enough money to buy so much land and build on it. Your wife's brother must have been very generous."

"I'd come into an inheritance from my father. And I had some other money waiting for me."

Thinking that an odd way of phrasing it, Lucy redirected the conversation. "That was a particularly bad time for the county, too, wasn't it? I mean, there was that September's big Nevada State Prison escape of a couple dozen prisoners. And there was a big shootout near Monte Diablo creek that flows into a lake."

Again, a long pause from J.B. "Yeah, they call it Convict Lake now. But they recaptured almost all of those who escaped."

"I heard some were hanged near Bishop at the north end of the Owens River Valley."

"Just two." His voice had taken on a raspy quality. "Various things have been written about it, some accurate and some not."

There was a long pause, and Lucy recognized his discomfort. Changing the subject, she said, "I wish the girl that works for me was as good a cook as Sing. She's good, but not nearly in Sing's class."

But what she had been thinking about during the long silence had nothing to do with cooking. She was thinking that some of the convicts had been in prison for robbery, and the stolen money had not all been recovered. She wondered if J.B. had known any of the prisoners, or if maybe he had even been related to one of them.

She concluded that whatever the cause of J.B.'s introspective mood, it would probably soon be pushed to the back of his mind where he didn't have to think about it. Even so, she wondered if he would someday recall their conversation about consequences when whatever guilty thing that plagued him finally caught up with him.

Since her youth, Lucy had thought much about this whole subject of consequences. She had once committed what society deemed the most unforgiveable sin. But when she looked back on what she had done, she knew it had been a situation of self-preservation, with no alternative action available. So, although she maintained regret, along with a slight scar on her cheek as a reminder, she carried no guilt.

Emily had a restless time getting to sleep that night, with strange ideas flitting through her mind. The hotel faced Main Street, but their room was upstairs and at the back, so night noise from the saloons was not a problem. When she did finally get to sleep, a bad dream awakened her. She could feel her heart beating hard even though she couldn't remember the particulars of the dream. For several minutes, she sat up in the bed with her mind racing. Finally, she pulled on a robe and raced to Lucy's room, knocking on the door, and not caring if she was disturbing anyone.

A bleary-eyed Jim opened the door a crack. "Emily? Is something wrong?"

"No. I need to talk to Lucy."

"I thought she was in your room. A while ago she put on her robe and left our room."

Emily stared at him for several seconds before managing a sharp "Oh!" She then fled down the steep stairs, finding Lucy alone in the chilly lobby, the glow of daylight just beginning to show through the window. Lucy was curled up at the end of a small sofa with her legs beneath a light throw pulled down from the back.

"Emily? Is something wrong?"

"No, no." Emily sat in the arm chair next to Lucy. "I just think I've solved what went on at the ranch that fateful weekend. And why."

"Yes. I think I have, too. And if we're both thinking the same thing, and we're right, it's very disturbing. That's why I came down here. I wanted to think it through before I said anything, even to you."

"I know what you mean. It seems so dastardly and yet tragic, too." She glanced at the big clock on the wall over the counter, the hands showing a quarter after five in the morning. No wonder there was no fire in the big pot-bellied stove. Her voice barely above a whisper, Emily said, "I think ..."

Gunfire erupted out on the street. Men shouted, horses and women screamed, and heavy boots pounded along the boardwalk. It brought the hotel's manager hurrying from his room behind the lobby while pulling on pants over his long-johns. He was in such a state that he didn't even notice the women in his lobby.

It also brought half a dozen people downstairs from the floor above, among which were Jim and Frank in the lead. More disturbing was the sight of a large, angry woman with gray hair in cloth curlers and face cream unsuccessfully hiding an angry scowl. Her left hand held a wad of flannel nightgown and robe, while also supporting a .40-44 Winchester rifle on her shoulder. Her other hand ran along the railing of the stairs.

The people from the hotel reached the front porch just as Emily and Lucy claimed the front window. They were in time to see Sheriff Cody restraining two young men who looked to be in their late teens. They were in the middle of the street with several people, both on horses and on foot, watching the source of commotion being subdued.

A man on the sidewalk called out, "Slap the cuffs on 'em! Then do the same to their parents!"

Another man shouted, "They both need a good tanning in the wood shed!"

A deputy put handcuffs on the larger and more vocal of the two boys, who was loudly proclaiming the injustice of the moment. The sheriff clamped a hand on the arm of the other one, a restraint more powerful than mere handcuffs would have been. In fact, the young miscreant's eyes were wide with fear and he was looking as though he deeply regretted that morning's activity.

As soon as the two boys had been led away, those from the hotel returned to their rooms, the large woman proclaiming with fervor her disappointment at having been unable to use her new shotgun. On her way up the stairs, she described a vivid and somewhat blood-thirsty picture of what she would have liked to do with that gun. Frank could be heard reassuring the woman that her mere presence most likely helped calm the boys enough that the sheriff could corral them, ignoring the fact that they were already under control when they exited the hotel. Whether or not she was pacified, the woman uttered a loud "Humph!" and slammed the door to her room.

The dawn having made a full appearance, Lucy told Emily, "We'd better get dressed."

"Why?" Emily asked in mocking wonder. "You don't think our presence in robes is appropriate attire for greeting those arriving for breakfast?"

Starting up the stairs, Lucy was quick to respond. "If it's men and they get a gander at you, my dear, they might stay through to supper."

Frank could hear them coming up the stairs, their laughter filling the upstairs corridor. He was used to hearing Emily and Vince's wife, Charlotte, laughing and joking with one another. He also knew that Emily would be missing Charlotte. So he was pleased that she and Lucy were enjoying one another's company. It made him feel a little less guilty about spending so much time with Vince and the other men.

Jim had lingered out front, enjoying the cool fresh air of the early morning. He was about to retreat inside when a stage pulled up out front, and he walked over to assist the driver unload the boot of luggage. Four men and a woman alighted, handed their dusters to the driver and stretched their limbs as they looked around at the town. One man among them waved to someone across the street, and Jim assumed he was a townsman.

By way of comment to no one in particular, one of the men said, "Those sure were some nice T-bones on the hoof that we passed coming into town. I'm hungry enough to eat a whole steer."

The stage driver nodded. "Yep, they'll be off to the slaughter house soon."

The woman gripped the arm of her husband. "Oh, Herbert! Those poor animals!"

The stage driver, his look one of disgust, shook his head and walked forward to his horses. But the local man turned to her, his impatience as clear as his sharp words. "If you don't weep at your dinner table as you cut into your meat, don't weep as you look at the animals in the pasture!" With that, he picked up a small satchel and walked toward nearby Sinclair Street.

The woman's husband hid his smile by turning away, commanding, "Come on, Edna." The chastened lady gathered her skirts, left to carry her own suitcase as she followed a bemused Herbert into the hotel, although she was careful to use the "Ladies Entrance". Jim hurried upstairs, eager to repeat to Lucy the exchange he had witnessed.

After a quick breakfast, Jim and Frank rode their horses back to the Double R. However, Lucy and Emily lingered over their coffee. The waiter hesitated as he refilled their cups, unsure if it was proper for him to allow two unescorted women to remain. Since they had been with men when entering, he decided not to make an issue of it. Besides, they had been staying in the hotel for several nights.

"I haven't heard anything about Sara's burial," Lucy said.

"Has the sheriff signed a death certificate?"

Lucy shrugged. "I don't know."

"Well, I'm sure we'll know when we need to know."

With that bit of philosophical acceptance, they decided to head out to the ranch. At the stable, Emily took up the reins of their rig after Mr. Waltze helped them climb in. There was never a scarcity of courteous men when a lady needed assistance, and Lucy and Emily always made sure to profusely thank any such gentleman. Courtesy toward women was an accepted code of behavior, such as a man walking on the street side of a woman, or rising when a lady entered or left their presence. And no man would ever think of preceding a woman through a door.

This being routine, Lucy had once commented to a friend, "I'd be happy to forego all of that if men would allow women to vote." Because until women did indeed have the vote, it would be men who would dictate much of how women lived their lives.

Emily decided to detour down Kingsley Street on their way out of town. Other than several well-maintained houses with big barns behind, and the schoolhouse near Kingsley and School streets, there wasn't much of interest. However, it was notable that one of the houses was in much more need of repair than the others, although the red barn behind it was in the process of receiving a new roof. They knew from Mrs. Turner that this was the home that had housed Sara, so they came to a stop.

Out front of the home's small front yard was an extremely thin young girl of about nine, hoeing weeds in a meager vegetable garden. Emily waved to the child. "Good morning. You're doing a fine job on those weeds."

The girl looked up, moved strands of pale hair aside from her damp face, and gave the women a shy smile. Her dark, smokey eyes and red lips promised a mature woman of some beauty, but at the moment she was simply a skinny child in a dirty brown dress trying to keep control of a hoe much taller than herself.

Emily told her, "My name's Emily, and this is Lucy." Lucy leaned across Emily and said, "Hello."

"What's your name?" Emily asked.

"Irene."

"Well, Irene, you're very pretty, and I think your garden will be happy with all your hard work."

Just as the girl smiled, standing up a little straighter, a large man with a long, whisp of a beard came out of the house. His white shirt hung loose almost to his knees, and his long white hair was uncovered. Slamming the door behind him, he stomped down the steps and in three strides was next to the girl. His words carried far beyond the yard. "Here, you worthless child, what's keeping you from your work?"

"Sorry, father." The girl quickly began working the hoe between the rows of stubby turnips. The man glared at the women with a scowl so venomous that it brought chills to them both.

Emily mumbled, "Sorry", and quickly encouraged the horse forward.

Having seen off the intruders, the man pounded his way back up the path and into the house, the strong breeze blowing his long beard sideways as his shirt flapped around him. Looking back at him as they rolled away, Lucy pictured a wrathful prophet having disbursed the heathens.

Emily had been deeply moved when noticing the look of disappointment on the child's woe-begone face as the kind ladies started forward. Feeling tears come to her eyes, Emily refocused on the road ahead.

But Lucy continued to watch her. And when the girl looked up at the house, Lucy saw something unexpected in the expression of one so young; something dark and dangerous. And once again she felt chills that were not prompted by the weather.

Upon reaching the ranch, one of the first things Lucy and Emily did was to ask Sing if he'd heard anything about a funeral for Sara. He looked down at the dough he was rolling out on the kitchen island, then over at Mrs. Lewis's bedroom door.

"She bury Miss Sara yesterday afternoon. No one invited. J.B. only find out this morning."

"Why keep it so secret?"

He shook his head, obviously upset about what had taken place. "Mrs. Lewis say she not want Sara to be a ...spectacle?" He looked at Lucy. "I don't understand word."

Lucy pulled out a chair at the kitchen table and sat heavily, feeling a deep sorrow for Mrs. Lewis. "I think she meant that she didn't want people who didn't know Sara to come to the funeral just out of curiosity. After all, she'd be the third person buried who died here at the ranch."

"And," Emily added, "Sara worked here, which in itself would garner curiosity. Poor Mrs. Lewis!"

Sing frowned. "Maybe, but it still not right!" His rolling pin pressed down hard on the dough until it was sheet thin.

"But Sing," Emily told him, "Mrs. Lewis was there to witness the burial, and she was Sara's only relative. And anyone who actually wants to show respect can visit the grave whenever they want to."

Sing took a deep breath and nodded. "Okay, yes."

Nothing more needed to be said. The rules of another game had been sufficiently explained to allow it to be put away.

# CHAPTER 11

## BLUFF OR FOLD?

It was a relief for the men to get into town on such a pleasant Saturday morning. The town was active, filled with wagons, horses, and people. Those from outlying ranches and homesteads had come in for supplies, and therefore a number of spring wagons were being loaded in front of shops and markets. Other wagons were being unloaded of home-grown produce, eggs, pork, and dairy. Most of it would be traded for staples like flour, sugar, salt, and leavening. Even spices would be obtained, most common of which was pepper, as well as nutmeg that came in the shape of a small nut that could be grated into the food.

As they rode down Main Street, J.B. raised a hand in greeting to men sitting on chairs outside the barber shop while awaiting their turn. All but two of them waved back. Mrs. McKinney, the milliner, was just opening her door to ladies wanting new bonnets, although one distressed woman carried a large straw hat in need of repair after what looked like a tussle with her dog. The talkative cooper in a small shed was banging together barrels and selling them as soon as they were completed, his customers laughing at his salty brand of humor.

Nearby, men visited outside the big, weathered shed of the Hughes Blacksmith Shop, its wide double doors fully open. The smell of wood smoke and hot iron carried on the breeze into town. Several horses were tied to a rail out front while waiting for new shoes, their owners enjoying refreshment at the nearby Stanton Saloon. More than one lady walking by cast a quick glance in the direction of the handsome and muscular blacksmith before passing on.

The night before, the street sweeper had cleared Main Street of the previous week's debris and dropping. He had been followed by the water wagon sprinkling the street to keep down the dust. It was therefore a good day to gather in small groups on the sidewalk for a quick chat, a bit of gossip, or inquiries about the health of friends. It was an accustomed opportunity to reestablish casual contacts while also getting errands done. In other words, a typical summer day in a small town where knowing as much as possible about what's going on, and who it's going on with, may at some point be useful knowledge.

J.B. was in an exceptionally good mood, noticed and wondered about by the others. What they didn't know was that he was feeling the lingering effect of an unexpected conversation with Lucy the evening before. She had joined him at the small corral where Hank and Mort were working with a young horse. After a few minutes, Lucy had apologized to him for them all staying such a long time beyond what he had originally planned.

"This was supposed to be a weekend gathering of men to play cards," she had told him. "But here we still are, intruding into your life."

J.B. had honored her with the rarity of a sincere smile, charmed by the warmth of her kindness. "My dear, it's been a pleasure. If you had not shown up, that might not be true. But your presence has made this week much more bearable than it otherwise would have been."

Although touched by his words, Lucy's lingering impression of that conversation had not been one of reassurance. J.B. had been pleased when she had received his comment with a gentle, demure smile. Little did he know that she had practiced such an ultra-feminine response in front of a mirror years before when she had realized that it softened her oft-expressed unfeminine opinions. It also served as a response when she knew someone was trying to influence her with nonsense.

Their conversation had left Lucy wondering why her approval was important to him. Of course, she was willing to do anything that would make their on-going ordeal of waiting a little easier, because she knew that as soon as the three deaths were dealt with appropriately, they would all depart for their respective homes. And J.B. would be alone to deal with the lingering repercussions of it all. There would always be those who would wonder if the resolution had been correct, and if maybe J.B. had been more involved than acknowledged by the law.

In fact, as the men from the ranch continued down Main Street that Saturday, they noticed every eye turn toward them. Although some raised a hand in greeting, others quickly turned away in a pretense of not having seen them. They turned down School Street and proceeded to the area behind the gleaming white court house.

J.B., Jim, Frank and Vince entered the sheriff's office next to the jail. It was actually the end of the house nearest the jail, allotted the current sheriff by the county. The men were eager to see if there was an update on the deaths so they could begin making plans to get back to the regular routine of their lives. They were disappointed to find the sheriff away, and his deputy not knowing when he would return.

Roger had remained with the horses out front on Bryant Street. His back to the courthouse, he looked at the stone jail with its webbed iron doors and barred windows. As small and cramped as it was, it was still better than the old wood and stone, two-cell jail that had held his father back in January of '79.

What his father had endured then and afterwards had resulted in a dire form of pneumonia that had taken over a year for his full recovery. It had followed the difficult war years of Jim being separated from Lucy and Roger. His long recovery had only lengthened Lucy's time of grief, since she had still thought her beloved husband dead.

But for Roger, who had secretly seen to his father's recovery in Bodie, it had been an opportunity to bring father and son together as men of equal standing. At the time, Roger's guilt at keeping his mother away from Jim had been balanced by his good intentions. It had been months before the doctor was sure that Jim would survive. And even then, the notorious town had been plagued by rampant disease to which Roger refused to expose his mother. Consequently, it had been a time of great trial and uncertainty, about which the family seldom referred. The stone jail was, however, an unavoidable reminder.

This was brought home as Roger watched the men return to their horses. Vince and Frank, unaware of remembered trauma by the others, barely glanced at the jail. Jim kept his eyes straight ahead as he walked, even averting his eyes from Roger as he took the reins from his son's outstretched hand. It was J.B. who couldn't hold back a slight shudder as he glanced at the jail, although only Roger observed this.

As soon as they were all mounted, they proceeded back to Main and ended up once again at the Court House Corner Saloon. Roger caught up to Vince, the last of them to enter, and drew him back to the porch. "Vince, would you mind telling the others that I have a headache? I'm going back to the ranch to lie down."

"Sure. No problem. You sure you'll be okay?"

"Oh, yeah. I just didn't sleep very well last night."

As Roger rode out of town and into the meadows, he urged his horse into a lope. His headache was actually very slight. He reasoned that he had just spent too much time around J.B. and his angst over all that had happened at the ranch. Roger had once been told that too much drama wasn't good for a man. It had been meant as a warning about spending too much time with women, but he now realized it was more general than that. However, once he was out in the cool, fragrant breezes of the meadows, his head almost miraculously cleared and he felt fit once again.

When the three men entered the saloon, only one man was standing at the near end of the bar. His spurs, dusty slouch hat, stained bandana and blue shirt buttoned to the neck, and denim pants crusted with what looked like blood labeled him as a cow hand. But the gun in his waist band at the back made them wonder what else he might be.

Vince, always keen to note details, saw that there were *jinglers* on the man's spurs so they would make a bell-like noise when he walked. Only someone who wanted to stand out, wore them. Or they might have been a gift from a sweetheart who wanted him to remember her always. Each of the men concluded that this was a man to be avoided, and they all headed to the far end of the bar, hoping the man wouldn't take offense.

Vince kept an eye on the man as he finished his beer, tossed two-bits on the bar, and walked out. The sound of his spurs may have faded away, but the smell of him lingered, and the bartender waved the air with a large paper fan. But not until he saw through the window that the stranger had mounted his horse and ridden east toward the bridge.

While the men were hearing from Jim a briefed explanation of why he had a mixed appreciation of Bridgeport, given his experiences there in the past, Lucy came down the steep stairs of the Leavitt House. She glanced into the dining room, but crossed to the entry door and ventured out onto the front porch. She always enjoyed the freshness of the early morning air.

Leaning against the corner post of the small overhang, she smiled while taking in the tableau of busy shops, men and women stopping for a quick visit, and wagons moving sedately down the street. Beyond the courthouse lot and the old cemetery behind Bryant Hall, she could see a sheep herder and his two dogs moving a small flock of sheep north down Emigrant Street.

There was no conflict here between sheep men and cattle men, as long as everyone understood that it was primarily cattle country. And as long as the Basque sheepherders made sure to never encroach into the pastures set out for cattle. It helped that there was enough pasturage north and south of town for any grass-eating critter.

Lucy's far view from the hotel porch was that of the Sweetwater Mountains, through which the East Walker River flowed toward and around the town. Lucy remembered it following their stage down the toll road. At the brief stop at the toll house, backed by the huge dark wall of the Dardanelles, the river had churned along its base as it continued on its way toward Bridgeport.

She chuckled at the fact that some hearing the word *river* might picture the wide Missouri. No, here in the West, it was more like a wide creek. But it was a life source for people of the tribes, towns and ranches; a twisting, writhing silver stream snaking its way through the rocky clefts of narrow canyons on its way through the meadows.

Lucy took a deep breath, feeling a welling up of contentment. There was an early morning tang to the meadow-scented air that belonged only to that area in summer, a combination of rich damp earth and lush vegetation of many varieties. A passing lumber wagon left behind the pitchy aroma of fresh cut wood. It mixed with the aroma of fresh bread baking in the hotel's kitchen, and the wet hay and horse coming from the stable next door. Surprisingly, it wasn't unpleasant.

She was reminded of her youth spent on the other side of the Sierra, traveling through so many of the gold rush camps back in the 1850's. Each town had offered its own identifying smell, not all of it appealing. But underlying each one had been the comforting tang of wood smoke and frying bacon.

After arriving on the east side, her favorite smell had become the pungency of rain-washed sagebrush. She chuckled at that, because when crossing the country by wagon train in her teens, she and so many others had loved that smell when first encountering it. Then, after days and days of its unrepentant presence, they had found it repugnant.

Three women walked past, two with their long skirts held out with several petticoats, something many women in the west had reduced to one. But all of the women's skirts were of a practical length above the dirt. It was easy to tell which of them wore a corset; they were the ones who stood more erect than those who did not. Otherwise, the boning would cut into flesh. Now that it was summer, women would be wearing their lightest cotton skirts and waists, although the collars would of course grip the throat and the sleeves extend to the wrists. And dress shields would be difficult to keep in stock on store shelves, easier to wash than a whole garment.

Lucy looked down at what she was wearing. It practically advertised her morning plans; a proper lady's riding outfit of tall boots, below-calf split skirt, white waste accented with a simple broach at the throat under a short leather vest in lieu of a jacket. A small, simple bonnet with no decoration was anchored by pins to hair that was swept back from her face. This was the prescribed simple apparel for a proper lady on horseback, even one so bold as to insist on riding astride.

A man came out from the hotel, his full beard neatly trimmed and his hair clean under an old hat that clearly wasn't She had seen him in town before, as well as every day in the hotel where he had his breakfast.

"Good morning, Mrs. Murphy."

"Good morning. Lovely morning, isn't it?"

He raised a brow as he said, "You're dressed for riding, I see."

Not hearing condemnation in his voice, she answered readily. "Yes. My husband and I are riding to Bodie for the day. I was just wishing that we were going up to the twin lakes for a picnic instead."

"Ah, yes. A visit to the old man of the mountain."

"I beg your pardon?"

"Haven't you noticed that the crest of the Sawtooth Range looks like a face looking up at the sky?"

"I have, actually. But I just thought it my vivid imagination."

The man laughed. "No, it's there. It's a Piute legend. You see, a very long time ago they say tribes on the other side of the mountain were a great danger to the local tribes of Piute, and it led to many battles. Then a big earthquake occurred, lasting several days and nights. When the mountain rose up, they claimed that the Great Spirit was throwing it up between the tribes so they couldn't reach each other to fight. When the shaking stopped, one ridge had a face looking up at the sky. The Indians claim it's a good spirit there to watch over and protect them from harm."

"I love stories like that. Although I must say that I think it looks more like a woman. Like a mother watching over her children."

"I think that says more about you than it does the legend. After all, fathers like to protect their children, too."

Lucy smiled at him. "You're absolutely right."

The man tipped his hat and crossed the street to Brown's Store, dodging between the traffic with practiced ease. Lucy entered back into the hotel and settled at a table in the dining room where she could look out the front window while waiting for Jim. He had wanted to see the sheriff with the others before joining Lucy for their ride. With a cup of coffee and a glorious sticky bun before her, she was content to wait as she contemplated the day ahead. Once back home, the one thing she would always comment on was the good food available in Bridgeport, no matter where you were.

Jim finished his beer, told the others he would see them the next day, and quickly headed out to join Lucy. Frank and Vince were left with J.B., who was sunk in thoughts he wasn't open to sharing. Therefore, seeing that the billiard table was free, the two friends moved over to it and began a game. Not long after, two men came in and, disappointed at finding the table in play, started to move away. Vince, however, recognized them as men who had attended Victor's funeral. The one with a short beard and buckskin pants, in his early forties, had been the man Lucy had engaged in conversation. Vince told him that he and Frank would be happy to start over with a new game. The men were pleased to accept.

These men had been friends since the early 1860's, back when there had been only a few buildings on the east side of the river. In those first years, the building of a real town on the west side had been more a goal than an imminent reality.

Introducing themselves as Amasa Bryant and By Day, the men shook hands all around, sliding immediately and comfortably into first names, usually done only after some acquaintance. Amasa Bryant, or

A.F. as everyone in town called him, was a man in his early sixties, with muttonchop sideburns that were less full than they once had been, and a hairline that had receded to the back of his head. However, there was about him a youthful energy, and a kindness, that immediately made one want to be his friend.

A.F. offered to get beers for them all. Noting his slight Boston accent, Vince asked him if he had indeed hailed from that part of the country. He received in answer a big smile and a nod. When A.F. returned with their drinks, Vince declared that his generosity gave him the first break.

"Thank you, sir. I'd be delighted." And A.F. bent over the table, his cue sending the ivory balls scattering in all directions. Several fell into the open-weave, crocheted pockets hanging below the table's dark wood frame.

Seeing this, By Day nodded with approval. In contrast to his friend, he had only a moderately full moustache, his blond hair giving him the appearance of relaxed casualness. That is, until one looked at his eyes, which reflected a shrewdness that had been the bulwark of a successful life. But it had been one underlain with great compassion. The local tribes told stories about the time when they were getting to know, and trust, the white men arriving in their territory. By Day and N. B. Hunewill, along with a few others, had shown them that there was such a thing as an honorable white man.

After they had played for several minutes, Vince asked By Day, "Is it true that you were one of the early settlers here who smoked a peace pipe with the local Indians?"

Mr. Day chuckled. "Oh, yes, it's true. Several of us. Like West Towle, who sawed the wood to build his fine home at the east end of town. And Dave Hays, whose store you might have visited. And old Napolean Hunewill of the Circle H. We smoked their pipe and they ate our food, and everything's been fine between us since."

A.F. nodded. "It helps that we regularly give them new blankets and hire their women to work in our homes."

It was typical of their modesty that the two men didn't add details that would have shown themselves in a greater light. In 1863, after blacksmith T. B. Severence had erected a shop for the shoeing of oxen near the footbridge on the East Walker River, Mr. Bryant had built a store there. His friend Louis Ladd had followed suit by putting up a hotel frequented by freighters traveling up the Walker River Canyon. Then Joseph Kingsley had built an inn that would be used as the courthouse until a real one would be built.

A.F. had eventually owned enough land that he could give some of it to the County. It had included an acre of land on the north edge of town for a cemetery, and the land for the courthouse and jail. Even the corner with Bryant's Hall had been his, as was the building itself, brought there from Bodie. Years later his grandson would build a motel on that site called Slick's Court, and which would eventually become the Maple Leaf Inn. Most of Bryant's remaining land was north of the town in the lowlands surrounding the river flowing through the ranches there.

Besides being a landowner, however, he had also been the Post Master until the previous year; had been responsible for bringing telegraph lines to the town; and had been the County Supervisor responsible for moving Mono County records from Aurora after the settling of the boundary dispute between California and Nevada. No wonder, Vince thought, that the town had named a street after him.

George Byron "By" Day was acknowledged locally as one of the first white men to have settled in the meadows in the summer of 1859. In his late teens when he had left Gold Hill, Nevada, he wound up on an Indian trail through the Sweetwater Valley with pack animals for company. Upon reaching the meadows, he had worked for the area's first lumber company, whipsawing lumber and building fences. Meanwhile, he had recognized the possibility not only for abundant pasturage, but also for rich farmland where hay could be raised and cut for winter use. Over the years, he had hauled much of that hay to the mining towns of Monoville, Aurora and Bodie. He now owned 400 acres of land called The Upper Day Ranch, where he raised sheep and cattle with his wife Harriet, whom he had married in 1868.

Hank had given much of this background to Vince and Frank while they had been helping him in the barn. Hank had told them about several other townsmen as well, but not in the same detail as when he had talked about Bryant and Day. Having realized that it wasn't easy to earn respect from Hank, Vince and Frank knew they were in special company.

Trying to find a conversational opener, Frank commented to A.F., "I saw you with your granddaughter the other day."

A.F. laughed. "That was my nine-year-old daughter. I married a woman seventeen years my junior twenty years ago this October. She gave me Amasa Scott first, back in '75. We call him Ammi." He looked up at Vince. "And now I have my sweet Annie. You have kids?"

Frank nodded. "A daughter, Whitney. She'll be eight this December. Vince here has a boy, seven year old Steven."

"It's a real pleasure watching them grow up, isn't it?" A.F. chuckled. "Of course, Eliza does most of the raising. I've always had my businesses. Ole By here, he has two sons, Charlie and Harv."

"Kids are fun," Mr. Day told them. "I keep a couple very tame horses for little kids to ride. They have to learn sometime, and not all families can afford to keep more than one or two. Often, they're for pulling, not riding.'

Frank looked closer at Mr. Bryant. "We met before. Back when you had the West and Bryant Store in Bodie. My wife and I lived there back in '79 and '80." He looked over at Vince at the far end of the table. "And you must have known Vince Perry, too."

A.F. scratched one of his abundant side whiskers and looked more closely at Vince. "That's who you are! I thought I recognized you from somewhere. I used to store supplies in your warehouse. Well, isn't this like an old Bodie home-coming!"

Vince smiled, happy that he had finally been recognized. "It's okay. You used to interact with my workers most of the time."

By Day asked, "What are you fellas up to now?"

"We live in Lone Pine," Frank explained, "raising cattle mostly. And still doing a little gambling now and then."

Mr. Bryant turned to Frank. "You were a mining engineer when you lived in Bodie, weren't you?"

"Right. And I did some work up at Cerro Gordo before it shut down."

Mr. Day cut in. "About the gambling. You part of those staying at the Double R?"

"Yes." Frank's crooked smile accented his next statement. "Where three deaths have occurred lately."

A.F. looked at his new friends. "Well, I didn't want to say, but it has gotten tongues wagging."

"I'm sure it has. But it's taken place more around us than with us." Frank shot a look over at the bar where J.B. was slowly sipping a small glass of amber liquid and chatting with the bartender. "It's been particularly hard on him."

By Day nodded, put down his cue and walked over to stand at the bar. "Good morning, J.B. Can I buy you another?"

Somewhat surprised, J.B. simply said, "Thank you. That's very kind of you."

"Not at all. You've stood me a few over the years." Changing the subject, he said, "How are those horses doing after being returned?"

"Oh, they're fine."

"They didn't catch who stole 'em, did they?"

"Well, yes and no. We think it was Otto."

"The guy who died at your place? The one they say was poisoned?"

J.B. rolled his eyes. "That's gotten out there, has it?"

"Sure. Not something that's ever happened around here before. But why would he steal the horses?"

"We think he did it on behalf of someone else."

By Day shook his head, more in sadness than in surprise. He was too old not to have witnessed some odd acts of human nature. "If Otto was poisoned, who would have done that?"

J.B. finished the rest of the drink already in front of him as the bartender placed the second one next to it. "That's what we're trying to figure out. There were a number of people around. A couple of which are no longer with us."

It took Mr. Day a few seconds to catch on. "Oh, the wind is blowing in that direction, is it?" When J.B. merely shrugged, By Day asked, "How well did you know Victor?"

"Not very. We had a falling out some time ago. For the last few years, we seldom spoke even when we ran into each other in town."

"Well, he was a strange one." Mr. Day looked out the front window. "Hard to get to know him. My wife liked Mrs. Turner well enough, but was never comfortable around Victor for some reason." When he noted J.B.'s jaw tighten he wondered about it, but only added, "He could be pretty vindictive if he felt that he hadn't been treated right. I know that."

"Were he and Otto close?" J.B. had been wondering just how good a friendship had existed between the two men.

"I don't know about that. Oh, they knew each other. Drank together when Otto could get away from the ranch where he worked. Otto wasn't married, so they didn't socialize."

"Hey, it's your turn!" Amasa called out. By Day gave J.B. a pat on the shoulder and returned to the game.

Meanwhile, Jim and Lucy had started for Bodie, eager to visit a friend in the County Hospital located there. They were riding the horses hired by Frank and Vince at Bodie's Kingsley Stables so they could turn them in before the hire rate went up higher. They planned to take a stage back to Bridgeport late in the day. Jim several times commented that they had to be sure not to miss it, as few stages worked the town now, unlike during the boom when eight departures a day was common. J.B. had assured Frank and Vince that if they needed to use a horse after their return, he would provide them.

All of this had been Vince's idea after he had received a telegram from his wife, Charlotte, saying that she was on her way to join him in Bridgeport. J.B. was looking forward to meeting Vince's wife, having heard glowing accounts of her kindness and beauty. It made him wonder how these men had managed to find women of such high caliber when he had found it impossible both in his youth as well as after losing his wife.

Frank and Vince were pleased with Charlotte's arrival, as it meant they could accompany their wives back to Lone Pine. At least when they were allowed to leave Bridgeport. Not that they were legally constrained from leaving, but they knew it wouldn't look good for themselves or J.B. if they left before the deaths were fully resolved.

And, although none of them spoke of it, they all felt J.B. deserved some show of loyalty from someone. The townspeople didn't seem eager to supply it. However, those same townspeople wondered if the Double R guests were staying because they liked J.B., or if it was just something in their pioneer character that didn't allow them to abandon a wounded comrade.

The ride to Bodie was an enjoyable one, down Aurora Canyon over Table Mountain. This took them over the older route that by-passed Aurora and hit the Aurora/Bodie toll road north of Sunshine Station. There they stopped, glad of the rest at Hank Blanchard's big stone station that the old-timers called Half-Way House. It had been built as a main house with a separate row of small rooms that served as overnight accommodations for travelers and freighters. And all of it made from native stones, along with Aurora brick and mortar.

Lucy and Jim's first act was to water their horses at the big trough out front before turning their mounts out to feed in the corral. Only then did they allow themselves to enjoy a bite to eat, graciously offered them by Hank's wife. It was her art work on the walls, and Lucy took the time to admire each one of her paintings.

When Hank went out to greet another arrival, Jim turned to Lucy as she finished her coffee. "We're acting like the problems at the Double R have all been solved. It's like we've moved on from it."

"Oh, I don't know." She considered a moment. "But it is interesting that you referred to three suspicious deaths as *problems*. Still, we haven't moved on. We're just taking a break from the tension."

"And using a visit to Peter as our excuse."

"Well, dear, I really do want to meet your friend. You've talked about his kindness to you back when you were arrested. I think the least we can do is visit him in the hospital."

"You're right. I guess I'm just feeling a little guilty about leaving Roger behind to deal with it all. But Frank and Vince are with him."

"They're not that much older than Roger." She laid her hand on his and smiled up at him. "They've just developed a little more settled maturity."

Jim put a hand over hers. "Is that a polite way of saying that they've left behind their reckless youth, and our son hasn't?"

Lucy got up and walked to the stove, picking up the coffee pot with a cloth to protect her hand from the hot enamel. "More coffee, dear?"

Jim's only response was to laugh at his wife's refusal to be baited. But they had to be getting on anyway, so he let it pass. Thankfully, it was only a short ride into Bodie, at which point Jim gave a low whistle as they passed down the town's wide main street to the Kingsley Stables.

Jim pictured how packed the street had been only seven years before. "Boy, Bodie sure has changed."

"So have we," Lucy laughed. "The first time I was here was just before the boom. That was with Roger, who was displaying his gambling prowess in the few saloons that were here. You lived here for over a year right at its peak in '79 into '80." The minute the words were out of her mouth, she regretted it. She didn't want him thinking she was sniping at him for having kept her in the dark about his whereabouts back then. She had long ago let go of any resentment about that.

"Yeah, I saw it at its wildest time. Its best, as well as its worst, all at the same time." His tone didn't indicate that he had taken offense, and Lucy relaxed. "But I didn't see much of it for months. I was too sick." He shrugged, thinking of the jail in Bridgeport as he said, "And, well, other reasons to stay out of sight." He glanced up and down Main Street. "Most of these buildings were here, with some name changes since then, of course. And back then, we couldn't have ridden down Main without encountering dozens of wagons. There's only a population of 500 now, they say. Back then there was at least 8,000."

"And there was mud," Lucy laughed. "Oh my, the mud! But it's the dry season now, thank goodness."

"Back then, that didn't matter. Not with all the animals on the road."

Choosing to avoid that disgusting topic, they stopped in front of the stable, gave up their horses and began walking south on the sidewalk edging Main Street. The hollow thud of their boots on wood accompanied them as they walked, several times finding it necessary to step over a loose board higher than the rest.

Lucy stopped to look in the window of Harvey Boone's Store. Mr. Boone had a ranch in Bridgeport in the lowlands north of town and was courting Ada Stewart, the widow of pioneer rancher John Stewart. Ada had a house on the south side of Main Street at the west end, not far from the Turner house.

Preparing to turn right off Main onto Green Street, they came to an abrupt stop. Lucy pointed to the far corner. The Bodie House was gone. It had burned down only two months before, and all of its charred remnants had not yet been removed. Nothing would be built there again, eventually becoming just a weed-strewn lot about which future visitors would wonder. On the other side of that was a funeral home, and beyond that was The Miner's Union Hall just this side of a brick building that had once been the post office, which had moved further north. Jim smiled when he saw a number of men gathered outside of the Hall, glad that it was still a busy place.

"Oh, that reminds me," he told Lucy. "I got a telegram from our friend in Genoa who loaned us his horses for our ride to Bridgeport. He wanted to know if J.B. would like to buy them."

"Are they what J.B. might want?"

"He was fine with it and wired back his offer. I think it was fair."

"So that means we'll be taking the stage home?"

"I guess."

Jim was focused on navigating their path between the wagon ruts in the road, and leading Lucy around puddles. They were there to visit Peter Nye, a friend of Jim's from years before when both men had worked at the same sawmill. They turned down Fuller and looked into the distance at the two-story brick hospital where several horses and a spring wagon were tied to the railing out front.

Until recently, Peter had been one of Bridgeport's most esteemed citizens. It was Peter who had fashioned many of the architectural corbels and other details inside the Bridgeport Court House. Now, after a mild stroke and other health problems, Peter was a resident of the County Hospital.

Not always a favored place to be, those in charge when the hospital opened in 1879 on Mills Street had been Dr. Summers, responsible for staffing. Dr. Rogers, who had successfully treated dozens of cases of a particularly virulent form of pneumonia in its early years, had been his partner. However, after the death of an over-flow patient housed in a nearby hotel, the County's Board of Supervisors had established a County Medical Society with Doctors Davidson, Deal and Robertson as officers. In fact, Dr. Davidson had been the medic who had cared for Jim during his long illness.

In 1881, after continued complaints, Dr. Summers had barely managed to keep his contract with the County, and had been required to hire a nurse to be on duty at all times. The hospital, due to a need for greater sanitation, had also been moved to an empty brick building at the end of Fuller Street. It had at one time been the large home of the infamous Joseph DeRoche, who had owned a brickyard at that location during the boom. That was before he killed his mistress's husband, and ended up as the town's only vigilante hanging.

Peter Nye looked up from where he was sitting at a small table next to a window at the far end of the ward. Lucy's first impression was the word *thin*, both in physique, hair, and the hand that turned the pages of a newspaper spread out on the table where it caught the light. His other hand rested on his lap, the fingers curled as though not quite able to open all the way.

Peter looked up at Jim, frowning with the effort to recall how he knew this somewhat familiar man. Lucy held back by the door to the ward, not wanting to confuse him. Suddenly, Peter's brow cleared and he grinned.

"Jim Murphy, you old sun of a gun! How the hell are you?"

Jim sat down at the table and held out his hand to be shaken. "I'm fine, Peter. I see you've found a plum spot to come to rest." He didn't mention that Peter had been resting there for three years, partly because he was too ill and poor to be anywhere else.

"Ah, well, they say I had a little stroke. But I'm getting better all the time, and soon I'll be out of here. You still in Virginia City?"

"Yes." He looked over at Lucy still in the door of the ward. "And I want you to meet my wife." He motioned to Lucy and she joined them at the table while Jim dragged over another chair from beside an empty bed. "Peter, this is my wife, Lucy."

"Please, don't bother rising," she told him. "I'd rather sit. I'm so happy to meet you. Your friends in Bridgeport send their best regards."

"Oh, you've been there, have you?"

"Yes. We're staying out at the Double R with J. B. Roberts."

His face clouded. "Oh, him. Friends, are you?"

Jim was quick to answer before Lucy could reply. "Not really. My son and I were invited to play poker with him and two other men we know. That's all."

"Good." He ran his hand down his face, as though he had once had a long beard. "I shouldn't pass judgement on him, I guess. It's just that he's a bit too good at cards, and everyone knows so little about him."

Lucy leaned forward. "He was married when he came to the meadows, wasn't he?"

"Oh, yeah. The women folk said his wife was nice enough, but very shy and quiet. Didn't join in much. Then she got expecting with the boy, and she stayed out at the ranch the whole of her time. She did bring the baby into town once and the women went crazy over him. Then there was a long time when she wasn't seen, and then news came that she had died."

"That's so sad."

He looked at Lucy for a moment before speaking. "Well, don't be too sad."

"Why not?"

"Some said she didn't die, but that she just disappeared. Maybe left J.B. and the kid behind."

Lucy felt a tightening in her chest as the words of J.B. came flooding back to her whenever his wife had been mentioned. He had never used the word *dead*, or any of its related synonyms, such as *passed on*. But he had used the word *gone*.

# CHAPTER 12

## TWO PAIRS, QUEENS & KINGS

Jim didn't know how to respond to Peter's insinuations about J.B., but he did know how people loved to gossip about unfounded rumors that grew into fantastic theories. So he simply cleared his throat and looked around the room. "The hospital seems to have been cleaned up considerably since the County started doing regular inspections."

"Yeah. It helps that there's a nurse on hand all the time now."

Lucy asked, "When was the last time you were in Bridgeport?"

Peter frowned at the effort to be exact, settling for, "Not for some time."

"I was in the courthouse the other day," she told him. "The wood work you and the other workers did in the lobby downstairs is simply beautiful."

"Yeah, I'm right proud of that." After a brief recollection of memory, he said, "We used Spanish cedar on the stairs. Ten feet wide it is, so folks coming down from trials don't have to brush against those going up."

Indeed, the builders had presented the town with a magnificent structure, and one that would still be in use over 150 years later. The second floor was elegantly laid out with sixteen-foot vaulted ceilings, tall windows that reached almost that height and were framed in dark wood. Polished, dark wooden floors flowed throughout. The handsomely carved judges' benches in the two upstairs courtrooms were only slightly raised, and built long so the judge and his clerk could easily fit behind.

The judges' chambers were comfortably furnished, and there was a room set aside in which attorneys could work. Space downstairs allowed for eight offices, two fireproof vaults for important papers, storerooms, and a pump room to run the 3,000-gallon water tank on the roof. In this important County building, fire protection was important, but it also allowed for water to flow into bathroom basins, a rare luxury when the courthouse was completed in 1881. More practical were the twenty cords of wood kept out back in winter to feed the stoves and allow business to continue even when the temperatures dipped below zero.

Peter smiled with pride as he thought back on his days working on the courthouse. Other parts of his memory might be gone, but he was grateful that this one was still with him. "Glad you like it. A lot of Bodie money helped build it. 'Course, most of its trials in the beginning were because of Bodie troubles." He chuckled with great enjoyment at the thought. "There was a six percent property tax levied on the properties here just to help pay for it."

"Oh, dear." Lucy knew how much citizens in Bodie hated taxes.

"Oh, I don't remember anyone complaining too much about that. We all knew we needed a courthouse, and Bridgeport was after all the county seat. I had helped remodel the old American Hotel so it could be used as a courthouse, but it just wasn't big enough."

"You were the primary builder of the Allen House, weren't you?"

"Oh, yeah. Among other buildings, but I really enjoyed running the shingle mill with my brother Josiah. It was west of the river, just south of the new bridge. We had to sell out when I had my stroke in '74 that left me partially paralyzed."

Jim nodded. "Yeah, that was really tough."

"I recovered from that with Josiah's help. Well, enough that I could get around. The folks here and in Bridgeport raised money to help with my medical expenses. They said it was to show their gratitude for all I had done for the town when it was just starting out." His smile was bittersweet as he said, "I'm still here because I've had some kind of stomach problem. I should be going back to Bridgeport any day now." He jumped to another memory, saying, "I helped build the Allen House, too."

Remembering that the man had suffered a small stroke, and had forgotten that they had already acknowledged his work on the Allen House, Lucy changed the subject. "It's very nice. We're staying at the Leavitt House."

But Peter wasn't ready to move on. It had been a time in his life when he had been surrounded by friends, and memories of them had not been wiped away by the stroke. "Yeah, me and Charley Anton did much of the work. He makes coffins now. His house is just west of the Allen House. He used to have a saloon across the street from the Leavitt House, but in '83 he sold out to Fred Grimmer."

There was a dreamy, far-away look on his face, and Lucy was concerned that they were over-tiring him. But he was enjoying his memories. "Ole Sam Hopkins worked with us, too. He learned how to build at a shipyard in Maine. His granddaddy had owned a shipyard and was the first Commander-in Chief of the Navy when it was created by Congress at the beginning of the Revolutionary War. Sam served in the Civil War before coming out here. He wants to build boats for use on the twin lakes." He smiled and shook his head. "Lots of fine fellas I worked with. I miss 'em all."

After a long pause where Peter was visibly fighting for control of a quivering chin, he perked up and looked at Jim. "But I remember you, too. Back when you were here in Bodie during the boom. You and your son. How's he doing?"

"Very well. Married and with a little girl."

"So you're a granddaddy." His smile was warm and a little sad. "That must be real nice." A thought occurred to him then. "Say, didn't I hear about some people dying out at the Double R in Bridgeport?"

Jim told him briefly about what had taken place. Instead of Peter asking questions, he nodded his head several times. "Victor. Oh, yeah, Victor."

Before he could jump to another subject, Lucy asked, "Did you know Victor Turner?"

"Oh, sure. He came out to the hospital a couple of months ago. After he got through talking to Dr. Davidson, he stopped by to visit."

"What kind of mood was he in?"

Peter frowned in an effort to recall. "Funny you should ask. He was very down. Preoccupied, I guess you could say. But then he suddenly became agitated and muttered something about it being a good time for getting even. I asked him what he was talking about, but he just shook his head."

Jim asked carefully, "He didn't give you a hint as to what he had in mind?"

"No, but he did say something strange. He asked me if I thought him a clever man. Before I could answer him, he left right sprightly."

Lucy put a hand on his arm. "We mustn't tire you out. The nurse told me we shouldn't stay longer than half an hour and it's been all of that."

After saying their good-byes, all the while trying to ignore Peter's misty eyes, Jim and Lucy walked back into town. The first thing they did was purchase tickets out on the stage due to arrive in two hours "or there abouts". The ticket agent had learned the wisdom of never committing himself further than that.

Thinking the stage could arrive either earlier or later than what was chalked on the blackboard outside Boone's Merchandise Store, Jim and Lucy purchased crackers and cheese along with bottles of sweet sarsaparilla. Sitting on a sidewalk bench, they leaned against the rough wood planks of the building and settled down to watch the traffic on Main Street. They couldn't help but compare it to what they would have seen during the boom. What they had witnessed then had been a compaction of thousands of people on and along the street, day and night. In 1879, the Carson City to Bodie stage had run eight daily coaches through town. To maintained such a schedule, they had kept fifty-four horses stationed along the route at nine changing stops. On the street now were a few wagons, several riders and only a couple dozen people on the sidewalks. Which, they noted, were in desperate need of repair throughout the town.

Observing Lucy's frown as she scanned the area, Jim sought to draw her attention away from the town's deterioration. "It was nice to see Peter again. He's sure had a hard luck life."

"Oh?" Lucy turned to her husband with her curiosity sparked.

"He followed the gold camps back in '50, but not very successfully. He had a small ranch for a short time, but the crop failed the first year and although he made good money the second year, the next year he lost everything in floods."

"Oh, the poor man. How did he survive?"

"Well, after that he started a sawmill." He looked away from her. "But it broke down the next year. What with his mounting debts, and lumber depreciation, he was forced to sell out for what he could get, which wasn't much. When he came to Mono County in '58, he decided to work for wages by packing with Mr. Luther in Monoville. But he borrowed on his wages and fell behind repaying, so until the Aurora boom, he continued to work on commission for Luther. He followed the rush to Aurora, but eventually had to declare insolvency."

"Didn't he ever find success?"

"Oh, yes. In Bridgeport, where they valued his carpentry skills. And for a short time, when they were building businesses and homes, his shingle mill was pretty successful. Much of that was also shipped to Bodie during its growth. But, of course, all mining towns stop expanding at some point."

Lucy was glad she hadn't known all this about Mr. Nye before the visit, or she might have shown how badly she felt for him. And she was sure he wouldn't have appreciated any sign of pity. She would, however, have cause to remember this visit in '93 when Peter would suffer another stroke. He would return as a resident of the hospital, after which it would become the Poor Farm at the back of a small meadow on Green Creek Road. Not far from Bridgeport, it allowed old friends to visit him often. Peter would stay there his last seven years, the only resident of the facility.

On the way back to Bridgeport on the late afternoon stage, Jim and Lucy were accompanied by two men in old suits badly in need of a cleaning. The stage took the route out the south end of town, and stopped at John Murphey's station. He was the president of the Big Meadows and Bodie Toll Road, and his station at Murphey Springs had been the most popular rest stop on the route since the beginning of the boom in the '70's. Jim had met Mr. Murphey and his wife in the past, and was looking forward to introducing them to Lucy.

John had crossed the plains in a covered wagon, where he had met and married his wife. They had three sons, Ed, Lew and John, as well as a daughter, Birdie. Young John would someday be elected District Attorney and later a Superior Court Judge of Mono County.

While the stage driver watered the horses, it gave Jim and Lucy time to visit with the Murphey family. However, sooner than Lucy preferred, they climbed back into the coach and continued the lurching ride down the hill to Dogtown. After a short stop, they turned north toward Bridgeport on a good road. Two new passengers had replaced the previous two, but no one bothered to introduce themselves, so Lucy focused on the view from the window next to her.

Jim had placed her there so it would be his knees knocking into the men across from them. Stages were built to allow only fifteen inches for each passenger, and woe to anyone sitting across from a long-legged man, or next to someone wider than those allowed inches.

Lucy was suddenly filled with a longing to see Roger. However, it was not a case of simple maternal fondness. She was overcome by a general sense of disquiet, and it made her wonder what Roger might be getting up to while they were away. This near-psychic, disconcerting connection had occurred before, so Lucy knew better than to deny its validity.

"Jim, was Roger okay this morning?"

He looked at her in surprise, not for the first time wondering about the close affinity between his wife and son that had developed while he was absent from their lives. But he was also quick to reassure her. "Other than a little headache, he was fine. He went back to the ranch after our failed attempt to find the sheriff."

"Where did you and the others go?"

"The Court House Corner Saloon. But I didn't stay long, since I wanted to join up with you."

Lucy turned away from Jim and looked out the window. But she was smiling, having a hunch as to why Roger had returned to the ranch. Although it did nothing to quiet her anxiety.

When Roger arrived back at the ranch after leaving the other men at the saloon, he chatted with Hank and Mort while stabling his horse. Consequently, as he walked back to the house he had in mind a mental inventory of everyone's whereabouts. His parents were gone for the day, and everyone else was in town visiting or shopping. Most importantly, they were away from the house or were busy outside. Roger had decided to do a little sleuthing. He didn't fool himself into thinking that he was doing more than simple snooping, but *sleuthing* sounded better. Because it was to J.B.'s study that he boldly made his way.

He had seen J.B. lock his study every time he left it, even when remaining in the house. To Roger this seemed excessive, and his curiosity begged to be satisfied. Thankfully, when Sing had needed to get into the study to clean or retrieve dirty dishes, Roger had seen him reach into a beautifully woven Piute basket. It sat on a narrow table in the hall outside J.B.'s study door, where Sing could rest a tray while dealing with the door. Finding the key still in the basket, Roger used it and then put it back before carefully closing the door behind him. He considered locking it from the inside, but decided that if caught, it wouldn't allow him to offer a casual explanation that the door had already been open.

Roger wasn't looking for anything in particular, and didn't know what he expected to find that made such an invasion of his host's privacy necessary. He was simply working off a hunch that was too strong to deny. Part of his justification was that he thought he and his father had been used. He wasn't sure how or by whom, but it was a feeling that persisted. Not knowing how much time he had before possibly being discovered, he went first to the large mahogany desk facing the door, its back to a wall between two windows.

The wall was lined with shelves of books, some with tooled leather covers and others covered in stamped cloth. But it was a tall, gray ledger that attracted Roger's attention. He sat at the desk and opened it, finding columns of numbers under headings that reflected ranch expenses. A check mark next to each one evidently indicated those that had been paid. He quickly flipped through those pages, as it was the very last pages that he sought, knowing more about how those on the edge of legality functioned than would have pleased his parents.

He was proved correct, because he found a list of numbers with no title heading the page. There were three columns, one of initials substituting for names and two columns of figures. It was arranged so that across from each set of initials was a number, quite possibly a dollar amount. To the right of that was either a blank, the same number, or several small numbers that sometimes added up to the first, large number. When it did, a line underscored the accumulation.

It wasn't difficult to decipher this as loans of money that had been paid back, some over time, or not yet. He scanned the list of initials, looking for one set that started with a "V" and ended with a "T". Not far past the middle of the list he found them, and had to keep from whistling. The first, large column number was 500. The other column was blank and yet had a slash through it.

Seeing that the entry had been treated that way, unlike any other entry, Roger's mind raced with questions. If the debt had been paid back, why wasn't the full amount entered in that column? If it had not been paid back, what was the meaning of the slash? Roger realized that he was calling it a slash because that's the way the mark appeared; not a neat little dash, but rather placed with an almost violent application of the pen. Assuming that J.B. was the only one to have access to the ledger, it revealed him having been in a bad temper when he had made that mark.

After opening the drawers of the desk, which he was surprised to find unlocked, he found in the deepest drawer to the right nothing but a neatly arranged stack of papers. The top one had a set of initials in the upper right corner, the second letter being "A". Roger had seen those initials on the list in the ledger, and assumed that the stack corresponded in alphabetical order.

Feeling his heart beat harder, he started to reach into the drawer. But when a gleam of light from the near window caught something in the drawer, he froze. Looking closer, he saw that there was a long, pale hair lying across the pile from corner to corner. Roger pulled back as quickly as if it had been a snake with a rattling tail.

He took a deep breath and held it as he took up the hair and laid it carefully on the desk. Without removing any of the drawer's contents, he quickly and carefully peeled back the upper corner of the papers until he came to one with a VT on it. It was only a single sheet of paper, a note written on cheap paper in a scratchy schoolboy hand. It was short and to the point.

*"June '88 -- Ok, you SOB, you have me. I told you I would have the money for you soon, but since that is not good enough for you, I will go along with what you want. Then we are even. Friday night it is. You know where to find them. VT"*

Roger was rocked back in the chair, immediately seeing the note's implications. But he didn't take the time to think it through. He quickly replaced the note and the hair just as he had found them, then wasted no time getting out of the study. First, however, he made sure the ledger and the desk chair were exactly as they had been when he entered. He relocked the door, dropping the key into the basket before hurrying down to the great room. On his way, he grabbed a book off the hall shelf without even looking at it and flopped on a sofa with the open volume on his lap. Fortunately, he realized before anyone arrived back that the book was upside down.

His thoughts were reeling. As hard as he tried, he couldn't shake the conclusion that J.B. had colluded with Victor to steal the horses. But why? And why was there no mention of Otto in Victor's note? Roger could come up with no answers that made sense. Then he thought of his mother. Lucy would have reminded him that there was more involved, about which he simply didn't yet know. And that comforted him. *Yet* was the key word.

There was more to be uncovered, and he was determined to find whatever it was.

Meanwhile, Lucy had been glad of the brief stop in Dogtown, as she had found the rocking and jostling of the coach as it descended from Murphey Station unsettling to her stomach. Their two fellow passengers alighted from the coach near a trail to a cabin, just as they left the rock walls of Bridgeport Canyon. Being now the only passengers, it gave them a chance to talk without being overheard, and Jim was glad of it.

"I had a chance to visit with John Murphey outside when you were inside with his wife and kids. It seems that he knows...er...knew Victor. John saw Victor in town at the Wedertz Store the day before Victor left for the Double R tournament. John thought Vic looked nervous, and not at all well."

"In what way?"

"He said Vic had lost a lot of weight in a short time. When he was at the counter paying, Vic was pacing around behind him. After John paid for his supplies, he stood outside on the porch waiting for Vic. When he came out, John asked Vic to have a beer with him. He put a hand on John's shoulder and said, 'I'd better not. I'm feeling a little sorry for myself and I might not stop at one. I need to keep my courage up and my head clear.' And then he just walked down the street toward his house."

Lucy remained thoughtful for several minutes. "That could mean many things, but I'm beginning to see more clearly a pattern in all of this."

"What's that?"

Lucy was kept from replying when the stage came to an abrupt halt. Their first thought was that a hold-up was taking place, although such a thing had not happened in that area for a long time. They were reassured when the driver hollered, "Hi there. Climb on in."

The door opened and a Basque sheepherder lunged inside, plopping down on the bench seat across from them. He introduced himself and told Lucy, "I hope my clothes don't offend. I've been with my flock for several days without help. He just arrived and now I can go into town and see my wife." He grinned. "And the inside of a tub, if you'll excuse my boldness."

Lucy and Jim laughed, but they didn't deny that the man needed a scrubbing. Lucy told him, "We spent the day in Bodie visiting a friend in the hospital. So we're pretty dusty ourselves."

"Do you mean Peter Nye by any chance?"

"Yes. You're a friend of his, too?"

"Oh, sure." He ran a hand over his heavy beard. "Grand fella. How was Bodie?"

"Lots of buildings gone," Jim answered. "Others needing paint. But overall, the town's still pretty active. About 500 people there, they say."

The man nodded, turned and banged on the roof under the driver, although they were still half a mile out of town. "Nice meeting you folks, but I'm getting out here." He leapt out the door, waved to the driver, and the coach continued on at a sedate pace.

Lucy forgot all her discomfort as Jim continued to talk about his visit with John Murphey at his station. "What was most interesting was that John later saw Victor with Otto behind Bryant's Hall on the edge of the cemetery. They were arguing about something, and then it ended suddenly when Victor handed Otto some money and shook his hand."

The coach rolled over a pothole, throwing them against each other. As they righted themselves, Lucy laughed. "That was indeed jarring information, but I didn't need it emphasized like that!"

Jim put his arm around his wife's shoulders and held her tightly to him, saying with a suggestive leer, "Just in case we hit another rough spot."

She managed a chuckle, but she was thinking about what Jim had just told her, eager to pass it on to Emily. It fit in with their idea of what had happened at the ranch, at least in part.

But upon reaching Bridgeport, there was no time for Lucy to share any of that with anyone. The dining room at the hotel was emptying of the last of the diners, so they asked for whatever was left in the kitchen. They quickly ate what the chef set before them, the man expressing his appreciation of their consideration, something he claimed was seldom shown him.

As they readied themselves for bed, Lucy told Jim, "When I think of Bodie, I think of wood. Can you imagine how devastating a big fire would be there?"

"The hook and ladder company has a Babcock Engine. If they maintain the hydrants, they should be okay. I'm picturing it under snow. Most winters, the buildings are buried."

"Wasn't the area out front of the Miner's Union a marsh early on?"

"That's right. But the Standard drained it for water needed at their first mill. After that, the area was used as a cemetery before they moved all the graves south of town."

"Why did they do that?"

"They needed that space for building onto the town. Boarding houses, a blacksmith, a brewery, and ... well, you remember."

"Yes, for progress." Lucy looked out the window, the darkness having swallowed anything visible during the day. "When Roger and I first lived in Bodie, several years before the boom, there was a big hay yard south of the Miner's Union Hall, where now there's the brick post office and I.O.O.U. building. When the breeze was in our direction, you could smell the fresh hay right after it was delivered by the freighters."

Jim's thoughts were more prosaic. "Good to know that the Standard and Bodie mines have merged now. And especially that they're doing well. Maybe Bodie will be around for a long time."

Lucy turned her thoughts to all those awaiting them at the Double R. "Do you realize that everyone who came together for the tournament has a connection to Bodie?"

That got his attention. "How so?"

"I lived there with Roger in late '75 for a brief time before we moved to Virginia City. He came back to live there for a few years starting in '78, meeting Amanda there in '80. He even owned a saloon there a few years ago. You were there all of '79 into '80. Frank and Vince, with their wives, lived in Bodie then, too, even if you didn't know them. Emily told me about the big explosion on the hill in July of '79, and how she almost lost Frank. Even Mike Cody lived there first as a miner and then as the Land Receiver before moving to Bridgeport last year." After a pause, she went on. "So, one way or another, for various reasons, we've all lived in Bodie."

"But not J.B."

She turned and looked at her husband with a raised brow. "But has he spent much time there?"

"You mean because we know so little about his past? We do know that he has business interests there. But as to the rest of his associations there, male or female, I doubt anyone knows."

"I bet Hank does."

Jim nodded and crawled under the covers of a very welcome bed, feeling his muscles relax. "I bet Hank knows a whole lot about J.B. But he'll never tell."

"Humph! I bet they both go to Bodie whenever they have an itch that needs scratching."

"Lucy! What a thing for a genteel lady to say!"

Lucy turned down the wick on the lamp and crawled under the covers, snuggling up to Jim. "Now, kind sir, when have you ever known me to be genteel?" She proceeded to show him why she also wasn't always a lady.

The next morning, even though a Sunday, those at the Double R rose early. It seemed that no one had slept well. Vince was missing his wife Charlotte more than he'd admit to anyone. Roger was uneasy about what he had found in J.B.'s study. Mrs. Lewis was dealing with grief and self-recrimination. And J.B. had so many dreads and fears filling his dreams that each one caused him to wake in a cold sweat.

But as early as it was when Roger and Vince came downstairs, they found Sing already at work in the kitchen. It was lit by a lantern on the center island, gleaming in the pre-dawn gloom and giving off a slight kerosene smell. They sat at the kitchen table by another lantern, reading the latest newspaper once again.

This time, however, Roger focused on the advertisements, finding them a combination of goods and services not all of which were available in Bridgeport. Carson City had purchased considerable advertising space. It was a reminder to Bridgeport readers that Carson, although eighty miles to the north in Nevada, was the closest trading hub for farming equipment, stoves, and the latest in medicines. They also had a "circulating library at the news depot", fancy restaurants, a surfeit of gambling halls, and a surprising abundance of lawyers.

It was obvious that the Folger brothers, the owners of the newspaper, were astute businessmen. Robert was the shorter of the two and dubbed locally as "Uncle Bob", and his taller, younger brother was Alex. One of their most popular columns, a humorous play on their odd appearance when walking together, was called "*The Long and Short of It*". They had published the *Bodie Chronicle* when living in Bodie during its boom years, but had moved to Bridgeport in 1880, calling their paper the *Bridgeport Chronicle-Union*. Their office was a small one-story, peaked roof building with a long sign across its face reading *Chronicle-Union*. It was a short walk to work every day, as the office was in front of their home and barn, and not far behind the courthouse. In fact, they shared the large courthouse wood lot between them.

Unlike most of the newspapers, the brothers avoided sarcasm and vitriol, and instead carried serious topics that supported their belief that ethics should apply in journalism. Along with this, their staunch patriotism was emphasized by the American flag they flew outside their office building each day. People credited their efforts as the reason why the County had established the protocol of the American flag flying in front of all school buildings.

Not long after breakfast had been enjoyed at the Double R and the dishes cleared away, a spring wagon could be heard pulling up outside the back door. Sing looked out the kitchen window and exclaimed, "It's Mr. and Mrs. Murphy!"

When Jim and Lucy had the day before climbed out of the stage in Bridgeport just after dusk, Dave Hays had come over to Jim and announced that he had supplies ordered by Sing ready to be delivered. He asked if in the morning Jim would take his loaded wagon out to the ranch so he wouldn't have to leave the store. His delivery boy's parents insisted he attend church with them in the morning.

Not having to rent a rig to take them out to the ranch saved Jim money, so he had happily agreed. Besides, they both knew that Frank and Emily had taken a buggy to the ranch earlier, and knew he and Lucy could return to town with them. Transportation, whether by horse, buggy or spring wagon, was always something local people had to keep in mind. After all, the ranches were a mile or more out from town, and it wasn't as though they could easily cover such a distance in only a few minutes, or at all in the dark of a moonless night.

As they left town the next morning, Mr. Hays assured Jim, "I'll send my boy out to retrieve the wagon as soon as possible."

It was a pleasant ride through the cattle-packed meadows and Jim took his time. Dozens of oxen were keeping company with the cattle in the pastures, along with a few large freighting mules. There was also present a group of men with shovels making sure the network of small streams, known as *stringers*, were flowing unheeded. The animals were already drinking the influx of fresh water. Ravens and black birds, along with black and white magpies, lined the fences. They were none too patiently waiting for whatever the men would stir up that might fly in their direction. Their excited rasping squawks filled the air with harsh caterwauling. A nearby steer lifted his head from the wet grass, seeming to glare at the birds, but his jaws never stopped moving from side to side.

"Not exactly the melody of sparrows, is it?" Jim commented. "But I'd still rather linger here than go back to the ranch."

Lucy agreed, but simply repeated the old saying, "Needs must."

Jim nodded and swallowed the temptation to sigh. Flicking the reins, he commanded the two horses, "Get along on."

When Jim stopped the wagon near the back door, Lucy looked across the kitchen garden to the house. "And now our lovely break is over."

Jim heard the funeral tone of her voice and wondered at it. He realized with a jolt that Lucy might know more about what was to follow than she had thus far told him, and he wondered about that, too. But before he could question her, the back door burst open and Sing, followed by Roger and Vince, rushed out to begin unloading the wagon. Not far behind came Frank, with Emily holding open the door for everyone. Within a few minutes all the bags, barrels and crates had been deposited either in the kitchen or along the back hallway.

Sing directed Frank to the great room with the crate in his arms that was shedding straw. "That one go over by liquor cabinet. Set down gentle." After Sing looked down at the straw strewn on the floor, Frank could hear his repeated "tsk" as he hurried back to the kitchen.

Once the goods were unloaded, and while Jim took the wagon out to the front to await retrieval, Sing began the inventory of everything on his list. Seeing Roger lift a burlap sack onto the kitchen table, Sing flew at him with arms flapping. "No, no." He then pulled himself up, lowered his voice and told Roger as politely as he could that it might be best if Roger relaxed in the other room. "But thank you for help. Very kind."

Roger got the point that Sing wanted no help in putting away the supplies. Having experienced similar moments with his mother, he simply smiled and walked into the great room with the newspaper that had been among the supplies.

While all of this was taking place, Lucy pulled Emily aside, suggesting they go for a walk. They headed out to the hog pens where they could be assured to be left alone. Lucy admired the hop vines over the shed at the back of the pens. They were lush and green, giving the hogs a cool retreat in the heat of summer.

"We used to keep hogs." Emily didn't look pleased at the memory. "It just became too much work. J.B. must have more help on the ranch than we've seen."

Lucy laughed as she said, "He probably has them trained to stay out of the way of guests."

"And, of course, there's always Hank to keep track of everyone." Emily looked sideways at Lucy. "They sure have a strange relationship."

Instead of replying to that, Lucy relayed what Peter Nye and John Murphey had said about Victor. Emily in return repeated the pertinent parts of the conversation Frank and Vince had enjoyed with Bryant and Day while playing billiards.

Lucy nodded. "It all fits in with our assumption of what led up to the deaths."

"If you think all that fits in, wait until I tell you what your clever son did. I'm the only one he's told, by the way."

When Emily had finished talking, Lucy was torn between being appalled that Roger would do something so discourteous, and yet glad that he had. "That gives us the solution to the horse stealing."

Emily wasn't as sure. "Maybe that tells us that J.B. was back of it, but not why he would cancel such a large debt of Victor's for doing it. What was the monetary value in that for J.B.?"

Lucy tried to ignore how disturbed she was at the thought that J.B. might have nefarious motives such that they could hurt others. She had grown fond of the man, even while knowing that there was much about him that was unknown. But she remained convinced that there was goodness in him, no matter what else might be mixed with it.

She told Emily, "Maybe there was more to it that we don't know about. Or that didn't happen because the horses were found so quickly."

Lucy remembered J.B.'s heated declaration that he would gladly have charged Victor with horse stealing. Had that been his plan? If so, it fell apart when the horses were found so quickly, followed by Victor's death. Or had Victor's death been J.B.'s alternate plan when the thefts couldn't be laid at Victor's feet? Lucy didn't want to think of J.B. as capable of such a thing, but she somehow felt that he was. Still, for some reason she couldn't define, she kept all this to herself.

Emily broke into her thoughts. "We've assumed that the horses being stolen was the precipitating event to everything that followed. Which is the death of three people." Emily couldn't keep the amazement from her voice. "And all on just one weekend! But maybe it wasn't. Maybe there was something else at play."

"And don't forget," Lucy added, "if we hadn't figured out that Otto was poisoned by the flowers, and Sara by an over-whelming reaction to ingesting so much mint, both deaths would have been thought natural. Or at the most, accidental."

Emily turned to Lucy with a frown. "They still might. A lot of people now claim that Otto had heart problems, which was in fact only what Victor had been passing around. So Otto's death as natural might indeed be the final judgment. Especially if it can't be proved that he ingested plant parts."

Lucy frowned. "You're right, of course. But we know differently. And I think the sheriff agrees with us." She stamped her foot in frustration. "There's just no conclusive evidence." Lucy pursed her lips and shook her head. "So Victor wins on that."

"And the events leading up to Sara's death are so subtle, and seemingly happenstance, that her death will probably be called an accident." Emily rested a fist on the railing around the hog pen, her frustration also evident. Two of the youngest hogs came over to them, flat noses quivering hopefully as they sniffed around for food.

"Or," Lucy continued, "they'll call Sara's death an undiagnosed medical condition that no one could have foreseen. Especially since no one has come up with a clear reason why Victor wanted her dead."

Lucy longed for a place to sit down. She spotted a tree stump at the edge of the willow grove and walked over to it with Emily following. As she sat and stretched her back, she said, "There'll be judgment aimed at J.B., for sure. But also everyone who lives at the ranch, even Sing and Mrs. Lewis. They'll always be looked at differently by those in town because what happened has no clear explanation. It allows for questions to remain in people's minds, and therefore suspicions to fester and grow. I think that'll bother J.B. much more than he'd be willing to admit."

Emily cocked her head to the side and looked at Lucy. "Maybe that answers the question as to *why* it happened the way it did. Living with suspicion and loss of face is for J.B. a form of punishment. I don't think Victor had forgiven J.B. for going back on his word about selling him back his horses. It was years ago, but he could have been waiting for the right time to visit his revenge on J.B. for that. Or maybe Victor's desire for revenge only began after things went sour in his life, culminating in what seems to be a terminal diagnosis."

"Yes, if Victor was going to die soon, it might be the reason he told J.B. 'no time like the present' about having a tournament."

"What if J.B. wanted to hurt Victor by getting him to steal the horses, and then get him arrested for it?" Emily thought a moment about what she had just said as it triggered another thought. "But if so, Victor must have figured out that he was being set up."

Lucy completed the thought. "And turned the tables on J.B. by getting Otto to do the rustling."

"But why would J.B. want to hurt Victor so badly?"

"I think I know." Lucy told Emily about Victor's harassment of J.B.'s wife, who evidently wasn't very stable to begin with.

Emily frowned. "I wonder how far such *harassment* went. It may have been much more serious than that." Women of their era might have understood the concept of rape, but it was a word they would avoid, even among themselves. Inference was sufficient.

Lucy shook her head. "If so, I can't imagine that J.B. wouldn't have gone after Victor at the time. Beat him up, at least."

"Unless, because his wife was unstable, he held himself back. He might have been waiting for a day when he could get his revenge without the possibility of arrest for assault. He'd have to give a reason for it, and he'd never give the true one."

Lucy stood up and stretched again. "Well, if he was out to get even with Victor, he sure waited a long time. Although maybe that's the real reason he refused to sell Victor's horses back to him years ago."

"Which angered Victor and made him seek his own revenge." Emily shook her head and sighed. "I think that Victor and J.B. would never have felt fully satisfied that things were even between them. Not until one of them was either in jail or dead."

The two women walked over to the turkey run and watched the big males strutting around, several unfurling their wings to show off their fine feathers. Finally, Emily broke the silence. "If Victor killed Otto, I think it was because Otto couldn't be trusted to keep his mouth shut about the theft. He knew it was Victor who hired him to do the rustling, and maybe even that J.B. had come up with the plan. So, Otto had to be gotten out of the way, or Victor's debt with J.B. might not be cancelled. Even more important to Victor, he wouldn't be able to proceed with his own plans if the truth about the horse theft was revealed. Even though Roger didn't see it, I'll bet there's an IOU somewhere proving that Victor owed J.B. the $500 listed in the ledger."

Lucy didn't like where that led, but she also couldn't ignore the logic of it. "That gives J.B. a motive, too. To kill Otto, I mean." Lucy stopped herself. "But, no, not really. No one would have believed Otto even if he had accused J.B. of planning the theft."

"They might have if Otto knew why J.B. would do that, which would bring Victor into the picture and what he did to J.B.'s wife. Victor wouldn't have liked that any more than J.B. would."

Lucy nodded. "And it's another reason why Victor would think it a good idea to get Otto out of the way."

"What about the note in J.B.'s desk drawer? Would Otto have known about that?"

"I don't think it would have mattered," Lucy mused. "The note didn't say anything about stealing. Just an unspecified agreement to do something on a certain night."

The women stood up sharply, hearing the arrival at the front of the house of a light carriage. The boy from the store would be riding a horse so he could tie it onto the back of the wagon, so it couldn't be him. With the single thought of "What now?", the two women hurried in that direction. No one being around to see, Emily picked up her skirts with both hands and ran lightly forward.

Lucy moved at a more sedate pace, feeling a stab of regret that she was past that time in her life when she could run without care over uneven ground. Grousing to herself, she thought, "Is there anything as cruel as having a quick mind and a slow body?" The answer came immediately.

"Yes. To have a quick body, but a mind that is failing. Or worse yet, both failing, like Peter Nye."

Ashamed of her moment of uncharacteristic self-pity, Lucy lifted her skirts and stepped over a puddle, full of gratitude that she could.

# CHAPTER 13

## A QUICK SHUFFLE OF THE CARDS

As curious as Emily and Lucy were, considering everything that had taken place over the last week, they both slowed down and approached somewhat cautiously. When they reached the front corner of the house, they heard the front door slam and saw the driver of the hired rig already heading down the long drive to the road.

Emily was the first of the two women to recognize the new arrival, a dark-haired, petit woman in her early thirties, wearing a smart traveling suit and bonnet of relatively current fashion. And she was being enthusiastically hugged by Vince.

Emily hurried forward. "Charlotte!"

The two close friends embraced as Sing came down the steps. But before he could pick up the new arrival's luggage, Vince beat him to it. Sing was reduced to following up the steps after a brief introduction to Mrs. Perry. Lucy caught up with the group, and welcomed Charlotte to the Double R.

"It's good to see you again, Lucy." Charlotte's smile was warm, even though she was beginning to feel the fatigue of the trip and was longing for a place to sit that wasn't moving. "Before I forget, Lucy, Amanda told me to immediately inform you that she and the baby are well and looking forward to your return."

Lucy laughed. "And in the meantime, she'll enjoy being taken care of by Kathryn. I can't believe Kathryn has been working for me for a dozen years now, even though she's married."

"She is indeed a jewel," Charlotte agreed. "She thinks the sun rises and sets on you, and having no children of her own, she's in heaven being around your granddaughter."

"Well, come on in." Lucy looked up at the porch, surprised not to see Mrs. Lewis in her usual place to greet a new arrival. But Lucy reminded herself that the housekeeper had been through a lot of trauma this last week. She also thought that the Double R could now stand for *Rage* and *Revenge*. Aloud, she declared, "I'm sure Sing will have a tea tray waiting for us."

Emily led the way, turning to Charlotte before they entered. "There's so much we have to catch you up on. But first, you have to sample Sing's baking."

True to his reputation, Sing had waiting for them a tray loaded with a big pot of tea under a quilted cozy, an array of mugs, a plate of butter and jam sandwiches, and shortbread cookies. The women encouraged Charlotte to help herself to the sandwiches, while they chose tea and a cookie.

From the hallway above and behind them, J.B. looked down on the three friends, listening to their laughter and excited chatter about travel to his ranch and Charlotte's time with Amanda. He didn't know whether to think of them as what he pictured a quilting bee must be like, or the three cackling witches from Macbeth. But he did know that he was filled with a strange longing to be part of the close-knit comradery that these women obviously shared. He had never had a friendship anywhere as close. There was no man he could trust to care about him without some degree of self-interest underlying. He'd like to think that wasn't true of Hank, but he wasn't absolutely sure.

As he observed the women, he could see why Emily and Lucy had become fast friends, as they were similar in disposition. But it struck him how very different this new woman was from the other two. There was a gentleness and soft femininity about Charlotte Perry that was missing in her friends. She too would draw people to her, but it wouldn't be for the quickness of her opinions or strength of leadership, although he perceived that she was not without such qualities. Rather it would be because of her innate genuineness, her kindness giving people an assurance that she was sincerely interested in whatever they had to say. Even more important, they would sense that she was sincerely interested in *who* they were. Whether she was viewed as a maternal substitute or a supportive friend, she would be trusted, and would never disappoint.

J.B. descended the stairs slowly. Seeing him, Charlotte stood up and looked him in the eyes, her smile one of pleasurable anticipation. "Good afternoon, Mr. Roberts. I'm delighted to meet you."

She extended her hand, and the carefully prepared attitude of nonchalance that J.B. had carefully prepared melted away. It was replaced by a smile of sincere welcome.

Emily and Lucy watched J.B.'s reaction with amused interest as Charlotte told him, "I'm sorry to impose one more person on your household."

"Oh, please. You're as welcome as an ace-high straight."

Lucy almost laughed aloud, and Emily had to resist rolling her eyes. They were not unaware of how instantly taken people were with Charlotte's warmth and charm. Even those obtuse souls unaffected by it, didn't miss her lovely ivory skin, thick lashes over dark eyes, and her purposeful yet graceful movement when simply walking through a room.

Vince returned downstairs and focused on J.B. holding his wife's hand. Aware of his host's cavalier gestures when meeting women, he hurried to stand next to Charlotte, one arm placed around her waist. "I'm glad you've met my wife. She's going to love your ranch."

J.B.'s smile at Vince was a little stiff as he released Charlotte's hand. He moved to his chair just as Sing approached with the master's coffee mug that always held more than just coffee. J.B. took such a large swallow that he had to struggle to keep from choking. He nevertheless managed to look as suave as ever as he sat back and gazed at those gathered before him, a slight smirk of satisfaction visible for anyone paying attention.

As the tea tray was depleted, Frank, Jim and Roger arrived, and so did Sing with another tray. This one was had more cookies, along with a pot of coffee. The men expressed their appreciation of Sing catering to their appetites, going for the coffee first.

The afternoon proceeded with casual discussion about Charlotte's trip to Bridgeport, the weather, and some background about the town. When the men began a discussion about news of a stage holdup near Sweetwater, Lucy took the opportunity to suggest that Charlotte might like to freshen up. It was the best she could come up with in order to get the three of them up to the room Charlotte would now share with Vince.

Immediately upon entering the room, Lucy said, "I'm so glad you'll be staying here instead of in town. This way, you can keep an eye on what might be happening."

Standing before a large oval mirror above the dresser, Charlotte stopped in the process of removing the hat pins that anchored her small traveling bonnet. "You don't expect any more deaths, do you?"

"Oh, no. But, well, there's just a lot that's been happening in that regard."

Emily helped Charlotte remove the form-fitting jacket of her traveling suit, hanging it in the tall armoire. Seeing the clay bed warmer on the floor of the closet, she was reminded of the below freezing winters in Bridgeport. She had a moment of intense gratitude that it was summer.

Emily moved over to the far side of the bed and stretched out with her back to the headboard, making room for Charlotte who did the same. Lucy pulled up a small velvet chair from the corner so it was closer to the bed, and proceeded to bring Charlotte up-to-date with recent events. This included the conclusions which she and Emily had that day reasoned out. Emily admired how quickly, yet thoroughly, Lucy laid out both what had happened and what it meant, knowing that she would never have been so succinct.

Charlotte nevertheless challenged some of it. "Victor might have planned the deaths of Otto and Sara, but he did hang himself."

"Maybe," Lucy said. "The sheriff still thinks someone killed Victor, although he admits he doesn't know how they could have gotten him up there without help."

"Lucy and I are toying with a crazy idea," Emily broke in. "That Victor set it up to look like murder, but actually did commit suicide." Emily showed her excitement at the idea as she spoke. "He was sick and dying anyway, so it was something someone might do."

"But," Charlotte posed, "didn't you say that the sheriff explained that if he had, the chair would have been closer to him?"

Emily and Lucy exclaimed in unison, "Sara!"

Lucy followed through with the idea that she and Emily had been discussing. "It's possible that Sara moved the chair when she went and found him."

Charlotte frowned at Lucy. "But if she did, which is something anyone might do in the shock of the moment of finding him, why didn't she just say so? Didn't anyone ask her?"

Lucy said, "I brought that up to Jim. He said everyone was asked if they'd touched anything in the bunk house. And Sara said nothing."

Emily jumped off the bed and began to pace. "When she went out to the tack room earlier in the day, she could have gone out the back and met up with Victor, telling him where everyone was. And he would have known it was the perfect time to do the deed because everyone was scattered. He could have told her when to come back, too."

Charlotte wanted more clarity. "Did she tell him where everyone was because he'd asked her to tell him whenever that occurred? Or did she just happen to mention it in a casual way?"

"We don't know." Emily stopped pacing and looked at Lucy.

Charlotte asked another question before Lucy could respond. "Did Sara know Victor was going to kill himself?"

Lucy shrugged. "We don't know that either, not for sure. But she might have. The whole thing could have been planned out very carefully. He was that kind of man."

Charlotte sat forward. "You mean he was the kind of man who wouldn't mind a young girl finding his body hanging there?"

"Yes." Emily realized such a quick answer wasn't enough. "Maybe he didn't care. After all, if his plans worked out, he was going to be dead, and she was going to die soon after. We're not talking about a caring person."

Lucy nodded. "I'm sorry to say that he was indeed that kind of man. I think he was so full of hate and anger and pain, that he didn't care about anyone else."

"Because of the wrongs he thought had been done him by J.B.?" Charlotte asked.

"That, and maybe by life itself." Lucy recalled what others had told her. "Every time he had thought his life was going to improve, something had occurred to make it go in the other direction."

"Poor man!"

"Maybe, but Charlotte, he had become someone who thought nothing of involving a young girl in his plan. He could be sure that at some point she wouldn't confess to moving the chair. That one little thing could have ruined all his efforts to make people think J.B., possibly with the help of our men, had killed him. Sara was, after all, a somewhat foolishly naïve girl. So, we think it's possible that he set her up to die right after him by getting her over-stimulated with mint. And with his being already dead, he would escape suspicion of involvement."

Emily still found it difficult to believe that any girl would have agreed to such an undertaking. "I wonder what he promised her to get her to do such a thing. Especially since she knew him well."

Charlotte, compassionate but also a realist, told them, "Maybe that's why. She did know him, and liked him. She might also have known that he was going to die in a lot of pain not too far in the future. If so, maybe she thought it an act of mercy on her part."

Emily considered that. "Maybe, at least partly. But she had to realize that he was setting it up to look like he was killed by someone. Although, considering what we've found out about Victor's manipulative ways, he probably told Sara some outrageous story of how J.B., and some of the others at the tournament, had treated him badly."

Charlotte got the point. "And therefore, she would think they deserved his twisted revenge."

"Yes. And," Lucy added, "he probably sweetened the pot, giving her enough money to quell any reservations she still might have had." Being older, with a multitude of rough experiences behind her, Lucy had developed a good degree of cynicism. "Just because money wasn't found in her room, that doesn't mean she didn't put it somewhere."

"Mrs. Lewis?" Charlotte suggested. "Is she the type to hold back that bit of information?"

Lucy pictured the woman's grief at the death of her sister. "She might not say anything about it if she didn't know where the money came from. And if Sara was still under Victor's influence, she wouldn't have told Mrs. Lewis the truth."

"But," Charlotte persisted, "if she does have money given her by Sara not long before her sister's death, wouldn't she have said something about it by now? She'd have to wonder where Sara got any sizeable sum."

Lucy shrugged. "On the other hand, why should she? Wherever it came from, she's sharp enough to realize that it legally belongs to her now as Sara's only relative."

"Let's go ask her." Emily was always eager for action.

"No," Lucy cautioned. "Let's go tell the sheriff our conclusions, and let him ask her. He has authority. We don't."

Accepting the reasonableness of this, the women turned their desire for answers into action. They told Sing they were going into town, and asked him to tell the others where they were. When the three women entered the horse barn and asked Hank to hitch up the larger, two-seat carriage, he couldn't help notice their excitement.

After they had left, Hank stood and watched the dust on the road slowly clear in the rising breeze. He wondered if he should tell the boss. Or maybe he should just mind his own business. It wasn't the first time he'd been caught in the middle of events surrounding J.B., and although his loyalty was absolute, he didn't want anything untoward to happen to such nice ladies. And with J.B., he reminded himself, you just never knew. He decided to treat their request as not unusual, and went back to work.

Such an anxiety-filled debate with himself was unnecessary. J.B. had been watching from the back window of his study. And he was wondering why the women had hurried away from the ranch without taking their shopping bags with them. Should he be concerned? Had they figured out something he would prefer they had not? Had Lucy shared with the women her suspicions about his activities in the fall of 1871? Hank knew the truth about the mass escape of convicts from the Nevada State Prison, but he sure as hell wouldn't talk. J.B. tried to calm down by reasoning with himself, knowing that he wasn't wanted by the law for anything. But he also knew that people had long memories. "No," he murmured aloud, "I don't like this at all."

His solution was to hurry into Alex's room, make his way down the outside stairs, and run to the barn. Thankful that Hank and Mort were down by the pond, he quickly saddled his horse. Instead of catching up with the women, however, he stayed well back from them all the way into town. When the carriage turned in behind the courthouse, he watched Emily tie the horse to the rail in front of the sheriff's office. But he stayed down the street next to a small house between Bryant's Hall and the cemetery. There, he had the advantage of seeing the women, without their being aware of him.

The three women walked boldly into Sheriff Cody's office, thankful to find him in. After introducing him to Charlotte, they arranged themselves in front of his desk in his rickety chairs. For some reason, both Emily and Charlotte turned to Lucy, who in turn looked at the sheriff.

That man was trying to arrange his face to look respectfully alert. He didn't want to do or say anything they might interpret as patronizing.

On the other hand, he didn't want them to see how eager he was to hear whatever they had to say. If what he had concluded about the deaths at the Double R was true, it wasn't going to be easily explained, and there might be no one who could be prosecuted. Yet he felt that somehow justice needed to be served.

After listening to Lucy, with several interjections by Emily, Sheriff Cody realized they had deduced much of what he too had been thinking. He had struggled with the idea that such a young girl would have agreed to Victor's plan, but after listening to Lucy and Emily, he began to see how Victor could have persuaded her. And he began to see Victor as an even greater villain than he had before. His previous sense of compassion for a man facing his mortality was now gone.

The sheriff's life experiences had taught him that it was in the difficult times in people's lives that their true character emerged. And he now thought he had a pretty clear picture of Victor, not as a victim but as a user of other people. Maybe as a youth, in order to get what he needed or even in order to survive harsh treatment, he had found such behavior expedient. And maybe that had developed into the way he had achieved whatever he wanted as an adult. Cody was willing to give him that, even understanding how Victor might have talked Sara into moving the chair.

But he wasn't able to justify how Victor could kill Sara and Otto just to make sure that his scheme was carried out against J.B., and possibly Jim and Roger. After all, how big a deal would it have been if his plan had failed and J.B. wasn't shunned by the townspeople?

He expressed his doubts to them. "Do you think that discrediting J.B., and maybe even Jim and Roger, was the whole of his plan?"

Charlotte leaned forward. "I see what you mean. It doesn't seem like so momentous a goal that it was worth killing two people to keep it hidden."

Lucy sat silent as the sheriff and her friends discussed this further. Did she know, or think she knew, what Victor might have been holding over J.B.'s head? Or was it the other way around? Would J.B. have killed Victor to keep his past from coming out, if Victor was threatening to reveal it? Did J.B.'s long-held resentment about Victor's treatment of his wife add justification for a lethal solution? But surely, J.B. couldn't have gotten a stunned man up into the noose by himself. The picture of Hank flashed into her mind.

"Lucy, are you okay?" The concern in the sheriff's voice brought Lucy back to the moment with a start.

"Oh, yes. Yes, of course." Lucy fanned herself with her hand. "I think the horror of all these deaths just caught up with me for a moment."

The sheriff smiled kindly. "That's understandable." But the way Emily and Charlotte looked at Lucy, with surprised disbelief, made the sheriff wonder. But he said nothing more about that. "Who else have you explained all this to?"

Three lovely heads moved back and forth in the negative as Emily mumbled, "No one."

"Not even your husbands?" Mike Cody found it difficult to believe that a woman wouldn't run her opinions past her husband for his approval, or at least advice. He might have admired their intelligence, but he was still a man of his generation.

The women understood his motivation for the question only too well, and they laughed. The sheriff's reaction to that was to turn red and offer a quick explanation. "Oh, my surprise isn't from any idea that women aren't able to keep a secret." Then, realizing that probably had nothing to do with their laughter, he turned a little deeper red. "I mean, I'm surprised that anyone having reached these conclusions wouldn't share them with those closest to them."

Lucy smiled, albeit somewhat pitiably because of his obvious lack of insight regarding women. "But we did." Glancing at the women on either side of her, she added, "With each other."

And in that moment, Mike Cody had an epiphany regarding the difference between men and women. The bond between women, even those who barely knew one another, had underlying it a common affinity that didn't exist among men, even those with life-styles and experiences in common. When men shared with one another, it was about ideas and experiences, about which they had made free and independent choices. Some outcomes might be brilliant or courageous, and others incurring loss and disappointment. But whatever their choices, society would not judge them based on their gender.

However, whatever women might do, no matter how brave or clever, their gender would always be a factor when it was commented upon, and judged. This was just one challenge shared by all women, simply by existing in a male-dominated world. Above all else, they had to be constantly mindful of what they said or did in order to avoid being chastised or outcast by society, or their own families. The consequence could be harsh. With so few well-paying jobs open for a woman on her own, she could find herself in a life-threatening situation. Such desperation had led many a woman to thievery or prostitution. So accepted by women was this fundamental awareness, that there was never a need for them to verbally acknowledge it among themselves.

Whether or not Mike would give this insight about women further consideration, no one but himself would ever know. But at least for a few moments he had seen clearly how women must live every day, because of a universal lack of male acceptance of their intelligence and capability. And why only a relatively few exceptional women had so far been courageous enough to challenge society's dictates.

Charlotte realized that the sheriff's thoughts were in turmoil, although not the reason for it, and wanted to reassure him. "When we did decide to share it with someone else, you were the first person we thought of. And that's why we're here."

Greatly humbled by their trust in him, Mike grinned. "Well, I do think we've made some good progress. But there're still some questions I have." He turned to Lucy. "When I showed you the bunk house, why were you walking around the room looking at the walls?"

"Oh, that." She cocked her head to the side and asked a question in return. "Did the Coroner ever explain the redness he called bruising on Victor's head?"

"Uh, no." Realization came upon the sheriff with a jolt. "Of course! He'd been slammed up against a wall, maybe during the struggle that ended on his bed."

"Well, yes, that's possible. If, that is, there was a struggle with someone."

"But hitting his head on the wall would have created what Doc and I saw on the body."

"Oh, we're not contradicting that." Lucy gave Emily the opportunity to jump in, but she simply smiled back at Lucy, who accepted her assigned role as speaker. "What if he hit his head against the wall himself, in order to make it look like he was injured during a struggle?"

The sheriff blinked a few times. "That would mean that he did commit suicide. But that he was trying to set it up to look like murder."

Emily finally spoke up. "Victor could be pretty sure that the question would arise as to who it was at the ranch who might want him dead. And the question would also be asked about who could have assisted him in lifting Victor up to the noose."

The sheriff nodded. "People would have inevitably thought of J.B. and Hank."

"Or," Lucy interjected, "Jim and Roger. I'm sure someone by now has wondered if their run-in with Victor in Bodie had more substance to it than my fellas have said."

"Do you think there's more?" Mike watched her carefully as she answered.

Lucy found the question disquieting, so merely answered, "No."

She wasn't sure her face had matched her denial. There was something about the way Roger didn't look at her whenever the subject came up. She wasn't sure how much more there was to the event, but she thought there was something about the run-in with Victor in Bodie that hadn't been told her. Whether or not the sheriff noted her unease, he said nothing. Nevertheless, Lucy stood up and was followed in this by her friends.

The sheriff also stood up, saying, "I'll be coming out to the ranch this evening so I can talk to Mrs. Lewis about any money Sara might have given her. And maybe to make sure there isn't anything else she's holding back."

The women smiled, nodded to him as they thanked him for his time, and made it out to the buggy without saying a word more. Charlotte, the first one to climb in, settled herself onto the back seat. As she did, she noted a man mounting his horse next to Bryant's Hall. By the time she called attention to the rider, however, he had entered the street and disappeared from view behind the courthouse.

Lucy looked in that direction, but saw no one. "Was it someone we know?"

"I thought it looked like J.B., but why would he be there?"

"Probably not him," Lucy reassured them.

But she didn't discount the possibility that J.B. had followed them off the ranch. She said nothing of this to the others, but she noted that Emily was frowning as she arranged the long ribbons of leather in her gloved hands. With a quick glance in the direction mentioned, and carefully avoiding looking at Lucy, Emily urged the horse forward.

# CHAPTER 14

## FOLD!

Traveling up the long drive to the house, the women were surprised to find two buggies and two buckboards with their horses still in the traces parked out front of the house. Four horses were also tied at the railing.

Emily exclaimed, "Uh, oh!" Not sure if what was happening inside the house was a protest or a party, she brought their carriage to the barn.

First to be helped down by Hank, Lucy asked, "What's happening?"

"You mean all the people?"

"Of course!"

"It's okay. Nothing to be worried about." She relaxed at the laughter underlying his words. "It seems that when J.B. was in town with Frank and Vince, they met up with Mr. Day and Mr. Bryant. And they got to talking, and well, J.B. invited them and their wives to lunch at the ranch. And then a few others came in, and they too were invited. It got so many that Mr. Day suggested they turn it into a pot luck. So that's what's happened." He followed this explanation with a shrug and shake of the head, expressing a lack of understanding from a man who thought all social interaction a waste of time.

Lucy tried not to show her surprise. "Does this kind of thing happen often?"

"Never before." And with that declaration, Hank followed Mort as he led the team away to the barn.

The three women stood together looking at the house as though not sure they should join whatever was taking place inside it. Charlotte, trying to be positive, murmured, "What a good way to win over at least a portion of the town."

"I suppose it could be." Lucy shook her head as she added, "They'll certainly think him a grand fellow for his generosity."

Emily nodded. "The coffee and alcohol will be his contribution. And that's what the men will remember. While the women will be charmed by Sing and whatever he adds to the table full of their dishes."

Charlotte took Emily by the arm and pulled her forward. "Come on. I'm sure it'll be a gay time, and we don't want to miss the fun."

Lucy added with a smirk. "Hopefully, something like this can help balance the disparaging comments currently circulating in town."

They jumped as they heard laughter behind them. Hank had returned and had heard what they were saying. "You ladies are a hoot! You put into words what I bet J.B. only sensed in a general way as helping his reputation." Music suddenly broke out up at the house, supplied by a banjo, a fiddle and J.B.'s piano. Hank removed his hat and banged it on his thigh. "Well, I'll be damned! We haven't had music here in years. J.B. got the piano for Mrs. Roberts not long before she...well, you know. Mrs. Lewis only plays the piano when she's sure J.B.'s gone. Last Christmas she and I and Sing had fun singing some carols around it when he was in town."

It was obviously a nice memory for him, because Lucy had never seen him smile. "I bet you have a very nice voice. Maybe before we leave, you'll grace us with a song."

His face fell as he shook his head. "Oh, no, I don't think so."

Lucy decided to be bold. "Wouldn't J.B. like that?"

"No." And with that terse response, he turned on his heel and strode purposefully to the bunk house. He didn't slam the door, but it closed with a bang nevertheless.

"Come on!" Charlotte pleaded. "I bet they've started the dancing, and if I know Vince, he's wishing I was there."

With that, she reached down with her left hand to lift her skirts while pushing Emily forward with her right. Lucy followed them a little more sedately, but she wasn't far behind. She was still unsure whether or not this shindig was a good idea. People, especially those in a town as small as Bridgeport, enjoyed anything that added a welcome break from their daily routine. But they were also savvy people. They had to be in order to survive the harsh demands of rural life, and they didn't like being played.

Not only was Vince overjoyed to see the women return, but so were Frank and Jim. And all three women were soon moving around the floor in their husband's arms to the tune of Mr. Strauss's 1866 *Blue Danube* waltz, which was new enough in the West to be considered a modern dance.

Lucy found it almost impossible to keep her eyes off the trio at the piano. Two men from town stood next to the housekeeper, the one with a fiddle under his chin adding harmony to her surprisingly proficient playing. The man with the banjo stood silently by, awaiting his turn during a livelier dance. But it was Mrs. Lewis who held Lucy's interest. The woman was actually smiling.

When Jim, Frank and Vince moved to the liquor cabinet to join other men gathered there, their wives moved to the dining room table. But first, Lucy watched J.B. handing out bottles of beer from a tub of ice. She couldn't help smile, as he wasn't sharing his precious stock of whiskey. He was obviously willing to take the bounty of his hospitality only so far.

The food on the table was a collection of sandwiches, a platter of fried chicken, and bowls of fruit, beans and potato salad. There were also two pies, already missing pieces. It was obviously a hodge-podge of food that the women put together when told by their husbands to grab something for a last-minute pot luck.

Of course, it had been supplemented by Sing with plates, flatware, and glasses, along with pitchers of water and pots of coffee. But just because it was called a pot luck, didn't mean there wouldn't be a lot of cleaning up afterwards. Emily and Charlotte immediately saw this and made up their minds to help Sing when the party was over.

When popped out of the kitchen and surveyed the table while holding a platter of cookies, Emily hurried to rearrange several of the items to make room. Sing gave her one of his brightest smiles and disappeared back into the kitchen. Picking up some dirty cups from the side board, she followed him. He was resting in one of the chairs at the corner table.

He started to rise, but Emily held up her hand. "No, please, take a few minutes for yourself."

Sing looked at her with a mixture of surprise and gratitude as she walked over to the crockery water filter on the kitchen's center island. Noting that it was almost empty, she brought a pitcher to the sink and used the iron pump handle on the side of it with energy. After filling the pitcher with the water that gushed out, she poured it into the top of the filter so the water could percolate down through charcoal to the bottom where it would be syphoned off for drinking.

Sing spoke up. "Ranch well water good. But Mrs. Lewis say we need be careful. She buy crock filter when in Virginia City two year ago. She not let J.B. pay her back for it."

Surprised at this spurt of confidential information, Emily sat at the table, hoping for more. She handed one of two glasses of water to Sing. "Are you trying to impress me with the idea that Mrs. Lewis isn't as unfeeling as she sometimes appears to be?"

His smile was shy as he looked down and straightened the cloth on the table. "She not easy woman. But she mean well. She love the ranch."

And, Emily realized, that was what was most important in Sing's estimation of anyone. As he drained his glass, she asked, "You didn't have much time to prepare for this party, did you?"

"No," he gasped out, setting the empty glass down with regret. Emily got up and fetched him another. He only drank half of it this time.

"You poor man. You must have been running off your feet the last couple of hours. I'm sorry Lucy and I weren't here to help you." Then she quickly added, "And Charlotte, too."

"Oh, no, you guests here. I did fine."

"I have no doubt of that." She couldn't help but smile at the thought that Sing could be anything less than capable. "Didn't any of the women who showed up help you?"

"They put food on table. But they here to have good time. Your good man put barrel in great room while Hank chop ice in ice house. Mr. Perry bring in cases of bottled beer. Roger move furniture so there was room to dance. They big help."

Emily noted that Sing always called Lucy's son by his first name, but not the other men. And, although she had not heard him speak their names, she knew he would never be comfortable calling any of the women by their first names.

"Well, Sing, when this is over, Charlotte and I will definitely help you clear up." He started to object, but she held up a hand. "No argument. I'll make Lucy rest, and then we'll pitch in." She moved his glass of water closer to him, rose up and headed back to join the others.

The party continued until four in the afternoon. In fact, it ended only because Sing cleared the dining room table, then lined up the town lady's empty dishes, now washed, along its length. He then closed the doors of the liquor cabinet, and with Roger's assistance, hauled the remaining beer bottles to the back hall. Once the townsmen saw that the ice barrel was empty, they tended to lose interest in the party and gathered their wives. Of course, there were a few who lingered. But even they finally got the hint when Frank and Vince hauled the barrel out the back door. It had been a grand party and word would soon get around town. So, a successful party, too.

Emily insisted Lucy retire to the front porch while she and Charlotte help Sing. Charlotte dried dishes while Emily swept the black-and-white checked, linoleum floor. Sing was so tired that he didn't even pretend to object.

Emily put the broom in the closet by the door to the hall and announced. "I think the men should take us into town for supper tonight."

Sing perked up at that, but said nothing. Noticing this, Charlotte agreed, dried the last plate, and went in search of Vince. Emily smiled at Sing and left the kitchen. When she broached the subject of supper to Lucy, she readily fell in with the plan. None of these women had eaten more than half a sandwich, wanting to make sure there was enough for everyone else.

J. B. was upstairs as usual. Roger, Vince and Frank, having had their share of the beer, were in the great room sprawled out on the sofas they had moved back into place. They were deep into a nap.

Letting them sleep, Jim joined the wives on the front porch where they could enjoy the late afternoon shade. They weren't there long before a rider was seen to be approaching, quickly recognized as Mike Cody by the ladies, who had expected him even earlier.

Jim, however, was surprised. "What the hell is this about?" He was tired and still feeling the effects of too much beer. He glanced at Lucy, but was rewarded by a stoic silence. Recognizing her poker face, he realized she probably had a good idea what was about to happen. And he wondered why she had not shared it with him.

Cody greeted everyone and removed his hat. Jim told him, "We missed you at the party."

"So it seems. I passed a number of happy people going into town."

"There's food left over in the kitchen," Lucy told him. "Can I get you a plate?"

"No, thanks, ma'am. I'm here to see Mrs. Lewis."

The fact that none of the women looked in the least surprised told Jim all he needed to know. Lucy stood up and led the way into the house. When Jim started to rise, Emily shook her head at him and motioned for him to stay seated.

Lucy knocked on the door of the housekeeper's room after checking briefly in the kitchen. When the door opened and Mrs. Lewis saw who was standing there, the look of surprise immediately turned to irritation. And in that moment Lucy was sure that this woman had a clear conscience. It might be based on self-justification, but she was feeling no guilt about anything she thought must be hidden.

Convinced that there was nothing to be gleaned from the interview, Lucy turned to leave. However, the sheriff stopped her, formally stating, "If you don't mind, Mrs. Murphy, would you stay with us? It would be better if a woman was present."

"Oh, of course." Mrs. Lewis might be formidable, but Lucy felt the sheriff didn't need protection from her. Then she realized her mistake. He was protecting himself from any accusations of improper or harsh treatment.

"Would you prefer to talk at the kitchen table?" Mrs. Lewis asked. "I'm sure Sing would be happy to give us privacy and it would be more comfortable." Without waiting for an answer, she walked across the hall and into the kitchen. "Sing, why don't you rest for a while? You've had a very busy afternoon."

Sing glanced at the assembled group and nodded. He went to his room across the hall and closed the door just hard enough to make it clear that he was giving them their privacy. However, the transom over the door was open just enough to allow for air, and the sound of voices.

As soon as everyone was seated, Mrs. Lewis rested her eyes on Mike Cody, a man she did not know well, but about whom she had heard good things. "Now, sheriff, what's this all about?"

He met her attitude head-on and didn't mince words. "In our investigations regarding both Sara and Victor's deaths, it's come to light that Victor might have given Sara a considerable amount of money. We were wondering if you came across any money belonging to her."

Her surprise was genuine. "No. Well, she had a little in a small leather purse she kept in her underwear drawer. But nothing more than what she had earned from her first two paychecks. Actually less, because she'd recently purchased a few personal things."

"Is there any other place she might have put a larger amount of money?"

Mrs. Lewis stared at him. "You mean from Victor, don't you? What are you implying?"

Mike glanced at Lucy, unsure how to formulate an answer. She came to his rescue. "Mrs. Lewis, Sara was sweet and kind, but also very young. Young people often have high ideals, and sometimes their sense of justice is not yet tempered by life experiences. They don't always see the wider, bigger picture of what's being told them. Or asked to do."

Mrs. Lewis's frown was deepening by the second. "Just come to the point."

"Okay." Lucy took a deep breath. "It seems quite possible that Sara knew about Victor's illness and that he didn't have long to live. She might also have been told by Victor a story of his ill treatment by J.B. in the past. Those two things together might have gained for Victor her cooperation in making his suicide look like murder."

The woman was aghast. "Why would he want to do such a thing?"

B  "Because he hated J.B. and wanted to implicate him in a murder. And possibly also Jim and Roger, who he deeply resented. He blamed them for the death of a friend. Unfairly, I might add."

"But," she reasoned, "without very strong evidence, they wouldn't even be arrested, much less convicted."

"No, but suspicion would linger, and maybe grow over time. J.B.'s reputation would be harmed, and it's a little fragile to begin with. It might affect his ability to get loans or do any kind of business deal. It certainly would make a difference with those who gamble with him from time to time."

This Mrs. Lewis did understand. She sat back and looked out the kitchen window. Lucy and Sherrif Cody let her think it through. When she spoke again, her voice was soft. "When I came to work for J.B., Victor had just come to the valley. He had a wife, a few acres west of town leased from By Day, and he was building up a nice herd of horses. But then everything went wrong for him when the recession of 1882 continued into '83. And as we know, it didn't end until the summer of '85. His wife found she was expecting in '83."

Lucy nodded. "I lived through the other long depression, that of '73 to '75. Such times hit some people really hard."

"Yes. The one just passed didn't affect everyone badly here. We're very self-sufficient, what with the cattle and the agriculture north in Antelope Valley."

"And," Lucy interjected, "the sheep."

Mrs. Lewis said nothing, but the pursing of her lips expressed well her attitude. "The lowering of prices might have been good for the purchasers, but it certainly wasn't good for those trying to sell horses, or the farmers and ranchers selling their crops and cattle. The value of so many things was affected. And Victor was caught up in that. J.B. helped him by buying some of his horses, but then Vic's wife gave birth late in '83, and the child didn't survive for long. His wife never fully recovered, and she died in '84. Vic just fell apart. He drank, sold all but a few of his remaining herd, and lost his lease on the pasture."

Lucy didn't comment on it, but she was taken aback by the dates being referenced. For some reason, she had thought of this transaction between Victor and J.B. as happening further back in time. But when she stopped to think about it, she remembered that Alex was almost thirteen years old, and J.B.'s wife had died when he was a baby. That meant that everything that had followed between J.B. and Victor had started after 1877.

"But," Mike was saying, "Vic did snap back."

"Yes. Some of the men in town took him in hand, and he sobered up. They helped him gather mustangs, and even gave him free breeding rights to some of their mares. The townspeople were wonderful to him. And he did, as you say, bounce back. He married again, this time to a local widow with two girls and her own house. And his life was back on track." She looked at Lucy and asked. "Why would he put all that in jeopardy?"

"Because he'd never forgiven J.B. for not selling the horses back to him for the same amount he'd received for them. And some other things, too, I believe."

"And," Sheriff Cody added, "there was the time factor. Victor was running out of it. He was out to revenge himself on those he thought had wronged him before he died." He shrugged. "Maybe for him, it was something to focus on instead of his impending painful death."

"And then Sara died." Mrs. Lewis didn't try to hide her sadness. "He was very fond of her. What a terrible coincidence."

"Um," Lucy hesitated. "Not really."

"What do you mean?" She looked from Lucy to the sheriff.

Knowing he couldn't sufficiently soften his words, he simply said, "We think Victor manipulated the circumstances that brought about her death."

"No! Sara was his friend. And if she did something to help his revenge plan, why kill her?"

Lucy started to put her hand over that of Mrs. Lewis lying on the table, but changed her mind. This wasn't a woman who would receive well a show of sympathy. "Because she was young and chatty, and he couldn't be sure she wouldn't talk to someone about what she had done for him."

"Which was what, exactly?"

"We think she told him when everyone was gone from the ranch, making it the perfect time for him to end his life." Responding to her puzzled frown, Lucy explained. "That way, everyone staying at the ranch could be suspected."

"Sara did that?"

"Quite possibly. And also that when she found him, per his instructions, she moved the chair that he would have had to stand on. Noticing it so far from his body was the first thing those who found him saw that triggered their thinking that he had been murdered. And he'd staged the area around him in a way that such a suspicion would be heightened."

"Oh, my poor Sara!" She buried her face in her hands for a moment, but then looked up. "You said he manipulated her death. How could that be? She choked on one of the chocolates he'd given her. That's just a terrible accident."

The sheriff looked exceedingly uncomfortable. "About that. She didn't choke on one of the candies. She had developed a bad reaction to mint, especially strong peppermint."

Mrs. Lewis nodded her head. "That explains the rash." She looked at Lucy and back at the sheriff. "But people don't die from a rash."

The sheriff hated to say it, but Mrs. Lewis needed to understand what had happened. "They do if they've taken in more of something they're allergic to than their system can handle. It affects their breathing and even their heart. At least that's what Doc says. It's an affliction that's been known about for hundreds of years, but just beginning to be seriously studied."

"She was exposed to a lot of mint," Lucy told her. "Not only in the candy, but also in mint tea after earlier in the day also handling the plants in the kitchen garden. It was just too much for her system to handle."

"Are you saying all that was not by accident?"

The sheriff took a deep breath. "We're saying that Victor knew of her sensitivity to mint and used it to eliminate her, and therefore the possibility of anyone finding out he really had committed suicide."

Mrs. Lewis sat and stared at the two people before her with an expression of dawning acceptance mixed with horror. Lucy walked over to the hot water kettle simmering on the back of the stove, and made a pot of tea in a large, white tea pot on the counter. She then poured out a cup, dumping in a good amount of sugar before taking it to Mrs. Lewis. Placing it in front of the woman, she told her, "Drink this. You've had a shock."

While the housekeeper did just that, slowly and carefully while deep in thought, the sheriff got up and poured himself a cup of coffee from the morning's pot also on the stove. His reaction to his first swallow told her it was cold, but he didn't seem to mind and took another.

But Lucy was also deep in thought. She was hoping no one would ask questions that would lead in J.B.'s direction; such as why J.B. refused to sell Victor's horses back to him for the price they had originally discussed. Lucy now saw this as J.B.'s first attempt at revenge for what Victor had done to his wife, and not simply a business decision. The fact that this had occurred over a decade earlier only showed J.B.'s capacity for holding a grudge, equal only to that of Victor.

It occurred to Lucy that Victor's life had gone wrong almost at that same time. Why hadn't J.B. considered that sufficient punishment? "Maybe," she thought, "because it had not been meted out by his own hand." Then a more disturbing thought occurred to her. Was it possible that some of Victor's misfortunes had been caused, or at least enhanced, by J.B.? So abhorrent was such a thought to her that she rejected it outright. And when she later remembered J.B.'s comments about guilt and retribution, she pushed those away, too.

"Mrs. Lewis," Lucy began, "I have one question. Sara's last name was Dulong. Was that your maiden name before you became Mrs. Lewis?"

The housekeeper put the cup and saucer on the table and looked Lucy in the eyes. It wasn't a look of attentiveness, but rather one of someone having been challenged. "Our family name is Lewis. Sara took our mother's maiden name when she left home in order to distinguish herself from the family. She didn't explain herself and I never asked. I am called *Mrs.* out of respect for my position, not because I was ever married."

This was a common tradition. Most women who ran rooming houses were called *Mrs.*, mainly to give them a status of respectability that an unmarried woman would not have. A single woman might be accepted as a teacher, a milliner or a seamstress, but there were few other means of their earning respectable money. In rural communities, this was more relaxed, and women did own businesses as well as ranches. Still, many of them were known as *Mrs.* when the census-taker came around.

Sheriff Cody thanked Mrs. Lewis for her time, and she quickly returned to her room. As she did, the sheriff turned to Lucy. "Can you walk with me to my horse, Mrs. Murphy?"

Outside, he took from his pocket a folded piece of paper and handed it to her. "I want you to review this and let me know if I've left something out, or included something not accurate. It was gathered together from several sources." He said nothing more as he mounted his horse, tipped his hat to her, and turned his horse toward the road.

Lucy walked out to the grove of willows at the back of the house and sat on the old tree stump. He had given her a summary of everyone's whereabouts the day of Victor's death.

*VICTOR:*   *Bunk house with newspaper*
*Frank:*   *In town with J.B., then to ranch and his room*
*Vince:*   *Chess with Roger, then nap in great room*
*Roger:*   *Chess with Vince, kitchen with Sing & playing*
      *solitaire, then to back porch*
*Jim:*   *In town with J.B., then to ranch and his room*
*Mrs. Lewis:*   *At Hunewill ranch*
*Sara:*   *Weeding kitchen garden, tack room, house*
*Sing:*   *Kitchen garden with Sara, kitchen cleaning harvest*

*J.B.:   In town, house, barn, study, then bedroom for nap.*
*Hank:   Pond with 2 new men. Saw J.B. enter barn, then right*
*          back out.*
*Mort:   Nap, blacksmith shop*

Lucy folded the paper and slipped it into the side pocket of her dress. There was much to think about, because it looked to be accurate. And yet, to accept every part of it as true meant an act of faith, as little of it could be proved by any actual evidence. Everyone was either by themselves or with another who would be only too happy to lie on their behalf.

Lucy felt her head begin to ache and she went in search of Jim. Not finding him, she decided to lie down on Roger's bed for a few minutes and rest her eyes. There was much she wanted to think through, and the quiet was welcome. But, as is no surprise, she immediately fell asleep.

# CHAPTER 15

## NO MORE CARDS, NO MORE PLAYS

Jim joined Roger at the barn early Monday morning so they could ride out the back road toward Buckeye Canyon. They had heard it mentioned several times, and were curious about it. The canyon started up at the back of the valley at the tree line, not far before reaching the first of the Twin Lakes. Having reached it, they crossed a sturdy wooden bridge over Robinson Creek and continued up through sagebrush and a scattering of trees. At a small collection of pines, an island amidst the sagebrush, they stopped to rest in the shade.

Roger took off his hat and brushed the sleeve of his shirt across his damp forehead. "I wonder why these were left uncut."

"The Hunewill Sawmill is further along. That's where most of the cutting has been done."

They got off their horses and rested themselves on some boulders, letting the breeze ruffle through their hair and enjoying the call of birds in the branches above them.

"Dad, I want to talk more about you and me and Victor."

"What do you mean?"

"Back in Bodie last year. After the game."

"I told you about that. We must have passed..."

"Don't!" Roger's voice was sharp, but also pleading. "Don't lie to me. I don't care what you did to him. He obviously survived it."

"Oh, for heaven's sake!" Jim ran his fingers through his hair, and slammed his hat back on his head. "It's just that I'm not proud of what happened." Roger said nothing, letting his father find his way forward in the telling. "After you watched him get on his horse and head out of town,

I saw you head to the privy out back. But I also saw Victor turn around and return. He rode into the alley next to the saloon. You couldn't have seen him there. He dismounted, and I followed him. I told him I knew he'd cheated in the game at your table. He tried to deny it, but when I explained what I saw him do, he knew I wasn't faking my claim."

"He cheated during the game with me? How in hell did I miss that?"

"He waited until you were distracted."

"When was that?"

"When a man at the bar dropped his glass of beer and began swearing. A lot of people turned to see what was happening. Even you. But I didn't. I watched the people at my table and yours just beyond."

"Was the man at the bar in cahoots with him?"

"I don't think so. But what matters is that Victor was sharp enough to take that moment to switch a card he had parked just under his sleeve for another in his hand. He won the pot with four of a kind."

"But wasn't he taking a chance that someone else had that card?"

"Sure. But how often does that happen?"

"I guess that's why it's called gambling." Roger looked at his father and tried not to sound reproachful. "Why didn't you tell me about all this at the time?"

"For one thing, I couldn't prove it. And for another, I wasn't sure you wouldn't go after him. But the main reason is because he began yelling threats in my face. So I punched him."

"You punched him? Wow! I never thought you could be pushed that far."

"I didn't either." But Jim didn't look proud of himself. "I don't know where all my rage came from. But in that moment, I felt like I was getting even for every time I'd backed down or backed off. Haven't you ever said to yourself, 'I wish I'd said or done this-or-that'? But instead, you backed off, telling yourself you didn't want to make things worse?"

"Well, of course."

Jim picked up a small branch and snapped it in half, tossing it back on the ground and grinding it under his boot. "I've lived longer than you, so I guess I've had more of those situations stored up. In the exact moment I struck out at him, I felt every missed opportunity I'd ever felt clutched in the fist that hit his jaw."

"Was he hurt?"

"I didn't wait to find out. He was still on his ass in the dirt when I walked back into the saloon. I ordered a stiff whiskey, kept my bruised hand out of sight, and waited for him to come storming in after me. We met J.B., and got to talking, and then went to dinner with him. Thankfully, I didn't have to hold cards the rest of that night. I never saw Victor again until he walked into J.B.'s house."

"But he didn't act like he remembered either one of us."

"No, he didn't." Jim looked Roger straight in the eyes. "And that's why I'm sure he knew we were going to be there. I think it was part of his plan to have it come out that he knew us, and that I'd attacked him."

Roger laughed. "You didn't attack him. You simply punched him."

"That's the way it happened. But how do we know what he said about it to other people? Or who he might have paid to lie about it? Don't forget, son, I've been down that road before."

Roger felt his stomach clench, as it did every time he thought of his father sitting in the old Bridgeport jail. As dreary as the current four-cell jail might be, the smaller one before it had been worse, especially in winter. "I guess he could have done anything, especially if he was manipulating this weekend the way we think."

"But so far," Jim reminded Roger, "other than vague suspicions of his death not being suicide, there hasn't been any fallout for J.B. or us."

"I think Victor's real hatred was for J.B. and not us." Roger hesitated, but expressed his thoughts anyway. "Although I don't like to think it, J.B. could have killed Victor. I mean, after we returned from town, J.B. says he was alone in his study before going into his room for a nap. But I wonder if that's true."

"It's not."

"What?"

"I saw him from my room's window. He went out to the barn before going up to his office. He was only in there a few minutes before returning, probably looking for Hank. But he never mentions that when we're all talking about where we were at the time Victor died."

"And then he returned for a nap, fostered by the sleeping powder put in his whiskey bottle."

"So he says," Jim reminded his son, "but he could have done that to himself. Or not at all, only saying he had been out cold. I like the man, but we have to keep in mind the facts."

Oddly, that had been the last thought entertained by Lucy before drifting into sleep on Roger's bed. But thoughts come with feelings, and the one Lucy experienced as she awoke a few minutes later was a sinking in the pit of her stomach. With it came questions. Why did she feel a loyalty towards J.B. such that she had told no one about their conversations? Even the ones that had led her to suspect his involvement in events of the past considered terrible enough that they had already become part of Eastern Sierra legend?

The Perrys and Murphys retired early to their rooms at the Leavitt House that night. Lucy didn't know, nor care, what the others staying at the ranch did that evening. Her nap in Roger's room had been short and she was tired. Jim, too, seemed played out, or maybe he just sensed Lucy's need for quiet. Whatever the case, he kept mostly silent and was happy to turn out the light early.

But Lucy didn't immediately fall asleep. Questions continued to plague her that she simply didn't know how to answer. Was her reticence to suspect J.B. because he had confided in her about his regrets? Or was it that he thought of himself now as a completely different man than he was as an impressionable and wayward youth? Hadn't she done things in her youth that would be considered by some as inexcusable? Her hand brushed against the slight scar on her cheek. She was saved from further contemplation of her motives by the enshrouding escape of sleep.

With the warm weather of summer having melted the snow in the passes, freight wagons were traveling through town more frequently. Some stopped to off-load supplies at the shops, but all continued on to towns further north or south. Before they did, however, they refreshed themselves in the local saloons. There were only five, but their scarcity kept them full and profitable, especially those that offered light bar food. Summer business balanced out those winter months when the passes over the Sierra were blocked with snow, as was access in and out of Bridgeport.

Freighters also took advantage of the opportunity for a good meal before heading out onto the trail where they did their own dubious cooking. The dining rooms in the Leavitt House and Allen House, and one small café, were full of these loud men that night. Most of their time spent out in the open, none of them knew how to speak below a near shout.

Maybe it was the noise both inside and outside the hotel, but Lucy's dreams that night were violent ones. Awakening suddenly from one such dream, it was still clear in her memory. She had been swimming across a lake surrounded by high mountains streaked in hues of brown, lavender and gray. They sloped down to the water's edge that was lined with large boulders. Somehow, she knew that these had been placed there at the end of the ice age. The glacier creeping over the Sierra had chosen this spot to melt, forming a deep, clear oasis of water. At first, she had been having a wonderful time. Then something grabbed her from below and began pulling her down. Thankfully, she had struggled to the surface of the water, as well as her dream. Sitting up in the bed, she tried to overcome the sense of desperation that lingered.

After several minutes, Lucy realized that the lake was one she had seen in paintings, and about which she had heard other people talk. It was the lake into which Monte Diablo Creek flowed, although it was now being called Convict Lake because of the deadly shoot-out there in the fall of 1871.

Refusing to ponder what might have been earlier thoughts that could have triggered such a dream, and seeing the first glow of dawn through the window, Lucy got out of bed and began to dress. Soon Jim too was up and dressed, and they headed to the dining room. Frank and Emily had informed them the night before that they were going out to the ranch for breakfast, so they were alone on this morning. Jim didn't say anything, but he noticed that Lucy consumed her first cup of coffee more rapidly than usual.

When Jim and Lucy arrived at the Double R, they found everyone half way through their breakfast, but joined them for coffee. Conversation was pleasantly light. Most of it was about events upcoming in the town throughout that summer, but mainly the Fourth of July commemoration just around the corner. It was, and would always be, a spectacular celebration for the town.

Lucy asked Sing as he brought in a fresh pot of coffee, "Where's Mrs. Lewis?"

"She in town with friend." He glanced around the table. "She need time away from ranch." Although he didn't say so, he looked like the idea greatly appealed to him.

They were all startled by a knock on the front door. It wasn't a hard knock, and no one had heard a wagon or rider pull up out front. When the door was opened by Sing, Sheriff Cody walked in. He stood at the edge of the great room, facing everyone seated at the table, hat in hand. And although he didn't look upset, he didn't look happy.

"I'm sorry to interrupt your breakfast, but when you're finished, I'd like everyone to join me." He didn't wait for a response, but instead turned and walked into the great room, sitting in the large chair with its back to them.

Breakfast was hastily finished, but with no conversation. Immediately after, they settled themselves in their usual places on the sofas, with J.B. in his chair facing them all. No one invited Sing, but everyone knew he would be listening from some vantage point.

Fidgeting with his hat, the sheriff took a deep breath. As he let it out, he dropped the hat on the floor next to his chair and cast his eyes around the room. "I've come to a conclusion about what took place that culminated in the deaths of three people at this ranch. I'm going to lay it out for you and then you can return home whenever you like. It's going to be difficult for some of you to hear, but I can't help that. Blame Victor, if you need to blame someone." His eyes scanned Lucy, Emily, and Charlotte, then moved to the men on the other sofa. "Some of you are more involved than you'd like to be known."

There was a general squirming among the men, but no eye contact between them. Cody almost smiled, knowing how much control it must have taken on their part for that.

"Now, much of what I've pieced together was given me by a number of others. For instance, that on the day Victor arrived at the ranch and joined you men in this room, Sara knew to add brown sugar to the tray. Victor immediately put it in his coffee. No one else did, not then or later."

Roger spoke up. "I told you about that. Of course, it wasn't until later that it occurred to me that it meant Sara knew him already."

"One thing you don't know," the sheriff told them, "is that Mrs. Turner found among Victor's papers an IOU to you, J.B., for a large sum of money."

"That's right. I told you I'd helped him out several times."

"How were you expecting him to pay it back?"

"His circumstances had improved, and after he sold some of his horses, he planned to pay me then." J.B. sat relaxed in his chair, fingers laced over his stomach. "I didn't think it a big risk."

Cody didn't seem totally satisfied, but he continued. "The whole thing, from your perspective, started with Sara finding Victor's body. But I think it actually started before that. It's my opinion that Victor asked Sara to help him commit suicide so that he didn't have to face a long, painful death. We'll never know how he convinced her, or why she agreed, but she did."

Roger said, "She didn't act like someone who expected to find what she did. She was pale and trembling, and ran up to the house like one being pursued."

"I think the word there is *act*," Jim put in.

"I don't know." The sheriff took back his narrative. "She was young and probably didn't realize what someone who had just been hanged would look like." It wasn't something any of them wanted to think about, so Cody hurried on. "As soon as you men arrived at the bunk house after she screamed, you began to question what you were seeing. The chair Vic would have had to stand on in order to hang himself was too far from where it would have landed if he'd kicked it away. We later realized that Sara moved it, as she had been told to do."

Again, the men variously shook their heads and mumbled over the fact that Sara had been involved at all.

"Beyond that," the sheriff told them, "when I looked over the room, there appeared to have been a struggle. And that Vic had been interrupted when about to enjoy a drink and smoking his pipe. That's what we were supposed to think. But the whiskey glass had been wiped clean of any hand prints."

Roger asked, "Did he just want to confuse us, or did he suppose it would make us think of murder?"

The sheriff shrugged. "He would've had to know about hands leaving traces. But whether or not it was done for our benefit, I don't know for sure."

"He'd have had to think you smart enough to know about such an advanced idea." J.B. smirked, waiting for the sheriff to react.

But if he had wanted to unnerve Cody, he was disappointed. Mike simply smiled and nodded, not at all offended. "True. So, I tend to think he did it for no real good reason. Maybe just to confuse, if it was noticed at all."

"Also," Frank chimed in, "there was that mark on his head. What was that about?"

"Ah, that." Cody looked at Lucy and smiled. "Mrs. Murphy figured that out before I did. It was part of Vic's setup. He purposely smacked his head on the wall so it would look like he had been hit on the head. Which might lead to the idea that he had been stunned and then lifted up into the noose. That way there would be medical evidence on the neck that looked like suicide, but suspected as murder because of the staging of the room. More confusion and more suspicion."

Lucy couldn't hold back any longer. "So that J.B., Jim and Roger could be suspected of his murder?"

Cody nodded. "I don't know what kind of anger or hate had been eating away at Victor, but that and his illness had turned him into a twisted man who couldn't see beyond his need to strike back at those he felt had wronged him. He hatched a plan that gave no quarter to anyone. Not Otto, a friend of long standing, or Sara, someone he had grown close to."

He gave everyone a moment to absorb the gravity of what he had just said. "But it still must have been difficult for him to climb up on that chair, because Doc said the autopsy showed that he had ingested a lot of pain medication and whiskey shortly before he died."

Charlotte asked, "Why did he have to kill Otto?"

"Because he knew too much. He knew that Vic owed a lot of money to J.B. that he couldn't repay. He knew that Victor had asked him to steal the horses, which if that had gotten out might spoil his plan to ruin J.B.'s reputation. It would also have put him in jeopardy with the law. He had probably already planned his suicide to look like murder, which Otto may have known about, too. And Otto was known to have a big mouth."

He turned to J.B. "Was there something else about that affair you might know about? For instance, who had put Victor up to the idea in the first place?"

J.B. looked at Mike without flinching. "Did someone do that? I'd think it was the kind of thing he'd come up with all on his own."

"Yeah. I guess so." But the sheriff was clearly not satisfied.

"What about Sara?" Charlotte wasn't as familiar with everything that had happened as the others. She certainly didn't know what J.B. had in his desk drawer, Lucy and Emily having told Roger their knowledge of that should remain with only the three of them.

"Sara's death is more unforgiveable, if you ask me." Cody ran a hand down his face before getting up to pour himself a glass of water at the dining table. He returned to his seat and took several swallows. "Whether or not Victor had ever had any warm feelings toward Sara, I don't know. If he did, he managed to overcome them in order to fulfill his plan. He talked her into telling him when everyone was scattered around the ranch, and on their own."

J.B. leaned forward. "Maybe that's what Hank heard. He told me that when Sara was in the tack room, he heard three odd bangs. Like something heavy was hitting the wall nearest the bunk house. Was that some kind of signal?"

Frank liked the idea. "It would keep her from being seen going into the bunk house if questioned about it later." He looked at Roger. "Which you did."

"Yeah. She said she was looking for an awl."

"Yes," Cody told them. "Hank mentioned that. I think it was a signal that it was Victor's window of opportunity. But the most important thing he told her to do was to move the chair a considerable distance from him when she came in to find the body, and scream really loud for help. She followed his instructions to the letter."

Emily spoke up. "We think he might have given her a large amount of money, but it hasn't come to light."

"Mrs. Lewis says she hasn't found it," Lucy said. "It occurred to me that instead of giving Sara cash, Victor might have told her that he was leaving money to her in his will. She'd believe something like that."

The sheriff nodded. "What she didn't know was that the candy waiting for her in her room was loaded with mint, and that Sing and Mrs. Lewis were both primed to give her mint tea at the first sign of illness. And we now know that it was at Victor's suggestion that she help in the kitchen garden, cutting back the mint there. By the time she was breaking out in a rash, her reaction was advanced enough that a lot of mint infused candy and a big cup of strong mint tea could put her over the edge of simple illness."

Charlotte sat forward. "But he couldn't be sure that would kill her."

"No, and maybe that wasn't his intent. But he could be sure that it would immobilize her for some time, especially during the investigation into his death. At the least, she would have been taken into town or out to the hospital in Bodie."

"Wow!" Roger exclaimed. "A lot of hate must have been festering in him for a long time."

The sheriff leaned back and stared at Roger. "As to that, you haven't exactly been up-front about your connection to Victor, have you?"

"Um..."

"Before you say anything, you might like to remember that I was still living in Bodie last year. I didn't realize something until recently when talking to some friends. One of them referred to what we saw one night between Victor and the 'slick gambler' who used to work at Wagner's. That was you, right?"

"Yeah." Roger's smile showed his pride.

"You didn't just watch Victor ride away. You stopped him, grabbed him by his shirt front and threatened him. Then he got on his horse and headed out of town."

"I kind of lost my temper when he yelled all those terrible things at my father."

Jim shook his head and sighed. "I didn't know at the time that he thought Roger and I had killed his friends Jimmy and Terry. What with his run-in with us in Bodie, and that, no wonder he wanted us to be under suspicion of murder, too."

Roger looked at his father, wondering if he would include his punching Victor when he had returned to town. Jim looked at his son, shook his head. He left it to the others to interpret that as they may. But he knew Roger would realize he wasn't going to say anything more unless Mike and his friends had seen him with Victor, too.

Sheriff Cody surprised everyone by asking, "Did either of you kill Terry in Virginia City? That was late in '81, not long after you'd returned from the dead, right?"

Together, the men answered, "No," and "Not us." Roger added, "No one ever did find out who shot him. It was from behind him, and straight through his neck. We didn't see anyone, but we'd ducked for cover. For all we knew, the shot was meant for us."

Jim added nothing. He was staring past the women opposite him, but could still see them clearly while making them think he couldn't. Because Lucy had suddenly gone very pale, and was sitting with her hands clasped in her lap so tightly that her knuckles were white. She was also looking almost serenely detached, the best of her poker faces.

A strange memory popped into Jim's mind. When they had come home after the shooting of Terry, who had been about to shoot both Jim and Roger, Lucy had been in the kitchen. He had vaguely noticed that she was pale and a little trembly, but had thought little of it at the time with all the excitement of the event.

Now, recalling what a good shot she had always been, the absurd thought that followed caused him to choke. He coughed hard, and Cody brought him a glass of water. Jim drank it down, then gasped out, "Sorry. Swallowed wrong."

Cody stood at the head of the group, wondering why J.B. had so far said little. On the other hand, he was twisting the snake-head ring like it was burning his skin. "Look everyone, I know that all of this is raking up uncomfortable events in your pasts. But these are the events that were feeding Victor's planned revenge. Not only for J.B., but also Roger and Jim. After all, it was Victor's idea that this poker game take place now, and that Roger and Jim be invited." He turned to Frank and Vince. "You guys just got dragged into all this, maybe as witnesses. After all, you didn't know the other men, or at least not well. So you could be considered impartial."

Vince couldn't hold back any longer. "But why did Victor hate J.B. so much that he'd go to such lengths?"

Cody turned to J.B., but said nothing. J.B. sat up straighter and took a deep breath. "It started before I even lived here. He thought I cheated him out of this land by marrying the sister of the man who owned it. Then, more out of resentment about that than anything else, he was very rude to my wife. Years later, when he was in desperate need of money, I bought his herd of horses. When he wanted to buy them back, I wanted their current value and he thought I should sell them back for what I'd paid."

"That's ridiculous," Frank scoffed.

J.B. smiled. "Yes, I thought so, too. But he held it against me, and went so far as to spread it around town that I welched on my gambling debts. For a while, it was almost impossible for me to get into a game here in Bridgeport. That's when I started traveling to Bodie, Carson or Virginia City, when I wanted to gamble."

"Maybe because you could do that," Emily suggested, "he felt he hadn't hurt you enough."

"Possibly," J.B. said. "Then about a year ago, he needed money and his wife wouldn't give him any more of hers. He'd married her mostly because she had quite a bit inherited from the girls' father. So I gave him a small loan."

Roger thought to himself that $500 was more than a small loan. He remembered just in time that he shouldn't know about the amount, and kept silent.

"Well," Charlotte began, "from what I've been told, I don't think he ever got over the loss of his first wife and their child. It seems his life spiraled down after that and never quite fully recovered."

Emily added, "His current wife even admitted to Lucy and me that there's was a marriage of convenience for both of them. His small attempts over the years to get even with J.B. hadn't come to anything, so when he realized he didn't have long to live, I think he became obsessed with doing whatever it took to get even." She turned to J.B. "And you made it easier for him when you asked him to steal your horses. You did, didn't you?"

All eyes turned to their host. That Mike Cody said nothing, showed his wisdom. Let these people do some of the confrontation for him. After all, he had to continue to live in this town. They would soon be leaving.

J. B. laughed, somewhat derisively. "Oh, yeah, I did that. I told him it was a prank for my arriving guests. That it would distract them, and give him and me an advantage at the first game. Then I'd have him go out and find the horses, and he'd be the hero of the day." He looked around at them. "Obviously, he saw through what I was doing. It would have set up a pretty risky situation for him if I didn't admit to it as a prank, or if I accused him of outright horse stealing. Which I would have done."

Charlotte was aghast. "He could have gone to prison, or even been hanged for that."

J.B.'s response was a casual shrug and a smirk that showed undisguised satisfaction at the thought. "Obviously, he didn't trust me, so he had Otto take the horses. I had no reason to have poor Otto arrested."

Frank asked, "If you had accused him, wouldn't it have been your word against Victor's? Did you count on everyone taking your word over his?"

"No. I had a friend who would have seen him take them."

Roger cut him off. "A friend who also owed you money?"

"Not anymore." J.B. got up and went to the liquor cabinet, pouring himself a small glass of his whiskey. He didn't offer it to anyone else.

"Oh, J.B.," Cody sighed.

Returning to his chair, J.B. appeared completely relaxed. "It makes no difference now. Victor didn't take them, the man who did is dead, and I didn't falsely accuse anyone."

"Okay." The sheriff looked resolute. "We'll let all that pass. But if Victor thought you were setting him up for being falsely accused, it would have just added to his determination to bring off his plan."

"I know."

Charlotte asked, "Why would you do that to him?"

"I had my reasons." He sat back in his chair, glanced at Lucy, and then at the sheriff.

Realizing that whatever those reasons were, they were not relevant now, Cody simply said, "I guess it all comes down to character. And a really big desire for revenge nursed over years, and backed up by a lot of justification. For Victor, it had evidently become intolerable to think of his dying while those he hated continued to live their customary lives. He needed to get even with someone, whether it was J.B., or even Jim and Roger. And quickly."

They sat together, weighed down by the realization of how grotesque it was for one person to carry in their heart so much hatred for another individual for so long. It might have been open for debate whether Victor or J.B. had harbored the greater proportion of this, but J.B. had not put at risk the lives of innocent people. Victor had done that without hesitation, although only those present in the room would ever know about it.

J.B. was not looking exactly ashamed, but there was a sheepish quality to him as he arose and walked around the sofas to the water in the dining table. On his way back, he stopped by Mike Cody, a friend he valued. "I'm sorry, Mike. I've justified my anger with Victor for years. My actions because of it probably only served to increase Vic's resentment of me."

"When it comes down to it, three people are dead. And no one can be held to account for it. I find that pretty damn frustrating!" But he shook

J.B.'s hand before reaching down for his hat. He turned to Lucy, Emily and Charlotte. "Ladies, it's been a pleasure to know you. I hope your memories of Bridgeport are pleasant ones, despite all that's happened."

"Most assuredly," Lucy told him. The others smiled and nodded.

"Mr. Perry and Mr. Eastman, I hope your trip back to Lone Pine is a nice one."

Vince and Frank mumbled their thanks as the sheriff turned to Jim and Roger. "Gentlemen, it's been a pleasure, despite all that has happened." He turned to Jim and smiled. "You're a very lucky man."

With that enigmatic comment, Mike Codey walked out of the house. Jim looked at Lucy, who was smiling in a manner that for a change he couldn't interpret.

There was then an immediate scattering of those present. Emily and Charlotte went out the back door and headed for the Creekside sheds and the chairs there. J.B. headed to the liquor cabinet and then up to his study. Roger went into the kitchen to visit with Sing. Jim, Frank and Vince went out to the bunk house where they invited Hank and Mort for a game of hearts. They had actually had enough of poker for the time being.

Lucy decided to retire to the front porch with a glass of water, where J.B. unexpectedly joined her. For several minutes, neither of them spoke. Lucy was dealing with a torrent of emotions, some exacerbated because she wanted to express them to J.B. However, she wasn't sure it was her place to do so, considering that they had been his guest. On the other hand, if she didn't speak her mind, she knew that she would always look back on this moment and regret that she had kept quiet.

J. B. broke the silence before Lucy could. "My wife didn't die here on the ranch. I'd sent her away to her brother for care. She was wandering away, and the last time, I almost didn't find her. I had to face the fact that she needed medical care."

"So, you weren't with her when she died. It must have been very difficult for you to not be with her at such a time."

He hesitated a long moment, considering his next words. But he only said, "I really don't want to talk about it."

"Of course. I understand."

She wanted to snap back at him that he was the one who had brought up the subject, just as he always did. She was getting tired of J.B. darting in with comments close to confessions, and then darting away again. As though she was supposed to somehow glean from his vague comments a deeper truth. If he was trying to paint himself as a victim in her eyes, he wasn't succeeding. She too had made choices she wished she hadn't had to make, but she accepted them as life lessons, from which she had learned and grown. She wasn't about to play into his attempts to make himself out as a pitiful victim.

"Actually, J.B., I don't understand." She turned and confronted him square on, so he couldn't avoid looking at her. "You made the choice you did because you thought it best for her. Or at least I hope that was the reason you sent her away. But maybe you did it because it was the easier choice and she could become someone else's problem. Yes, you had a boy to raise. But let's face it, that's easier than taking care of a wife who is mentally unstable. You're trying to rewrite what happened in your mind so you can think of yourself as the poor husband who was saddled with a decision wherein you had no other choice."

"Lucy! I can't believe you'd think of me that way."

"Why not? I don't really know you." She made a conscious effort to keep her tone casual, but she could feel her ire rising. "I know no more than what I've seen in your actions, and what you've told me, and that's very little. You've kept me at bay like you probably have everyone else. The closest you've come is to hint at a disreputable past about which you have many regrets. Well, so do we all."

"I've done what I can to make up for my bad choices," he declared, doing a poor job of masking his ego-based pride. "I give money to projects helpful to the town, and I allow my men to help on other ranches during the haying season."

"Yes, you give of your money and your employees. But you don't give of yourself. And that's why, when the townspeople heard negative things about you, they were primed to believe them. Because you never allow them to know the real you, to see your warmth, your humor, and your humanity."

"When I have free time, I spend it with Alex."

"You do things *with* Alex, but you don't open yourself up to him, either. You talk about the ranch, or relate events from your past that show you in a good light. But does he know about your hopes, your vulnerabilities, your regrets? Does he know how you *feel* about anything?"

"He's only twelve!"

"Oh, please. You usually refer to him as a young *man*. The openness between you, or the lack of it, is being put in place now." She softened her voice. "Oh, J.B., I understand how hard it is to talk to our children about our past, or our fears. But if you don't change now, when he's a man in his twenties, you'll be communicating the same way. You'll be talking about things related to the ranch, and little else. And that's going to be your downfall. There's so much goodness in you. Let him see it."

Lucy didn't want to leave this exchange as their last conversation, but they were interrupted by Alex arriving home from school. And unfortunately, there was no other opportunity for them to be alone.

# CHAPTER 16

## LAST ACE UP THE SLEEVE

All the guests were gone. And J.B. found the silence in the house oppressive. Alex was in town spending the night with Amasa Bryant's son, Scott. Mrs. Lewis had been given a week's holiday in Carson City, along with Sing. They both had friends with whom they were going to be staying. J. B. told them that he felt it was the least he could do after all they had been through over the past week.

They had been surprised at his generosity, but had accepted it gratefully. He had even driven them in the spring wagon into town in time for the morning stage, Mrs. Lewis on the seat with him and Sing in the back with their luggage.

J.B. had returned to the ranch straight away, not stopping in town for supplies at the Bump Market, even though he had claimed that was why he was taking them instead of Mort or Hank.

But that was this morning. He sat at the kitchen table drinking a cup of coffee and wondering why it had felt so necessary to see for himself that they were well and truly gone. He was feeling adrift, unable to concentrate. Nothing in the newspaper held his attention. There was nothing pressing in his office.

He wanted to feel relief that they had all survived the past week, but he couldn't even do that. He found himself revisiting the conversations he'd had with Lucy, and discovered that he missed her more than he thought he would.

Hank was out riding fence, checking for breaks or weaknesses, and at the same time doing a general check on the younger calves. Mort was in town helping his friend P. G. Hughes at his blacksmith shop, after which they would have a good meal at the Allen House. For the first time in years, J.B. was completely alone on the ranch. Maybe, he thought, that's why I'm feeling so restless and unsettled.

Or maybe it was his conscience.

He didn't immediately deny it, although the concept somewhat surprised him. He knew he had a conscience, but it hadn't bothered him for a very long time. Not since he said good-bye to his wife. Well, best not to think about that.

Some people would have said there were lots of things in his life that he could regret, but he scoffed at the thought. Everything in business was fair game, wasn't it? The town women he had taken to dinner or a dance had no business expecting anything more than that. He'd certainly not led them on. Of course, the fair but frail women he spent time with out of town might hope for a prince to come along and rescue them, but he always made it clear that it wasn't going to be him. So, what did he have to feel uneasy about?

"Damn Lucy Murphy! She's got me thinking there's goodness in me. I'd like to think that's true, of course. But I don't think it is." His sigh as he looked out the kitchen window was a deep one. "I wish I'd had the courage to tell her everything."

He went back out to the barn, unhitched the horses from the wagon and led them to their stalls. He wiped them down and gave them hay. After checking to be sure their buckets were full of water, he closed the barn door and started for the house.

He tried not to look over at the bunk house door, but he felt himself drawn to it as though he were metal and it was a magnet. Even the dread he felt in the pit of his stomach, and the hard beating of his heart didn't stop him, although both slowed him down a bit.

Or maybe it was his conscience.

When he opened the door and saw the light flooding in, he realized it was after all just the same old bunk house and nothing more. But his anxiety didn't subside. He stepped into the big room, sweeping his eyes over the row of beds and tables along the left wall. Nothing different there.

The wardrobe closets were still across from the beds on the right wall. The old cooking stove next to the back door, now locked, had been cleaned and was shining. The table was in the corner and the chairs around it were pushed in. Glass jars full of flatware were nestled in the middle, along with a stack of freshly laundered napkins. The door to Hank's small room was closed, although probably not locked. And sun was streaming in through the window on the far back wall. The tidiness of the bright interior should have been enough to bring cheer to the room, and alleviation of his anxiety.

But it wasn't. Because the rough beam where Victor's body had hung was still there, too. And always would be. For those who had been his guests, it was this picture they would always see in their minds; Victor's body swinging in the breeze from the open door.

They thought J.B. hadn't seen it, having arrived after the body had been cut down. But he had. He thought he would always see it. After all, it wasn't exactly something one expects to discover on one's property.

So maybe it was his conscience, after all.

Because he had seen Victor's dead body before any of the others. The sudden clarity of the memory pushed him back a step, pressing him against the wall next to the entry with a suddenness that tightened his chest and made his breath catch in his throat. Before J.B. could stop himself, he was back in the room watching what had taken place, like a stage play with him as the only audience.

* * *

*The curtain goes up with J. B. Roberts, looking through the back window into the room. Victor is swallowing a handful of pills that he takes from his shirt pocket, downing it with a large glass of whiskey. Somewhat surprising, Victor wipes off the glass before putting it back on the table by his bed. Victor then walks up to the flat of the wall near the head of his bed, turns his head parallel to the wall, and slams his head into it. It sends him stumbling back, falling onto his bed. But he doesn't pass out. Instead, he opens a newspaper and spreads it out, part of it hanging off the bed.*

*By the time J.B. comes in through the back door, Victor has placed an armless wooden chair under one of the ceiling beams, from which hangs a rope with a hangman's noose at the end. J.B. quickly enters the room and approaches Victor, who is standing next to the wooden chair.*

*Victor sees J.B. and their eyes meet. J.B. says the logical thing. "What the hell are you doing?"*

"I'm doing what I have to do!" Victor stands by the chair with his hand on its doweled back as though it's holding him up. "I'm sick, J.B. Very sick. Not much time left and I can't stand the pain anymore."

"So then take an overdose of something. Why this, and why here?"

"Don't try to stop me!" He steps up onto the chair, grabbing the dangling loop in his hand to balance himself.

J.B. takes a slow step forward as he says, "I'm not going to stop you." He doesn't come closer than about six feet from Victor. "I'd like to see you dead. I've wanted that ever since you dishonored my wife."

"That was a misunderstanding!" Victor reaches out a hand, as though begging for understanding. "I thought she was giving me the come-on. I didn't get carried away like that again, not even when I could have with Sara. When the little bitch turned me down, I just laughed it off."

"It doesn't sound like you thought it funny."

"Yeah, well, Sara's only worth one thing to me now. But you don't need to know about that."

J.B. is still fixated on the subject of his wife, speaking in a rush of emotion held in check for years. "The thing is, you didn't stop when my wife told you to. You pushed her down, ripped off her dress, and then pulled the top of her chemise down and grabbed her breast so hard it left a bruise."

"But that's all I did. I got hold of myself and backed off. I told her I was sorry and I left her there in the shed."

J.B. takes a step closer. "She was never the same after that. She was afraid of every man she saw, including me. I couldn't touch her. Her brother was the only man she could bear to be near."

"Jesus, I didn't know she was that loopy. Is that why you refused to sell me back my horses?"

"I did agree to sell them back." J.B. takes another step closer, but Victor doesn't seem to notice. "Why should I have sold them back for the same money after breaking and training them, and increasing their value?"

Victor ignores the question. "Don't think I couldn't see through your plan to have me steal the horses. I didn't buy your 'it'll be a good joke on my guests' bullshit. Even when you promised to cancel my debt. I figured you'd have me arrested for horse theft. No one would believe me if I said it was a put-up job by you. Ole Otto believed it was all a joke, of course, and fell in with it when I told 'em to do it instead. He was always an ounce shy of a pound."

"*Oh, by the way, Vic. Where did you get the flowers you used to poison Otto?*"

"*Oh, that. Simple. They were right outside my front door. I told him they were a surprise for Sara, and he put them in his saddlebags. I told him I was trying to make time with her.*"

"*So, something else he could have told someone if he'd lived.*"

*Victor is putting more of his weight on the rope and the beam squeaks under his weight.* "*Yeah.*"

"*Well, I guess you've taken care of me.*" *J.B. shrugs, as though he doesn't care.* "*And I guess that means you win after all.*"

"*Oh, no, I win when they find my body hanging here, and they think it's murder. And you're suspected.*"

"*Did you have all of this worked out when you manipulated me into having this poker weekend?*"

"*Somewhat. I added details after you said yes.*"

"*Is that why you hit your head on the wall? Was that a detail that got added? So the sheriff and the Doc will think someone hit you and strung you up there?*"

"*Yeah.*"

"*But they won't buy it. And since I haven't killed you, there's no evidence that I have. I won't be arrested for something I didn't do, if that's what you think.*"

"*Maybe. But if not, at least there'll always be the suspicion that you put it over on the sheriff. Who, by the way, everyone knows is a friend of yours. Besides, I did something that'll enhance suspicion.*"

"*What?*"

"*You'll know when it comes to light. No one will ever fully trust you again. Especially in this God-forsaken town. But rumors travel. You'll have to go a very long way from here for your little gambling trips in the future, in order to find people willing to gamble with you.*"

*J.B. doesn't argue.* "*So, what are you waiting for? Do you want me to leave?*"

"*No.*" *Victor turns to the front window, puts the noose around his neck, and stands rigid on the chair.*

*After several minutes, J.B. frowns and crosses his arms across his chest. Then he realizes that Victor is crying.*

*"I can't do it!" Victor sobs. "I just can't."*

*"Yes, you can." J.B.'s voice is soft and almost kind. "It's the best way. Think of the pain to come."*

*"No!" Victor starts to reach up to the rope around his neck, but his hand never reaches it. The chair shoots out from under him, and his body drops heavily. And J.B. returns his foot to the floor.*

*He then simply turns and walks out the back door. He goes in the back door of the barn and straight out the front, less than five minutes since he entered. Long strides bring him to the house. Seeing Roger over on the back porch, he starts to say something, then realizes he's still asleep in his chair, the same as when J.B. went out to the barn.*

*J.B. climbs the outside stairs slowly, making no sound and quietly closing the door at the top behind him. Leaving Alex's room, he hears the back door close, realizing that it must be Sara by the swish of her skirts.*

*Safe in his room, he laughs out loud. He goes to a drawer of his dresser and removes a folded piece of paper from an envelope given him by N.B. Hunewill. He had told J.B., "Victor told me to open this if anything unexpected happens to him and to do what I think best. I didn't like the way he laughed when he said not to let you know I have the this. I don't trust whatever is in this envelope, and I think you should have it."*

*J.B. had been surprised, but had simply thanked his neighbor and friend. Now, he opens the envelope again. Inside is a note from Victor, addressed as "To whom it may concern". The note lays out a fantastic tale of evil-doing by J.B., tying him into the September 1871 prison break and a number of hideous events that still shocks J.B. as he reads it.*

*He remembers that when he had first read the note, he had broken out in a cold sweat. But not this time, knowing that Victor is now beyond the ability to hurt him. He walks to the black warming stove and opens its door. He then touches the flame of a match to the note, and tosses it into the stove. He lies down on the bed and sinks into a peaceful nap, awaiting the discovery of Victor's body.*

*   *   *

J.B. took a deep breath, opened his eyes and faced the empty bunk room, murmuring to himself, "And the curtain falls."

Of course, he now knew that within a few minutes, Sara had arrived at the bunk house, picked up the fallen chair, and moved it well away from the body. And the scene had been set for someone to think it couldn't have been suicide, just like Victor had wanted.

A week later, J.B. joined Doc and Mike at the Court House Corner Saloon for a drink. As Doc finished his beer, he chuckled. It was full of mirth, and Mike was curious.

"What's so funny?"

"I didn't say anything before, but about Victor's death." Mike and J.B. waited impatiently for him to take a drink of his beer and continue. "He'd swallowed so many pain pills with a large quantity of whiskey, that he would have died of an overdose if he hadn't hanged himself. It's a wonder it didn't happen before he even dropped. Just think about that. If he'd died on his bed, people would still have thought murder a possibility because of the way he'd set up the room around him. But he wouldn't have had to involve Sara, and she wouldn't have had to die. It's like someone said about him. Victor was a bad gambler because he had a terrible lack of imagination."

Doc didn't see J.B.'s reaction to this, but Mike did. Confusion and horror were there on J.B.'s face, but also something akin to disbelief. After claiming to be ill, J.B. walked out of the saloon. Through the front window they saw him get on his horse and head west toward the end of town and the meadows.

What they didn't see was that J.B. continued past his ranch, past the Hunewill ranch, and rode on to the first of the twin lakes. Dismounting, he leaned against a large, gnarled pine and focused on breathing. From the first time he had seen this lake, it had felt like a place of sanctuary. And over the years, whenever he had needed solace in times of tribulation, he had found peace right here next to the lake. The mountains in the distance, crusted with snow as they were right now, cooled his spirit. The Old Man of the Mountain seemed to smile with acceptance, and he could feel his heart beating normally again.

Did what Doc said mean that he hadn't killed Victor after all? Or if so, only seconds before he would have passed out and dropped on his own? "Yes, I saw Victor reach up to the rope, and a second later the rope would have been removed. But Victor would probably have passed out in that second, even if I hadn't kicked the chair away."

Somehow in the morass of this justification, J.B. arrived at the conclusion that he had not killed Victor. He watched a fish jump out of the water in its primal joy, and matched the exuberance of his own relief to it. When the rings of water around the fish disappeared, J.B. climbed on his horse and rode calmly back to his ranch. Passing under the Double R medallion with his conscience at rest, he smiled as he thought of the lovely Lucy and her faith in his goodness.